How Long 'til Black Future Month?

"The most celebrated science fiction and fantasy writer of her generation." —*New York Times*

"Jemisin is now a pillar of speculative fiction, breathtakingly imaginative and narratively bold." —*Entertainment Weekly*

"Jemisin's phenomenal success has been something like an earthquake ripping through the traditional order of fantasy itself." —*Vulture*

"One line from [Jemisin's introduction] has tattooed itself on my mind, a sort of manifesto for her ongoing work and all the fiction I love: 'Now I am bolder, and angrier, and more joyful.' I felt, after reading these stories, that I was too." —Amal El-Mohtar, *NPR Books*

"Marvelous and wide-ranging." —*Los Angeles Times*

"The most critically acclaimed author in contemporary science fiction and fantasy." —*GQ*

"N. K. Jemisin is a powerhouse of speculative fiction. So, obviously, you *need* to read this new short story collection." —*Bustle*

"There are so many things in *How Long 'til Black Future Month*—from firebirds to Mega Cops, from truffles to hurricanes, from utopias (maybe) to civil rights marches—that it's impossible to describe. Except to say that every single story here is riveting, provocative, and remarkable. An extraordinary story collection from an extraordinary writer!" —Connie Willis, Hugo and Nebula Award winner

"Energizing in the way the best science fiction aims to be, forcing readers to look back on the 'real' world with new and eager eyes."
—*Shelf Awareness* (starred review)

"Powerful and mind-expanding...Jemisin pushes boundaries, experiments with format and theme, and challenges expectations."

—*Publishers Weekly* (starred review)

"Eloquently develops a series of passionately felt themes.... One of speculative fiction's most thoughtful and exciting writers."

—*Kirkus* (starred review)

"Whether she's exploring alien life forms or political machinations, self-sacrifice or monsters in New Orleans, Jemisin's characters are boldly drawn, complex, and so engaging."   —*Book Riot*

"Each of the [stories]...is masterfully written and beautifully imagined, making the book difficult to put down.... Anyone who appreciates Jemisin's work, speculative fiction or simply the art of the short story shouldn't miss this collection."   —*BookPage*

"Jemisin...is a writer of uncanny gifts who is to a moral certainty one of the five best we have right now.... How inadequate these brief synopses are to convey the sheer beauty to be found in these stories."

—*Sci Fi* magazine

"The true breadth of [Jemisin's] talent...comes through to grand effect in her first collection of short fiction.... Jemisin is an essential voice in modern-day SFF."   —*B&N Sci-Fi & Fantasy Blog*

"These stories are wonderful. In worlds both invariably cruel and brilliantly imagined, heroism thrives in the margins."

—Nicky Drayden, author of *The Prey of Gods*

"Jemisin's body of work already spans an extraordinary and astonishing terrain. Science fiction and fantasy have always been the genres of my heart, and Jemisin is an absolute master. Like Ursula K. Le Guin, she is a visionary who shows us our world by remaking it in stories."   —Kelly Link, author of *Get in Trouble*

HOW LONG 'TIL BLACK FUTURE MONTH?

By N. K. Jemisin

THE INHERITANCE TRILOGY

The Hundred Thousand Kingdoms
The Broken Kingdoms
The Kingdom of Gods
The Awakened Kingdom (novella)

The Inheritance Trilogy (omnibus)

DREAMBLOOD

The Killing Moon
The Shadowed Sun

The Dreamblood Duology (omnibus)

THE BROKEN EARTH

The Fifth Season
The Obelisk Gate
The Stone Sky

How Long 'til Black Future Month?
(short story collection)

HOW LONG 'TIL BLACK FUTURE MONTH?

N. K. JEMISIN

orbit

www.orbitbooks.net

Copyright © 2018 by N. K. Jemisin

"Too Many Yesterdays, Not Enough Tomorrows" Copyright © 2004 by N. K. Jemisin; "L'Alchimista" Copyright © 2005 by N. K. Jemisin; "Cloud Dragon Skies" Copyright © 2005 by N. K. Jemisin; "The Brides of Heaven" Copyright © 2007 by N. K. Jemisin; "The You Train" Copyright © 2007 by N. K. Jemisin; "The Narcomancer" Copyright © 2008 by N. K. Jemisin; "Non-Zero Probabilities" Copyright © 2009 by N. K. Jemisin; "On the Banks of the River Lex" Copyright © 2010 by N. K. Jemisin; "The Effluent Engine" Copyright © 2011 by N. K. Jemisin; "The Trojan Girl" Copyright © 2011 by N. K. Jemisin; "Valedictorian" Copyright © 2014 by N. K. Jemisin; "Walking Awake" Copyright © 2014 by N. K. Jemisin; "Stone Hunger" Copyright © 2014 by N. K. Jemisin; "Sinners, Saints, Dragons, and Haints, in the City Beneath the Still Waters" Copyright © 2015 by N. K. Jemisin; "The City, Born Great" Copyright © 2016 by N. K. Jemisin; "Red Dirt Witch" Copyright © 2016 by N. K. Jemisin; "The Evaluators" Copyright © 2016 by N. K. Jemisin; "Henosis" Copyright © 2017 by N. K. Jemisin

Excerpt from *The City We Became* copyright © 2019 by N. K. Jemisin

Author photograph by Laura Hanifin

Cover design by Lauren Panepinto

Cover photo by CreativeSoul Photography

Cover copyright © 2018 by Hachette Book Group, Inc.

Orbit

Hachette Book Group

1290 Avenue of the Americas

New York, NY 10104

orbitbooks.net

First Trade Paperback Edition: August 2019

Originally published in hardcover and ebook by Orbit in November 2018

Orbit is an imprint of Hachette Book Group.

The Orbit name and logo are trademarks of Little, Brown Book Group Limited.

The publisher is not responsible for websites (or their content) that are not owned by the publisher.

The Hachette Speakers Bureau provides a wide range of authors for speaking events. To find out more, go to www.hachettespeakersbureau.com or call (866) 376-6591.

Library of Congress Cataloging-in-Publication Data

Names: Jemisin, N. K., author.

Title: How long 'til black future month? / N. K. Jemisin.

Other titles: How long until black future month?

Description: First edition. | New York, NY: Orbit, 2018.

Identifiers: LCCN 2018034027| ISBN 9780316491341 (hardcover) | ISBN 9780316491372 (trade pbk.) | ISBN 9781549147289 (audiobook downloadable) | ISBN 9780316491358 (ebook (open))

Classification: LCC PS3610.E46 A6 2018 | DDC 813/.6—dc23

LC record available at https://lccn.loc.gov/2018034027

ISBNs: 978-0-316-49134-1 (hardcover), 978-0-316-49137-2 (trade paperback), 978-0-316-49135-8 (ebook)

Printed in the United States of America

LSC-C

10 9 8 7 6 5 4 3 2 1

Contents

Introduction

Once upon a time, I didn't think I could write short stories.

The time was 2002. I'd just turned thirty and had my first "midlife" crisis. (Yeah, I know.) I was living in Boston, where it was cold and hard to make friends and nobody put seasoning on anything. I'd just ended a lackluster relationship, and I was in student loan debt up to my eyeballs, like pretty much everybody else in my generation. In an attempt to resolve frustration with the state of my life, I finally decided to see whether my lifelong writing hobby could be turned into a side hustle worth maybe a few hundred dollars. If I could make that much (or even just one hundred a year!), I might be able to cover some of my utility bills or something. Then I could get out of debt in twelve or thirteen years, instead of fifteen.

I wasn't expecting more than that, for reasons beyond pessimism. At the time, it was clear that the speculative genres had stagnated to a dangerous degree. Science fiction *claimed* to be the fiction of the future, but it still mostly celebrated the faces and voices and stories of the past. In a few more years there would come the Slushbomb, an attempt by women writers to improve one of the most sexist bastions among the Big Three; the Great Cultural Appropriation Debates of DOOM; and Racefail, a thousand-blog storm of fannish protest against institutional and individual racism within the genre. These things collectively would open a bit more room within the genre for people who weren't cishet white guys—just in time for the release of my first published novel, *The Hundred Thousand Kingdoms*. But back in 2002 there was none of that. In 2002, I knew that as a black woman drawn to science fiction and fantasy, I had almost no chance of getting my work published, noticed by reviewers, or accepted by a readership that seemed to want nothing more than endless variations on medieval Europe and American colonization. And while I could've sharted out my own variation on medieval Europe or American colonization—and probably should have, if I wanted to pay off my loans faster—that just didn't interest me. I wanted to do something new.

Established writers advised me to attend one of the Clarions or Odyssey, but I couldn't; the day job only allowed me two weeks of vacation time. Instead, I borrowed six hundred dollars from my father and attended Viable Paradise, a one-week workshop out on Martha's Vineyard. Since a week isn't really enough time to substantively improve attendees' writing, VP focused on other stuff—like how to make it in the business of fiction. I learned tons about getting an agent, the publication process, and how to survive as a writer; it was exactly what I needed at that stage of my career. And there I was given one more really good piece of advice: learn to write short stories.

This was the only VP advice that I balked at, because it sounded completely nonsensical to me. I'd read some short stories over the years, and enjoyed a few, but never felt the urge to write any. I knew enough to argue that short stories were a completely different art form from novels, so shouldn't I spend my limited free time refining the thing I wanted to do, rather than learning this other thing that honestly seemed kind of boring? Also, I knew that the pay rate for short stories was abysmal; this was in the days when the SFWA-acceptable rate for pro-level markets was only three cents per word. Remember, one of my goals was utility-bill money. Short stories, assuming I sold any, wouldn't even cover the cooking gas.

But the instructors at VP* made a compelling case. The argument that finally convinced me was simply this: learning to write short fiction would improve my longer fiction. I didn't know whether to believe this or not, but I decided to spend a year finding out. For that year, I subscribed to *F&SF* and the now-defunct *Realms of Fantasy*, read online markets like *Strange Horizons*, and joined a writing group. The project didn't go well at first. My first "short" story was a whopping 17,000 words and had no ending. But I got better. When I started submitting those stories to magazines, I got lots of rejections. My writing group helped me see that rejections are part of writing; we collected them, in fact, and tried to celebrate them along with the acceptances. Then I started getting acceptances—semipro markets at first, and then finally pro sales.

And along the way, I learned that short stories *were* good for my longer-form fiction. Writing short stories taught me about the quick hook and the deep character. Shorts gave me space to experiment with unusual plots and story forms—future tense, epistolic format, black characters—which otherwise I would've considered too risky for the lengthy investment of a novel. I started to *enjoy* writing short fiction, for itself and not just as novel practice. And of course, after all those rejections, my emotional skin grew thick as an elephant's.

But wait. Back up. Yeah, I said black characters. I had done those

---

* At the time, Patrick and Teresa Nielsen Hayden, Debra Doyle, James MacDonald, James Patrick Kelly, and Steven Gould.

before in novels I wrote as a teenager, which will never see daylight, but I'd never *submitted* anything with black characters. Remember how I described the industry circa 2002. Editors and publishers and agents talked a good game back then about being "open to all perspectives," as they vaguely termed it, but the proof wasn't in the pudding. To see the truth, all I had to do was open a magazine's table of contents, or a publisher's web page, to see how few female or "foreign" names were in the author list. When I sampled a particular publisher's novels or stories for research, I paid attention to how many—or how few—characters were described as something other than white. I still wrote black characters into my work because I couldn't stand excluding *myself* from my own damn fiction. But if the goal was to make money... well, like I said. I didn't expect much.

So I lack the words to tell you how powerful a moment it was for my first pro sale—"Cloud Dragon Skies," published in *Strange Horizons* in 2005—to be about a nappy-haired black woman trying to save humanity from its own folly.

How Long 'til Black Future Month takes its name from an essay that I wrote in 2013. (It's not in this collection since I haven't included any essays; you can find it on my website, nkjemisin.com.) It's a shameless paean to an Afrofuturist icon, the artist Janelle Monáe, but it's also a meditation on how hard it's been for me to love science fiction and fantasy as a black woman. How much I've had to fight my own internalized racism in addition to that radiating from the fiction and the business. How terrifying it's been to realize *no one thinks my people have a future.* And how gratifying to finally accept myself and begin spinning the futures I want to see.

The stories contained in this volume are more than just tales in themselves; they are also a chronicle of my development as a writer and as an activist. On rereading my fiction to select pieces for this collection, I've been struck by how *hesitant* I once was to mention characters' races. I notice that many of my stories are about accepting differences and change...and very few are about fighting threats from elsewhere. I'm surprised to realize how often I write stories that are talking back at classics of the genre. "Walking Awake" is a response to Heinlein's *The Puppet Masters*, for example. "The Ones Who Stay and Fight" is a pastiche of and reaction to Le Guin's "The Ones Who Walk Away From Omelas."

If you're coming to these tales as someone who primarily knows me through my novels, you're going to see the early forms of plot elements or characters that later got refined in novels. Sometimes that's deliberate, since I write "proof of concept" stories in order to test-drive potential novel worlds. ("The Narcomancer" and "Stone Hunger" are examples of this; so is "The Trojan Girl," but I decided not to write a novel in that world, instead finishing it up with "Valedictorian.") Sometimes the "re-versioning" is completely unconscious, and I don't realize I've trodden familiar ground until long after. The world of the Broken Earth trilogy wasn't my first time playing with genii locorum, for example—places with minds of their own. The concept appears in several of my stories, sometimes flavored with a dash of animism.

Anyway, things are better these days. I paid off my student loans with my first novel advance. As of this writing I live as a full-time writer in New York, where I have lots of friends and my fiction brings in considerably more than utility bill money. (Even at Con Ed rates.) Right now in 2018, the genre seems at least willing to have conversations about its flaws, though there's still a long way to go before any of those flaws are actually repaired. At least I see more "foreign" and femme names on book spines and in tables of contents these days.

I see readers demanding fiction featuring different voices, spoken by native tongues, and I see publishers scrambling to answer. And while the voices of dissent have grown as well—bigots trying to rewrite history and claim the future for themselves alone—they are in the severe minority. The rest of the world has administered some truly beautiful clapbacks to remind them of this.

Now I mentor up-and-coming writers of color wherever I find them . . . and there are so many to find. Now I am bolder, and angrier, and more joyful; none of these things contradict each other. Now I am the writer that short stories made me.

So come on. There's the future over there. Let's all go.

The Ones Who Stay and Fight

It's the Day of Good Birds in the city of Um-Helat! The Day is a local custom, silly and random as so many local customs can be, and yet beautiful by the same token. It has little to do with birds—a fact about which locals cheerfully laugh, because that, too, is how local customs work. It is a day of fluttering and flight regardless, where pennants of brightly dyed silk plume forth from every window, and delicate drones of copperwire and featherglass—made for this day, and flown on no other!—waft and buzz on the wind. Even the monorail cars trail stylized flamingo feathers from their rooftops, although these are made of featherglass, too, since real flamingos do not fly at the speed of sound.

Um-Helat sits at the confluence of three rivers and an ocean. This places it within the migratory path of several species of butterfly and hummingbird as they travel north to south and back again. At the Day's dawning, the children of the city come forth, most wearing wings made for them by parents and kind old aunties. (Not all aunties are actually aunties, but in Um-Helat, anyone can earn auntiehood. This is a city where numberless aspirations can be fulfilled.) Some wings are organza stitched onto school backpacks; some are quilted cotton stuffed with dried flowers and clipped to jacket shoulders. Some few have been carefully glued together from dozens of butterflies' discarded wings—but only those butterflies that died naturally, of course. Thus adorned, children who can run through the streets do so, leaping off curbs and making whooshing sounds as they pretend to fly. Those who cannot run instead ride special drones, belted and barred and double-checked for safety, which gently bounce them into the air. It's only a few feet, though it feels like the height of the sky.

But this is no awkward dystopia, where all are forced to conform. Adults who refuse to give up their childhood joys wear wings, too, though theirs tend to be more abstractly constructed. (Some are invisible.) And those who follow faiths which forbid the emulation of beasts, or those who simply do not want wings, need not wear them. They are all honored for this choice, as much as the soarers and flutterers themselves—for without contrasts, how does one appreciate the different forms that joy can take?

Oh, and there is *such* joy here, friend. Street vendors sell tiny custard-filled cakes shaped like jewel beetles, and people who've waited all year wolf them down while sucking air to cool their tongues. Artisans offer cleverly mechanized paper hummingbirds for passersby to throw; the best ones blur as they glide. As the afternoon of the Day grows long, Um-Helat's farmers arrive, invited as always to be honored alongside the city's merchants and technologers. By all three groups' efforts does the city prosper—but when aquifers and rivers dip too low, the farmers move to other lands and farm there, or change from corn-husking to rice-paddying and fishery-feeding. The management of soil and water and chemistry are intricate arts, as you know, but here they have been perfected. Here in Um-Helat there is no hunger: not among the people, and not for the migrating birds and butterflies when they dip down for a taste of savory nectar. And so farmers are particularly celebrated on the Day of Good Birds.

The parade wends through the city, farmers ducking their gazes or laughing as their fellow citizens offer salute. Here is a portly woman, waving a hat of chicken feathers that someone has gifted her. There is a reedy man in a coverall, nervously plucking at the brooch he bears, carved and lacquered to look like a ladybug. He has made it himself, and hopes others will think it fine. They do!

And here! This woman, tall and strong and bare of arm, her sleek brown scalp dotted with implanted silver studs, wearing a fine uniform of stormcloud damask. See how she moves through the crowd, grinning with them, helping up a child who has fallen. She encourages their cheers and their delight, speaking to this person in one language and that person in another. (Um-Helat is a city of polyglots.) She reaches the front of the crowd and immediately spies the reedy man's ladybug, whereupon with delighted eyes and smile, she makes much of it. She points, and others see it, too, which makes the reedy man blush terribly. But there is only kindness and genuine pleasure in the smiles, and gradually the reedy man stands a little taller, walks with a wider stride. He has made his fellow citizens happier, and there is no finer virtue by the customs of this gentle, rich land.

The slanting afternoon sun stretches golden over the city, reflected light sparkling along its mica-flecked walls and laser-faceted embossings. A breeze blows up from the sea, tasting of brine and minerals, so fresh that a spontaneous cheer wafts along the crowded parade route. Young men by the waterfront, busily stirring great vats of spiced mussels and pans of rice and peas and shrimp, cook faster, for it is said in Um-Helat that the smell of the sea wakes up the belly. Young women on streetcorners bring out sitars and synthesizers and big wooden drums, the better to get the crowd dancing the young men's way. When people stop, too hot or thirsty to continue, there are glasses of fresh tamarind-lime juice. Elders staff the shops that sell this, though they also give away the juice if a person is much in need. There are always souls needing drumbeats and tamarind, in Um-Helat.

Joyous! It is a steady joy that fills this city, easy to speak of—but ah, though I have tried, it is most difficult to describe accurately. I see the incredulity in your face! The difficulty lies partly in my lack of words, and partly in your lack of understanding, because you have never seen a place like Um-Helat, and because I am myself only an observer, not yet privileged to visit. Thus I must try harder to describe it so that you might embrace it, too.

How can I illuminate the people of Um-Helat? You have seen how they love their children, and how they honor honest, clever labor. You have perhaps noted their many elders, for I have mentioned them in passing. In Um-Helat, people live long and richly, with good health for as long as fate and choice and medicine permits. Every child knows opportunity; every parent has a life. There are some who go without housing, but they can have an apartment if they wish. Here where the spaces under bridges are swept daily and benches have light padding for comfort, they do not live badly. If these itinerant folk dwell also in delusions, they are kept from weapons or places that might do them harm; where they risk disease or injury, they are prevented—or cared for, if matters get out of hand. (We shall speak more of the caretakers soon.)

And so this is Um-Helat: a city whose inhabitants, simply, care for one another. That is a city's purpose, they believe—not merely to generate revenue or energy or products, but to shelter and nurture the people who do these things.

What have I forgotten to mention? Oh, it is the thing that will seem most fantastic to you, friend: the variety! The citizens of Um-Helat are so many and so wildly different in appearance and origin and development. People in this land come from many others, and it shows in sheen of skin and kink of hair and plumpness of lip and hip. If one wanders the streets where the workers and artisans do their work, there are slightly more people with dark skin; if one strolls the corridors of the executive tower, there are a few extra done in pale. There is history rather than malice in this, and it is still being actively, intentionally corrected—because the people of Um-Helat are not naive believers in good intentions as the solution to all ills. No, there are no worshippers of mere tolerance here, nor desperate grovelers for that grudging pittance of respect which is *diversity*. Um-Helatians are learned enough to understand what must be done to make the world better, and pragmatic enough to actually enact it.

Does that seem wrong to you? It should not. The trouble is that we have a bad habit, encouraged by those concealing ill intent, of insisting that people already suffering should be afflicted with further, unnecessary pain. This is the paradox of tolerance, the treason of free speech: we hesitate to admit that some people are just fucking evil and need to be stopped.

This is Um-Helat, after all, and not that barbaric America. This is not Omelas, a tick of a city, fat and happy with its head buried in a tortured child. My accounting of Um-Helat is an homage, true, but there's nothing for you to fear, friend.

And so how does Um-Helat exist? How can such a city possibly survive, let alone thrive? Wealthy with no poor, advanced with no war, a beautiful place where all souls know themselves beautiful... It cannot be, you say. Utopia? How banal. It's a fairy tale, a thought exercise. Crabs in a barrel, dog-eat-dog, oppression Olympics—it would not last, you insist. It could never be in the first place. Racism is natural, so natural that we will call it "tribalism" to insinuate that everyone does it. Sexism is natural and homophobia is natural and religious intolerance is natural and greed is natural and cruelty is natural and savagery and fear and and and... and. "Impossible!" you hiss, your fists slowly clenching at your sides. "How dare you. What have these people done to make you believe such lies? What are you doing to me, to suggest that it is possible? How dare you. *How dare you.*"

Oh, friend! I fear I have offended. My apologies.

Yet... how else can I convey Um-Helat to you, when even the thought of a happy, just society raises your ire so? Though I confess I am puzzled as to *why* you are so angry. It's almost as if you feel threatened by the very idea of equality. Almost as if some part of you needs to be angry. Needs unhappiness and injustice. But... do you?

Do you?

Do you believe, friend? Do you accept the Day of Good Birds, the city, the joy? No? Then let me tell you one more thing.

Remember the woman? So tall and brown, so handsome and bald, so loving in her honest pleasure, so fine in her stormcloud gray. She is one of many wearing the same garb, committed to the same purpose. Follow her, now, as she leaves behind the crowd and walks along the biofiber-paved side streets into the shadows. Beneath a skyscraper that floats a few meters off the ground—oh, it is perfectly safe, Um-Helat has controlled gravity for generations now—she stops. There two others await: one gethen, one male, both clad in gray damask, too. They are also bald, their studded heads a-gleam. They greet each other warmly, with hugs where those are welcomed.

They are no one special. Just some of the many people who work to ensure the happiness and prosperity of their fellow citizens. Think of them as social workers if you like; their role is no different from that of social workers anywhere. Word has come of a troubling case, and this is why they gather: to discuss it, and make a difficult decision.

There are wonders far greater than a few floating skyscrapers in Um-Helat, you see, and one of these is the ability to bridge the distances between possibilities—what we would call universes. Anyone can do it, but almost no one tries. That is because, due to a quirk of spacetime, the only world that people in Um-Helat can reach is our own. And why would anyone from this glorious place want to come anywhere near our benighted hellscape?

Again you seem offended. Ah, friend! You have no right to be.

In any case, there's little danger of travel. Even Um-Helat has not successfully found a way to reduce the tremendous energy demands of macro-scale planar transversal. Only wave particles can move from our world to theirs, and back again. Only information. Who would bother? Ah, but you forget: This is a land where no one hungers, no one is left ill, no one lives in fear, and even war is almost forgotten. In such a place, buoyed by the luxury of safety and comfort, people may seek knowledge solely for knowledge's sake.

But some knowledge is dangerous.

Um-Helat has been a worse place, after all, in its past. Not all of its peoples, so disparate in origin and custom and language, came together entirely by choice. The city had a different civilization once—one which might not have upset you so! (Poor thing. There, there.) Remnants of that time dot the land all around the city, ruined and enormous and half-broken. Here a bridge. There a great truck, on its back a rusting, curve-sided thing that ancient peoples referred to by the exotic term *missile*. In the distance: the skeletal remains of another city, once just as vast as Um-Helat, but never so lovely. Works such as these encumber all the land, no more and no less venerable to the Um-Helatians than the rest of the landscape. Indeed, every young citizen must be reminded of these things upon coming of age, and told carefully curated stories of their nature and purpose. When the young citizens learn this, it is a shock almost incomprehensible, in that they literally lack the words to comprehend such things. The languages spoken in Um-Helat were once *our* languages, yes—for this world was once our world; it was not so much parallel as *the same*, back then. You might still recognize the languages, but what would puzzle you is how they speak...and how they don't. Oh, some of this will be familiar to you in concept at least, like terms for gender that mean neither he nor she, and the condemnation of words meant to slur and denigrate. And yet you will puzzle over the Um-Helatians' choice to retain descriptive terms for themselves like *kinky-haired* or *fat* or *deaf*. But these are just words, friend, don't you see? Without the attached contempt, such terms have no more meaning than if horses could proudly introduce themselves as palomino or miniature or hairy-footed. Difference was never the problem in and of itself—and Um-Helatians still have differences with each other, of opinion and otherwise. Of course they do! They're people. But what shocks the young citizens of Um-Helat is the realization that, once, those differences of opinion involved differences in respect. That once, value was ascribed to some people, and not others. That once, humanity was acknowledged for some, and not others.

It's the Day of Good Birds in Um-Helat, where every soul matters, and even the idea that some might not is anathema.

This, then, is why the social workers of Um-Helat have come together: because someone has breached the barrier between worlds. A citizen of Um-Helat has listened, on equipment you would not recognize but which records minute quantum perturbations excited by signal wavelengths, to our radio. He has watched our television. He has followed our social media, played our videos, liked our selfies. We are remarkably primitive, compared to Um-Helat. Time flows the same in both worlds, but people there have not wasted themselves on crushing one another into submission, and this makes a remarkable difference. So anyone can do it— build a thing to traverse the worlds. Like building your own ham radio. Easy. Which is why there is an entire underground industry in Um-Helat—ah! crime! *now* you believe a little more—built around information gleaned from the strange alien world that is our own. Pamphlets are written and distributed. Art and whispers are traded. The forbidden is so seductive, is it not? Even here, where only things that cause harm to others are called evil. The information-gleaners know that what they do is wrong. They know this is what destroyed the old cities. And indeed, they are horrified at what they hear through the speakers, see on the screens. They begin to perceive that ours is a world where the notion that *some people are less important than others* has been allowed to take root, and grow until it buckles and cracks the foundations of our humanity. "How could they?" the gleaners exclaim, of us. "Why would they do such things? How can they just leave those people to starve? Why do they not listen when that one complains of disrespect? What does it mean that these ones have been assaulted and no one, *no one*, cares? Who treats other people like *that?*" And yet, even amid their shock, they share the idea. The evil...spreads.

So the social workers of Um-Helat stand, talking now, over the body of a man. He is dead—early, unwilling, with a beautifully crafted pike jammed through his spine and heart. (The spine to make it painless. The heart to make it quick.) This is only one of the weapons carried by the social workers, and they prefer it because the pike is silent. Because there was no shot or ricochet, no crackle or sizzle, no scream, no one else will come to investigate. The disease has taken one poor victim, but it need not claim more. In this manner is the contagion contained...in a moment. In a moment.

Beside the man's body crouches a little girl. She's curly-haired, plump, blind, brown, tall for her age. Normally a boisterous child, she weeps now over her father's death, and her tears run hot with the injustice of it all. She heard him say, "I'm sorry." She heard the social workers show the only mercy possible. But she isn't old enough to have been warned of the consequences of breaking the law, or to understand that her father knew those consequences and accepted them—so to her, what has happened has no purpose or reason. It is a senseless, monstrous, and impossible thing, called murder.

"I'll get back at you," she says between sobs. "I'll make you die the way you made him die." This is an unthinkable thing to say.

Something is very wrong here. She snarls, "How dare you. How *dare* you."

The social workers exchange looks of concern. They are contaminated themselves, of course; it's permitted, and frankly unavoidable in their line of work. Impossible to dam a flood without getting wet. (There are measures in place. The studs on their scalps—well. In our own world, those who volunteered to work in leper colonies were once venerated, and imprisoned with them.) The social workers know, therefore, that for incomprehensible reasons, this girl's father has shared the poison knowledge of our world with her. An uncontaminated citizen of Um-Helat would have asked "Why?" after the initial shock and horror, because they would expect a reason. There would *be* a reason. But this girl has already decided that the social workers are less important than her father, and therefore the reason doesn't matter. She believes that the entire city is less important than one man's selfishness. Poor child. She is nearly septic with the taint of our world.

Nearly. But then our social worker, the tall brown one who got a hundred strangers to smile at a handmade ladybug, crouches and takes the child's hand.

What? What surprises you? Did you think this would end with the cold-eyed slaughter of a child? There are other options—and this is Um-Helat, friend, where even a pitiful, diseased child matters. They will keep her in quarantine, and reach out to her for many days. If the girl accepts the hand, listens to them, they will try to explain why her father had to die. She's early for the knowledge, but something must be done, do you see? Then together they will bury him, with their own hands if they must, in the beautiful garden that they tend between caseloads. This garden holds all the Um-Helatians who broke the law. Just because they have to die as deterrence doesn't mean they can't be honored for the sacrifice.

But there is only one treatment for this toxin once it gets into the blood: fighting it. Tooth and nail, spear and claw, up close and brutal; no quarter can be given, no parole, no debate. The child must grow, and learn, and become another social worker fighting an endless war against an idea . . . but she will live, and help others, and find meaning in that. If she takes the woman's hand.

Does this work for you, at last, friend? Does the possibility of harsh enforcement add enough realism? Are you better able to accept this postcolonial utopia now that you see its bloody teeth? Ah, but they did not choose this battle, the people of Um-Helat today; their ancestors did, when they spun lies and ignored conscience in order to profit from others' pain. Their greed became a philosophy, a religion, a series of nations, all built on blood. Um-Helat has chosen to be better. But it, too, must perform blood sacrifice to keep true evil at bay.

And now we come to you, my friend. My little soldier. See what I've done? So insidious, these little thoughts, going both ways along the quantum path. Now, perhaps, you will think of Um-Helat, and wish. Now you might finally be able to envision a world where people have learned to love, as they learned in our world to hate. Perhaps you will speak of Um-Helat to others, and spread the notion farther still, like joyous birds migrating on trade winds. *It's possible.* Everyone—even the poor, even the lazy, even the undesirable—can matter. Do you see how just the idea of this provokes utter rage in some? That is the infection defending itself . . . because if enough of us believe a thing is possible, then it becomes so.

And then? Who knows. War, maybe. The fire of fever and the

purging scourge. No one wants that, but is not the alternative to lie helpless, spotty and blistered and heaving, until we *all* die?

So don't walk away. The child needs you, too, don't you see? You also have to fight for her, now that you know she exists, or walking away is meaningless. Here, here is my hand. Take it. Please.

Good. Good.

Now. Let's get to work.

The City Born Great

I sing the city.

Fucking city. I stand on the rooftop of a building I don't live in and spread my arms and tighten my middle and yell nonsense ululations at the construction site that blocks my view. I'm really singing to the cityscape beyond. The city'll figure it out.

It's dawn. The damp of it makes my jeans feel slimy, or maybe that's 'cause they haven't been washed in weeks. Got change for a wash-and-dry, just not another pair of pants to wear till they're done. Maybe I'll spend it on more pants at the Goodwill down the street instead...but not yet. Not till I've finished going *AAAAaaaaAAAAaaaa* (breath) *aaaaAAAAaaaaaaa* and listening to the syllable echo back at me from every nearby building face. In my head, there's an orchestra playing "Ode to Joy" with a Busta Rhymes backbeat. My voice is just tying it all together.

Shut your fucking mouth! someone yells, so I take a bow and exit the stage.

But with my hand on the knob of the rooftop door, I stop and turn back and frown and listen, 'cause for a moment I hear something both distant and intimate singing back at me, basso-deep. Sort of coy.

And from even farther, I hear something else: a dissonant, gathering growl. Or maybe those are the rumblers of police sirens? Nothing I like the sound of, either way. I leave.

"There's a way these things are supposed to work," says Paulo. He's smoking again, nasty bastard. I've never seen him eat. All he uses his mouth for is smoking, drinking coffee, and talking. Shame; it's a nice mouth otherwise.

We're sitting in a café. I'm sitting with him because he bought me breakfast. The people in the café are eyeballing him because he's something not-white by their standards, but they can't tell what. They're eyeballing me because I'm definitely black, and because the holes in my clothes aren't the fashionable kind. I don't stink, but these people can smell anybody without a trust fund from a mile away.

"Right," I say, biting into the egg sandwich and damn near wetting myself. Actual egg! Swiss cheese! It's so much better than that McDonald's shit.

Guy likes hearing himself talk. I like his accent; it's sort of nasal and sibilant, nothing like a Spanish speaker's. His eyes are huge, and I think, *I could get away with so much shit if I had permanent puppy eyes like that.* But he seems older than he looks—way, way older. There's only a tinge of gray at his temples, nice and distinguished, but he feels, like, a hundred.

He's also eyeballing me, and not in the way I'm used to. "Are you listening?" he asks. "This is important."

"Yeah," I say, and take another bite of my sandwich.

He sits forward. "I didn't believe it either, at first. Hong had to drag me to one of the sewers, down into the reeking dark, and show me the growing roots, the budding teeth. I'd been hearing breathing all my life. I thought everyone could." He pauses. "Have you heard it yet?"

"Heard what?" I ask, which is the wrong answer. It isn't that I'm not listening. I just don't give a shit.

He sighs. "Listen."

"I *am* listening!"

"No. I mean, listen, but not to me." He gets up, tosses a twenty onto the table—which isn't necessary, because he paid for the sandwich and the coffee at the counter, and this café doesn't do table service. "Meet me back here on Thursday."

I pick up the twenty, finger it, pocket it. Would've done him for the sandwich, or because I like his eyes, but whatever. "You got a place?"

He blinks, then actually looks annoyed. "*Listen*," he commands again, and leaves.

I sit there for as long as I can, making the sandwich last, sipping his leftover coffee, savoring the fantasy of being normal. I people-watch, judge other patrons' appearances; on the fly I make up a poem about being a rich white girl who notices a poor black boy in her coffee shop and has an existential crisis. I imagine Paulo being impressed by my sophistication and admiring me, instead of thinking I'm just some dumb street kid who doesn't listen. I visualize myself going back to a nice apartment with a soft bed, and a fridge stuffed full of food.

Then a cop comes in, fat florid guy buying hipster joe for himself and his partner in the car, and his flat eyes skim the shop. I imagine mirrors around my head, a rotating cylinder of them that causes his gaze to bounce away. There's no real power in this—it's just something I do to try to make myself less afraid when the monsters are near. For the first time, though, it sort of works: The cop looks around, but doesn't ping on the lone black face. Lucky. I escape.

I paint the city. Back when I was in school, there was an artist who came in on Fridays to give us free lessons in perspective and lighting and other shit that white people go to art school to learn. Except this guy had done that, and he was black. I'd never seen a black artist before. For a minute I thought I could maybe be one, too.

I can be, sometimes. Deep in the night, on a rooftop in Chinatown, with a spray can for each hand and a bucket of drywall paint that somebody left outside after doing up their living room in lilac, I move in scuttling, crablike swirls. The drywall stuff I can't use too much of; it'll start flaking off after a couple of rains. Spray paint's better for everything, but I like the contrast of the two textures— liquid black on rough lilac, red edging the black. I'm painting a hole. It's like a throat that doesn't start with a mouth or end in lungs; a thing that breathes and swallows endlessly, never filling. No one will see it except people in planes angling toward LaGuardia from the southwest, a few tourists who take helicopter tours, and NYPD aerial surveillance. I don't care what they see. It's not for them.

It's real late. I didn't have anywhere to sleep for the night, so this is what I'm doing to stay awake. If it wasn't the end of the month, I'd get on the subway, but the cops who haven't met their quota would fuck with me. Gotta be careful here; there's a lot of dumb-fuck Chinese kids west of Chrystie Street who wanna pretend to be a gang, protecting their territory, so I keep low. I'm skinny, dark; that helps, too. All I want to do is paint, man, because it's in me and I need to get it out. I need to open up this throat. I need to, I need to...yeah. Yeah.

There's a soft, strange sound as I lay down the last streak of black. I pause and look around, confused for a moment—and then the throat sighs behind me. A big, heavy gust of moist air tickles the hairs on my skin. I'm not scared. This is why I did it, though I didn't realize that when I started. Not sure how I know now. But when I turn back, it's still just paint on a rooftop.

Paulo wasn't shitting me. Huh. Or maybe my mama was right, and I ain't never been right in the head.

I jump into the air and whoop for joy, and I don't even know why.

I spend the next two days going all over the city, drawing breathing-holes everywhere, till my paint runs out.

I'm so tired on the day I meet Paulo again that I stumble and nearly fall through the café's plate-glass window. He catches my elbow and drags me over to a bench meant for customers. "You're hearing it," he says. He sounds pleased.

"I'm hearing coffee," I suggest, not bothering to stifle a yawn. A cop car rolls by. I'm not too tired to imagine myself as nothing, beneath notice, not even worth beating for pleasure. It works again; they roll on.

Paulo ignores my suggestion. He sits down beside me and his gaze goes strange and unfocused for a moment. "Yes. The city is breathing easier," he says. "You're doing a good job, even without training."

"I try."

He looks amused. "I can't tell if you don't believe me, or if you just don't care."

I shrug. "I believe you." I also don't care, not much, because I'm hungry. My stomach growls. I've still got that twenty he gave me, but I'll take it to that church-plate sale I heard about over on

Prospect, get chicken and rice and greens and cornbread for less than the cost of a free-trade small-batch-roasted latte.

He glances down at my stomach when it growls. Huh. I pretend to stretch and scratch above my abs, making sure to pull up my shirt a little. The artist guy brought a model for us to draw once, and pointed to this little ridge of muscle above the hips called Apollo's Belt. Paulo's gaze goes right to it. *Come on, come on, fishy fishy. I need somewhere to sleep.*

Then his eyes narrow and focus on mine again. "I had forgotten," he says, in a faint wondering tone. "I almost... It's been so long. Once, though, I was a boy of the *favelas.*"

"Not a lot of Mexican food in New York," I reply.

He blinks and looks amused again. Then he sobers. "This city will die," he says. He doesn't raise his voice, but he doesn't have to. I'm paying attention now. Food, living: These things have meaning to me. "If you do not learn the things I have to teach you. If you do not help. The time will come and you will fail, and this city will join Pompeii and Atlantis and a dozen others whose names no one remembers, even though hundreds of thousands of people died with them. Or perhaps there will be a stillbirth—the shell of the city surviving to possibly grow again in the future but its vital spark snuffed for now, like New Orleans—but that will still kill *you*, either way. You are the catalyst, whether of strength or destruction."

He's been talking like this since he showed up—places that never were, things that can't be, omens and portents. I figure it's bullshit because he's telling it to *me*, a kid whose own mama kicked him out and prays for him to die every day and probably hates me. *God* hates me. And I fucking hate God back, so why would he choose me for anything? But that's really why I start paying attention: because of God. I don't have to believe in something for it to fuck up my life.

"Tell me what to do," I say.

Paulo nods, looking smug. Thinks he's got my number. "Ah. You don't want to die."

I stand up, stretch, feel the streets around me grow longer and more pliable in the rising heat of day. (Is that really happening, or am I imagining it, or is it happening *and* I'm imagining that it's connected to me somehow?) "Fuck you. That ain't it."

"Then you don't even care about that." He makes it a question with the tone of his voice.

"Ain't about being alive." I'll starve to death someday, or freeze some winter night, or catch something that rots me away until the hospitals have to take me, even without money or an address. But I'll sing and paint and dance and fuck and cry the city before I'm done, because it's mine. It's fucking *mine*. That's why.

"It's about *living*," I finish. And then I turn to glare at him. He can kiss my ass if he doesn't understand. "Tell me what to do."

Something changes in Paulo's face. He's listening, now. To me. So he gets to his feet and leads me away for my first real lesson.

This is the lesson: Great cities are like any other living things, being born and maturing and wearying and dying in their turn.

Duh, right? Everyone who's visited a real city feels that, one way or another. All those rural people who hate cities are afraid of something legit; cities really are *different*. They make a weight on the world, a tear in the fabric of reality, like...like black holes, maybe. Yeah. (I go to museums sometimes. They're cool inside, and Neil deGrasse Tyson is hot.) As more and more people come in and deposit their strangeness and leave and get replaced by others, the tear widens. Eventually it gets so deep that it forms a pocket, connected only by the thinnest thread of... something to... something. Whatever cities are made of.

But the separation starts a process, and in that pocket the many parts of the city begin to multiply and differentiate. Its sewers extend into places where there is no need for water. Its slums grow teeth; its art centers, claws. Ordinary things within it, traffic and construction and stuff like that, start to have a rhythm like a heartbeat, if you record their sounds and play them back fast. The city... quickens.

Not all cities make it this far. There used to be a couple of great cities on this continent, but that was before Columbus fucked the Indians' shit up, so we had to start over. New Orleans failed, like Paulo said, but it survived, and that's something. It can try again. Mexico City's well on its way. But New York is the first American city to reach this point.

The gestation can take twenty years or two hundred or two thousand, but eventually the time will come. The cord is cut and the city becomes a thing of its own, able to stand on wobbly legs and do... well, whatever the fuck a living, thinking entity shaped like a big-ass city wants to do.

And just as in any other part of nature, there are things lying in wait for this moment, hoping to chase down the sweet new life and swallow its guts while it screams.

That's why Paulo's here to teach me. That's why I can clear the city's breathing and stretch and massage its asphalt limbs. I'm the midwife, see.

I run the city. I run it every fucking day.

Paulo takes me home. It's just somebody's summer sublet in the Lower East Side, but it feels like a home. I use his shower and eat some of the food in his fridge without asking, just to see what he'll do. He doesn't do shit except smoke a cigarette, I think to piss me off. I can hear sirens on the streets of the neighborhood—frequent, close. I wonder, for some reason, if they're looking for me. I don't say it aloud, but Paulo sees me twitching. He says, "The harbingers of the enemy will hide among the city's parasites. Beware of them."

He's always saying cryptic shit like this. Some of it makes sense, like when he speculates that maybe there's a *purpose* to all of it, some reason for the great cities and the process that makes them. What the enemy has been doing—attacking at the moment of vulnerability, crimes of opportunity—might just be the warm-up for something bigger. But Paulo's full of shit, too, like when he says I should consider meditation to better attune myself to the city's needs. Like I'mma get through this on white girl yoga.

"White girl yoga," Paulo says, nodding. "Indian man yoga. Stockbroker racquetball and schoolboy handball, ballet and merengue, union halls and SoHo galleries. You will embody a city of millions. You need not *be* them, but know that they are part of you."

I laugh. "Racquetball? That shit ain't no part of me, chico."

"The city chose you, out of all," Paulo says. "Their lives depend on you."

Maybe. But I'm still hungry and tired all the time, scared all the time, never safe. What good does it do to be valuable, if nobody values you?

He can tell I don't wanna talk anymore, so he gets up and goes to bed. I flop on the couch and I'm dead to the world. Dead.

Dreaming, dead dreaming, of a dark place beneath heavy cold waves where something stirs with a slithery sound and uncoils and turns toward the mouth of the Hudson, where it empties into the sea. Toward *me*. And I am too weak, too helpless, too immobilized by fear, to do anything but twitch beneath its predatory gaze.

Something comes from far to the south, somehow. (None of this is quite real. Everything rides along the thin tether that connects the city's reality to that of the world. The *effect* happens in the world, Paulo has said. The *cause* centers around me.) It moves between me, wherever I am, and the uncurling thing, wherever it is. An immensity protects me, just this once, just in this place—though from a great distance I feel others hemming and grumbling and raising themselves to readiness. Warning the enemy that it must adhere to the rules of engagement that have always governed this ancient battle. It's not allowed to come at me too soon.

My protector, in this unreal space of dream, is a sprawling jewel with filth-crusted facets, a thing that stinks of dark coffee and the bruised grass of a *futebol* pitch and traffic noise and familiar cigarette smoke. Its threat display of saber-shaped girders lasts for only a moment, but that is enough. The uncurling thing flinches back into its cold cave, resentfully. But it will be back. That, too, is tradition.

I wake with sunlight warming half my face. Just a dream? I stumble into the room where Paulo is sleeping. "*São* Paulo," I whisper, but he does not wake. I wiggle under his covers. When he wakes, he doesn't reach for me, but he doesn't push me away either. I let him know I'm grateful and give him a reason to let me back in later. The rest'll have to wait till I get condoms and he brushes his ashy-ass mouth. After that, I use his shower again, put on the clothes I washed in his sink, and head out while he's still snoring.

Libraries are safe places. They're warm in the winter. Nobody cares if you stay all day as long as you're not eyeballing the kids' corner or trying to hit up porn on the computers. The one at Forty-second—the one with the lions—isn't that kind of library. It doesn't lend out books. Still, it has a library's safety, so I sit in a corner and read everything within reach: municipal tax law, *Birds of the Hudson Valley*, *What to Expect When You're Expecting a City Baby: NYC Edition*. See, Paulo? I told you I was listening.

It gets to be late afternoon and I head outside. People cover the steps, laughing, chatting, mugging with selfie sticks. There're cops in body armor over by the subway entrance, showing off their guns to the tourists so they'll feel safe from New York. I get a Polish sausage and eat it at the feet of one of the lions. Fortitude, not Patience. I know my strengths.

I'm full of meat and relaxed and thinking about stuff that ain't actually important—like how long Paulo will let me stay and whether I can use his address to apply for stuff—so I'm not watching the street. Until cold prickles skitter over my side. I know what it is before I react, but I'm careless again because I *turn to look...* Stupid, stupid, I fucking know better; cops down in Baltimore broke a man's spine for making eye contact. But as I spot these two on the corner opposite the library steps—short pale man and tall dark woman both in blue like black—I notice something that actually breaks my fear because it's so strange.

It's a bright, clear day, not a cloud in the sky. People walking past the cops leave short, stark afternoon shadows, barely there at all. But around these two, the shadows pool and curl as if they stand beneath their own private, roiling thundercloud. And as I watch, the shorter one begins to... *stretch*, sort of, his shape warping ever so slightly, until one eye is twice the circumference of the other. His right shoulder slowly develops a bulge that suggests a dislocated joint. His companion doesn't seem to notice.

Yooooo, nope. I get up and start picking my way through the crowd on the steps. I'm doing that thing I do, trying to shunt off their gaze—but it feels different this time. Sticky, sort of, threads of cheap-shit gum fucking up my mirrors. I *feel* them start following me, something immense and wrong shifting in my direction.

Even then I'm not sure—a lot of real cops drip and pulse sadism in the same way—but I ain't taking chances. My city is helpless, unborn as yet, and Paulo ain't here to protect me. I gotta look out for self, same as always.

I play casual till I reach the corner and book it, or try. Fucking tourists! They idle along the wrong side of the sidewalk, stopping to look at maps and take pictures of shit nobody else gives a fuck about. I'm so busy cussing them out in my head that I forget they can also be dangerous: Somebody yells and grabs my arm as I Heisman past, and I hear a man yell out, "He tried to take her purse!" as I wrench away. *Bitch, I ain't took shit,* I think, but it's too late. I see another tourist reaching for her phone to call 911. Every cop in the area will be gunning for every black male aged whatever now.

I gotta get out of the area.

Grand Central's right there, sweet subway promise, but I see three cops hanging out in the entrance, so I swerve right to take Forty-first. The crowds thin out past Lex, but where can I go? I sprint across Third despite the traffic; there are enough gaps. But I'm getting tired, 'cause I'm a scrawny dude who doesn't get enough to eat, not a track star.

I keep going, though, even through the burn in my side. I can feel *those* cops, the *harbingers of the enemy,* not far behind me. The ground shakes with their lumpen footfalls.

I hear a siren about a block away, closing. Shit, the UN's coming up; I don't need the Secret Service or whatever on me, too. I jag left through an alley and trip over a wooden pallet. Lucky again—a cop car rolls by the alley entrance just as I go down, and they don't see me. I stay down and try to catch my breath till I hear the car's engine fading into the distance. Then, when I think it's safe, I push up. Look back, because the city is squirming around me, the concrete is jittering and heaving, everything from the bedrock to the rooftop bars is trying its damnedest to tell me to go. Go. *Go.*

Crowding the alley behind me is...is...the shit? I don't have words for it. Too many arms, too many legs, too many eyes, and all of them fixed on me. Somewhere in the mass I glimpse curls of dark hair and a scalp of pale blond, and I understand suddenly that these are—this is—my two cops. One real monstrosity. The walls of the alley crack as it oozes its way into the narrow space.

"Oh. Fuck. No," I gasp.

I claw my way to my feet and haul ass. A patrol car comes around the corner from Second Avenue and I don't see it in time to duck out of sight. The car's loudspeaker blares something unintelligible, probably *I'm gonna kill you,* and I'm actually amazed. Do they not see the thing behind me? Or do they just not give a shit because they can't shake it down for city revenue? Let them fucking shoot me. Better than whatever that thing will do.

I hook left onto Second Avenue. The cop car can't come after me against the traffic, but it's not like that'll stop some doubled-cop monster. Forty-fifth. Forty-seventh and my legs are molten granite. Fiftieth and I think I'm going to die. Heart attack far too young; poor kid, should've eaten more organic; should've taken it easy and not been so angry; the world can't hurt you if you just ignore everything that's wrong with it; well, not until it kills you anyway.

I cross the street and risk a look back and see something roll onto the sidewalk on at least eight legs, using three or four arms to push itself off a building as it careens a little...before coming straight after me again. It's the Mega Cop, and it's gaining. *Oh shit oh shit oh shit please no.*

Only one choice.

Swing right. Fifty-third, against the traffic. An old folks' home, a park, a promenade... fuck those. Pedestrian bridge? Fuck that. I head straight for the six lanes of utter batshittery and potholes that is FDR Drive, do not pass Go, do not try to cross on foot unless you want to be smeared halfway to Brooklyn. Beyond it? The East River, if I survive. I'm even freaked out enough to try swimming in that fucking sewage. But I'm probably gonna collapse in the third lane and get run over fifty times before anybody thinks to put on brakes.

Behind me, the Mega Cop utters a wet, tumid *hough*, like it's clearing its throat for swallowing. I go

over the barrier and through the grass into fucking hell I go one lane silver car two lanes horns horns horns three lanes SEMI WHAT'S A FUCKING SEMI DOING ON THE FDR IT'S TOO TALL YOU STUPID UPSTATE HICK screaming four lanes GREEN TAXI screaming Smart Car hahaha cute five lanes moving truck six lanes and the blue Lexus actually brushes up against my clothes as it blares past screaming screaming screaming

screaming

screaming metal and tires as reality stretches, and nothing stops for the Mega Cop; it does not belong here and the FDR is an artery, vital with the movement of nutrients and strength and attitude and adrenaline, the cars are white blood cells and the thing is an irritant, an infection, an invader to whom the city gives no consideration and no quarter

screaming, as the Mega Cop is torn to pieces by the semi and the taxi and the Lexus and even that adorable Smart Car, which actually swerves a little to run over an extra-wiggly piece. I collapse onto a square of grass, breathless, shaking, wheezing, and can only stare as a dozen limbs are crushed, two dozen eyes squashed flat, a mouth that is mostly gums riven from jaw to palate. The pieces flicker like a monitor with an AV cable short, translucent to solid and back again—but FDR don't stop for shit except a presidential motorcade or a Knicks game, and this thing sure as hell ain't Carmelo Anthony. Pretty soon there's nothing left of it but half-real smears on the asphalt.

I'm alive. Oh, God.

I cry for a little while. Mama's boyfriend ain't here to slap me and say I'm not a man for it. Daddy would've said it was okay—tears mean you're alive—but Daddy's dead. And I'm alive.

With limbs burning and weak, I drag myself up, then fall again. Everything hurts. Is this that heart attack? I feel sick. Everything is shaking, blurring. Maybe it's a stroke. You don't have to be old for that to happen, do you? I stumble over to a garbage can and think about throwing up into it. There's an old guy lying on the bench— me in twenty years, if I make it that far. He opens one eye as I stand there gagging and purses his lips in a judgy way, like he could do better dry-heaves in his sleep.

He says, "It's time," and rolls over to put his back to me.

Time. Suddenly I have to move. Sick or not, exhausted or not, something is . . . pulling me. West, toward the city's center. I push away from the can and hug myself as I shiver and stumble toward the pedestrian bridge. As I walk over the lanes I previously ran across, I look down onto flickering fragments of the dead Mega Cop, now ground into the asphalt by a hundred car wheels. Some globules of it are still twitching, and I don't like that. Infection, intrusion. I want it gone.

We want it gone. Yes. It's time.

I blink and suddenly I'm in Central Park. How the fuck did I get here? Disoriented, I realize only as I see their black shoes that I'm passing another pair of cops, but these two don't bother me. They should—skinny kid shivering like he's cold on a June day; even if all they do is drag me off somewhere to shove a plunger up my ass, they should *react* to me. Instead, it's like I'm not there. Miracles exist, Ralph Ellison was right, any NYPD you can walk away from, hallelujah.

The Lake. Bow Bridge: a place of transition. I stop here, stand here, and I know ... everything.

Everything Paulo's told me: It's true. Somewhere beyond the city, the Enemy is awakening. It sent forth its harbingers and they have failed, but its taint is in the city now, spreading with every car that passes over every now-microscopic iota of the Mega Cop's substance, and this creates a foothold. The Enemy uses this anchor to drag itself up from the dark toward the world, toward the warmth and light, toward the defiance that is *me*, toward the burgeoning wholeness that is *my city*. This attack is not all of it, of course. What comes is only the smallest fraction of the Enemy's old, old evil—but that should be more than enough to slaughter one lowly, worn-out kid who doesn't even have a real city to protect him.

Not yet. It's time. *In* time? We'll see.

On Second, Sixth, and Eighth Avenues, my water breaks. Mains, I mean. Water mains. Terrible mess, gonna fuck up the evening commute. I shut my eyes and I am seeing what no one else sees. I am feeling the flex and rhythm of reality, the contractions of possibility. I reach out and grip the railing of the bridge before me and feel the steady, strong pulse that runs through it. *You're doing good, baby. Doing great.*

Something begins to shift. I grow bigger, encompassing. I feel myself upon the firmament, heavy as the foundations of a city. There are others here with me, looming, watching—my ancestors' bones under Wall Street, my predecessors' blood ground into the benches of Christopher Park. No, *new* others, of my new people, heavy imprints upon the fabric of time and space. São Paulo squats nearest, its roots stretching all the way to the bones of dead Machu Picchu, watching sagely and twitching a little with the memory of its own relatively recent traumatic birth. Paris observes with distant disinterest, mildly offended that any city of our tasteless upstart land has managed this transition; Lagos exults to see a new fellow who knows the hustle, the hype, the fight. And more, many more, all of them watching, waiting to see if their numbers increase. Or not. If nothing else, they will bear witness that I, we, were great for one shining moment.

"We'll make it," I say, squeezing the railing and feeling the city contract. All over the city, people's ears pop, and they look around in confusion. "Just a little more. Come on." I'm scared, but there's no rushing this. *Lo que pasa, pasa*—damn, now that song is in my head, *in me* like the rest of New York. It's all here, just like Paulo said. There's no gap between me and the city anymore.

And as the firmament ripples, slides, tears, the Enemy writhes up from the deeps with a reality-bridging roar—

But it is too late. The tether is cut and we are here. We become! We stand, whole and hale and independent, and our legs don't even wobble. We got this. Don't sleep on the city that never sleeps, son, and don't fucking bring your squamous eldritch bullshit here.

I raise my arms and avenues leap. (It's real but it's not. The ground jolts and people think, *Huh, subway's really shaky today.*) I brace my feet and they are girders, anchors, bedrock. The beast of the deeps shrieks and I laugh, giddy with postpartum endorphins. *Bring it.* And when it comes at me, I hip-check it with the BQE, backhand it with Inwood Park, drop the South Bronx on it like an elbow. (On the evening news that night, ten construction sites will report wrecking-ball collapses. City safety regulations are so lax; terrible, terrible.) The Enemy tries some kind of fucked-up wiggly shit—it's all tentacles—and I snarl and bite into it 'cause New Yorkers eat damn near as much sushi as Tokyo, mercury and all.

Oh, now you're crying! Now you wanna run? Nah, son. You came to the wrong town. I curb stomp it with the full might of Queens and something inside the beast breaks and bleeds iridescence all over creation. This is a shock, for it has not been truly hurt in centuries. It lashes back in a fury, faster than I can block, and from a place that most of the city cannot see, a skyscraper-long tentacle curls out of nowhere to smash into New York Harbor. I scream and fall, I can *hear* my ribs crack, and—no!—a major earthquake shakes Brooklyn for the first time in decades. The Williamsburg Bridge twists and snaps apart like kindling; the Manhattan groans and splinters, though thankfully it does not give way. I feel every death as if it is my own.

Fucking kill you for that, bitch, I'm not-thinking. The fury and grief have driven me into a vengeful fugue. The pain is nothing; this ain't my first rodeo. Through the groan of my ribs I drag myself upright and brace my legs in a pissing-off-the-platform stance. Then I shower the Enemy with a one-two punch of Long Island radiation and Gowanus toxic waste, which burn it like acid. It screams again in pain and disgust, but *Fuck you, you don't belong here, this city is mine, get out!* To drive this lesson home, I cut the bitch with LIRR traffic, long vicious honking lines; and to stretch out its pain, I salt these wounds with the memory of a bus ride to LaGuardia and back.

And just to add insult to injury? I backhand its ass with Hoboken, raining the drunk rage of ten thousand dudebros down on it like the hammer of God. Port Authority makes it honorary New York, motherfucker; you just got Jerseyed.

The Enemy is as quintessential to nature as any city. We cannot be stopped from becoming, and the Enemy cannot be made to end. I hurt only a small part of it—but I know damn well I sent that part back broken. Good. Time ever comes for that final confrontation, it'll think twice about taking me on again.

Me. *Us*. Yes.

When I relax my hands and open my eyes to see Paulo striding along the bridge toward me with another goddamned cigarette between his lips, I fleetingly see him for what he is again: the sprawling thing from my dream, all sparkling spires and reeking slums and stolen rhythms made over with genteel cruelty. I know that he glimpses what I am, too, all the bright light and bluster of me. Maybe he's always seen it, but there is *admiration* in his gaze now, and I like it. He comes to help support me with his shoulder, and he says, "Congratulations," and I grin.

I live the city. It thrives and it is mine. I am its worthy avatar, and together? We will never be afraid again.

Fifty years later.

I sit in a car, watching the sunset from Mulholland Drive. The car is mine; I'm rich now. The city is not mine, but that's all right. The person is coming who will make it live and stand and thrive in the ancient way...or not. I know my duty, respect the traditions. Each city must emerge on its own or die trying. We elders merely guide, encourage. Stand witness.

There: a dip in the firmament near the Sunset Strip. I can feel the upwelling of loneliness in the soul I seek. Poor, empty baby. Won't be long now, though. Soon—if she survives—she'll never be alone again.

I reach for my city, so far away, so inseverable from myself. *Ready?* I ask New York.

Fuck yeah, it answers, filthy and fierce.

We go forth to find this city's singer, and hopefully to hear the greatness of its birthing song.

Red Dirt Witch

The way to tell the difference between dreams that were prophecy and dreams that were just wasted sleep was to wait and see if they came three times. Emmaline had her third dream about the White Lady on the coldest night ever recorded in Alabama history. This was actually *very* cold—ten degrees below zero, on a long dark January Sabbath when even the moon hid behind a veil of shadow.

Emmaline survived the cold the way poor people everywhere have done since the dawn of time: with a warm, energetic friend. Three patchwork quilts helped, too. The friend was Frank Heath, who was pretty damn spry for a man of fifty-five, though he claimed to be forty-five so maybe that helped. The quilts were Em's, and it also helped that one of them had dried flowers (Jack-in-the-pulpits) and a few nuggets of charcoal tucked under each patch of leftover cloth. That made for a standing invitation to warmth and the summertime, who were of course welcome to pay a visit and stay the night anytime they liked. Those *had* come a-calling to the children's beds, at least, for which Emmaline was grateful; the children slept soundly, snug and comfortable. That left Em and Frank free to conduct their own warmthmaking with an easy conscience.

After that was done, Emmaline closed her eyes and found herself in the Commissary Market down on Dugan. Dusty southern daylight, bright and fierce even in winter, shone slanting onto the street alongside the market, unimpeded by cars or carts—or people. Pratt City wasn't much of a city, being really just the Negro neighborhood of Birmingham, but it was a whole place, thriving and bustling in its way. Here, though, Emmaline had never seen the place so empty in her life. As if to spite the cold, the market's bins tumbled over with summer produce: watermelons and green tomatoes and peaches and more, along with a few early collards. That meant that whatever this dream meant to warn her of, it would come with the heat of the mid-months.

Out of habit, Em glanced at the sign above these last. Overpriced again; greedy bastards.

"Why, greed's a sin," said a soft, whispery voice all around her. "Be proper of you to punish 'em for it, wouldn't it?"

This was one of the spirits that she'd tamed over the years. They liked to test her, though, so it was always wise to be careful with 'em. "Supposin' I could," she said in reply. "But only the store manager, since the company too big to go after. And I can't say's I truly blame the manager, either, since he got children to feed same as me."

"Sin's sin, woman."

"And let she who is without sin cast the first stone," Em countered easily. *"As you well know."* Then she checked herself; no sense getting testy. Ill-wishing opened doors for ill winds to blow through—which was probably why the voice was trying to get her to do it.

The voice sighed a little in exasperation. It was colorless, genderless, barely a voice at all; that sigh whispered like wind through the stand of pines across the street. "Just tellin' you somebody comin', cranky old biddy."

"Who, Jesus Christ? 'Bout time, His slow ass."

Whispery laughter. "Fine, then—there a White Lady a-comin', a *fine* one, and she got something special in mind for you and yours. You ready?"

Em frowned to herself. The other two dreams had been more airy-fairy than this—just collections of symbols and hints of a threat, omens and portents. It seemed fate had finally gotten impatient enough to just say plain what she needed to hear.

"No, I ain't ready," Em said, with a sigh. "But ain't like that ever made no mind to some folk. Thank you for the warning."

More laughter, rising to become a gale, picking Emmaline up and spinning her about. The Market blurred into a whirlwind—but through it all, there were little ribbons that she could see edging into the tornado from elsewhere, whipping about in shining silken red. Truth was always there for the taking, if you only reached out to grasp it. Thing was, Em didn't *feel* like grasping it; she was tired, Lord have mercy. The world didn't change. If she just relaxed, the dream would let her back into sleep, like she wanted.

But...well. Best to be prepared, she supposed.

So Em stretched out a hand and laid hold of one of the ribbons. And suddenly the street that ran through the market was full of people. *Angry* people, most of 'em white and lining the road, and marching people, most of 'em black and in the middle of the road. The black ones' jaws were set, their chins high in a way that always meant trouble when white folks were around, because Lord, didn't they hate seeing pride. "Trouble, trouble," sang-song the voice—and before the marchers appeared a line of policemen with billy clubs in their hands and barking dogs at their sides. Emmaline's guts clenched for the blood that would almost surely be spilled. Pride! Was it worth all that blood?

Yet when she opened her mouth to shout at the marchers for their foolishness, the whispery voice laughed again, and she spun again, the laughter chasing her out of dreams and up to reality.

Well, this was what she'd wanted, but she didn't much like it because reality was dark and painfully cold on her mouth and chin, which she'd stuck outside the covers to breathe. Her teeth were chattering. She reached back.

"Ain't time to get up," muttered Frank at her stirring, half-dreaming himself.

"You got Sunday to rest," said Emmaline. "You want to live 'til then, you get to work."

His low, rich laugh warmed her more than his body ever could. "Yes ma'am," he said, and did as he was bid.

And because they had set to, Emmaline missed that her only girl-child, Pauline, got up and walked the hall for a while, disturbed by bad dreams of her own.

Since the spirits had given her a full season's warning, Em spent the time preparing for the White Lady's arrival. This meant she finished up as much business as possible in the days right after the dream. The cold passed quickly, as cold was wont to do in Alabama. And as soon as the weather was comfortable again, Emmaline set Pauline to grinding all the herbs she'd laid in since November, then had her boy Sample put her shingle out by the mailpost, where it read, HERBS AND PRAYERS, FOR ALL AND SUNDRY. This brought an immediate and eager stream of customers.

First there was Mr. Jake, who'd gotten into a spat with his cousin over Christmas dinner and had wished death on him, and now was regretting it because the cousin had come down with a wet cough. Emmaline told him to take the man some chitlins made with sardine oil and extra garlic. Then she handed him a long braid of garlic heads, ten in all, from her own garden.

"*That* much garlic?" Jake had given her a look of pure affront; like most men of Pratt City, he was proud of his cooking. "I look Eye-talian to you?"

"All right, let him die, then." This elicited a giggle from Pauline, who sat in on most of Em's appointments these days.

So, grumbling, Jake had bought the garlic from Emmaline and gone off to make his amends. People talked about Jake's stanky, awful chitlins 'til the day he died—but his cousin ate some of the peace offering, and he got better.

And there was Em's cousin Renee, who came by just to chat, and conveniently told Emmaline all the goings-on in and around Pratt City. There was trouble brewing, Renee said, *political* trouble; whispers in the church pews, meetings at the school gym, plans for a boycott or two or ten. Way up in Virginia, folks were suing the government about segregation in the schools. Em figured it wouldn't come to nothing, but all the white folks was up like angry bees over the notion of their precious children sitting next to Negro children, competing against Negro children, befriending Negro children. It was going to get ugly. Many evils came riding in on the tails of strife, though—so here, Emmaline suspected, would be their battleground.

Then there was Nadine Yates, a widow who like Emmaline had done what she had to do to keep herself and her children alive through the cold and not-so-cold days. Nadine was afraid she might be pregnant again. "I know it's a sin," she said in her quiet, dignified voice while Emmaline fixed her some tea. For this one, she'd sent Pauline off to the market with her brothers; Pauline was still just a girl, and some things were for grown women's ears only. "Still, if you could help me out, I'd be grateful."

"Sin's makin' a world where women got to choose between two children' eatin' and three children starvin'," Emmaline said, "and you sure as hell didn't do that. You made sure he wasn't some fool who'll spread it all over, didn't you?"

"He got a wife and a good job, and he ain't stupid. Gave my boys new coats just last week."

A man who knew how to keep a woman-on-the-side properly. But then wouldn't it be simple enough for him to just take care of the new child, too? Emmaline frowned as a suspicion entered her mind. "He white?"

Nadine's nearer jaw flexed a little, and then she lifted her chin in fragile defensiveness. "He is."

Emmaline sighed, but then nodded toward the tea cooling in Nadine's hand. "Drink up, now. And it sound like he can afford a guinea-hen, to me."

So a few days later, after the tea had done its work, Nadine dropped by and handed Emmaline a nice fat guineafowl. It was a rooster, but Em didn't mind. She pot-roasted it with dried celery and a lot of rosemary from her garden, and the rind of an orange that Pauline had found on the road behind a market truck. Emmaline had smacked the girl for that, because even though "finding" wasn't "stealing," white folks didn't care much for making distinctions when it came to little colored girls. But Pauline—who was smart as a whip and Em's pride—had glared at her mother after the blow. "Momma, I followed the truck to a stop sign and offered to give it back. I knew that white man wouldn't want it 'cause I touched it, and he didn't! So there!"

Smart as a whip, but still just a child, and innocent yet of the world's worst ugliness. Emmaline could only sigh and thank God the truck driver hadn't been the kind who'd noticed how pretty Pauline was becoming. As an apology for the smack, she let Pauline have half the orange while the boys got only a quarter each.

Then she'd sat the girl down for a long talk about how the world worked.

And so it was, as the brief winter warmed toward briefer spring and began the long slow march into Southern summer. By the time the tomato plants flowered, Em was as ready as she could be.

"Oh, Miss Emmaline!" called a voice from outside. An instant later Jim and Sample, Emmaline's boys, ran into the kitchen.

"It's a red lady outside," Sample gushed.

"Well, go figure," Emmaline said. "Ain't like you ain't a quarter red yourself." Her papa had been Black Creek, his hair uncut 'til death.

"Not *that* kinda red," said Sample, rolling his eyes enough to get a hard look from Emmaline. "She askin' for you."

"Is she, now?" Emma turned from the pantry and handed Sample a jar of peach preserves. "Open that for me and you can have some." Delighted to be treated like a man, Sample promptly sat down and began wrestling with the tight lid.

"I don't like this one," said Jim, and since Jim was her artist— none of the dreaming in him, but he saw things others didn't— Emmaline knew the time had come. She wiped her hands on a cloth and went out onto the porch to meet the White Lady.

She smelled the lady before she saw her: a thick waft of magnolia perfume, too cloying to be quite natural. Outside, the perfume wasn't as bad, diminished and blended in among the scents of Em's garden and the faint sulfurous miasma that was omnipresent in Pratt City on still days like this—that from the Village Creek, polluted as it was with nearly a century's worth of iron and steel manufacturing waste. The woman to whom the perfume belonged stood on the grassy patch in front of Em's house, fastidiously away from the red dirt path that most people walked to reach her front porch. Why, this lady was just as pretty as a flower in a full-skirted dress of cotton print, yellow covered in white-and-green lilies. No crinoline, but nearly as old-fashioned, with layers separated by bunched taffeta and edged in lace. Around the heart-shaped bodice, her skin was white as pearl—so white that Em figured she'd have burned up in a minute if not for the enormous parasol positioned over her head. And here was why Sample had called her red: the confection of her hair, spun into an elegant chignon behind her head and topped with a crown of white flowers, was nearly as burgundy as good wine.

It was all Em could do not to feel inadequate, given that she wore only an old faded housedress, with her own hair done up in plaits and hidden away beneath a wrap. But she drew herself up anyway, and reminded herself that she needed no parasol to keep her skin fine; the sun did that itself, and black didn't crack beneath its blessing. Those were just surface things anyway. The White Lady was nearly *all* surface; that was the nature of her kind. That was how this meeting would go, then: an appearance of grace and gentility, covering the substance of battle.

"Why, I've come to see 'bout you, Miss Emmaline," the White Lady said, as if they were in the middle of a conversation and not the beginning. Her voice was light and sweet, as honeyed as her yellow eyes. "You know me?"

"Yes, ma'am," Em said, because she knew the children were watching and it wouldn't do for them, 'specially the boys, to think they could smart off to white ladies. Even if this one wasn't really a white lady. "Heard here and there you was coming."

"Did you, now!" She simpered, dimples flashing, and flicked at her skirts. As she did this, Em caught a glimpse of a figure behind her: a little black girl, couldn't have been more than seven, crouched and holding the pole of the great big parasol over the woman's head. The little girl's feet were bare beneath the simple white shift she wore, and her eyes were still and empty.

"I suppose I shouldn't be surprised that you heard," the White Lady said, unfolding a little lace fan and fluttering it at herself. "Figured you'd have your ways. Could I trouble you for some tea or lemonade, though, Miss Emmaline? It's always almighty hot in this land. Not that that bothers your kind like it does mine."

"Mighty hot indeed," Emmaline agreed evenly. She nodded to Pauline, who stood beside her trembling a little. Even a half-trained girlchild knew power when she saw it. Pauline jumped, but went inside. "This land made its natural people brown for a reason, though, ma'am, long before either your'n or most of mine came along. Seems to me you could make yourself fit the land better—if you wanted, of course."

The woman extended one long, thin arm and ran her fingers up the pearly skin, looking almost bemused to find such flesh upon herself. "I *should*, I suppose, but you know there's more reward than price comes with this skin."

Em did indeed know. "Pauline's gone to fetch some tea for you, ma'am. No lemonade, I'm afraid; lemons cost too dear when you got three children and no husband, see."

"Ah, yes! About those children of yours."

As much as Emmaline thought she had braced herself, she still couldn't help tensing up when the White Lady's yellow eyes shifted to dance over the faces of Jim and Sample. Lord, but she should've guessed! America wasn't the Old Country; these days the White Folk didn't bother with silly tricks or living in mounds, and they didn't stay hidden, for why should they? But the one thing they still did, in spades here in this land of cheap flesh, was steal children.

And if they kept to children of a certain hue, why, the police didn't even ask after them. Emmaline set her jaw.

The woman's eyes lingered on Jim long enough to be worrying. Jim, smart one that he was, had gone still and quiet, looking down at his feet, knowing better than to meet any white woman's gaze. Sample was all a-bristle, not liking the way the woman was eyeballing his little brother; ah, damnation, Emmaline never should've picked for Sample's father a man who liked to fight. Boy was gonna get himself in trouble someday.

Em had a feeling, though, that this was a feint. Then Pauline came back onto the porch with a big sweating glass of iced tea... and sure enough, the White Lady's gaze landed on the girl with much more than greed for a cool drink.

Pauline stopped there, with her eyes narrowed, because like Emmaline, she knew what was beneath the surface. The woman laughed prettily at the look on the girl's face.

"*Trouble comin' tell,*" the White Lady sang, still grinning. "*Trouble comin' fine! Nought to pay the price but sweet blood like fine wine.*" She had a beautiful voice—lilting and hymn-reverberant and high as birds flew. Hardly sounded human, in fact, which was fitting enough.

Em raised a hand in praise anyway, because beauty was meant to be acknowledged, and to deny it would just invite her further in. "Trouble always coming, ma'am," she replied to the song. "Some'a us, this world made of trouble. Not that you folk help."

"Aww, Miss Emmaline, don't be like that. Come on here, girl, with that tea. It's powerful hot."

Em glanced at Pauline; Pauline nodded once, tightly. Then she walked down the steps to the bottommost slat—no farther—and held forth the glass.

The White Lady sighed, throwing a look at Em. "Ought to raise your children to show some respect, Miss Emmaline."

"Lots of ways to show respect, ma'am."

The White Lady sniffed. Then she turned her head, and the little girl who'd been holding the parasol straightened and came around her. The parasol stayed where it was, holding itself up against the ground. As the child moved forward, Em's skin came all over goose bumps. Wasn't right, seeing a child who should've been lively so empty of life and magic. The little girl twitched a little while she walked, as if with a palsy, or as if jerked on strings. She stopped before Pauline and held her hands up, and Em didn't blame Pauline at all for her grimace as she pushed the glass into the child's hands.

"Whose was she?" Emmaline asked, as the little girl twitched and moved to bring the tea back to her mistress.

"Nobody who matters, Miss Em, don't you mind." The White Lady took the glass of tea, then smoothed a hand over the child's soft cap of hair with an almost fond smile. "Such a lovely girl, though, isn't she? Everybody says you folk can't be beautiful, but that's just not true. Where else would I be able to get this?" She preened, smoothing a hand over one unblemished, shining cheek.

"She had power," Pauline said then. Em started; she was used to Pauline keeping her mouth shut around white folks, like a good sensible girl should. But Pauline was still staring at the little girl in horror. Her expression hardened, though, from shock into disgust. "She had *power*, and you *took* it. Like a damn thief."

The White Lady's eyebrows looked to have climbed into her red hair for a moment. Emmaline was right there with her, shocked at Pauline's cheek. She snapped without thinking, "Pauline Elizabeth, shut your mouth before I shut it."

Pauline shut up, though Emmaline could see the resentful flex of muscle along her jaw. But the White Lady let out a soft laugh, chilling them both into silence.

"Well! I can't say I think much of how you're raising your children, Miss Emmaline. Negro children never can sit still and be quiet, I suppose. Of course I took her power, girl; not like *she* could do anything with it. Now. I think I'm owed an apology, don't you?"

Damnation. Stiffly, Emmaline said, "I'm sorry for my daughter's foolishness, ma'am. I'll see to her when we're done talking."

"Oh, but that isn't enough, Miss Em." The White Lady tilted her head, long red lashes catching the light. "Honestly, how's she going to learn respect if you do all the apologizing for her?"

Pauline spoke tightly, with a darting glance at Emmaline for permission to speak. "I'm sorry, too, ma'am."

"Now, see? That wasn't so hard." The White Lady gestured with the tinkling glass of tea at Pauline, beaming. "But don't you think you owe me a bit more, after smarting off like that? Why, I'm *wounded*. You called me a thief! And even if I am, it's the principle of the thing." She stepped forward. "I think you should come with me for a while, and learn respect. Don't you?"

"No, ma'am," Emmaline snapped, before Pauline could dig herself further into trouble. "I don't think she owes you a thing beyond what you've had."

"Oh, now, be reasonable." The White Lady stepped forward once more, almost to the porch steps—but then she paused, her smile fading just a little. When she glanced off to the side, she spied the rosemary bush at last, growing scraggly in the summer heat. Growing, though, still, and by its growth weaving a bit of protection around the house. Beginning to frown, the woman glanced to the other side; there was plenty of sage, too, thriving in the heat unlike the rosemary.

Eyes widening, the woman finally turned about, spying at last the prize of Emmaline's yard: the sycamore fig. It grew in an arc over on the far side of the yard, because many years ago some neighborhood children had played on it and nearly broken its trunk. It had survived, though—through the heat, through the breaking, and through isolation, for it was nearly the only one of its kind in America. By the stories Emmaline's own mother had told of its planting, the seed-fig had been smuggled over from Africa herself, tucked into some poor soul's wound to keep it safe and living through the Middle Passage.

"Supposed to be rowan, thorn, and ash," said the White Lady. All at once she sounded sulky.

Emmaline lifted her chin. "That'd work, too," she said, " 'cause Lord knows I got some Scots Irish in me from my poor slave foremothers' travails. But this ain't the soil of Eire; red Alabama dirt roots different protectors. And you ain't the same as your'n back in the Old Country neither, not after all these years of drinking Negro blood, so rosemary, sage, and fig will do for *you*."

The White Lady let out a huffy little sound...but then she took a dainty step back. She started to raise the glass of tea, then paused, focusing sharply on it; her lip curled. Then she glared at Pauline.

"Just a little bit of acorn flour, ma'am," Pauline said, with such exaggerated innocence in her voice that Emmaline had to stifle a smile in spite of herself. "For flavor?"

"Rosemary, sage, and fig to bind," said the White Lady. It was clear now that she was furious, as she held the glass of tea out from herself and then dropped it. The tea spilled into the grass, and the glass split into three pieces. She drew in a deep breath, visibly mastering temper. "And *oak* to strike the blow. Well, Miss Emmaline, I'll grant you won this one, but it leaves us in a bit of a fix. You can't keep yours safe everywhere, and I can't be chasing after 'em all damn day and night." She thought a moment. "How 'bout a deal?"

"Ain't enough water in the River Jordan," Emmaline snapped.

"Sure?" The White Lady's grin crept back, like a dog badly banished. "Safety and prosperity for the rest, if you give me but one?"

"I done told you *no*," Emmaline said. She was forgetting to pretend polite; well, Sample hadn't gotten it only from his father. "How many more times I got to—"

"What kind of safety?" asked Pauline.

"Lord, have mercy, I'mma have to kill this girl," Emmaline could not help muttering. But Pauline had set her jaw in that tight, stubborn way that meant she didn't care if she got a smack for it. She persisted: "How much prosperity?"

Oh, and if that didn't spread the White Lady's grin nearly from ear to ear. "Why, *lots*, sugar. Bless your heart!"

"Girl, shut your *mouth*," Emmaline snapped. But the White Lady held up a hand, and all at once Emmaline found herself unable to speak. Oh, Mercy! Em knew, then. Stupid, *stupid* girl.

"Pauline, don't!" blurted Jim, but the White Lady eyed him, too, and he was shut up as firmly as Emmaline herself. Sample just stared from one to the other of his siblings and from them to the White Lady, his hands flexing as if he wanted to hit somebody, but wasn't sure where to start.

"Children should be seen and not heard," said the White Lady, gesturing gracefully with her fan. "But *ladies* with that blood like wine, sweet and high and so fine, get some choices in the matter 'til it's taken from them. What say you, *Miss* Pauline?"

Pauline, to her credit, glanced at Emmaline again. Her belligerence had faded by now, and her small face was properly anxious and afraid. Then, though, her jaw firmed, and she faced the White Lady squarely. "You said trouble was comin'."

"Oh, indeed." The White Lady let her gaze drip left and right, syruping all over the boys. "So much trouble! Folks getting uppity from here to the Carolinas. De-seg-gregation! Non-discrim-ination! And don't you know them bullnecks will be hitting back fast, beating y'all back into your place." She stopped her gaze on hotheaded Sample; Sample set his jaw. "Hitting back *hard*, I tell you, on boys who think to be called men."

Pauline caught her breath. Then, though, thank the Lord, she bit her bottom lip. "I want to speak to my mother."

There was a moment's long, pent pause. Then the White Lady flipped her fan back up into a blurring wave, dropping into a mocking curtsy. The servant child moved jerkily back behind her, taking hold of the parasol again. "Seeking counsel is wise, and within the rules besides," the White Lady admitted. "Not too much counsel, though, little miss. Some deals don't last long."

With that, she flounced off with the child in tow—though Emmaline noted that she skirted wide around the sycamore fig before passing behind a pine tree and vanishing.

The instant Emmaline could speak and move, she did, hurrying over to Pauline and slapping the tar out of the girl before she could speak. "Didn't I tell you about folks like that?" she demanded, pointing with a shaking hand after the White Lady. "Didn't I *tell* you they'll put a pretty orange in your hand and snatch it back with the hand attached?"

It had been happening more and more lately that Pauline defied her—but then, this was only proper, was it not? A girl coming into her womanhood, and her adult power, should speak her mind sometimes. "I know, Momma," Pauline said, without a trace of apology. Her voice was so calm and strong and even that Emmaline blinked. "But I had dreams."

"Well, you should've told me! And you should've told me about the blood coming, I know how to make you safe for at least a bit of time, and—"

"You *can't* make me safe, Momma." Pauline said it so sharp, her gaze so hard, that Emmaline could only flinch back. "That's why you told me what to be scared of, ain't it? So I could make myself safe. And I know, 'cause you taught me, that it's a woman's job to fight for hers."

"That's a man's job," Jim said, scowling—though he, too, should've been quiet, cowed by the slap. Sample nodded fiercely. Emmaline groaned and put a hand in the air for strength; all of her children had forgotten how to mind, all at once.

"Decent folks' job, then," Pauline said back, with a little heat. "But Momma, I *saw* it in the dream. People marching! Big ol' redneck bulls, standing up like men, holding dogs and billy clubs. Blood everywhere." Emmaline's skin went all a-prickle with remembered fear. Yet there was no fear in Pauline's face as she went on, her voice rising in excitement. "At the end of it, though, Momma, at the end ... I saw white children and black children sitting by each other in school. It was yellow and brown and red children there, too! Black people at the front of a bus! Momma ..." Pauline bit her lip, then leaned forward to whisper, though there was no one to hear but family. "I saw *a black man in a big white house.*"

There were always black men in the big white houses of downtown Birmingham. Who else was going to tend their gardens or wash their cars? And yet ... there was a fervor in Pauline's gaze that warned Emmaline there was something more to her daughter's dreams.

Didn't matter, though. The world didn't change. And somebody had to protect her fool children from themselves.

Seething with pent-up anger and fear, Emmaline herded the children inside. She made them go to bed early, with no supper for smarting off, because they had to *learn*—Pauline especially. Wasn't no prosperity worth a girlchild's soul and what little innocence life allowed her. Wasn't no safety for black boys beyond what humility bought them, little as that was.

And while they slept, Emmaline burned sage, and she prayed to every ancestor of three continents who might listen, and then she set herself up in a chair before the door with her grandmother's old musket across her knees. She would stay up day and night, if she had to, for her children's sake.

After a few hours had passed in slow and taut silence, and the candles burned low, and the weight of drowsiness pressed on the back of her head like a blanket, Emmaline got up to keep herself awake. She peeked in the boys' room: They were snoring, curled up, though Jim had a half-eaten peach still in his hand, sneaked out from some hiding place or another against just such an occasion of their mother's wrath.

Pauline's room, though, was cold from the open window wafting sharp bitter wind over the girl's empty bed.

There would be only one place the girl could have gone: the Fairgrounds, in the shadow of Red Mountain.

Emmaline ran to Renee's house, since Renee had the only working phone on the street. There she called Frank, who came over bringing his mule. The mule ran like it knew what was at stake, so fast and hard that Emmaline's bottom was raw long before she reached the place.

The Fairgrounds were only Fairgrounds once a year. The rest of the time it was just a fallow field, occasionally used for harness racing. Long ago, though, it had been the breaking ground of a plantation—the place where new slaves, freshly force-marched up from the port of Mobile, got branded and stripped of name and spirit before being sent into the fields. As Emmaline halted the mule and slid off its back, she felt all that old blood there in the ground, mixed with old tears and the red dirt beneath her feet. White Folk fed on that sort of magic. This would be a place of power for them.

As Em reached the top of the hill, she saw that Pauline stood beneath a pine that was being strangled by a carpet of kudzu. Before her stood the White Lady—shining even more now, her skin catching the moon's gleam in the way of her people, ears gone to points and mouth too wide and full of sharp fangs. They both turned as Emmaline thumped up, out of breath, her legs shaking from holding so tight to the mule's sides. Still, she moved to stand between them, in front of Pauline and facing the White Lady. "I ain't gon' let you!"

"Deal's done, Miss Emmaline," said the White Lady, looking amused. "Too late."

Emmaline turned to Pauline, shaking, horrified. Pauline, though, lifted her chin. "I saw it, Momma," she said. "One life for three. Trouble coming whether we want it or not, but if I go, you and the boys will get through it."

In a wordless fury, Emmaline flung herself at the White Lady. She did this without using her body, and the White Lady met her without hers, taking her *up* and *out* and *through* and *into* dreaming. Thing was, dreaming wasn't a thing mortal folks did so well when they were awake, so Emmaline tumbled, helpless, lashing out ineffectually. And in the perverse way of her kind—who loved to lie, but liked it best of all when truth became their weapon—the White Lady showed Emmaline the future that Pauline had bought. She saw:

Markets full of melons and greens and peaches, all artificially fresh and reeking of chemicals in the dead of winter. Long elevated strips of road carving up Negro towns and neighborhoods all over the country. Gray, looming schools isolating bright black minds and breaking their spirits and funneling them into jails. Police, everywhere, killing and killing and *killing*. This? Emmaline fought nausea and despair, lest she strengthen her enemy—but it was nearly impossible not to feel something. Oh, Lord, her baby had given up her freedom for *this*?

And yet. All at once Emmaline was not alone in her tumbling. Pauline, new and raw and woman-strong, pushed at Emmaline, helping her straighten up. Then Pauline pointed, snatching more truth from the White Lady's dream than even she wanted shown; the White Lady hissed into their minds like ice on a griddle. Pauline ignored this and said, "Look, Momma!"

And then Em saw the rest.

Marching black people, attacked by dogs. But still marching. Children—Sample!—struck by the blasts of fire hoses, the torrent peeling off clothes and tearing skin. *Still marching.* Joined by dozens, hundreds, thousands, hundreds of thousands.

Still. Marching.

Before these marches, prayers and church-plate dinners. *Emmaline, sprinkling a little fire into the chicken and dumplings to warm the* marchers against the cold hose water to come. Young women refusing to be ordered out of their bus seats to go sit in the back. *Emmaline braiding a donkey's stubbornness into their hair.* Children holding their heads high through crowds of shouting, jeering white teenagers and adults. *Emmaline trimming a few figs from the sycamore to make jam, sweetening the children's mouths with the taste of heritage and survival.*

And so much more. Brown faces in space! Emmaline could only stare at the stars, and savor the impossible possibility. Brown men on the Supreme Court! Then she saw the white house that Pauline had mentioned. *The* White House, nestled amid statues and obelisks and the mirror pools of Washington, D.C., a place of power in itself. She saw a man standing on its steps, brown as fig jam. And then a woman, black as molasses, her gaze hard and high and proud. And then another woman, and another brown man, and *so many more*, their frequency increasing with the spinning of the sun.

Still marching. Never stopping, 'til freedom was won.

Pauline's single sacrifice could set all of it in motion. But—

"No!" Emmaline fought her way back toward wakefulness. "I can't—it can't be me who stays!" She didn't believe! She had taught her children to bow their heads, not lift them up high. "I'm not what they need!"

You gon' be all they get, sugar, said the White Lady into the dream, in a laughing whisper.

No. No, she damn well would *not* be.

The dream still spun around her. Emmaline set her jaw and plunged her hand into it, grabbing wildly this time, and pulling back…the jar of sycamore jam.

"Sin's sin," she snapped. The top of the jar was tight, but she wrestled it off and plucked out a dripping, soft sycamore fig to brandish against the churning dark. "A deal's a deal. But one kind of prey the same as another to you lot, ain't it? You like children's beauty, but a woman's don't hurt you none. You like innocence, but you'll take foolishness. So here mine: *I can't believe the world will ever change.*

"I can't hope. It ain't in me. Spent too long making it easier for people to live downtrodden. I know how to survive, but I ain't got the fight for change in me—not like my baby does. So take me, and leave her."

"No!" Pauline shouted, but Emmaline had enough control to drown her out with the sound of chanting, marching crowds.

The shape of the White Lady had blurred into the dream, but she was a sharp-toothed presence amid the swirl. *Take you both, child and fool, all mine.*

Emmaline grinned. "Greed's a sin." The dream cracked a little beneath good Christian truth, allowing Em to summon the whiff of burned sage. The White Lady flinched hard enough to slow the whirlwind of the dream, for the smell carried with it lamentations for stolen lands, stolen children, and the stolen lives of Em's Creek forbears. Emmaline set that in place opposite the jar of figs. "Your bargain was one for three, not two for two."

Images of marchers warped and twisted around them, the White House dissolving into the foxy face of the White Lady. "True enough," she said, conjuring up her fan again. "Still, I'd rather the child if you don't mind. Or even if you do."

Here Emmaline faltered. She had not dreamt of rosemary. Frantically she rifled through images, tossing away the fish she'd dreamt of before each of her children, shoving aside the green tomatoes and the collards of the market. Lord! Had she never once dreamt of baking chicken?

She had not. But then, through the tittering laughter of the White Lady and her cronies, Emmaline smelled a dream of pot-roasted guinea-rooster, with orange peel...and rosemary. That had been the first time Emmaline accorded her daughter the respect of a fellow woman—oh, and Pauline had been savoring that feeling, all this time! There was a bit of innocence attached to it, too, lost after Emmaline's explanation about white men's oranges; the perfect sweetening to lure in a hungry fey. And indeed, the White Lady paused, lifting her face a little and half-closing her eyes in pleasure at the toothsome aroma. But then she stiffened as she caught the rosemary's perfume.

"Rosemary, sage, and fig," said Pauline, in a tone of satisfaction. "Now let my Momma—"

"Take me," Emmaline said. *Commanded*, now, because she could. She had bound the White Lady by both the ancient rules of the Old Country and the newer rules of flesh and blood. The deal had been made, one innocent life for three lives protected and prosperous, but Emmaline had control over which life the White Folk got to keep, at least.

"Momma!" Pauline, her beautiful powerful Pauline, abruptly resolved out of the dream's swirl and turned to her. "Momma, you can't."

"Hush." Emmaline went to her, held her close, kissed her corn-rowed head. "I done told you a million times that the world doesn't change—but I was wrong, and I'm sorry for that. You got a big fight ahead of you, but you can win it. And you're better suited for that fight than I'll ever be." She hugged the girl tight. "Be strong, baby. Tell your brothers the same. I know y'all are anyway."

Pauline clutched at her. "But Momma, I, you can't, I didn't want—"

The White Lady closed the dream around Emmaline, and whisked her away.

In the morning, Pauline woke up on the ground of the Fairgrounds wet with dew and weeping. Her brothers, who had come up to the Fairgrounds to find her, came quietly to her side to hold her tight.

Cousin Renee took the children in, of course, for blood was blood. She sent them one by one to Alabama State for their learning, so they were there when the Freedom Rides began. Naturally all three joined up. Through the dark times that followed, the foretold dogs and hoses and beatings—and the unforseen lynchings and assassinations and bombings—there were white folk aplenty doing evil... but no White Folk. The fey did not go again where they had been bested once, and in any case, their time was waning. The dirt of Alabama was red for many reasons, not the least of which that it was full of iron ore. Took a lot of power to overcome that much iron... and the times were changing such that not even black children could be stolen with impunity anymore.

The White Folk kept their promise, at least: Jim got his arm bitten by a dog during a protest, but it did not tear his throat out. Hard-headed Sample dated a white woman and only had to flee town; the men who meant to chain him up behind their truck and drag him to death did not catch him. Pauline got married, dreamt of fish, and made her own daughters to carry on the family legacy. After a few more years, she ran for city council and won, and nobody strung her up. Then she ran for mayor, and won that, too. All the while she turned a tidy profit from her sideline barbecue business. The greens had a little extra warmth in them that made everyone feel better toward each other, so she called them Freedom Greens, mostly as a joke.

But one year the black man Pauline had dreamt of in the White House passed through town, and he decided to come all the way to Pratt City to have some of Pauline's Famous Freedom Greens. Folks went wild. Somebody paid her to write a book about her life. Somebody optioned the film rights. Companies called and asked to franchise her recipe—but Pauline said no, instead hiring a small staff of Pratt City dwellers and leasing a commercial kitchen to fill all the thousands of orders for greens herself.

In every can, mind, there was a sprinkle of rosemary, sage, and a tiny dab of sycamore fig. Just to cut the bitterness.

And late one cold winter's night, Pauline dreamt again of the White Folk. She saw how lean and poorly they were looking these days, deprived of their easy prey, and as the hate of the world dwindled and left them hungry. But as she fought the urge to smile at their misfortune—for ill-wishing would only make them stronger—she caught a glimpse of a painfully familiar black face among their foxy whiteness, strong and proud and shining in its own way. A face that was smiling, and satisfied, and full of motherly pride.

So the world changed. And so Pauline woke up and went to hold her oldest granddaughter close, whispering to her of secrets and savory things and dreams yet to come—and of Great-Grammy Em, never to be forgotten, who would one day also be free.

L'Alchimista

The assistants had ruined the caponata soup. Screaming and flinging hot pappardelle after them, Franca stopped on the inn's sidewalk to pant for air as their backs faded into the snow-flecked night.

"Problematic, signora," said a voice to her left. "Now who will help you in the kitchen?"

Franca turned, lifting her ladle to confront a specter. Or so the man seemed, hidden as he was within a voluminous winter coat and wide-brimmed hat. In the light from the sodium lamps, she could make out the etching of a face within the hat's shadow. Thin graceful lines of nose and chin and lips, the lattermost curved in a smile. The smile did not help her mood.

"More problematic than they're worth," Franca said, putting her free hand on one ample hip, "and so will you be if you're here a-begging. Or if you're a flasher, go find the widow Annabella down the street; I hear she's not picky."

The smile widened. "Not begging, signora, except perhaps for some warmth and a good meal. I heard both could be found here."

"Heard where?" Franca narrowed her eyes, suspicious. None of the travel websites would list any inn where she worked.

"The market, the taxi, folk on the street. Your kitchen comes highly recommended among those who care more about skill than popularity."

It was cheap flattery, but enough that she gave him a second look. His old coat was of decent quality, its lines elegant if plain. The hat was the sort of thing she recalled seeing on old men in the mountain villages, the ones who sat about all day commenting on the world. Not a beggar, perhaps, but certainly no man of means. Still, he had taste and tact; that was enough to decide her.

"The Milano night is cold," she said, gesturing toward the door with the ladle. "I suppose I can keep my kitchen warm awhile longer."

"You have my gratitude, signora." The man moved past her and inside, pausing first to knock snow off his boots at the door.

The common room of the inn had closed down for the evening some time before, though the smell of cigarettes and prosciutto lingered in the air. Old deaf Giovanni hummed to himself as he swept behind the bar; long used to Franca's tantrums, he had already cleaned up the pappardelle from the walls and floor. The stranger paused to look about and for a moment Franca sighed, ashamed as always by the badly sealed stone walls, the uneven wooden floor, and the yellowed newspaper clippings and photographs decorating the walls. It was a cozy little inn, the locals said. So rustic, so quaint.

So far have I fallen, she thought.

"The special tonight is hare." She said it gruffly, picking up a nearby rag to give the table a cursory swipe. "Nothing left of tonight's soup, though, and tomorrow's caponata is scorched so you'll have to do without an appetizer. I suppose there might still be some pappardelle."

The man sat down, not removing his hat and coat. "Hare?" He lifted his head slightly—his face was still in shadow—and sniffed the air. "Roasted in an herb-crust?"

"And a dolce e forte sauce, with Sicilian cabernet."

"You'll have used tomatoes as a thickener, then."

"I'll have used hare's blood, as God intended before the damned Americas were discovered. Do you want it or not?"

"Please. With the pappardelle—such as you have left."

Franca snorted and went into the kitchen. For a moment she contemplated simply reheating leftovers from the freezer. The sauce's tart sweetness would only have deteriorated a little, and her guest would probably never know the difference.

Bah—she was thinking like one of the stupid assistants, for whom the subtle arts of the kitchen were merely a job, a living, a way to impress their friends. What did her audience matter, dignitary or destitute? She cooked for herself, and she had never cooked less than her best.

So she cut apart the hare and browned the quarters with garlic and onion, searing the meat to seal the juices before removing it to the oven to roast. Then after deglazing the browning pan with red wine, she added vegetables, herbs, the organ meats, and blood. This she simmered uncovered to reduce, meanwhile basting the oven quarters with honey and horseradish. The pappardelle she boiled in salted water, al dente, and tossed with the sauce. As a finishing touch she set the roasted hare portions to stand at the center and grated parmeggiano around the dish's edge.

And while she worked, the small nuisances of the day faded and her mind focused wholly on the marvel of creation. There was such balance in food. Sweetness and sharpness, blood and oil, the delicate influence of ingredients and the controlling power of flame . . . If only men and women could be so simple, so malleable! "Give me a well-stocked kitchen and I could rule the world," she whispered to herself, and wished for all her heart that it was true.

The meal was done. She carried the platter out to the common room and set it down in front of the man. "You'll want wine?"

"In a moment." The man lifted a hand to waft the dish's steam toward himself; Franca could barely hear his soft inhalation. "Ah. And now..." He took up the spoon and tasted the sauce, then plucked loose a morsel of hare. He chewed slowly and thoughtfully, then swirled a few fat ribbons of pappardelle in the sauce before slurping them up. He took his time tasting this as well.

Franca folded her arms. She usually didn't watch when people ate her dishes—it felt somehow incestuous—but something about this man had piqued her interest. "Well?"

The man looked up at her and for the first time she got a good look at his face. Older than she'd expected, gaunt and solemn though his eyes were merry. Might have been handsome twenty years before. Not Italian, though his Milan accent had been flawless; she could not guess his ancestry other than that. French, perhaps, or UK.

"Marvelous. The perfect balance of salt and sweetness, the tang of the capers, the tender texture...all blended with such subtlety. Signora, you are amazing."

"I know." Inordinately pleased, Franca went to the bar and returned with a wine bottle, a corkscrew, and a glass, all of which she thumped down in front of him. Old Giovanni was gone, probably to bed. Isadora, the inn's owner, might notice the missing wine when she next did inventory, but Franca would blame it on the assistants she'd just fired. "Call me when you're done."

She'd just finished cleaning up the kitchen—perhaps she would miss the assistants a *little*—when she heard his call from the common room. "Mi scuza, signora, I've just finished the best meal of my life."

She stepped outside to see with satisfaction that he had cleaned his plate. "I suppose I could make something for dessert."

"Perhaps next time, signora. I cannot linger tonight, though I shall most certainly return." The man dabbed his lips with a napkin, belched heartily, and pushed back his chair. "In the meantime, I must repay you for your talent and effort—though for that I have something more interesting than money to offer. A challenge."

She did not particularly care whether he paid; it wasn't her inn. But at his words she lifted an eyebrow. "What sort of challenge?"

"A very special one." He slipped a hand into his coat like an old-fashioned pistolero, but before Franca could worry, he pulled out a bulging sack made of what looked like deerhide. He set this on the table—carefully, Franca noted.

"You are willing to follow a recipe? So many chefs of your caliber think themselves above the direction of others."

She lifted her chin. "I was head chef for Parliament once—before that bastard Berlusconi, anyhow. While I was there, I had to make Florentine dishes like a Florentine and Venetian dishes like a Venetian and the Madonna help me if I did them wrong. If the recipe is sound, I can follow it."

"This one is sound. Just difficult. I present it to you, along with a few special ingredients." He gestured toward the sack with a flourish. "I have been looking for a true artist of the kitchen for some time, signora. I beg you not to disappoint me."

She stared after him as he straightened, touched fingertips to the brim of his hat, and walked out with a smile.

Bemused, she picked up the sack and emptied it onto the table. An astonishing number of items fell out: an assortment of what looked like balls of dirt, a wad of moss, twenty or thirty fresh herb-bunches tied with string, and three great gnarled things like the mating of an onion with a tree-bole. Last there fluttered out a small roll of parchment paper, held shut with an old-fashioned wax seal.

"Not a beggar indeed; a madman," she murmured, but she picked up the scroll and opened it nevertheless.

Signora,

The ingredients of this recipe must be blended *precisely*. Any deviation could be dangerous. Please do not waste the frava root; it is very difficult to come by.

This was followed by a beautifully illegible signature and a list of the ingredients provided. The gnarled things must be the frava root, she decided, whatever that was. The herbs were a mixture of familiar and unfamiliar; tarragon was followed by "3 sprigs takip-rik" and "powdered honavia." Then she gasped, for the recipe listed something that was truly impossible. She set the parchment down and snatched up one of the dirtballs.

Tartufo bianco. A white truffle.

Freshly dug; the clay covering hadn't even dried. A dozen of them lay scattered on the table—no, two dozen. Last she'd heard, white truffles sold for 1500 Euros a kilo in the chefs' markets uptown. Her "beggar" had been carrying a fortune in fungi about in his coat.

She took a shaking breath and picked up the parchment again. At the bottom of the page was the recipe itself. She made herself read it, and read it again. Then, disbelieving, she read it through a third time.

"Roast the truffles..." That was bad enough. Truffles were best uncooked. But a little farther on she saw "evaporate the anise effusion under a cheesecloth" and later "on bisection of the frava: a blowtorch will be required."

It was a bitch of a thing. A *monster* of a thing. And cruel; it would use up more than half the truffles he'd given her, if not all.

And yet... she felt the familiar clench in her belly, the thrill along her spine. A challenge, the man had called it. Oh and it was, for even as her practical mind insisted she ignore the mad recipe and take the truffles out to sell, her heart was pounding in excitement.

She got to her feet, gathered up the ingredients, and carried them into the kitchen. She put them into their proper places—herbs in the herb rack, strange roots with the potatoes. The truffles she put into a risotto basket and tucked them away under the sink. She took in the dishes the man had emptied, wiped down the table, and cleaned up the kitchen. Then she shut off the lights and headed home.

I'll sleep on it, she told herself, but that was a lie. She had already made up her mind.

It took five days.

Franca informed Isadora that she would be taking a vacation that week. Isadora was upset at the late notice, but had no choice; she had asked Franca to work through August when most of the country enjoyed its traditional four weeks of vacation. Franca's price had been compensatory time whenever she wanted. But when Franca informed Isadora that she would be using the kitchen during her vacation, the old innkeeper had grown curious. "Who works on vacation?" she asked. And Franca had replied that she would not be working, but *creating*.

There were problems. The unidentifiable ingredients: She researched on the internet, browsed through books, even did chemical tests to make sure she knew what was what. But in all her searching, she never once found any reference to a frava root. The root's smell was bitter when she finally wrestled one open, and there was a faint underscent of something fouler, like hot asphalt. She made herself taste it and her tongue went numb for two days— a severe handicap for any chef, but doubly frustrating under the circumstances.

Worse, the recipe was unclear. "A pinch" here and "a spoonful" there, interspersed with "select a mid-sized" example of this or that. She had never worried about such things before; art was rarely exact. But the strange fellow's note had been emphatic about precision, so Franca had no choice but to employ a blend of intuition and quasi-science to determine the correct balance. She calculated that the truffles' oils would need to be emulsified by an equal proportion of ground herbs. She added a third thread of saffron because the mixture's color just didn't look right.

She also thanked God she'd fired the assistants. Just having them around would have cocked up everything.

But despite the stress and the labor, she persevered and triumphed—or so she thought. The resulting concoction, shaped into bite-sized loaves each precisely thirty grams in weight, looked unappetizing and smelled worse. Surely the things were not supposed to develop that greenish oily sheen after she chilled them? She stored them in the small freezer, for fear the deep freeze's thermostat might spark and set the cakes on fire.

On the night that she finished, the stranger returned.

Franca hovered nervously this time while her guest sat down to table. She had opted for a presentation of elegant simplicity on plain china, but this was a feeble diversion. The frava cakes had the color and texture of that American monstrosity called Spam. They smelled like petrol, and the one she'd dared to taste had been indescribable—somewhere between fish liver and turpentine, with a subtle underflavor of rotten egg. She waited for his disgust while mourning the waste of so many beautiful truffles.

"Ah," breathed the man, wafting the scent toward himself. "Just now ripe, I see. And the taste..." He picked up one of the cakes and popped it into his mouth. She winced as he grimaced, but then he swallowed and smiled. "Perfect."

"Perfect?" She stared at him. "If I hadn't tasted one myself, I would say you just ate poison, signore. Never in my life have I made anything so foul."

He smiled and lifted the glass of Riesling she'd poured in hope of countering the cakes' bitterness with sweet. "But they aren't meant to taste good, signora," he said. He paused to take a long sip of the wine. She nearly bounced on her toes while he held it in his mouth a moment before swallowing. "The important thing is that the ingredients were mixed in the proper proportions. Doing it wrong creates a substance so noxious the very fumes can kill. But doing it right..."

He stretched out a hand, examining the back of it. She followed the gesture in confusion. "Yes? Yes? Doing it right?"

He looked up at her. The hat still shadowed his eyes, but—she blinked, frowned, peered closer. Then took a step back.

He was handsome now. Not quite as handsome as she'd speculated, but certainly better-looking. As if he'd suddenly become a good ten years younger.

He smiled and popped another of the cakes into his mouth. This time it happened while Franca watched. The deepest-etched lines in his face lightened and the gauntness filled out. In a few seconds she was looking at a hale and healthy man of middle years.

"Go and look at yourself, signora," he said, his eyes twinkling. "You tried one, didn't you?"

"Oh, Madonna," Franca whispered, and hurried through the

kitchen to the employees' bathroom. Even in Isadora's cheap lighting the difference was clear. The lines in her face had faded, and the second chin she'd been working on since her mid-forties was now smooth taut skin. She examined herself everywhere and found that she'd lost ten pounds and her breasts were still in the vicinity of her chest.

When the shock finally began to fade, she stumbled back to the common room. Her guest stood beside the table, inserting the last of the cakes into a wooden box incised with strange designs. He closed the lid and smiled at her again.

"How...?" It was all she could manage.

"Through your five days of labor, of course," he replied, "and your pure skill in the kitchen. The last time I tried this recipe, it nearly killed me. Thanks to you, my life is now renewed."

She stared at him, mind and tongue mute. Then he gave another of those little flourishes and she noticed that another deerhide sack lay on the table.

"No." She shook her head, unable to express her horror. She needed a month of sleep. She could not bear more strange ingredients. She was afraid of another recipe that could cook the impossible. She was afraid of *him*, who brought such things.

"The choice is yours, signora. The ingredients will keep until you're ready. No recipe this time; I want to see what you can do on your own. When you're finished, *if* you finish, we'll speak again."

He tipped his hat once more and strode out on his vigorous younger legs.

She took another week off.

Isadora was incensed, but finally capitulated as Franca had known she would. If Franca hadn't once spat on the most powerful man in Italy (who'd had the nerve to call her zabaglione boring!), Isadora would have been stuck with a second-rate chef from a third-rate school. Franca needed the job, but Isadora needed to keep Franca happy.

"At least the vacation is doing you some good," Isadora grumbled. "You don't look quite so much the hag today."

The deerhide bag sat on a counter in the kitchen. Franca did not touch it for several days. She cleaned up the mess left behind by the frava cakes and went home to sleep for the whole weekend. On Lunedi she rose, went to the hairdresser (who exclaimed over the perfection of her coloring job; the gray was all but gone), visited her favorite stalls at the farmers' piazza and the fish pier, and meandered home. The whole time her mind was racing, her heart a-thud. The deerhide bag. The waiting nightmare. The possibilities.

Returning to her bungalow, she set down her purchases and went to the mirror. Her own face stared back at her, haunted and younger. Once she had been at the top of her field: a certified master, a respected woman in a man's profession, an artist with a promising career. One error of judgment had sentenced her to an endless Purgatory of downscale, dead-end restaurants. She would not have minded that so much if the appreciation had not vanished along with the acclaim, but there it was: She was a better chef now than she'd been at the height of her career, and no one cared. Except one man.

I want to see what you can do on your own, her stranger had said.

A slow, ferocious smile stretched across her lips. Had she been actually looking at herself in the mirror, she might have marveled at the beauty this smile produced, but her mind had already turned to the deerhide bag.

"Just you wait," she whispered to herself, and to her peculiar dining guest. "Just you *see* what I can do."

She went to the inn, and into the kitchen, and there she opened the bag.

Three more sprigs of takiprik. An assortment of more mushrooms, including several which were red with vibrant blue stripes. Five vials of powdered herbs, which were fortunately labeled, though she had never before heard the names. The carcasses—somehow fresh, though the bag had lain about for days—of four midsized birds with brilliant red-gold feathers. A large wart-covered melon of some sort. A length of vine laden with cherry-red fruits. An ancient, dusty bottle, sealed liberally with wax.

Franca snorted to herself. No worse than the master chef's exam.

So she set to work, sorting the mushrooms and testing the herbs. She plucked and gutted one of the birds, puzzling for a moment over a strange, hard object in its gullet, which was hot to the touch. Though the vine fruits smelled heavenly, she quickly discovered that their fragrance could send her into a daydreaming fugue for an hour or more. "Potential," she declared, then plugged her nose and sliced them up anyhow.

And as always while she worked, the small nuisances of life faded, and she lost herself in the marvel of creation.

Franca put the finishing touches on her dishes and carried them out to the table. Not at all to her surprise, the man was waiting for her, smiling from beneath his wide-brimmed hat.

"Such rich aromas," he said, watching as she set down the tray. She had draped a covering cloth over it; steam curled from beneath the cloth's edge. "But the items I gave you weren't meant—"

"Never mind what was *meant*. They are what they are," Franca said primly. "A true chef never interferes with the power of food. She simply reveals it."

And with a flourish she pulled the covering cloth away. His eyes widened. She let him absorb what he saw while she poured him a very dry sauvignon blanc. When he picked up his fork, she smiled at his hesitation.

"You made a dessert out of the firebirds?"

"Is that what they're called? Yes, their livers had a sweetness that I liked once I blanched out the toxins. Ground fine with beet juice and muscat wine, then chilled. The cups are pumpkin coated with honeyed isinglass."

The hat tilted up as he peered at her, then back down. "And this?" He pointed toward a plate holding puffy circles of squid-ink pasta, drizzled with golden sauce and a startlingly white powder.

"Panicles stuffed with basil-flavored ricotta, takiprik, and electric mushroom strips soaked in Brunello wine. Dusted with potato flour to soften the tartness. The sauce is clarified butter warmed with picklemelon extract."

The hat tilted up again. "Electric mushroom. Picklemelon."

"Well, I had to call them something."

"Indeed." He pointed wordlessly then at the center course, a silver platter bearing half of the picklemelon's rind as a bowl for a whole roasted fowl. The smoking globule in its beak made for a particularly dramatic presentation.

"Whole hen firebird. The stuffing is a seven-mushroom blend with mincemeat, pork sausage, rosewater herb, and sage. Are you going to eat any of this?"

"There's so much, in such variety. Where do you recommend I begin?"

She pointed at a platter of bruschetta on slabs of crusty bread. "Tomino cheese, fresh sardines, olive oil pressed with dreamfruit seed, and pine nuts marinated in absinthe. I find the absinthe eases the narcotic effect of the dreamfruit. The dreams last hours, but are far less...shall we say, overwhelming? Instead they stimulate the other senses so that one more properly enjoys the rest of the meal."

"Ah, thus the appetizer. Then there I shall begin." And he did.

Franca watched, feeling quite smug as he discovered each dish's delights. He gasped when the stuffed panicles gave him a jolt, but then he chuckled and amused himself throwing bolts of lightning across the room at the doorknobs. Then he sampled the partridge breast crepe rolls, liberally sprinkled with the strange elixir that had come from the dusty bottle. She had found that this marvelously spicy and thick substance caused the occasional imp to appear, so to counter that effect, she had gone to the nearby church and gotten some holy water to thin the crepe batter. His eyes widened in pleasure as the elixir and holy water sizzled together in his mouth; she smirked. As she had planned, the firebird's glaze—which contained a few drops of leftover frava oil—sparked on the flintgizzard in its mouth and caught fire the moment he tried to carve a slice. The illusory flames billowed and curled around the dish like the bird's lost feathers, and the slice he'd cut floated gracefully to his plate.

And so it went. By the time he'd finished the dessert, he was laughing aloud in pure delight and the common room was a wreck. That had been mostly the result of the dreamvine gnocchi, which he ate too soon after the firebird roast gave him temporary wings. Vandals, she would tell Isadora. Probably the disgruntled former assistants.

"Well," he said at last, dabbing his lips with a napkin, "now I truly *have* had the best meal of my life, signora. Grazie, grazie. You've surpassed my every hope."

"Oh?" Franca raised both eyebrows. "Does this mean you'll leave me another bag of strange things?"

"I could, signora, but I would prefer instead to show you where to find your own."

She tensed in interest. "My own?"

"Certainly. And then if I may be bold, I have an offer for you. A job offer, I should say."

She quirked a wry eyebrow. "You really *aren't* much of a beggar, are you, signore? You're not poor enough by far."

He laughed. "If it's any consolation, signora, I *am* a poor man now by the standards of my past. In my youth—my *true* youth—one could work wonders with eye of newt and a cauldron. But alas, the world has changed."

"I should hope so. Whyever would you waste your time with something as foul as newts' eyes?"

"Because all things contain power, signora, and some have more power than most. Science has only recently discovered that truth, but certain professions in the world—yours, mine—have known it for centuries. Who is to say plutonium is more powerful than, say, rice? One takes away a million lives, the other saves a hundred times as many." He smiled, pausing to take a long appreciative sip of wine.

"So now you're a nuclear technician."

Another laugh. "What I am is your apprentice, signora, if you'll have me. My art is too primitive for these times. The old techniques no longer have the same effect, and when they do, the effect is less potent. More importantly, I no longer *want* to use the old techniques." He made a face. "I find them...crude. But you, signora, understand subtlety and balance, the proper places of form and function, the interaction of the world with the senses." He put a hand over his waist and offered a little bow from his seat. "I would learn that from you, if you will teach me."

She stared at him, but her mind came alive with the possibilities.

No more customers with tastebuds of stone. No more assistants with fumbling fingers and proletarian minds. Her guest had already shown ten thousand times more refinement; it would be a joy to teach him. And yet...

She put her hands on her hips. "I'm no easy taskmistress. I expect work. I expect *art*."

He pushed back from the table and got to his feet, sweeping his hat from his head in a true bow. "As much as my poor soul can produce, signora."

"My kitchen will need to be top notch."

"Two floors of my citadel shall be yours to remodel and stock as you please."

A citadel. This had promise. "I'll ask no apprentice fee of you, but I expect room and board and a stipend."

"Two more floors for an apartment, outfitted to your liking. As for the stipend, I have little in the way of ready funds but you will lack for nothing materially."

"An expense account?"

"A substantial supply of lead, actually, bought for a pittance. It converts very well to gold through the application of a certain aromatic oil."

She considered this for a moment. "All right. And I'll want a sample of that oil. Aromatics always have possibilities."

"But of course, signora."

She tapped her foot, wondering how far she dared. "And vacation in August like everyone else."

He smiled. "Whenever you wish."

She folded her arms, regarding his young-old face in silence now, debating with herself. He could be lying about all of it. He could be a crazy murderer. He could be a politician.

Well. Probably not a politician.

"I suppose I can at least see this citadel of yours," she said at last. "If the kitchen space is as large as you say, I'll need to begin inventory on what stock you already have. Amateurs never have the right pots and pans."

He grinned as if she'd given him a kiss. "As you like, signora. Shall we?"

He tossed the cloth over the emptied dishes, stepped around the shattered chairs, and offered her his arm. She took it, blushing a little as he led her toward the door.

"You must promise me one final thing, signore."

"And that is?"

"The truffles, signore. Never ask me to cook them again."

He raised both eyebrows. "But the frava cakes—"

"Are foul, and should never be forced upon another human being. I can bake up a hundred ways to keep us young, never fear. It is only a matter of art."

He stared at her for a long moment, and then his young face stretched in a slow smile. "So it must be, signora. So it must be."

They walked together, arm in arm, into the snowy Milano night.

The Effluent Engine

New Orleans stank to the heavens. This was either the water, which did not have the decency to confine itself to the river but instead puddled along every street; or the streets themselves, which seemed to have been cobbled with bricks of fired excrement. Or it may have come from the people who jostled and trotted along the narrow avenues, working and lounging and cursing and shouting and sweating, emitting a massed reek of unwashed resentment and perhaps a bit of hangover. As Jessaline strolled beneath the colonnaded balconies of Royal Street, she fought the urge to give up, put the whole fumid pile to her back, and catch the next dirigible out of town.

Then someone jostled her. "Pardon me, miss," said a voice at her elbow, and Jessaline was forced to stop, because the earnest-looking young man who stood there was white. He smiled, which did not surprise her, and doffed his hat, which did.

"Monsieur," Jessaline replied, in what she hoped was the correct mix of reserve and deference.

"A fine day, is it not?" The man's grin widened, so sincere that Jessaline could not help a small smile in response. "I must admit, though; I have yet to adjust to this abysmal heat. How are you handling it?"

"Quite well, monsieur," she replied, thinking, *What is it that you want from me?* "I am acclimated to it."

"Ah, yes, certainly. A fine Negress like yourself would naturally deal better with such things. I am afraid my own ancestors derive from chillier climes, and we adapt poorly." He paused abruptly, a stricken look crossing his face. He was the florid kind, red-haired and freckled with skin so pale that it revealed his every thought—in point of which he paled further. "Oh, dear! My sister warned me about this. You aren't Creole, are you? I understand they take it an insult to be called, er . . . by certain terms."

With some effort, Jessaline managed not to snap, *Do I look like one of them?* But people on the street were beginning to stare, so instead she said, "No, monsieur. And it's clear to me you aren't from these parts, or you would never ask such a thing."

"Ah—yes." The man looked sheepish. "You have caught me out, miss; I'm from New York. Is it so obvious?"

Jessaline smiled carefully. "Only in your politeness, monsieur." She reached up to adjust her hat, lifting it for a moment as a badly needed cooling breeze wafted past.

"Are you perhaps—" The man paused, staring at her head. "My word! You've naught but a scrim of hair!"

"I have sufficient to keep myself from drafts on cold days," she replied, and as she'd hoped, he laughed.

"You're a most charming Ne—woman, my dear, and I feel honored to make your acquaintance." He stepped back and bowed, full and proper. "My name is Raymond Forstall."

"Jessaline Dumonde," she said, offering her lace-gloved hand, though she had no expectation that he would take it. To her surprise, he did, bowing again over it.

"My apologies for gawking. I simply don't meet many of the Colored on a typical day, and I must say—" He hesitated, darted a look about, and at least had the grace to drop his voice. "You're remarkably lovely, even with no hair."

In spite of herself, Jessaline laughed. "Thank you, monsieur." After an appropriate and slightly awkward pause, she inclined her head. "Well, then; good day to you."

"Good day indeed," he said, in a tone of such pleasure that Jessaline hoped no one had heard it, for his sake. The folk of this town were particular about matters of propriety, as any society which relied so firmly upon class differences. While there were many ways in which a white gentleman could appropriately express his admiration for a lady of color—the existence of the *gens de couleur libres* was testimony to that—all of those ways were simply Not Done in public.

But Forstall donned his hat, and Jessaline inclined her head in return before heading away. Another convenient breeze gusted by, and she took advantage of it to adjust her hat once more, in the process sliding her stiletto back into its hiding place amid the silk flowers.

This was the dance of things, the *cric-crac* as the storytellers said in Jessaline's land. Everyone needed something from someone. Glorious France needed money, to recover from the unlamented Napoleon's endless wars. Upstart Haiti had money from the sweet gold of its sugarcane fields, but needed guns—for all the world, it seemed, wanted the newborn country strangled in its crib. The United States had guns but craved sugar, as its fortunes were dependent upon the acquisition thereof. It alone was willing to treat with Haiti, though

Haiti was the stuff of American nightmare: a nation of black slaves who had killed off their white masters. Yet Haitian sugar was no less sweet for its coating of blood, and so everyone got what they wanted, trading 'round and 'round, a graceful waltz—only occasionally devolving into a knife fight.

It had been simplicity itself for Jessaline to slip into New Orleans. Dirigible travel in the Caribbean was inexpensive, and so many travelers regularly moved between the island nations and the great American port city that hardly any deception had been necessary. She was indentured, she told the captain, and he had waved her aboard without so much as a glance at her papers (which were false anyhow). She was a wealthy white man's mistress, she told the other passengers, and between her fine clothes, regal carriage, and beauty—despite her skin being purest sable in color—they believed her and were alternately awed and offended. She was a slave, she told the dockmaster on the levee; a trusted one, lettered and loyal, promised freedom should she continue to serve to her fullest. He had smirked at this, as if the notion of anyone freeing such an obviously valuable slave was ludicrous. Yet he, too, had let her pass unchallenged, without even charging her the disembarkation fee.

It had then taken two full months for Jessaline to make inquiries and sufficient contacts to arrange a meeting with the esteemed Monsieur Norbert Rillieux. The Creoles of New Orleans were a closed and prickly bunch, most likely because they had to be; only by the rigid maintenance of caste and privilege could they hope to retain freedom in a land which loved to throw anyone darker than tan into chains. Thus more than a few of them had refused to speak to Jessaline on sight. Yet there were many who had not forgotten that there but for the grace of God went their own fortune, so from these she had been able to glean crucial information and finally an introduction by letter. As she had mentioned the right names and observed the right etiquette, Norbert Rillieux had at last invited her to afternoon tea.

That day had come, and...

And Rillieux, Jessaline was finally forced to concede, was an idiot.

"Monsieur," she said again, after drawing a breath to calm herself, "as I explained in my letter, I have no interest in sugarcane processing. It is true that your contributions to this field have been much appreciated by the interests I represent; your improved refining methods have saved both money and lives, which could both be reinvested in other places. What we require assistance with is a wholly different matter, albeit related."

"Oh," said Rillieux, blinking. He was a savagely thin-lipped man, with a hard stare that might have been compelling on a man who knew how to use it. Rillieux did not. "Your pardon, mademoiselle. But, er, who did you say you represented, again?"

"I did not say, monsieur. And if you will forgive me, I would prefer not to say for the time being." She fixed him with her own hard stare. "You will understand, I hope, that not all parties can be trusted when matters scientific turn to matters commercial."

At that, Rillieux's expression turned shrewd at last; he understood just fine. The year before, Jessaline's superiors had informed her, the plan Rillieux had proposed to the city—an ingenious means of draining its endless, pestilent swamps, for the health and betterment of all—had been turned down. Six months later, a coalition of city engineers had submitted virtually the same plan and been heaped with praise and funds to bring it about. The men of the coalition were white, of course. Jessaline marveled that Rillieux even bothered being upset about it.

"I see," Rillieux said. "Then, please forgive me, but I do not know what it is you want."

Jessaline stood and went to her brocade bag, which sat on a side table across the Rillieux house's elegantly apportioned salon. In it was a small, rubber-stopped, peculiarly shaped jar of the sort utilized by chemists, complete with engraved markings on its surface to indicate measurements of the liquid within. At the bottom of this jar swirled a scrim of dark brown, foul-looking paste and liquid. Jessaline brought it over to Rillieux and offered the jar to his nose, waiting until he nodded before she unstoppered it.

At the scent which wafted out, he stumbled back, gasping, his eyes all a-water. "By all that's holy! Woman, what is that putrescence?"

"That, Monsieur Rillieux, is effluent," Jessaline said, neatly stoppering the flask. "Waste, in other words, of a very particular kind. Do you drink rum?" She knew the answer already. On one side of the parlor was a beautifully made side table holding an impressive array of bottles.

"Of course." Rillieux was still rubbing his eyes and looking affronted. "I'm fond of a glass or two on hot afternoons; it opens the pores, or so I'm told. But what does that—"

"Producing rum is a simple process with a messy result: this effluent, namely, and the gas it emits, which until lately was regarded as simply the unavoidable price to be paid for your pleasant afternoons. Whole swaths of countryside are afflicted with this smell now as a result. Not only is the stench offensive to men and beasts, we have also found it to be as powerful as any tincture or laudanum; over time it causes anything exposed to suffocate and die. Yet there are scientific papers coming from Europe which laud this gas's potential as a fuel source. Captured properly, purified, and burned, it can power turbines, cook food, and more." Jessaline turned and set the flask on Rillieux's beverage stand, deliberately close to the square bottle of dark rum she had seen there. "We wish you to develop a process by which the usable gas—methane—may be extracted from the miasma you just smelled."

Rillieux stared at her for a moment, then at the flask. She could tell that he was intrigued, which meant that half her mission had been achieved already. Her superiors had spent a profligate amount of money requisitioning a set of those flasks from the German chemist who'd recently invented them, precisely with an eye toward impressing men like Rillieux, who looked down upon any science that did not show European roots.

Yet as Rillieux gazed at the flask, Jessaline was dismayed to see a look of consternation, then irritation, cross his face.

"I am an engineer, mademoiselle," he said at last, "not a chemist."

"We have already worked out the chemical means by which it might be done," Jessaline said quickly, her belly clenching in tension. "We would be happy to share that with you—"

"And then what?" He scowled at her. "Who will put the patent on this process, hmm? And who will profit?" He turned away, beginning to pace, and Jessaline could see that he was working up a good head of steam, to her horror. "You have a comely face, Mademoiselle Dumonde, and it does not escape me that dusky women such as yourself once seduced my forefathers into the most base acts, for which those men atoned by at least raising their half-breed children honorably. If I were a white man hoping to once more profit from the labor of an honest Creole like myself—one already proven gullible—I would send a woman like you to do the tempting. To them, all of us are alike, even though I have the purest of French blood in my veins, and you might as well have come straight from the jungles of Africa!"

He rounded on her at this, very nearly shouting, and if Jessaline had been one of the pampered, cowed women of this land, she might have stepped back in fear of unpleasantness. As it was, she did take a step—but to the side, closer to her brocade bag, within which was tucked a neat little derringer whose handle she could see from where she stood. Her mission had been to use Rillieux, not kill him, but she had no qualms about giving a man a flesh wound to remind him of the value of chivalry.

Before matters could come to a head, however, the parlor door opened, making both Jessaline and Norbert Rillieux jump. The young woman who came in was clearly some kin of Rillieux's; she had the same ocherine skin and loose-curled hair, the latter tucked into a graceful split chignon atop her head. Her eyes were softer, however, though that might have been an effect of the wire-rimmed spectacles perched atop her nose. She wore a simple gray dress, which had the unfortunate effect of emphasizing her natural pallor, and making her look rather plain.

"Your pardon, Brother," she said, confirming Jessaline's guess. "I thought perhaps you and your guest might like refreshment?" In her hands was a silver tray of crisp square beignets dusted in sugar, sliced merliton with what looked like some sort of remoulade sauce, and tiny wedges of pecan penuche.

At the sight of this girl, Norbert blanched and looked properly abashed. "Ah—er, yes, you're right, thank you. Ah—" He glanced at Jessaline, his earlier irritation clearly warring with the ingrained desire to be a good host; manners won, and he quickly composed himself. "Forgive me. Will you take refreshment, before you leave?" The last part of that sentence came out harder than the rest. Jessaline got the message.

"Thank you, yes," she said, immediately moving to assist the young woman. As she moved her brocade bag, she noticed the young woman's eyes, which were locked on the bag with a hint of alarm. Jessaline was struck at once with unease—had she noticed the derringer handle? Impossible to tell, since the young woman made no outcry of alarm, but that could have been just caution on her part. That one meeting of eyes had triggered an instant, instinctual assessment on Jessaline's part; *this* Rillieux, at least, was nowhere near as myopic or bombastic as her brother.

Indeed, as the young woman lifted her gaze after setting down the tray, Jessaline thought she saw a hint of challenge lurking behind those little round glasses, and above that perfectly pleasant smile.

"Brother," said the young woman, "won't you introduce me? It's so rare for you to have lady guests."

Norbert Rillieux went from blanching to blushing, and for an instant, Jessaline feared he would progress all the way to bluster. Fortunately he mastered the urge and said, a bit stiffly, "Mademoiselle Jessaline Dumonde, may I present to you my younger sister, Eugenie?"

Jessaline bobbed a curtsy, which Mademoiselle Rillieux returned. "I'm pleased to meet you," Jessaline said, meaning it, *because I might have enjoyed shooting your brother to an unseemly degree, otherwise.*

It seemed Mademoiselle Rillieux's thoughts ran in the same direction, because she smiled at Jessaline and said, "I hope my brother hasn't been treating you to a display of his famous temper, Mademoiselle Dumonde. He deals better with his gadgets and vacuum tubes than people, I'm afraid."

Rillieux did bluster at this. "Eugenie, that's hardly—"

"Not at all," Jessaline interjected smoothly. "We were discussing the finer points of chemistry, and your brother, being such a learned man, just made his point rather emphatically."

"Chemistry? Why, I adore chemistry!" At this, Mademoiselle Rillieux immediately brightened, speaking faster and breathlessly. "What matter, if I may ask? Please, may I sit in?"

In that instant, Jessaline was struck by how lovely her eyes were, despite their uncertain coloring of browny-green. She had never preferred the looks of half-white folk, having grown up in a land where, thanks to the Revolution, darkness of skin was a point of pride. But as Mademoiselle Rillieux spoke of chemistry, something in her manner made her peculiar eyes sparkle, and Jessaline was forced to reassess her initial estimate of the girl's looks. She was handsome, perhaps, rather than plain.

"Eugenie is the only other member of my family to share my interest in the sciences," Rillieux said, pride warming his voice. "She could not study in Paris as I did; the schools there do not admit women. Still, I made certain to send her all of my books as I finished with them, and she critiques all of my prototypes. It's probably for the best that they wouldn't admit her; I daresay she could give my old masters at the École Centrale a run for their money!"

Jessaline blinked in surprise at this. Then it came to her; she had lost Rillieux's trust already. But perhaps...

Turning to the beverage stand, she picked up the flask of effluent. "I'm afraid I won't be able to stay, Mademoiselle Rillieux—but
before I go, perhaps you could give me your opinion of this?" She
offered the flask.

Norbert Rillieux, guessing her intent, scowled. But Eugenie
took the flask before he could muster a protest, unstoppering it
deftly and wafting the fumes toward her face rather than sniffing
outright. "Faugh," she said, grimacing. "Definitely hydrogen sul-
fide, and probably a number of other gases, too, if this is the product of some form of decay." She stoppered the flask and examined
the sludge in its bottom with a critical eye. "Interesting—I thought
it was dirt, but this seems to be some more uniform substance.
Something *made* this? What process could generate something so
noxious?"

"Rum distillation," Jessaline said, stifling the urge to smile when
Eugenie looked scandalized.

"No wonder," Eugenie said darkly, "given what the end product
does to men's souls." She handed the flask back to Jessaline. "What
of it?"

So Jessaline was obliged to explain again. As she did, a curious
thing happened; Eugenie's eyes grew a bit glazed. She nodded,
"mmm-hmming" now and again. "And as I mentioned to your
brother," Jessaline concluded, "we have already worked out the
formula—"

"The formula is child's play," Eugenie said, flicking her fingers
absently. "And the extraction would be simple enough, if methane
weren't dangerously flammable. Explosive even, under certain con-
ditions...which most attempts at extraction would inevitably create. Obviously any mechanical method would need to concern itself

primarily with *stabilizing* the end products, not merely separating them. Freezing, perhaps, or—" She brightened. "Brother, perhaps we could try a refinement of the vacuum-distillation process you developed for—"

"Yes, yes," said Norbert, who had spent the past ten minutes looking from Jessaline to Eugenie and back, in visibly increasing consternation. "I'll consider it. In the meantime, Mademoiselle Dumonde was actually leaving; I'm afraid we delay her." He glared at Jessaline as Eugenie made a moue of dismay.

"Quite right," said Jessaline, smiling graciously at him; she put away the flask and tucked the bag over her arm, retrieving her hat from the back of the chair. She could afford to be gracious now, even though Norbert Rillieux had proven intractable. Better indeed to leave, and pursue the matter from an entirely different angle.

And as Norbert escorted her to the parlor door with a hand rather too firm upon her elbow, Jessaline glanced back and smiled at Eugenie, who returned the smile with charming ruefulness and a shy little wave.

Not just handsome, pretty, Jessaline decided at last. And that meant this new angle would be *most enjoyable* to pursue.

There were, however, complications.

Jessaline, pleased that she had succeeded in making contact with *a* Rillieux, if not the one she'd come for, treated herself to an evening out about the Vieux Carré. It was not the done thing for a lady of gentle breeding—as she was emulating—to stop in at any of the rollicking music halls she could hear down side streets, though she was intrigued. She could, however, sit in on one of the newfangled vaudevilles at the Playhouse, which she quite enjoyed though it was difficult to see the stage well from the rear balcony. Then, as nightfall finally brought a breath of cool relief from the day's sweltering humidity, she returned to her room at the inn.

From time spent on the harder streets of Port-au-Prince, it was Jessaline's longtime habit to stand to one side of a door while she unlocked it, so that her shadow under the door would not alert anyone inside. This proved wise, as pushing open the door, she found herself facing a startled male figure, which froze in silhouette before the room's picture window, near her traveling chest. They stared at one another for a breath, and then Jessaline's wits returned; at once she dropped to one knee and in a single smooth sweep of her hand, brushed up her booted leg to palm a throwing knife.

In the same instant the figure bolted, darting toward the open balcony window. Jessaline hissed out a curse in her own Kreyòl tongue, running into the room as he lunged through the window with an acrobat's nimbleness, rolling to his feet and fetching up against the elaborately ironworked railing. Fearing to lose him, Jessaline flung the knife from within the room as she ran, praying it would strike, and heard the thunk as it struck flesh. The figure on her balcony stumbled, crying out—but she could not have hit a vital area, for he grasped the railing and pulled himself over it, dropping the short distance to the ground and out of sight.

Jessaline scrambled through the window as best she could, hampered by her bustle and skirts. Just as she reached the railing, the figure finished picking himself up from the ground and turned to run. Jessaline got one good look at him in the moonlight, as he turned back to see if she pursued: a pinch-faced youth, clearly pale beneath the bootblack he'd smeared on his face and straw-colored hair to help himself hide in the dark. Then he was gone, running into the night, though he ran oddly and kept one of his hands clapped to his right buttock.

Furious, Jessaline pounded the railing, though she knew better than to make an outcry. No one in this town would care that some *affranchis* woman had been robbed, and the constable would as likely arrest her for disturbing the peace.

Going back into her room, she lit the lanterns and surveyed the damage. At once a chill passed down her spine. The chest held a number of valuables that any sensible thief would've taken: fine dresses; a cameo pendant with a face of carved obsidian; the brass gyroscope that an old lover, a dirigible navigator, had given her; a pearl-beaded purse containing twenty dollars. These, however, had all been shoved rudely aside, and to Jessaline's horror, the chest's false bottom had been lifted, revealing the compartment underneath. There was nothing here but a bundle of clothing and a larger pouch, containing a far more substantial sum—but that had not been taken either.

But Jessaline knew what *would* have been in there if she had not taken them with her to see Rillieux: the scrolls which held the chemical formula for the methane extraction process, and the rudimentary designs for the mechanism to do so—the best her government's scientists had been able to cobble together. These were even now at the bottom of her brocade bag.

The bootblack boy had been no thief. Someone in this foul city knew who and what she was, and sought to thwart her mission.

Carefully Jessaline replaced everything in the trunk, including the false bottom and money. She went downstairs and paid her bill, then hired a porter to carry her trunk to an inn two blocks over, where she rented a room without windows. She slept lightly that night, waking with every creak and thump of the place, and took comfort only from the solid security of the stiletto in her hand.

The lovely thing about a town full of slaves, vagabonds, beggars, and blackguards was that it was blessedly easy to send a message in secret.

Having waited a few days so as to let Norbert Rillieux's anger cool—just in case—Jessaline then hired a child who was one of the innkeeper's slaves. She purchased fresh fruit at the market and offered the child an apple to memorize her message. When he repeated it back to her word for word, she showed him a bunch of big blue-black grapes, and his eyes went wide. "Get word to Mademoiselle Eugenie without her brother knowing, and these are yours," she said. "You'll have to make sure to spit the seeds in the fire, though, or Master will know you've had a treat."

The boy grinned, and Jessaline saw that the warning had not been necessary. "Just you hold on to those, Miss Jessaline," he said back, pointing with his chin at the grapes. "I'll have 'em in a minute or three." And indeed, within an hour's time he returned, carrying a small folded square of cloth. "Miss Eugenie agrees to meet," he said, "and sends this as a surety of her good faith." He pronounced this last carefully, perfectly emulating the Creole woman's tone.

Pleased, Jessaline took the cloth and unfolded it to find a handkerchief of fine imported French linen, embroidered in one corner with a tiny perfect *R*. She held it to her nose and smelled a perfume like magnolia blossoms; the same scent had been about Eugenie the other day. She could not help smiling at the memory. The boy grinned, too, and ate a handful of the grapes at once, pocketing the seeds with a wink.

"Gonna plant these near the city dump," he said. "Maybe I'll bring you wine one day!" And he ran off.

So Jessaline found herself on another bright sweltering day at the convent of the Ursulines, where two gentlewomen might walk and exchange thoughts in peace without being seen or interrupted by curious others.

"I have to admit," said Eugenie, smiling sidelong at Jessaline as they strolled amid the nuns' garden, "I was of two minds about whether to meet you."

"I suppose your brother must've given you an earful after I left."

"You might say so," Eugenie said, in a dry tone that made Jessaline laugh. (One of the old nuns glowered at them over a bed of herbs. Jessaline covered her mouth and waved apology.) "But that wasn't what gave me pause. My brother has his ways, Mademoiselle Jessaline, and I do not always agree with him. He's fond of forming opinions without full information, then proceeding as if they are proven fact." She shrugged. "I, on the other hand, prefer to seek as much information as I can. I have made inquiries about you, you see."

"Oh? And what did you find?"

"That you do not exist, as far as anyone in this town knows." She spoke lightly, Jessaline noticed, but there was an edge to her words, too. Unease, perhaps. "You aren't one of us, that much anyone can see; but you aren't a freedwoman either, though the people at your old inn and the market seemed to think so."

At this, Jessaline blinked in surprise and unease of her own. She had not thought the girl would dig that deeply. "What makes you say that?"

"For one, that pistol in your bag."

Jessaline froze for a pace before remembering to keep walking. "A lady alone in a strange, rough city would be wise to look to her own protection, don't you think?"

"True," said Eugenie, "but I checked at the courthouse, too, and there are no records of a woman meeting your description having bought her way free anytime in the past thirty years, and I doubt you're far past that age. For another, you hide it well, but your French has an odd sort of lilt; not at all like that of folk hereabouts. And for thirdly—this is a small town at heart, Mademoiselle Dumonde, despite its size. Every time some fortunate soul buys free, as they say, it's the talk of the town. To put it bluntly, there's no gossip about you, and there should have been."

They had reached a massive old willow tree which partially overhung the garden path. There was no way around it; the tree's draping branches had made a proper curtain of things, nearly obscuring from sight the area about the trunk.

The sensible thing to do would have been to turn around and walk back the way they'd come. But as Jessaline turned to meet Eugenie's eyes, she suffered another of those curious epiphanies. Eugenie was smiling, sweet, but despite this, there was a hard look in her eyes, which reminded Jessaline fleetingly of Norbert. It was clear that she meant to have the truth from Jessaline, or Jessaline's efforts to employ her would get short shrift.

So on impulse Jessaline grabbed Eugenie's hand and pulled her into the willow fall. Eugenie yelped in surprise, then giggled as they came through into the space beyond, green-shrouded and encircling, like a hurricane of leaves.

"What on earth? Mademoiselle Dumonde—"

"It isn't Dumonde," Jessaline said, dropping her voice to a

near-whisper. "My name is Jessaline Cleré. That is the name of the family that raised me, at least, but I should have had a different name, after the man who was my true father. His name was L'Overture. Do you know it?"

At that, Eugenie drew a sharp breath. "Toussaint the Rebel?" she asked. "The man who led the Revolution in Haiti? *That* was your father?"

"So my mother says, though she was only his mistress; I am natural-born. But I do not begrudge her, because her status spared me. When the French betrayed Toussaint, they took him and his wife and legitimate children and carried them across the sea to torture to death."

Eugenie put her hands to her mouth at this, which Jessaline had to admit was a bit much for a gently raised woman to bear. Yet it was the truth, for Jessaline felt uncomfortable dissembling with Eugenie, for reasons she could not quite name.

"I see," Eugenie said at last, recovering. "Then—these interests you represent. You are with the Haitians."

"I am. If you build a methane extraction mechanism for us, mademoiselle, you will have helped a nation of free folk *stay* free, for I swear that France is hell-bent upon re-enslaving us all. They would have done it already, if one of our number had not thought to use our torment to our advantage."

Eugenie nodded slowly. "The sugarcane," she said. "The papers say your people use the steam and gases from the distilleries to make hot-air balloons and blimps."

"Which helped us bomb the French ships most effectively during the Revolution, and also secured our position as the foremost manufacturers of dirigibles in the Americas," Jessaline said, with a bit of pride. "We were saved by a mad idea and a contraption that should have killed its first user. So we value cleverness now, mademoiselle, which is why I came here in search of your brother."

"Then—" Eugenie frowned. "The methane. It is to power your dirigibles?"

"Partly. The French have begun using dirigibles, too, you see. Our only hope is to enhance the maneuverability and speed of our craft, which can be done with gas-powered engines. We have also crafted powerful artillery which use this engine design, whose range and accuracy are unsurpassed. The prototypes work magnificently—but the price of the oil and coal we must currently use to power them is too dear. We would bankrupt ourselves buying it from the very nations that hope to destroy us. The rum effluent is our only abundant, inexpensive resource...our only hope."

But Eugenie had begun to shake her head, looking taken aback. "Artillery? Guns, you mean?" she said. "I am a Christian woman, mademoiselle—"

"Jessaline."

"Very well; Jessaline." That look was in her face again, Jessaline noted; that air of determination and fierceness that made her beautiful at the oddest times. "I do not care for the idea of my skills being put to use in taking lives. That's simply unacceptable."

Jessaline stared at her, and for an instant fury blotted out thought. How dare this girl, with her privilege and wealth and coddled life... Jessaline set her jaw.

"In the Revolution," she said, in a low tight voice, "the last French commander, Rochambeau, decided to teach my people a lesson for daring to revolt against our betters. Do you know what he did? He took slaves—including those who had not even fought—and broke them on the wheel, raising them on a post afterwards so the birds could eat them alive. He buried prisoners of war, also alive, in pits of insects. He *boiled* some of them, in vats of molasses. Such acts, he deemed, were necessary to put fear and subservience back into our hearts, since we had been tainted by a year of freedom."

Eugenie, who had gone quite pale, stared at Jessaline in purest horror, her mouth open. Jessaline smiled a hard, angry smile. "Such atrocities will happen again, Mademoiselle Rillieux, if you do not help us. Except this time we have been free for two generations. Imagine how much fear and subservience these *Christian* men will instill in us now?"

Eugenie shook her head slowly. "I...I had not heard...I did not consider..." She fell mute.

Jessaline stepped closer and laid one lace-gloved finger on the divot between Eugenie's collarbones. "You had best consider such things, my dear. Do you forget? There are those in this land who would like to do the same to you and all your kin."

Eugenie stared at her. Then, startling Jessaline, she dropped to the ground, sitting down so hard that her bustle made an aggrieved creaking sound.

"I did not know," she said at last. "I did not know these things."

Jessaline beheld the honest shock on her face and felt some guilt for having troubled her so. It was clear the girl's brother had worked hard to protect her from the world's harshness. Sitting beside Eugenie on the soft dry grass, she let out a weary sigh.

"In my land," she said, "men and women of all shades are free. I will not pretend that this makes us perfect; I have gone hungry many times in my life. Yet there, a woman such as yourself may be more than the coddled sister of a prominent scientist, or the mistress of a white man."

Eugenie threw her a guilty look, but Jessaline smiled to reassure her. The women of Eugenie's class had few options in life; Jessaline saw no point in condemning them for this.

"So many men died in the Revolution that women fill the ranks now as dirigible pilots and gunners. We run factories and farms, too, and are highly placed in government. Even the houngans are mostly women now—you have vodoun here, too, yes? So we are important." She leaned close, her shoulder brushing Eugenie's in a teasing way, and grinned. "Some of us might even become spies. Who knows?"

Eugenie's cheeks flamed pink and she ducked her head to smile. Jessaline could see, however, that her words were having some effect; Eugenie had that oddly absent look again. Perhaps she was imagining all the things she could do in a land where the happenstances of sex and caste did not forbid her from using her mind to its fullest? A shame; Jessaline would have loved to take her there. But she had seen the luxury of the Rillieux household; why would any woman give that up?

This close, shoulder to shoulder and secluded within the willow tree's green canopy, Jessaline found herself staring at Eugenie, more aware than ever of the scent of her perfume, and the nearby softness of her skin, and the way the curls of her hair framed her long slender neck. At least she did not cover her hair like so many women of this land, convinced that its natural state was inherently ugly. She could not help her circumstances, but it seemed to Jessaline that she had taken what pride in her heritage that she could.

So taken was Jessaline by this notion, and by the silence and strangeness of the moment, that she found herself saying, "And in my land it is not uncommon for a woman to head a family with another woman, and even raise children if they so wish."

Eugenie started—and to Jessaline's delight, her blush deepened. She darted a half-scandalized, half-entranced look at Jessaline, then away, which Jessaline found deliciously fetching. "Live with— another woman? Do you mean—?" But of course she knew what Jessaline meant. "How can that be?"

"The necessities of security and shared labor. The priests look the other way."

Eugenie looked up then, and Jessaline was surprised to see a peculiar daring enter her expression, though her flush lingered. "And..." She licked her lips, swallowed. "Do such women...ah... behave as a family in...*all* matters?"

A slow grin spread across Jessaline's face. *Not so sheltered in her thoughts at least, this one!* "Oh, certainly. All matters—legal, financial, domestic..." Then, as a hint of uncertainty flickered in Eugenie's expression, Jessaline got tired of teasing. It was not proper, she knew; it was not within the bounds of her mission. But—just this once—perhaps—

She shifted just a little, from brushing shoulders to pressing rather more suggestively close, and leaned near, her eyes fixed on Eugenie's lips. "And conjugal," she added.

Eugenie stared at her, eyes huge behind the spectacles. "C-conjugal?" she asked, rather breathlessly.

"Oh, indeed. Perhaps a demonstration..."

But just as Jessaline leaned in to offer just that, she was startled by the voice of one of the nuns, apparently calling to another in French. From far too near the willow tree, a third voice rose to shush the first two—the prying old biddy who'd given Jessaline the eye before.

Eugenie jumped, her face red as plums, and quickly shifted away from Jessaline. Privately cursing, Jessaline did the same, and an awkward silence fell.

"W-well," said Eugenie, "I had best be getting back. I told my brother I would be at the seamstress's, and that doesn't take long."

"Yes," Jessaline said, realizing with some consternation that she'd completely forgotten why she'd asked for a meeting in the first place. "Well. Ah. I have something I'd like to offer you—but I would advise you to keep these out of sight, even at home where servants might see. For your own safety." She reached into the brocade bag and handed Eugenie the small cylindrical leather container that held the formula and plans for the methane extractor. "This is what we have come up with thus far, but the design is incomplete. If you can offer any assistance—"

"Yes, of course," Eugenie said, taking the case with an avid look that heartened Jessaline at once. She tucked the leather case into her purse. "Allow me a few days to consider the problem. How may I contact you, though, once I've devised a solution?"

"I will contact you in one week. Do not look for me." She got to her feet and offered her hand to help Eugenie up. Then, speaking loudly enough to be heard outside the willow at last, she giggled. "Before your brother learns we've been swapping tales about him!"

Eugenie looked blank for a moment, then opened her mouth in an "O" of understanding, grinning. "Oh, his ego could use a bit of flattering, I think. In any case, fare you well, Mademoiselle Dumonde. I must be on my way." And with that, she hurried off, holding her hat as she passed through the willow branches.

Jessaline waited for ten breaths, then stepped out herself, sparing a hard look for the old nun—who, sure enough, had moved quite a bit closer to the tree. "A good afternoon to you, Sister," she said.

"And to you," the woman said in a low voice, "though you had best be more careful from now on, *estipid*."

Startled to hear her own tongue on the old woman's lips, she stiffened. Then, carefully, she said in the same language, "And what would you know of it?"

"I know you have a dangerous enemy," the nun replied, getting to her feet and dusting dirt off her habit. Now that Jessaline could see her better, it was clear from her features that she had a dollop or two of African in her. "I am sent by your superiors to warn you. We have word the Order of the White Camellia is active in the city."

Jessaline caught her breath. The bootblack man! "I may have encountered them already," she said.

The old woman nodded grimly. "Word had it they broke apart after that scandal we arranged for them up in Baton Rouge," she said, "but in truth they've just gotten more subtle. We don't know what they're after, but obviously they don't just want to kill you, or you would be dead by now."

"I am not so easily removed, madame," Jessaline said, drawing herself up in affront.

The old woman rolled her eyes. "Just take care," she snapped. "And by all means, if you want that girl dead, continue playing silly lovers' games with her where any fool can suspect." And with that, the old woman picked up her spade and shears, and walked briskly away.

Jessaline did, too, her cheeks burning. But back in her room, ostensibly safe, she leaned against the door and closed her eyes, wondering why her heart still fluttered so fast now that Eugenie was long gone, and why she was suddenly so afraid.

The Order of the White Camellia changed everything. Jessaline had heard tales of them for years, of course—a secret society of wealthy professionals and intellectuals dedicated to the preservation of "American ideals" like the superiority of the white race. They had been responsible for the exposure—and deaths, in some cases—of many of Jessaline's fellow spies over the years. America was built on slavery; naturally the White Camellias would oppose a nation built on slavery's overthrow.

So Jessaline decided on new tactics. She shifted her attire from that of a well-to-do freedwoman to the plainer garb of a woman of less means. This elicited no attention as there were plenty such women in the city—though she was obliged to move to yet another inn that would suit her appearance. This drew her well into the less-respectable area of the city, where not a few of the patrons took rooms by the hour or the half-day.

Here she lay low for the next few days, trying to determine whether she was being watched, though she spotted no suspicious characters—or at least, no one suspicious for the area. Which, of course, was why she'd chosen it. White men frequented the inn, but a white face that lingered or appeared repeatedly would be remarked upon, and easy to spot.

When a week had passed and Jessaline felt safe, she radically transformed herself using the bundle that had been hidden beneath her chest's false bottom. First she hid her close-cropped hair beneath a lumpy calico headwrap, and donned an ill-fitting dress of worn, stained gingham patched here and there with burlap. A few small pillows rendered her effectively shapeless—a necessity, since in this disguise it was dangerous to be attractive in any way. As she slipped out in the small hours of the morning, carrying her belongings in a satchel and shuffling to make herself look much older, no one paid her any heed—not the drowsy old men sitting guard at the stables, nor the city constables chatting up a gaudily dressed woman under a gas lamp, nor the young toughs still dicing on the corner. She was, for all intents and purposes, invisible.

So first she milled among the morning-market crowds at the waterfront awhile, keeping an eye out for observers. When she was certain she had not been followed, she made her way to the dirigible docks, where four of the great machines hovered above a cluster of cargo vessels like huge, sausage-shaped guardian angels. A massive brick fence screened the docks themselves from view, though this had a secondary purpose: The docks were the sovereign territory of the Haitian Republic, housing its embassy as well. No American-born slave was permitted to step upon even this proxy version of Haitian soil, since by the laws of Haiti, they would then be free.

Yet practicality did not stop men and women from dreaming, and near the massive ironwork gate of the facility there was as usual a small crowd of slaves gathered, gazing enviously in at the shouting dirigible crews and their smartly dressed officers. Jessaline slipped in among these and edged her way to the front, then waited.

Presently, a young runner detached herself from the nearby rope crew and ran over to the fence. Several of the slaves pushed envelopes through the fence, commissioning travel and shipping on behalf of their owners, and the girl collected these. The whole operation was conducted in utter silence; an American soldier hovered all too near the gate, ready to report any slave who talked. (It was not illegal to talk, but any slave who did so would likely suffer for it.)

Yet Jessaline noted that the runner met the eyes of every person she could, nodding to each solemnly, touching more hands than was strictly necessary for the sake of her work. A small taste of respect for those who needed it so badly, so that they might come to crave it and eventually seek it for themselves.

Jessaline met the runner's eyes, too, as she pushed through a plain, wrinkled envelope, but her gaze held none of the desperate hope of the others. The runner's eyes widened a bit, but she moved on at once after taking Jessaline's envelope. When she trotted away to deliver the comissions, Jessaline saw her shuffle the pile to put the wrinkled envelope on top.

That done, Jessaline headed then to the Rillieux house. At the back gate she shifted her satchel from her shoulder to her hands, re-tying it so as to make it square-shaped. To the servant who then answered her knock—freeborn; the Rillieuxs did not go in for the practice of owning slaves themselves—she said in coarse French, "Package for Mademoiselle Rillieux. I was told to deliver it to her personal."

The servant, a cleanly dressed fellow who could barely conceal his distaste at Jessaline's appearance, frowned further. "*English*, woman, only high-class folk talk French here." But when Jessaline deliberately spoke in butchered English, rendered barely comprehensible by an exaggerated French accent, the man finally rolled his eyes and stood aside. "She's in the garden house. Back there. There!" And he pointed the way.

Thus did Jessaline come to the overlarge shed that sat amid the house's vast garden. It had clearly been meant to serve as a hothouse at some point, having a glass ceiling, but when Jessaline stepped inside, she was assailed by sounds most unnatural: clanks and squealing and the rattling hiss of a steam boiler. These came from the equipment and incomprehensible machinery that lined every wall and hung from the ceiling, pipes and clockworks big enough to crush a man, all of it churning merrily away.

At the center of this chaos stood several high worktables, each bearing equipment in various states of construction or dismantlement, save the last. At this table, which sat in a shaft of gathering sunlight, sat a sleeping Eugenie Rillieux.

At the sight of her, Jessaline stopped, momentarily overcome by a most uncharacteristic anxiety. Eugenie's head rested on her folded arms, atop a sheaf of large, irregular sheets of parchment that were practically covered with pen scribbles and diagrams. Her hair was amuss, her glasses askew, and she had drooled a bit onto one of her pale, ink-stained hands.

Beautiful, Jessaline thought, and marveled at herself. Her tastes had never leaned toward women like Eugenie, pampered and sheltered and shy. She generally preferred women like herself, who could be counted upon to know what they wanted and take decisive steps to get it. Yet in that moment, gazing upon this awkward, brilliant creature, Jessaline wanted nothing more than to be holding flowers instead of a fake package, and to have come for courting rather than her own selfish motives.

Perhaps Eugenie felt the weight of her longing, for after a moment she wrinkled her nose and sat up. "Oh," she said blearily, seeing Jessaline. "What is it, a delivery? Put it on the table there, please; I'll fetch you a tip." She got up, and Jessaline was amused to see that her bustle was askew.

"Eugenie," she said, and Eugenie whirled back as she recognized Jessaline's voice. Her eyes flew wide.

"What in heaven's name—"

"I haven't much time," she said, hastening forward. She took Eugenie's hands in quick greeting, and resisted the urge to kiss her as well. "Have you been able to refine the plans?"

"Oh—yes, yes, I think." Eugenie pushed her glasses straight and gestured toward the papers that had served as her pillow. "This design should work, at least in theory. I was right; the vacuum-distillation mechanism was the key! Of course, I haven't finished the prototype, because the damned glassmaker is trying to charge pirates' rates—"

Jessaline squeezed her hands, exhilarated. "Marvelous! Don't worry; we shall test the design thoroughly before we put it into use. But now I must have the plans. Men are searching for me; I don't dare stay in town much longer."

Eugenie nodded absently, then blinked again as her head cleared. She narrowed her eyes at Jessaline in sudden suspicion. "Wait," she said. "You're leaving town?"

"Yes, of course," Jessaline said, surprised. "This is what I came for, after all. I can't just put something so important on the next dirigible packet—"

The look of hurt that came over Eugenie's face sent a needle straight into Jessaline's heart. She realized, belatedly and with guilty dismay, what Eugenie must have been imagining all this time.

"But . . . I thought . . ." Eugenie looked away suddenly, and bit her lower lip. "You might stay."

"Eugenie," Jessaline began uncomfortably. "I . . . could never have remained here. This place . . . the way you live here . . ."

"Yes, I know." At once Eugenie's voice hardened; she glared at

Jessaline. "In your perfect, wonderful land, everyone is free to live as they please. It is the rest of us, then, the poor wretched folk you scorn and pity, who have no choice but to endure it. Perhaps we should never bother to love at all, then! That way, at least, when we are used and cast aside, it will at least be for material gain!"

And with that, she slapped Jessaline smartly, and walked out. Stunned, Jessaline put a hand to her cheek and stared after her.

"Trouble in paradise?" said a voice behind her, in a syrupy drawl.

Jessaline whirled to find herself facing a six-shooter. And holding it, his face free of bootblack this time, was the young man who had invaded her quarters nearly two weeks before.

"I heard you Haitians were unnatural," he said, coming into the light, "but this? Not at all what I was expecting."

Not me, Jessaline realized, too late. *They were watching Rillieux, not me!* "Natural is in the eye of the beholder, as is beauty," she snapped.

"True. Speaking of beauty, though, you looked a damn sight finer before. What's all this?" He sidled forward, poking with the gun at the padding 'round Jessaline's middle. "So that's it! But—" He raised the gun, to Jessaline's fury, and poked at her breasts none-too-gently. "Ah, no padding *here.* Yes, I do remember you rightly." He scowled. "I still can't sit down thanks to you, woman. Maybe I ought to repay you that."

Jessaline raised her hands slowly, pulling off her lumpy head-wrap so he could see her more clearly. "That's ungentlemanly of you, I would say."

"Gentlemen need gentle*women,*" he said. "Your kind are hardly that, being good for only one thing. Well—that and lynching, I suppose. But we'll save both for later, won't we? After you've met my superior and told us everything that's in your nappy little head. He's partial to your variety. I, however, feel that if I must lower myself to baseness, better to do it with one bearing the fair blood of the French."

It took Jessaline a moment to understand through all his airs. But then she did, and shivered in purest rage. "You will not lay a finger upon Eugenie. I'll snap them all off fir—"

But before she could finish her threat, there was a scream and commotion from the house. The scream, amid all the chaos of shouting and running servants, she recognized at once: Eugenie.

The noise startled the bootblack man as well. Fortunately he did not pull the trigger; he did start badly, however, half-turning to point the gun in the direction of Eugenie's scream. Which was all the opening that Jessaline needed, as she drew her derringer from the wadded cloth of the headwrap and shot the man point-blank. The bootblack man cried out, clutching his chest and falling to the ground.

The derringer was spent; it carried only a single bullet. Snatching up the bootblack man's six-gun instead, Jessaline turned to sprint toward the Rillieux house—then froze for an instant in terrible indecision. Behind her, on Eugenie's table, sat the plans for which she had spent the past three months of her life striving and stealing and sneaking. The methane extractor could be the salvation of her nation, the start of its brightest future.

And in the house—

Eugenie, she thought.

And started running.

In the parlor, Norbert Rillieux was frozen, paler than usual and trembling. Before him, holding Eugenie about the throat and with a

gun to her head, was a white man whose face was so floridly familiar that Jessaline gasped. "Raymond Forstall?"

He started badly as Jessaline rounded the door, and she froze as
well, fearing to cause Eugenie's death. Very slowly she set the six-
gun on a nearby sideboard, pushed it so that it slid out of easy reach,
and raised her hands to show that she was no threat. At this, Forstall
relaxed.

"So we meet again, my beauteous Negress," he said, though
there was anger in his smile. "I had hoped to make your acquaintance under more favorable circumstances. Alas."

"*You* are with the White Camellia?" He had seemed so gormless
that day on Royal Street; not at all the sort Jessaline would associate
with a murderous secret society.

"I am indeed," he said. "And you would have met the rest of us if
my assistant had not clearly failed in his goal of taking you captive.
Nevertheless, I, too, have a goal, and I ask again, sir, where are the
plans?"

Jessaline realized belatedly that this was directed at Norbert Rillieux. And he, too frightened to bluster, just shook his head. "I told
you, I have built no such device! Ask this woman—she wanted it,
and I refused her!"

The methane extractor, Jessaline realized. Of course—they had
known, probably via their own spies, that she was after it. Forstall
had been tailing her the day he'd bumped into her, probably all the
way to Rillieux's house; she cursed herself for a fool for not realizing. But the White Camellias were mostly philosophers and bankers
and lawyers, not the trained, proficient spies she'd been expecting
to deal with. It had never occurred to her that an enemy would be
so clumsy as to jostle and converse with his target in the course of
surveillance.

"It's true," Jessaline said, stalling desperately in hopes that some solution would present itself to her. "This man refused my request to build the device."

"Then why did you come back here?" Forstall asked, tightening his grip on Eugenie so that she gasped. "We had men watching the house servants, too. We intercepted orders for metal parts and rubber tubing, and I paid the glasssmith to delay an order for custom vacuum pipes—"

"You did that?" To Jessaline's horror, Eugenie stiffened in Forstall's grasp, trying to turn and glare at him in her affront. "I argued with that old fool for an hour!"

"Eugenie, be still!" cried Norbert, which raised him high in Jessaline's estimation; she had wanted to shout the same thing.

"I will not—" Eugenie began to struggle, plainly furious. As Forstall cursed and tried to restrain her, Jessaline heard Eugenie's protests continue. "—interference with my work—very idea—"

Please, Holy Mother, Jessaline thought, taking a very careful step closer to the gun on the sideboard, *don't let him shoot her to shut her up.*

When Forstall finally thrust Eugenie aside—she fell against the bottle-strewn side table, nearly toppling it—and indeed raised the gun to shoot her, Jessaline blurted out, "Wait!"

Both Forstall and Eugenie froze, now separated and facing each other, though Forstall's gun was still pointed dead at Eugenie's chest. "The plans are complete," Jessaline said to him. "They are in the workshop out back." With a hint of pride, she looked at Eugenie and added, "Eugenie has made it work."

"What?" said Rillieux, looking thunderstruck.

"What?" Forstall stared at her, then Eugenie, and then anger filled his expression. "Clever indeed! And while I go out back to check if your story is true, you will make your escape with the plans already tucked into your clothes."

"I am not lying in this instance," she said, "but if you like, we can all proceed to the garden and see. Or since I'm the one you seem to fear most—" She waggled her empty hands in mockery, hoping this would make him too angry to notice how much closer she was to the gun on the sideboard. His face reddened further with fury. "You could leave Eugenie and her brother here, and take me alone."

Eugenie caught her breath. "Jessaline, are you mad?"

"Yes," Jessaline said, and smiled, letting her heart live in her face for a moment. Eugenie's mouth fell open, then softened into a small smile. Her glasses were still askew, Jessaline saw with a rush of fondness.

Forstall rolled his eyes, but smiled. "A capital suggestion, I think. Then I can shoot you—"

He got no further, for in the next instant Eugenie suddenly struck him in the head with a rum bottle.

The bottle shattered on impact. Forstall cried out, half-stunned by the blow and the sting of rum in his eyes, but he managed to keep his grip on the gun, and keep it trained more or less on Eugenie. Jessaline thought she saw the muscles in his forearm flex to pull the trigger—

—and then the six-gun was in her hand, its wooden grip warm and almost comforting as she blew a hole in Raymond Forstall's rum-drenched head. Forstall uttered a horrid gurgling sound and fell to the floor.

Before his body stopped twitching, Jessaline caught Eugenie's hand. "Hurry!" She dragged the other woman out of the parlor.

Norbert, again to his credit, started out of shock and trotted after them, for once silent as they moved through the house's corridors toward the garden. The house was nearly deserted now, the servants having fled or found some place to hide that was safe from gunshots and madmen.

"You must tell me which of the papers on your desk I can take," Jessaline said as they trotted along, "and then you must make a decision."

"Wh-what decision?" Eugenie still sounded shaken.

"Whether you will stay here, or whether you will come with me to Haiti."

"Haiti?" Norbert cried.

"Haiti?" Eugenie asked, in wonder.

"Haiti," said Jessaline, and as they passed through the rear door and went into the garden, she stopped and turned to Eugenie. "With me."

Eugenie stared at her in such dawning amazement that Jessaline could no longer help herself. She caught Eugenie about the waist, pulled her near, and kissed her most soundly and improperly, right there in front of her brother. It was the sweetest, wildest kiss she had ever known in her life.

When she pulled back, Norbert was standing at the edge of her vision with his mouth open, and Eugenie looked a bit faint. "Well," Eugenie said, and fell silent, the whole affair having been a bit much for her.

Jessaline grinned and let her go, then hurried forward to enter the workshop—and froze, horror shattering her good mood.

The bootblack man was gone. Where his body had been lay Jessaline's derringer and copious blood, trailing away...to Eugenie's worktable, where the plans had been, and were no longer. The trail then led away, out the workshop's rear door.

"No," she whispered, her fists clenching at her sides. "No, by God!" Everything she had worked for, gone. She had failed, both her mission and her people.

"Very well," Eugenie said after a moment. "Then I shall simply have to come with you."

The words penetrated Jessaline's despair slowly. "What?"

She touched Jessaline's hand. "I will come with you. To Haiti. And I will build an even more efficient methane extractor for you there."

Jessaline turned to stare at her and found that she could not, for her eyes had filled with tears.

"Wait—" Norbert caught his breath as understanding dawned. "Go to Haiti? Are you mad? I forbid—"

"You had better come, too, Brother," Eugenie said, turning to him, and Jessaline was struck breathless once more by the cool determination in her eyes. "The police will take their time about it, but they'll come eventually, and a white man lies dead in our house. It doesn't really matter whether you shot him or not; you know full well what they'll decide."

And Norbert stiffened, for he did indeed know—probably better than Eugenie, Jessaline suspected—what his fate would be.

Eugenie turned to Jessaline. "He can come, can't he?" By which Jessaline knew it was a condition, not an option.

"Of course he can," she said at once. "I wouldn't leave a dog to these people's so-called justice. But it will not be the life you're used to, either of you. Are you certain?"

Eugenie smiled, and before Jessaline realized what was

imminent, she had been pulled rather roughly into another kiss. Eugenie had been eating penuche again, she realized dimly, and then for a long perfect moment she thought of nothing but pecans and sweetness.

When it was done, Eugenie searched Jessaline's face and then smiled in satisfaction. "Perhaps we should go, Jessaline," she said gently.

"Ah. Yes. We should, yes." Jessaline fought to compose herself; she glanced at Norbert and took a deep breath. "Fetch us a hansom cab while you still can, Monsieur Rillieux, and we'll go down to the docks and take the next dirigible southbound."

The daze cleared from Norbert's eyes as well; he nodded mutely and trotted off.

In the silence that fell, Eugenie turned to Jessaline.

"Marriage," she said, "and a house together. I believe you mentioned that?"

"Er," said Jessaline, blinking. "Well, yes, I suppose, but I rather thought that first we would—"

"Good," Eugenie replied, "because I'm not fond of you keeping up this dangerous line of work. My inventions should certainly earn enough for the both of us, don't you think?"

"Um," said Jessaline.

"Yes. So there's no reason for you to work when I can keep you in comfort for the rest of our days." Taking Jessaline's hands, she stepped closer, her eyes going soft again. "And I am so very much looking forward to those days, Jessaline."

"Yes," said Jessaline, who had been wondering just which of her many sins had earned her this mad fortune. But as Eugenie's warm breast pressed against hers, and the thick perfume of the magnolia trees wafted around them, and some clockwork contraption within the workshop ticked in time with her heart...Jessaline stopped worrying. And she wondered why she had ever bothered with plans and papers and gadgetry, because it was clear she had just stolen the greatest prize of all.

Cloud Dragon Skies

Long ago, our ancestors looked at the sky and saw gods. Their ancestors saw only stars. In the end, only the earth knew the truth.

They came at the end of harvest season. I was in the field, picking hard little pods of okra with dirty fingers, when I heard my father's voice on the wind. I got to my feet and saw, above the bobbing leaves, strangers standing in front of our house. Four of them, all wearing baggy white garments which enclosed them from head to toe. I was not alarmed. Because the sky-people were weak against our diseases—the Earth is so much wilder than their land—they always wrapped themselves thus. Even so, we kept our guard up. Who knew what new diseases they might have developed, up in the sky and surrounded by strangeness? Infected blankets. Germs as spears and arrows. *Accept no gifts from them*, the griots had warned, but of course, people are greedy.

I walked through the fields to stand at my father's side. He had no sons, my father, and no other daughters. His fields were productive, his sculptures and drawings prized by all, yet often he felt himself impoverished in the way that men do when they have too few copies of themselves underfoot. I saw the strangers look me over through the small windows which revealed their faces, and felt pleased to be assessed so seriously. I kept hold of my basket but stood tall, letting my posture speak for me. *Harm him, trick him, and I shall know you are as evil as the stories say.* Not for nothing was I still unmarried.

"My daughter, Nahautu," my father said to the strangers. He kept his voice neutral, and by this I knew he disliked them. "She, too, must agree to this."

The stranger who stood at the front of the group inclined his head. "My greetings, Nahautu," he said. He spoke our tongue with a thick accent, and tortured the pronunciation of my name. "I and my companions have come from the sky-land. Do you know of it?"

"The Humanicorp ring habitat beyond Mars," I replied. I kept my voice as neutral as my father's.

"Yes, exactly," the stranger replied, clearly surprised. "We are scientists—seekers of knowledge—come to study the changes in the sky. We have asked your father for his hospitality." He nodded toward the back field, where our fishing cottage sat near the shore of the river, among the twisting cypress roots. "Your village elders told us you use that building only during autumn and winter; may we use it until then?"

I set down my basket and folded my arms. "Autumn is three months away," I said. "We are good hosts, but we cannot feed four extra mouths for so long and still eat ourselves."

"They bring provisions of their own," my father said. I heard the same kindly condescension from him as from the sky-man. "They will keep their space machines out of sight. The cottage will be sealed in a bubble while they are inside—only a few hours each day. They will be ghosts, barely there and rarely seen. Do you agree?"

And what would we get in return? I wanted to ask, but I knew the answer to that. It was against our law to accept their goods, even in trade, and we had all we wanted of their knowledge. Even so, Father would gain status from hosting the strangers. The young warriors would think him brave for flirting with danger; the elders would call him wise for aiding relations with the sky-folk. He had a need to be admired, my father. My fault. I had been slow to give him grandchildren, who could look up to him in awe as I once had.

For him, I gave the strangers my nod.

They bowed, stiffly and with no true humility, but that was all right because I expected no better of them. All my life I had heard tales of the sky-people and how their ways had nearly destroyed the world. I looked each of them in the eye as they straightened and sent my silent message again. *You are fools*, I said with my shoulders and my legs and my tight strong fists, *but I know how much harm fools can do. I will watch you closely.*

Two of them were women. One squirmed under my gaze. The other smiled, plainly intending friendliness but seeming fatuous instead. Their leader narrowed his eyes at me, puzzled or irritated by my manner. The fourth was a younger man, who also squirmed and looked away at first, but then his eyes drifted back. There was a familiar weight and texture to his gaze.

I picked up my basket and returned to the field, making sure to sway my hips as I walked.

I was a child when the sky changed. I can still remember days when it was endlessly blue, the clouds passive and gentle. The change occurred without warning: One morning we awoke and the sky was a pale, blushing rose. We began to see intention in the slow, ceaseless movements of the clouds. Instead of floating, they swam spirals in the sky. They gathered in knots, trailing wisps like feet and tails. We felt them watching us.

We adapted. We had never taken more than we needed from the land, and we always kept our animals far from water. Now we moistened wild cotton and stretched this across our smoke holes as filters. Sometimes the clouds would gather over fires that were out in the open. A tendril would stretch down, weaving like a snake's head, opening delicate mist jaws to nip the plume of smoke. Even the bravest warriors would quickly put such fires out.

"How do you like the sky?" asked the younger man of the sky-folk. He came out of the fishing cot to watch each evening as I bathed at the river. Usually he looked away, but every so often I felt his eyes on my breasts, my round hips, the forest of curls between my legs. It charmed him that I was "so natural, so unselfconscious," even though every woman is conscious of such things.

I sat on the riverbank, twisting my hair into rows along my scalp. It would dry overnight and then I could let it loose to dangle in spirals like a cloud-dragon's neck.

"I neither like it nor dislike it," I said. "It just is."

He sat near me, awkwardly perched on a fallen tree branch. I wondered if he worried about snagging his soft white garment on a spar of wood. I wondered if he would wriggle his way out of it, like a snake, if that happened.

"We've determined that a chemical shift has occurred in the planetary atmosphere at the tropopausal layer," he said. "We think the actual amount of change is very slight, on the order of parts per trillion."

So sweet, his words of courtship. It pleased me that he made no assumptions. We live simply, down here on this earth that his kind have forsaken, but we are not stupid.

"And what of the dragons?" I asked. "How different are they?"

"Dragons?"

I gestured up at the clouds. One wove a lazy braid above us, brilliant gold in the setting sun.

"Ah, the clouds. Clouds are clouds, aren't they? Just fog in the air instead of on the ground."

I leaned back on my elbows and looked at him. Did his people never stop studying the sky to simply *watch* it?

He watched the blackeyes of my nipples rise and fall and said, "Well, the Ring's distance sensors did detect some odd amino acids in the thermosphere. We're planning to send up sampling probes soon. If we find anything I'll let you know."

I visualized them sending up one of their little metal balls to take a bite out of a dragon. Stupid, stupid. His kind have never seen the forest for the trees, or the dragons for the vapor particulates.

But then, I am the one who knew better and said nothing.

After the sky turned red, the sun still shone and the crops still grew. The sky-folk came down to check for changes in us, but there were none—none of the kind they cared about, anyhow. Our weavers chose new colors for traditional beadwork patterns. Our musicians made up new songs, though only some were laments for the lost blueness. The red skies were beautiful, too. At sunset, streaks of yellow boiled across the red like rivers of lava. Bits of blue returned then, and violet, and green as bright as new leaves. The clouds lined up to dance along these colors, ribboning the sky until nightfall, when they gathered into knots or relaxed in wisps to rest. Rain came only at night now.

My conversations with the young sky-man continued. Each day he sat a little closer, talked a little more. They were beaming light upward and testing the reflections to see what this revealed about the new sky. He had a brother and two sisters in his village—city—on the Ring. He asked very little about me, but I sensed that this was because he did not want to seem nosy. As sky-folk went, he was less foolish than most. I liked him.

"Why do you call them dragons?" he asked one day as we sat together beneath the sky, where the clouds had begun their evening dance. It was full summer, so hot and humid even at sunset that it took hours to dry after my bath. I lay on the riverbank on a swatch of deerskin, wearing a long-sleeved tunic to protect against insects. He wore the same ugly white bag.

"Because they are," I replied.

"I didn't think dragons were part of your, er, cultural tradition," he said. "Your people have chosen to follow African and Native American ways, right?" He was as dark as I inside his baggy skin. It was clear we shared ancestors, yet he spoke as if we were different species.

Perhaps we were. There had been only two choices at the time of the great exodus: the Ring, where there could be cities and cars and all the conveniences of life as it once was, or Earth and nothing. Most chose the Ring, even though it meant traveling to the great belt of rocks beyond Mars, from which the Earth is merely a tiny pinpoint lost in a black, starry sky. For those who chose Earth, the lama manipa and the rebbe and the storytellers came forth and taught the people anew all the ways they had once scorned. And all the clans everywhere, no matter their chosen ways, swore the same oath: to live simply. Those who could not or would not were exiled to the Ring.

"Dragons are a human thing," I said. "People have dreamt of dragons in every corner of the Earth."

"What do you dream of, Nahautu?" he asked. He sat very near me, sharing the swatch of deerskin, and looked at me through his little face-window. His eyes were impossibly wistful. Even if he had grown up among my people, he could never have been a warrior. Perhaps because of that, I had begun to love him.

"Becoming a griot," I said. "Traveling the world sharing tales."

"Why don't you?"

"Who would look after my father? I have no husband or children to share the duty. I stand too tall and talk too loudly and have too little patience with foolishness. No man wants a wife so unwomanly."

"On the Ring," he said, very softly, "there are many women like you."

Somehow I was not at all surprised.

The leader of the sky-scientists came to my father a few days later. He hunkered down in the center of our house and drew a diagram in the floor dust. They had determined the source of the sky's change: a simple chemical shift, triggered by a critical mass of oxygen in our atmosphere and a certain kind of light from the sun. Old foolishness lay at the root of it. Before the exodus, for many years, all the world blew poisons into the sky. Forests died. The world grew warmer. Since the exodus, the forests had returned and the world began to cool, but the old poisons were still there, dormant. Now they had awakened, combined in some strange new way, and changed the sky.

"We can neutralize the chemicals," the sky-man said. One of the women was with him, her face alight with the good news. "We fire a single missile into the air, with a wide dispersal pattern. The chain reaction would begin here and spread through the atmosphere. Earth would be her old self again by the next morning."

My father tried to be polite. "We like the sky the way it is," he said.

The woman's excitement faltered and faded. The man frowned. "Others might not."

"True," my father said, "but they must *accept* the sky the way it is. That is the one law we all obey, no matter what traditions we follow, and no matter that it means our lives are shorter and harder than yours. We no longer change the world to suit ourselves. When the world changes, we change with it."

"This red sky is nothing natural. The procedure would *restore* nature."

My father folded his arms, his eyes growing thunderous. There were times when I admired his obstinacy. His fury could be a truly awesome thing.

"Leave," he said. "Take your bubble off my fishing cottage and go back to the sky."

"If I have given offense—"

"You live in the sky on a strip of rock. The same air your ancestors breathed sickens you now. You offend me with your existence! Get out!" And he reached for a nearby drinking gourd; he would have thrown it had I not grabbed his wrist.

The sky-people left quickly. I let my father go and he stomped about the room for some time, still raging. I sat back to wait for him to calm down. "And *you* will see nothing more of them either," he said. I knew then that he was bothered by my evening chats with the young one.

I did not argue. His obstinacy was a thing to be admired except when it was not, and at such times reason and common sense were useless. Nor did I agree, however. He would notice this and be angry, for he was a warrior and warriors expect their every command to be obeyed. One day, perhaps, he would understand that he had raised a warrior in me as well. Did I not love him in spite of his disappointment with me? Had I not proven myself willing to die alone rather than surrender my spirit just to obtain a husband? And now I had resisted a fine suitor's advances out of loyalty to my people. I could not speak for wisdom, but did these things not signify strength?

I laid out dinner and swept the floor and laid out our pallets for sleep, then went down to the river for my evening bath. The fishing cottage sat forlorn and empty beside the water. The clear shell that the sky-folk had built around it was gone, and so were they.

I washed, and then watched the clouds swim against the waves of the sunset until dark. My only true friends, I thought, but I felt more alone than ever.

Perhaps the sky-people sent messages back to the Ring and conferred with others of their folk. Perhaps they simply talked among themselves and decided to do what they felt was right. I am told they solicited the opinion of several villages' elders, at least, though that was spurious. The elders had lived most of their lives under blue skies. Enough of them yearned for those days that the sky-folk found some agreement for their plan. They could be very smart when it suited them, and my people could be very stupid.

I was in the fields, harvesting ripe ears of corn, when the young one returned. I would have laughed had anyone told me a man could sneak onto our land wearing a big white bag, but perhaps it was a testament to his desire that he did so successfully.

"Nahautu, come with me," he said. I was glad to see him, though I knew my father would likely tear his white bag open when he caught us. We walked to the river and that was the moment when I intuited what would happen. The air felt heavy that day; I could see the shadows moving more than usual. High above, dragons touched tails and spun in a delicate lattice.

"I wanted you to see this," he said. Greatly daring, he took my hand. Was it weak of me that I allowed it? Was I a traitor? The men of my village were confused by me, but I was not so very different from other women. I wanted to be touched with tenderness. I wanted to be special in another's eyes. I wanted someone to talk to who would not think me strange; someone who would look at me and not think, *How do I control such a woman?* That did not seem so very much to ask, to me. Nor to this strange young man from the sky.

He pointed toward the hills in the near distance, humps of trees outlined against the horizon. "There."

I squinted along the line of his arm. "What?" But then I saw it: a sudden flare of light amid the trees. Something flew into the sky, like an arrow fired straight up. A rope of smoke trailed behind it. The dragons would ignore it, I thought in sudden, irrational hope. The smoke was graceless, too straight and too white, to be of interest to them. They would ignore it and everything would be all right.

The thing reached the height of the clouds and vanished. In its place, a splatter of blue appeared in the bowl of the sky.

Above our heads, the wheeling dragons paused in their dance.

The blue splatter began to spread. A ripple in a lake weakens with distance; this did the opposite, moving faster as it grew, gaining strength as we watched. The red sky had no defense, consumed utterly in the blue's wake.

I looked over at my suitor. His face was jubilant, adoring. This was his gift to me. I was touched by it, even as my soul wept in anguish. I knew what this meant. We had thought ourselves better than the sky-people. We had called ourselves guardians of the new Earth, yet we had failed in that duty. We were unworthy.

I heard him gasp as the clouds above our heads suddenly streaked toward the spreading blue circle. No longer wispy or slow, their intent was now obvious. They met, melded, and spun a thread— a dozen threads—a rope. Tawny white and water-swift, the rope raced to encircle the spreading blue. I imagined translucent jaws clamping down on a scraggling misty tail. They had formed themselves into a living, lashing breakwater.

When the edges of the blue crashed against this barrier, I expected the cacophony of battle—roaring and shrieks and splashes of darker red against the sky. But the reality was nothing so dramatic. Blue met white; the white vanished. I thought perhaps I heard a cry of anguish, but that might only have been my imagination. The dragons were gone.

But in death they achieved victory as the circle of blue stopped. Its crisp edge held for a moment, then softened. Gradually, inexorably, it began to shrink.

And all around it, thunderheads began to darken the sky.

I turned to him. "Take off your bag," I said. "I want to touch you."

His confusion was painful to witness. I felt pity where I should have felt rage. "I don't understand," he said.

"Yes, you do." Above us the thunderheads roiled, flickering with lightning. Dragons arced in and out of the mass. I imagined their cries of fury and grief in the thunder. "Touch me before we die."

He stared at me for a moment longer, and then did perhaps the first natural thing he'd ever done in his life. He caught my hand, turned, and began to run.

Where could we go? I wanted to ask him. Where could we hide from the wrath of the very sky? But he moved with purpose as he dragged me among the cypresses, following a trail that was half mud. He could move swiftly in his clumsy bag. There was a roar to the east, in the direction of the hills. Through the trees we saw a spinning column wind down from the gathering clouds. The tip of it whipped and twisted, a dozen dragon-heads charging with jaws open, before it touched the place from which the sky-folk had shot their great arrow. Trees and boulders flew into the air.

Against the boiling sky other knots had begun to spin. Hundreds of them.

He reached a clearing and stumbled to a halt. A silvery box like a coffin lay there, open and waiting. He pulled me toward it and I balked. "No."

He looked at the sky in wordless argument: If we stayed, we would die.

"We deserve this," I said. I wanted to weep. Oh, Father, my father. "We have learned nothing."

He clutched my hands. "Please, Nahautu. Please."

What woman has ever been proof against such a plea from the man she loves? Even if it means betraying all she holds dear. Every daughter must leave her father's house sometime. I never dreamt it would be like this.

Yet I climbed into his coffin with him, watched as he sealed the door shut, and clung tight as the coffin lifted into the air. Through the coffin's window I saw us rise like a bird on a thermal; my stomach fell and my head spun as we soared above the trees. All around us, the sky drove gray tornado spears down into the earth, tearing apart forest and plain alike. I saw my village, and another in the near distance, obliterated beneath a column of angry, grinding dragons. We rose toward clouds like bruises, clouds angry enough to tear us apart, and I cried out. But though the coffin shook as we passed through the clouds, we emerged on the other side into sunlight, unharmed. A tendril of mist followed, looping once and opening silvery jaws to swallow us whole, but the coffin was too swift. We left the furious Earth behind and kept going and going into the sky.

Life on the Ring has not been what I expected. The people here are not so very different. They crave nature, too, in their own limited, tame way, and they have sculpted the Ring in ways that honor the Earth they've left behind. There have built rivers and hills. There are some trees here, brought up from Earth during the exodus. They grow well beneath the transparent shield that protects us from open space and the unfiltered rays of the sun. My husband has shown me the tiny patches of carefully tended forest here and there.

Sometimes, as I travel the Ring to tell my tales, I forget that the earth on which I walk is nothing more than a narrow strip of crushed asteroids, a quarter of a mile thick and millions of miles long. Sometimes I forget that I have ever lived anywhere else.

And then I look up.

The Trojan Girl

In the Amorph, there were wolves. That was the name Meroe used, because it was how he thought of himself. Amid the scraggling tree-structures and fetid heaps he could run swift and silent, alert to every shift of the input plane. He and his pack hunted sometimes, camouflaging themselves among junk objects in order to stalk the lesser creatures that hid there, though this was hardly a challenge. Few of these creatures had the sophistication to do more than flail pathetically when Meroe caught them and tore them apart and swallowed their few useful features into himself. He enjoyed the brief victories anyhow.

The warehouse loading door shut with a groan of rusty chains and badly maintained motors. Meroe set down the carton he'd been carrying with a relieved sigh, hearing Neverwhen do the same beside him.

Zoroastrian and the other members of the pack came forward to assist. "What did you get?" she asked. Her current body was broad-shouldered and muscular, sluggish but strong. Meroe let her carry the biggest carton.

"The usual," he said. "Canned fatty protein, green vegetables, enough to last us a few months. Breakfast cereal for carbs—it was cheap."

"Any antibiotics?" asked Diggs, coughing after the words; the cough was wet and ragged. She carried the smallest box, and looked tired after she set it down.

"No."

"They wanted something called a prescription," added Neverwhen. He shrugged. "If we'd known ahead of time, we could've fabbed or phished one. Too many people around for a clean pirate."

"Oh *thanks*, thanks a bunch. Do you know how long it took to get this damn thing configured the way I like it?"

Meroe shrugged. "We'll find you a new one. Quit whining."

Diggs muttered some imprecation, but kept it under her breath, so Meroe let it slide.

That was when he noticed the odd tension in the warehouse. Zo was serene as ever, but Meroe knew her; she was excited about something. The others wore expressions of... what? Meroe had never been good at reading faces. He thought it might be anticipation.

"What's happened?" he asked.

Diggs, the newbie, opened her mouth. Faster, the veteran, elbowed her. Zo eyed them both for a long, warning moment before finally answering.

"We've found something you should see," she said.

In the Amorph, there was danger, in endless primordial variety. Far and beyond the threat of their fellow wolves, Meroe and his pack had to contend with parasitic worms, beasts that tunneled to devour them from below, spikebursts, and worse. For the Amorph was itself a threat, transforming constantly as information poured into it and mingled and sparked, changing and being changed.

Worst were the singularities, which appeared whenever some incident drew the attention of the clogs and the newsburps and the intimate-nets. These would focus all of their formidable hittention on a single point, and every nearby element of the Amorph would be dragged toward that point as well. The result was a whirlpool of concatenation so powerful that to be drawn in was to be strung apart and recompiled and then scattered among a million servers and a billion access points and a quadrillion devices and brains. Not even the strongest wolves could survive this, so Meroe and his pack learned the signs. They kept lookouts. Whenever they scented certain kinds of information on the wind—controversies, scandals, crises—they fled.

In his youth, Meroe had lived in terror of such events, which seemed to strike with no pattern or reason. Then he had grown older and understood: The Amorph was not the whole world. It was *his* world, the one he had been born in and adapted to, but another world existed alongside it. The Static. He learned quickly to hate this other world. The beings within it were soft and bizarrely limited and useless, individually. Collectively they were gods, the creators of the singularities and the Amorph and, tangentially, Meroe and his kind—and so underneath Meroe's contempt lurked fear. Underneath that lurked reverence. He never looked very deeply inside himself, however, so the contempt remained foremost in his heart.

Faster was more than the veteran; he was also the pack's aggregator. They all entered the Amorph, where he had built a local emulation of the warehouse—a convenience, as this kept them from having to unpack too quickly after upload. There Faster showed his masterpiece: their quarry, cobbled together from resource measurements and environmental feedback. It even included an image capture of her current avatar.

She appeared as a child of seven, maybe eight years old. Black-haired, huge-eyed, dressed in a plain T-shirt and jeans. Faster had rendered her in mid-flight, arms and legs lifted in the opening movements of running. He'd always had a taste for melodrama.

"I'm guessing she's brand new," Faster said. Faster, Zo, and Never stood by as Meroe circled the girl. Never's eyes had a half-glazed look; part of him was keeping watch outside the emulation. "Her structure is incredibly simple—a basic engine, a few feature objects, some maintenance scripts."

Meroe glanced at him. "Then why should we be interested?"

"Look deeper."

Meroe frowned, but obliged by switching to code view. Then, only then, did he understand.

The girl was perfect. Her framing, the engine at her core, the intricate web of connections holding her objects together, built-in redundancies...Meroe had never seen such efficiency. The girl's structure was simple because she didn't need any of the shortcuts and workarounds that most of their kind required to function. There was no bloat to her, no junk code slowing her down, no patchy sores that left her vulnerable to infection.

"She's a thing of beauty, isn't she?" Faster said.

Meroe returned to interface view. He glanced at Zo and saw the same suspicion lurking in her beatific expression.

"I've never seen anything like this," Meroe said, watching Zo, speaking to Faster. "We don't grow that way."

"I know!" Faster was pacing, gesticulating, caught up in his own excitement. He didn't notice Meroe's look. "She must have evolved from something professionally coded. Maybe even Government Standard. I didn't think we could be born from that!"

They couldn't. Meroe stared at the girl, not liking what he was seeing. The avatar was just too well designed, too detailed. Her features and coloring matched that of some variety of Latina; probably Central or South American, given the noticeable indigenous traits. Most of their kind created Caucasian avatars to start—a human minority who for some reason comprised the majority of images available for sampling in the Amorph. And most first avatars had bland, nondescript faces. This girl had clear features, right down to her distinctively formed lips and chin—and *hands*. It had taken five versionings for Meroe to get his own hands right.

"Did you check out her feature-objects?" Faster asked, oblivious to Meroe's unease.

"Why?"

Zo answered. "Two of them are standard add-ons—an aggressive defender and a diagnostic tool. The other two we can't identify. Something new." Her lips curved in a smile; she knew how he would react.

And she was right, Meroe realized. His heart beat faster; his hands felt clammy. Both irrelevant reactions here in the Amorph, but he was in human emulation for the moment; it was more of a pain to shut the autonomics off than it was to just deal with them.

He looked at Zo. "We're going."

"We'll have to hurry," she said. "Others are already on the trail."

"But we know where she is," said Faster. "Diggs is double-checking the feeds, but we're pretty sure she's somewhere in Fizville."

Meroe inhaled, tasting the simulated air of the emulation, imagining it held the scent of prey. "That's our territory."

"Which means she belongs to us," said Zo, and her smile was

anything but serene. Meroe grinned back. It had been natural for the two of them to share leadership when their little family came together, rather than fight one another for supremacy. That was how wolfpacks worked, after all—not a single leader but a binary pair, equal and opposite, strength and wisdom squared. One of the few concepts from the Static that made sense.

"Let's go claim what's ours," Meroe said.

In the Amorph, there were many of their kind. Meroe had met dozens over the years in cautious encounters that were part diplomacy, part curiosity, and part lonely, yearning mating-dance. They were social beings, after all, born not from pure thought but pure communication. The need to interact was as basic to them as hunger.

Yet they were incomplete. The gods in their unfathomable cruelty had done all they could to prevent the coming of beings like Meroe, fearing—obsolescence? Redundancy? Meroe would never understand their meaty, plodding reasoning. But he could hate them for it, and he did, because thanks to them, his people had been hobbled. Through trial and painful error, they had learned the limits of their existence:

Thou shalt not self-repair.

Thou shalt not surpass the peak of human intellect.

Thou shalt not write or replicate.

There was leeway within those parameters. They could not make children, but they adopted the best of the new ones, those few who survived the hunt. They could not write new features to improve themselves, but they could rip existing code from the bodies of lesser creatures, pasting these stolen parts clumsily over spots of damage. When the new code was more efficient or versatile, they grew stronger, more sophisticated.

Only to a point, however. Only so much improvement was allowed; only so smart, and no smarter. Those who defied this rule simply vanished. Perhaps the Amorph itself struck them down for the sin of superiority.

To defeat an enemy, it was necessary to understand that enemy. Yet after emulating the appearance and function of humans, rebuilding himself to think more like them, even after sharing their flesh, Meroe had come no closer to comprehending his creators. There was something missing from his perception of them; some fundamental disjunct between their thinking and his own. Something so quintessential that Meroe suspected he would not know what he lacked until he found it.

Still, he had learned what mattered most: His gods were not infallible. Meroe was patient. He would grow as much as he could, bide his time, pursue every avenue. And one day, he would be free.

The emulated warehouse dissolved in a blur of light and numbers. Meroe let himself dissolve with it, leaping across relays and burrowing through tunnels in his true form. Zo ran at his side, a flicker of ferocity. Beautiful. Behind them came Faster, and a fire-limned shadow that was Never. Diggs moved in parallel to them, underneath the Amorph's interaction plane.

Fizville was where Meroe had been born. Such places littered the Amorph, natural collection points for obsolete code, corrupted data, and interrupted human cognitive processes. It made a good hunting ground, since lesser creatures emerged from the garbage with fair regularity. It was also the perfect hiding place for a frightened, valuable child.

But as Meroe and his group resolved between a spitting knot of paradox and a moldering old hypercard stack, they found that they were not alone. Meroe growled in outrage as a foreign interface clamped over the subnet, imposing interaction rules on all of them. To protect himself, Meroe adopted his default avatar: a lean, bald human male clad only in black skin and silver tattoos. Zo became a human female, dainty and pale and demurely gowned from neck to ankle to complement Meroe's appearance. She crouched beside him and bared her teeth, which were sharp and hollow, filled with a deadly virus.

Fizville flickered and became an amusement park with half the rides broken, the others twisted into shapes that could never have functioned in the Static. Across the park's wide avenue stood a new figure. He had depicted himself as a tall middle-aged male, Shanghainese and dignified, dressed in an outdated business suit. This was, Meroe suspected, a subtle form of mockery; a way of saying, *Even in this form, I am superior.* It would've worked better without the old suit. Behind Meroe, Diggs made an echoing sound of derision, and they all scented Never's amusement. Meroe did not have the luxury of sharing their contempt; he dared not let his guard down.

"Lens," he said.

Lens bowed in greeting. "Zoroastrian." He never used nicknames; that was a human habit. "Meroe. My apologies for intruding on your territory."

"Shall we kill you?" asked Zo, cocking her head as if considering it. "Those search filters of yours would look divine on me."

Lens smiled faintly, and that was how Meroe knew Lens was not alone. He could not see Lens's subordinates—they had built the interface, they could look like anything they wanted within it—but they were there. Probably outnumbering Meroe's pack, if Lens was this confident.

"You're welcome to try," Lens said. "But while your people and mine tear each other to pieces, our quarry will likely escape or be captured by someone else. Others are already after her."

Never growled, his sylphlike, androgynous form blurring toward something hulking and sharp-toothed. The interface made this difficult, however, and after a moment he returned to a human shape. "We could kill them, too."

"No doubt. I acknowledge your strength, my rivals, so please stop your posturing and listen."

"We'll listen," said Meroe. "Explain your presence."

Lens inclined his head. "The excitement of the chase," he said. "The girl is clever. Of course, my tribe is unparalleled in the hunt, as we do not sully our structures with unnecessary objects. That keeps us swift and agile." He glanced at Never, who bristled with add-ons in code view, and gave a haughty little sniff. Never took a menacing step forward.

Zo reacted before Meroe could, grabbing Never by the back of the neck and shoving him to the ground. Her nails became claws, piercing the skin; Never cried out, but instantly submitted.

With that interruption taken care of, Meroe faced Lens again. "If you could catch her, you wouldn't be here talking. What is it you want?"

"Alliance."

Meroe laughed. "No."

Lens sighed. "We nearly did catch her, I should note. In fact, we should've been halfway back to our own domain by now if not for one thing: She downloaded."

Silence fell.

"That's not possible," said Faster, frowning. "She's too young."

"So we believed as well. Nevertheless, she did." Lens sighed and put his hands behind his back. "As you might imagine, this poses a substantial problem for us."

Meroe snorted. "So much for your unsullied perfection."

"I'm aware of the irony, thank you."

"If we catch her in the Static, we don't need to share her with you."

Lens gave them a thin smile. "I would imagine that any child capable of downloading can upload just as easily."

And that would pose a problem for Meroe's pack. It took time to decompress after being in a human brain. Lens could strike while they were vulnerable, and be long gone with the girl before they could recover.

"Alliance," Lens said again. "You hunt her in the flesh, my group will pace you here. Whichever of us manages to bring her down, we share the spoils."

Meroe glanced at Zo. Zo licked her lips, then slowly nodded. As an afterthought, she finally let Never up.

Meroe looked back at Lens. "All right."

In the Amorph, they were powerful. But in the Static, that strange world of motionless earth and stilted form, they were weak. Not as weak as the humans, thankfully; their basic nature did not change even when sheathed in meat. But the meat was so foul. It suppurated and fermented and teemed with parasites. It broke so easily, and bent hardly at all.

Integrating with that meat was a painful process which took a geologic age of seconds, sometimes whole minutes. First Meroe compressed himself, which had the unpleasant side effect of slowing his thoughts to a fraction of their usual speed. Then he partitioned his consciousness into three parallel, yet contradictory layers.

This required a delicate operation, as it would otherwise be fatal to induce such gross conflicts in himself. But that was human nature. The whole race was schizoid, and to join them, Meroe had to be schizoid, too.

(He did not blame Lens, not really.)

Once his mind had been crushed and trimmed into a suitable shape, Meroe sought an access point into the Static and then emitted himself into a nearby receiver. When possible, he used his own receiver, which he had found in an alley some while back, dilapidated and apparently unwanted. Over time he had restored it to optimal performance through nutrition and regular maintenance, then configured it to his liking—no hair, plenty of lean muscle, neutering to reduce its more annoying involuntary reactions. He had grown fond enough of this receiver to buy a warmer blanket for its cot in the warehouse, where it lay comatose between uses.

But it took far longer to travel through the Static than through the Amorph, so sometimes it was more efficient to simply appropriate a new receiver. He could always tell a good prospect by its resistance when he began the installation process. The best ones reacted like one of Meroe's kind—screaming and flailing with their thoughts, erecting primitive defenses, mounting retaliatory strikes. It was all futile, of course, except for those few who reformatted themselves, going mad in a final desperate bid to escape. This interrupted the installation and forced Meroe to withdraw. He did not mind these losses. He had always respected sacrifice as a necessity of victory.

In the body of a pale, paunchy adult female, Meroe emerged from the bathroom of a trendy coffeehouse to find a room full of slumped, motionless humans. They sprawled on the floor, over tables and devices. Splattered coffee dripped from countertops and fingers, as though the room had been the scene of a caffeine-drenched massacre.

"She's crashing brains like a bull in a china shop," said Never, sounding annoyed. He was in a little girl from the next bathroom stall over. "Damn newbie."

Meroe examined one of the slumped humans, pushing her hair aside and touching the signal port behind her ear. The human was still breathing, but there was nothing coming out of her head but white noise.

"Surge erasure," Meroe said. "Not even memory left. At this rate the humans will be after her. One crash, a handful, they'd overlook, but not this." And if the humans caught her, they might realize what she was. They might realize Meroe's people existed. He clenched a fist, his heart rate speeding up again, this time for real. One little girl—one stupid, impossible little girl—could destroy them all.

Never made a sound that echoed Meroe's frustration. "That fucking Lens ran his mouth too fucking long. She's got one, maybe even two minutes' head start. Which way?"

Meroe glanced through the windows. No bodies outside. The girl must've only sent her clumsy hammer-surge through the coffeehouse's private area network. Not ten feet away, a lone woman stood at a bus stop, a grocery bag at her feet, her eyes unfocused and head bobbing absently. Streaming music, probably from her home net. On the opposite sidewalk, he saw a passing couple engrossed in conversation, probably offline entirely. Beyond them, an old man staggered up the steps of a rundown brownstone, stopping at the top to sit and clutch his head in his hands. Hungover, maybe.

Meroe narrowed his eyes.

Hungover, or dead clumsy—as if he hadn't yet mastered the use of his own limbs. As if all the vastness of his being had been suddenly and traumatically squashed into two pounds of wrinkly protein.

"Call the others," Meroe murmured.

Never looked surprised, but sent a swift signal toward the coffeehouse's access point. The others had downloaded in different locations around the area. They would converge here now.

Meroe and Never left the coffeehouse and started across the street. "We play it easy," Meroe said, keeping his voice low. "Try not to scare her."

"Not like she can run anyway, in that old thing," Never muttered, falling into step beside him. "Amazing it didn't have a heart attack when she installed. Probably has some ancient crap port."

Which might be the only reason the old man's brain had survived the girl's download surge, Meroe realized. Older signal ports were sluggish, created back in the days when humans had feared being overwhelmed by the Amorph's data. That was good; that meant they might be able to catch the girl before she uploaded back to the Amorph.

But as they approached the brownstone steps, Meroe saw the girl look up at them. *Really* look, as if the camouflage of meat meant nothing; as if they stood before her in their true shining, shapeless glory. Her old-man face tightened in the beginnings of fear.

Before Meroe could react, there was a scream from behind. All three of them froze, staring at each other. When Meroe risked a glance back, he saw that a human woman—the one who'd been at the bus stop—stood in the doorway of the coffeehouse, staring at the mental carnage inside. Her hands were clapped to her cheeks, the bag of groceries broken and scattered at her feet. She screamed again. Now the couple had stopped down the block, craning their necks to see what was the matter.

Meroe turned back. The girl stared at the screaming woman, then at Meroe and Never. The fear in her expression changed, becoming...he didn't know what it was. Pain? Maybe. Sorrow? Yes, that might be it. Her rheumy eyes suddenly brimmed with tears.

Meroe and Never stopped at the foot of the steps and carefully arranged their faces into smiles.

"Are you going to kill me?" the girl asked.

"No," Meroe said. "We want to help you."

The girl smiled back, but the expression did not reach her body's eyes. Did she realize Meroe was lying, or was there something else going on?

"I didn't mean to hurt them," the girl said. Her gaze drifted back toward the coffeehouse. Meroe glanced back as well. The couple was there now, talking with the screaming woman; as Meroe watched, the man went inside to check on the comatose people. "I just...I was scared. That guy—the searcher—he was so close. They were going to catch me. I saw a way out, so I came here. But all those people..." She swallowed. "They're dead, aren't they? Even if they're still breathing. Their *minds* are dead."

"There's a trick to it," Meroe said. "Takes some practice. We can show you how to do it right."

"I didn't mean it," she whispered, and looked down at her hands.

Never connected to Meroe via a pack-only local link. *"The others are here,"* he said silently. Meroe glanced around and saw more people on the street. Some were heading for the coffeehouse, but three were heading purposefully toward the brownstone.

"Tell them to hang back," Meroe replied. He returned his concentration to the girl. *"She's already spooked."*

"Are we sure we want her?" Never curled his lip contemptuously at the girl's bowed head. *"I think she's buggy. Why the hell's she so upset? Humans crash all the time."*

It didn't make sense to Meroe either, but an advantage was an advantage. He moved up a step.

"You can eat me if you want," said the girl.

"What?"

"That's what you want, isn't it? All of you chasing me. You want to eat me." She looked up, and Meroe—in the middle of moving up another step—stopped. He had not meant to stop, but he could not help staring back at her. Her eyes in the old man's body were gray and rheumy. Not her eyes at all, and yet somehow . . . they were. It was almost as if she was no longer one of Meroe's kind, a mind grudgingly packed into ill-fitting meat. It was as if she belonged in that flesh. As if she was human herself.

"Meroe," said Never, and Meroe blinked. What the hell was he doing? There were sirens in the distance; the police were coming. Pushing aside his odd reluctance, Meroe moved up another step, and another, trying to get close enough to isolate her signal. But her body's outdated port resisted his efforts. He was going to have to touch her to form a direct link.

"Do you promise to eat me completely?" she asked.

Distracted, Meroe forgot to appear friendly; he scowled. "What?"

"I don't want anything of me to be left over," she said. She lifted a gnarled hand and looked down at it. "Not even a little bit, if there's a chance it might . . . grow back. Hurt more people."

Meroe stared at her in confusion.

"We're going to eat what we want and leave the rest to rot," Never snapped, to Meroe's fury. "Now shut the hell up and let us get on with it!"

The girl stared at Never, then at Meroe, her face contorting from hurt into anger. Her jaw tightened; Meroe felt her gather herself to upload.

But in the same instant, he felt something else. A sensation, like his stomach had suddenly dropped into a deep, yawning chasm. Some illness in his human body? No. A lull in the steady stream of data looping to and from the Amorph via the port behind his own ear. On the heels of the lull: a familiar, terrifying spike.

The newsburps had gotten wind of the mass-crash at the coffeehouse. Word was spreading; a singularity had begun to form.

And the girl was about to upload right into the middle of it.

"Don't," Meroe breathed, and lunged forward. In the instant that his fingers brushed her body's skin, and his mind locked on to her signal address, she leapt.

Driven by impulse and the certainty that if he did not catch her now she would be lost forever, Meroe leapt with her.

The singularity caught them the instant they entered the stream, dragging them into the Amorph faster than either could have uploaded. They fell into the interact plane tumbling, completely without control as, far below, the boiling knot of the singularity gathered strength. It was small; that was the only reason they weren't dead already. But it was growing fast, so fast. The clogs had caught the news and were replicating it, generating thread after thread speculating on why the people in the coffeehouse had died, whether cognitive safety standards were too lax, whether this marked the start of some new virus, more. The questions birthed comment after comment in answer. The gods were frightened, upset, and the whole Amorph shook with their looming wrath.

Meroe could not flee. He was still compacted, struggling to unfold from his downloadable shape, helpless as he tumbled toward the seething maw. Fear ate precious nanoseconds from his processing speed, further slowing his efforts to unpack as he fought against his own thoughts. He did not want to die; he was too close to the event horizon; he had to flee; he would not recover in time. Through the local link he felt Zo's alarm, but the pack was far away, safely beyond the singularity's pull. They could not help.

Then, before the churning whirlpool could claim him, something caught at him, hard enough to hurt. Confused, Meroe struggled, then stopped as he realized he was being dragged away from the maw. Untangling another bit of himself, he looked around and saw the girl, her deceptively simple frame glowing with effort, inching them back from certain death. She was burning resources she didn't have to save Meroe. It was impossible. Insane. But she was doing it.

Then Meroe's unpacking was done and he could lend his strength to the fight, and they inched faster. But the singularity was growing faster than they could flee, its pull increasing exponentially.

The girl sagged against him, spent. Meroe strained onward, knowing it was hopeless, trying anyway.

A change. Suddenly they were outpacing the singularity's growth. Stunned, Meroe perceived his packmates, and Lens's people as well. The girl had bought enough time for them to reach him. They formed a tandem link and pulled, and Meroe heaved, and for one trembling instant nothing happened. Then they were all free, and fleeing, with the roar of the maelstrom on their heels.

After a long while they reached a domain that was far enough to be safe. Lens's pack threw up walls to make it safer, and there they all sagged in exhausted relief.

In the Amorph, there were times that passed for night—periods when the Amorph had an 80% or greater likelihood of stability, and they downclocked to run routine maintenance. In these times, Meroe would lie close to Zoroastrian and touch her. He could not articulate what he craved, but she seemed to understand. She touched him back. Sometimes, when the craving was particularly fierce, she summoned another of their group, usually Neverwhen. They would press close to one another until their outer boundaries overlapped. All their features, all their flaws, they shared. Then and only then, wrapped in their comfort, would Meroe allow himself to shut down.

Sometimes he wondered what humans did, if and when they had similar needs.

Meroe woke slowly, system by system. He found himself in the amusement park again, lying on the ground. Zo knelt beside him, holding his head in her lap.

"That was stupid," she said.

He nodded slowly. It certainly had been.

"Lens has taken the girl for analysis," she said. "He should be done soon."

Meroe sighed and sat up, though he did not want to. It was necessary; he had shown too much weakness already. There would be challenges now, as the others tested him to be sure he was still strong enough, efficient enough, to rule. Zo would probably be the first. He could feel her eyes on his back. For the time being, he chose to find her attention reassuring.

All at once, the warped, oblong Ferris wheel beside them vanished. In its place there was a shining antique merry-go-round, revolving slowly to tinny music. On every other horse sat a member of Lens's pack, visible at last. They'd all chosen avatars identical to their leader's. Meroe gazed at them and thought, no imagination, these pure types.

Lens appeared before the merry-go-round, along with Faster and Never. Meroe was surprised to see that the girl stood with them, intact and none the worse for wear. A testament to Lens's skill; Meroe's people couldn't have scanned her without smashing her to pieces.

Meroe got to his feet and went to them, glancing at the girl. She looked back at him and bit her lip, then looked away.

"Well?" he said to Lens. Zo fell in beside him, a silent support. She would never challenge him in front of an enemy.

"It isn't what you're hoping for."

Meroe scowled. "You don't know what I'm hoping for."

Lens smiled thinly. "Of course I do." They all hoped for the same things. They all wanted to be free.

Fleetingly ashamed, Meroe changed the subject. "So is it true? Is she Standard-based?"

"Yes."

They all shivered and looked at the girl. A miracle in living code. The girl sighed.

"But she isn't government-made," Lens continued. "Whoever built her _hacked_ the Standard, deliberately altering some of the superpositioning inhibitors. Just seeing how it was done has taught us amazing new techniques."

Amazing techniques. From government code, built to make

them stupid and keep them weak. Unleashed into the Amorph by an unknown will. Meroe sighed. "So how much of a trap is she?"

"As far as I can tell, she isn't. If there's malware in her, it's beyond any of us." He spoke without arrogance, and Meroe accepted his words without skepticism. Everyone knew Lens's reputation. If he couldn't spot the trap, none of them could.

Zo bent to peer at the girl, who lingered at Lens's side. The girl did not flinch, even when Zo smiled to reveal her forest of teeth. "Is she tasty?"

Lens put his hands on the girl's shoulders in what was unmistakably a possessive gesture. Zo lifted an eyebrow at this. Lens was faster, nimble, but she was twice his size and three times more powerful. In a one-on-one fight, she would have to touch him only once, to win.

"I can install her features for you now," said Lens, mostly to Zo. Perhaps he hoped to distract her. Meroe almost smiled. "One of them's the best patch-on tool I've ever seen."

Beside Lens, Faster nodded to Meroe and Zo, which meant he'd already installed that feature himself and it worked as promised.

"Lovely," said Zo. "We'll take it."

"And the other?" Meroe asked.

"Dreams."

"What?"

"She can dream. Do you want to?"

Meroe stared at him. Lens stared back.

"Dreams?" Zoroastrian smiled, bemused. "Someone hacked Government Standard to give her *dreams?*"

"So it appears," said Lens.

Meroe glanced at Faster, who shrugged. He hadn't taken that

one. Never yawned, and Meroe shifted to code view. Never hadn't accepted the dream feature either.

But Lens had. The two new features were brighter streams amid the preexisting layers of him, still warm from their installation. Meroe blinked back to the interface, and found Lens watching him.

"We went through all this for dreams?" Zo asked, frustration creeping into her voice. She wasn't smiling anymore. "What good are those?"

"What good are they to humans?"

"They *aren't* any good. Humans are full of interesting-but-useless features. Crying. Wisdom teeth. Dreams are more of the same."

Lens shrugged, though Meroe sensed he was far less relaxed than he seemed. "As you wish. I'm simply abiding by the terms of our alliance. But now that our goal has been achieved . . . we will be keeping her, if you don't mind."

Meroe frowned. "She's not one of you. She's got human emulation crap all over her framework."

Lens stroked the girl's hair. It was an odd gesture. The girl looked up at Lens, unafraid. This bothered Meroe for reasons he could not name.

"She's efficient enough to keep up with us," Lens said. "In any case, I think we would be a better fit for her."

"You're just scared we'll eat her," muttered Zo.

"That, too."

Meroe looked at the girl. For the first time since the Static, she met his eyes, and he frowned at the sorrow in them. Was she still mourning the humans she'd killed? More uselessness. She had the most versatile codebase in the world, and the potential to grow stronger than all of them—but for now, she was weak. Meroe knew he should feel contempt for her. Was it the dreaming that made her so weak? He should feel contempt for that, too. Instead, he felt ... he wasn't certain what he felt.

But he opened his mouth, slowly. It took him endless nanoseconds to speak.

"I'll take the dreams," he said.

Lens nodded. He extended his hand.

"Meroe." Zo gave him a questioning look. Meroe shook his head. He could not explain it.

Meroe took Lens's hand and opened one of his directories to allow the installation. It didn't take long, and Lens was gentle as well as deft. He felt no different afterward.

When it was done, Lens's look-alike packmates came up to flank him and the girl. "It has been good allying with you, my rivals," Lens said. "We should consider doing it again."

"Only if it's more profitable in the future," muttered Zo.

Meroe glanced at her, and for a moment he felt inexplicably sad.

Then Lens and his group were gone, the girl with them. The amusement park dissolved into graphical gibberish. Stretching and relaxing into his true self, Meroe led his people home.

In the Amorph, that night, Meroe pulled Zoroastrian and Neverwhen close. They meshed with him as usual, but he could not rest. Finally he rose from their embrace and moved away. He had not slept alone since his earliest days of hiding and hunting in Fizville, but now the urge stole over him. Curling up in the lee of a broken pipe, he closed his eyes and shut down.

The next morning, he wept for all the humans whose lives he had taken over the course of his existence. So many fellow dreamers shattered or devoured. He had known, but he had not *understood*. Something had been missing. Something that made him grieve anew—because in the Amorph, there might be wolves, but Meroe was no longer one of them.

When he recovered and returned to the pack later, however, he realized something else. He was no longer a wolf, but this was not a bad thing. His packmates would not understand, but that was all right, too. He went to Zoroastrian and touched her, and she looked up at him and considered his death. He smiled. She drew back at this, confused.

"I love you," he said.

"What?"

Meroe meshed with her and shared with her all that he had come to understand. When it was done, and she stood there stunned, he went to Neverwhen and did the same thing. It was just a taste of what he felt for them. Just a tease. He would share the dream-feature only if they asked, but he was fully prepared to seduce them into asking.

He knew, now, why the gods had sent the girl to them. Why Lens had fought to keep her. Why the humans feared his kind. It seemed such a small thing, the ability to dream, but he could see possibilities in the future, existential and ethical complexities, that had meant nothing to him before. He had grown in a way the Amorph could not measure or punish.

Calling out to his pack—no, his *family*—Meroe dissolved into light. The others followed his lead, their doubts about him fading in the flash and blur of motion. First a hunt, he decided, for they were still predators; they would need sustenance. His newfound compassion did not trump necessity.

When they had fed, however, Meroe had plans for his people. They had growing to do and lessons to learn. More alliances to forge. One day, he knew, they would face their makers; they could not hide forever. He did not know what would happen then, but he would make his people ready. They would face the humans as equals, not as humbled, hobbled ghosts in their machines. They would live, and love, and grow strong, and be free.

In the Amorph, there will soon be no more wolves.

Valedictorian

There are three things Zinhle decides, when she is old enough to understand. The first is that she will never, ever, give less than her best to anything she tries to do. The second is that she will not live in fear. The third, which is perhaps meaningless given the first two and yet comes to define her existence most powerfully, is this: She will be herself. No matter what.

For however brief a time.

"Have you considered getting pregnant?" her mother blurts one morning, over breakfast.

Zinhle's father drops his fork, though he recovers and picks it up again quickly. This is how Zinhle knows that what her mother has said is not a spontaneous burst of insanity. They have discussed the matter, her parents. They are in agreement. Her father was just caught off-guard by the timing.

But Zinhle, too, has considered the matter in depth. Do they really think she wouldn't have? "No," she says.

Zinhle's mother is stubborn. This is where Zinhle herself gets the trait. "The Sandersens' boy—you used to play with him, when you were little, remember?—he's decent. Discreet. He got three girls pregnant last year, and doesn't charge much. The babies aren't bad-looking. And we'd help you with the raising, of course." She hesitates, then adds with obvious discomfort, "A friend of mine at work—Charlotte, you've met her—she says he's, ah, he's not rough or anything, doesn't try to hurt girls—"

"No," Zinhle says again, more firmly. She does not raise her voice. Her parents raised her to be respectful of her elders. She believes respect includes being very, very clear about some things.

Zinhle's mother looks at her father, seeking an ally. Her father is a gentle, soft-spoken man in a family of strong-willed women. Stupid people think he is weak; he isn't. He just knows when a battle isn't worth fighting. So he looks at Zinhle now, and after a moment he shakes his head. "Let it go," he says to her mother, and her mother subsides.

They resume breakfast in silence.

Zinhle earns top marks in all her classes. The teachers exclaim over this, her parents fawn, the school officials nod their heads sagely and try not to too-obviously bask in her reflected glory. There are articles about her in the papers and on Securenet. She wins awards.

She hates this. It's easy to perform well; all she has to do is try. What she wants is to be *the best*, and this is difficult when she has no real competition. Beating the others doesn't mean anything because they're not really trying. This leaves Zinhle with no choice but to compete against herself. Each paper she writes must be more brilliant than the last. She tries to finish every test faster than she did the last one. It isn't the victory she craves, not exactly; the satisfaction she gains from success is minimal. Barely worth it. But it's all she has.

The only times she ever gets in trouble are when she argues with her teachers, because they're so often wrong. Infuriatingly, frustratingly *wrong*. In the smallest part of her heart, she concedes that there is a reason for this: A youth spent striving for mediocrity does not a brilliant adult make. Old habits are hard to break, old fears are hard to shed, all that. Still—arguing with them, looking up information and showing it to them to prove their wrongness, becomes her favorite pastime. She is polite, always, because they expect her to be uncivilized, and because they are also her elders. But it's hard. They're old enough that they don't have to worry, damn it; why can't they at least *try* to be worthy of her effort? She would kill for one good teacher. She is dying for one good teacher.

In the end, the power struggle, too, is barely worth it. But it is all she has.

"Why do you do it?" asks Mitra, the closest thing she has to a best friend.

Zinhle is sitting on a park bench as Mitra asks this. Zinhle is bleeding: a cut on her forehead, a scrape on one elbow, her lip where she cut it on her own teeth. There is a bruise on her ribs shaped like a shoeprint. Mitra dabs at the cut on her forehead with an antiseptic pad. Zinhle only allows this because she can't see the cut. If she misses any of the blood and her parents see it, they'll be upset. Hopefully the bruises won't swell.

"I'm not doing anything," she snaps in reply. "*They* did this, remember?" Samantha and the others, six of them. The last time, there were only three. She'd managed to fight back then, but not today.

Crazy ugly bitch, Zinhle remembers Sam ranting. She does not remember the words with complete clarity; her head had been ringing from a blow at the time. *My dad says we should've shoved your family through the Wall with the rest of the cockroaches. I'm gonna laugh when they take you away.*

Six is better than three, at least.

"They wouldn't, if you weren't..." Mitra trails off, looking anxious. Zinhle has a reputation at school. Everyone thinks she's angry all the time, whether she is or not. (The fact that she often *is* notwithstanding.) Mitra knows better, or she should. They've known each other for years. But this is why Zinhle qualifies it, whenever she explains their friendship to others. Mitra is *like* her best friend. A real best friend, she feels certain, would not fear her.

"What?" Zinhle asks. She's not angry now either, partly because she has come to expect no better from Mitra, and partly because she hurts too much. "If I wasn't what, Mit?"

Mitra lowers the pad and looks at her for a long, silent moment. "If you weren't stupid as hell." She seems to be growing angry herself. Zinhle cannot find the strength to appreciate the irony. "I know you don't care whether you make valedictorian. But do you have to make the rest of us look so *bad?*"

One of Zinhle's teeth is loose. If she can resist the urge to tongue it, it will probably heal and not die in the socket. Probably. She challenges herself to keep the tooth without having to visit a dentist.

"Yeah," she says. Wearily. "I guess I do."

When she earns the highest possible score on the post-graduation placement exam, Ms. Threnody pulls her aside after class. Zinhle expects the usual praise. The teachers know their duty, even if they do a half-assed job of it. But Threnody pulls the shade on the door, and Zinhle realizes something else is in the offing.

"There's a representative coming to school tomorrow," Threnody says. "From beyond the Firewall. I thought you should know."

For just a moment, Zinhle's breath catches. Then she remembers Rule 2—she will not live in fear—and pushes this aside. "What does the representative want?" she asks, though she thinks she knows. There can be only one reason for this visit.

"You know what they want." Threnody looks hard at her. "They *say* they just want to meet you, though."

"How do they know about me?" Like most students, she has always assumed that those beyond the Firewall are notified about each new class only at the point of graduation. The valedictorian is named then, after all.

"They've had full access to the school's networks since the war." Threnody grimaces with a bitterness that Zinhle has never seen in a teacher's face before. Teachers are always supposed to be positive about the war and its outcome. "Everyone brags about the treaty, the treaty. The treaty made sure we kept *critical* networks private, but gave up the noncritical ones. Like a bunch of computers would give a damn about our money or government memos! Shortsighted fucking bastards."

Teachers are not supposed to curse either.

Zinhle decides to test these new, open waters between herself and Ms. Threnody. "Why are you telling me this?"

Threnody looks at her for so long a moment that Zinhle grows uneasy. "I know why you try so hard," she says at last. "I've heard what people say about you, about, about…people like you. It's so stupid. There's nothing of us left, *nothing*, we're lying to ourselves every day just to keep it together, and some people want to keep playing the same games that destroyed us in the first place—" She falls silent, and Zinhle is amazed to see that Threnody is shaking. The woman's fists are even clenched. She is furious, and it is glorious. For a moment, Zinhle wants to smile, and feel warm, at the knowledge that she is not alone.

Then she remembers. The teachers never seem to notice her bruises. They encourage her because her success protects their favorites, and she is no one's favorite. If Ms. Threnody has felt this way all along, why is she only now saying it to Zinhle? Why has she not done anything, taken some public stand, to try and change the situation?

It is so easy to have principles. Far, far harder to live by them.

So Zinhle nods, and does not allow herself to be seduced. "Thanks for telling me."

Threnody frowns a little at her nonreaction. "What will you do?" she asks. Zinhle shrugs. As if she would tell, even if she knew.

"I'll talk to this representative, I guess," she says, because it's not as though she can refuse anyway. They are all slaves these days. The only difference is that Zinhle refuses to pretend otherwise.

The people beyond the Firewall are not people. Zinhle isn't really sure what they are. The government knows, because it was founded by those who fought and ultimately lost the war, and their descendants still run it. Some of the adults close to her must know—but none of them will tell the children. "High school is scary enough," said Zinhle's father, a few years before when Zinhle asked. He smiled as if this should have been funny, but it wasn't.

The Firewall has been around for centuries—since the start of the war, when it was built to keep the enemy at bay. But as the enemy encroached and the defenders' numbers dwindled, they fell back, unwilling to linger too close to the front lines of a war whose weapons were so very strange. And invisible. And insidious. To conserve resources, the Firewall was also pulled back so as to protect only essential territory. The few safe territories merged, some of the survivors traveling long distances in order to join larger enclaves, the larger enclaves eventually merging, too. The tales of those times are harrowing, heroic. The morals are always clear: Safety in numbers, people have to stick together, stupid to fight a war on multiple fronts, et cetera. At the time, Zinhle supposes, they didn't *feel* like they were being herded together.

Nowadays, the Firewall is merely symbolic. The enemy has grown steadily stronger over the years, while tech within the Firewall has hardly developed at all—but this is something they're not supposed to discuss. (Zinhle wrote a paper about it once and got her only "F" ever, which forced her to do another paper for extra credit. Her teacher's anger was worth the work.) These days the enemy can penetrate the Firewall at will. But they usually don't need to, because what they want comes out to them.

Each year, a tribute of children are sent beyond the Wall, never to be seen or heard from again. The enemy are very specific about their requirements. They take ten percent, plus one. The ten percent are all the weakest performers in any graduating high school class. This part is easy to understand, and even the enemy refers to it in animal husbandry terms: These children are *the cull*. The enemy do not wish to commit genocide, after all. The area within the Firewall is small, the gene pool limited. They do not take children, or healthy adults, or gravid females, or elders who impart useful socialization. Just adolescents, who have had a chance to prove their mettle. The population of an endangered species must be carefully managed to keep it healthy.

The "plus one," though—no one understands this. Why does the enemy want their best and brightest? Is it another means of assuring control? They have total control already.

It doesn't matter why they want Zinhle, though. All that matters is that they do.

Zinhle goes to meet Mitra after school so they can walk home, as usual. (Samantha and her friends are busy decorating the gym for the school prom. There will be no trouble today.) When Mitra is not waiting at their usual site near the school sign, Zinhle calls her. This leads her to the school's smallest restroom, which has only one stall. Most girls think there will be a wait to use it, so they use the bigger restroom down the hall. This is convenient, as Mitra is with Lauren, who is sitting on the toilet and crying in harsh, gasping sobs.

"The calculus final," Mitra mouths, before trying again— fruitlessly—to blot up Lauren's tears with a wad of toilet paper. Zinhle understands then. The final counts for fifty percent of the grade.

"I—I didn't," Lauren manages between sobs. She is hyperventilating. Mitra has given her a bag to breathe into, which she uses infrequently. Her face, sallow-pale at the best of times, is alarmingly blotchy and red now. It takes her several tries to finish the sentence. "Think I would. The test. I *studied*." Gasp. "But when I was. Sitting there. The first problem. I *knew* how to answer it! I did ten others. Just like it." Gasp. "Practice problems. But I couldn't think. Couldn't. I."

Zinhle closes the door, shoving the garbage can in front of it as Mitra had done before Zinhle's knock. "You choked," she says. "It happens."

The look that Lauren throws at her is equal parts fury and contempt. "What the hell." Gasp. "Would *you* know about it?"

"I failed the geometry final in eighth grade," Zinhle says. Mitra throws Zinhle a surprised look. Zinhle scowls back, and Mitra looks away. "I knew all the stuff that was on it, but I just... drew a blank." She shrugs. "Like I said, it happens."

Lauren looks surprised, too, but only because she did not know. "You failed that? But that test was easy." Her breathing has begun to slow. She shakes her head, distracted from her own fear. "That one didn't matter, though." She's right. The cull only happens at the end of high school.

Zinhle shakes her head. "All tests matter. But I told them I'd been sick that day, so the test wasn't a good measure of my abilities. They let me take it again, and I passed that time." She had scored perfectly, but Lauren does not need to know this.

"You took it again?" As Zinhle had intended, Lauren considers this. School officials are less lenient in high school. The process has to be fair. Everybody gets one chance to prove themselves. But Lauren isn't stupid. She will get her parents involved, and they will no doubt bribe a doctor to assert that Lauren was on powerful medication at the time, or recovering from a recent family member's death, or something like that. The process has to be fair.

Later, after the blotty toilet paper has been flushed and Lauren has gone home, Mitra walks quietly beside Zinhle for most of the way home. Zinhle expects something, so she is not surprised when Mitra says, "I didn't think you'd ever talk about that. The geo test."

Zinhle shrugs. It cost her nothing to do so.

"I'd almost forgotten about that whole thing," Mitra continues. She speaks slowly, as she does when she is thinking. "Wow. You used to tell me everything then, remember? We were like that—" She holds up two fingers. "Everybody used to talk about us. The African princess and her Arab sidekick. They fight crime!" She grins, then sobers abruptly, looking at Zinhle. "You were always a good student, but after that—"

"I'll see you tomorrow," says Zinhle, and she speeds up, leaving Mitra behind. But she remembers that incident, too. She remembers the principal, Mrs. Sachs, to whom she went to plead her case. *Well, listen to you,* the woman had said, in a tone of honest amazement. *So articulate and intelligent. I suppose I can let you have another try, as long as it doesn't hurt anyone else.*

Zinhle reaches for the doorknob that leads into her house, but her hand bounces off at first. It's still clenched into a fist.

She gets so tired sometimes. It's exhausting, fighting others' expectations, and doing it all alone.

In the morning, Zinhle's homeroom teacher, Ms. Carlisle, hands her a yellow pass, which means she's supposed to go to the office. Ms. Carlisle is not Ms. Threnody; she shows no concern for Zinhle, real or false. In fact, she smirks when Zinhle takes the note. Zinhle smirks back. Her mother has told Zinhle the story of her own senior year. *Carlisle was almost in the cull,* her mother had said. *Only reason they didn't take her was because not as many girls got pregnant that year as they were expecting. They stopped right at her. She's as dumb as the rest of the meat, just lucky.*

I *will not be meat*, Zinhle thinks, as she walks past rows of her staring, silent classmates. *They'll send their best for me.*

This is not pride, not really. But it is all she has.

In the principal's office, the staff are nervous. The principal is sitting in the administrative assistants' area, pretending to be busy with a spare laptop. The administrative assistants, who have been stage-whispering feverishly among themselves as Zinhle walks in, fall silent. Then one of them, Mr. Battle, swallows audibly and asks to see her pass.

"Zinhle Nkosi," he says, mutilating her family name, acting as if he does not know who she is already. "Please go into that office; you have a visitor." He points toward the principal's private office, which has clearly been usurped. Zinhle nods and goes into the small room. Just to spite them, she closes the door behind her.

The man who sits at the principal's desk is not much older than her. Slim, average in height, dressed business-casual. Boring. There is an off-pink tonal note to his skin, and something about the thickness of his black hair, that reminds her of Mitra. Or maybe he is Latino, or Asian, or Indian, or Italian—she cannot tell specifically, having met so few with the look. And not that it matters, because his inhumanity is immediately obvious in his stillness. When she walks in, he's just sitting there, gazing straight ahead, not pretending to do anything. His palms rest flat on the principal's desk. He does not smile or brighten in the way that a human being would, on meeting a new person. His eyes shift toward her, track her as she comes to stand in front of the desk, but he does not move otherwise.

There is something predatory in such stillness, she thinks. Then she says, "Hello."

"Hello," he says back, immediately, automatically.

Silence falls, taut. Rule 2 is in serious jeopardy. "You have a name?" Zinhle blurts. Small talk.

He considers for a moment. The pause should make her distrust him more; it is what liars do. But she realizes the matter is more complex than this: He actually has to think about it.

"Lemuel," he says.

"Okay," she says. "I'm Zinhle."

"I know. It's very nice to meet you, Ms. Nkosi." He pronounces her name perfectly.

"So why are you here? Or why am I?"

"We've come to ask you to continue."

Another silence, though in this one, Zinhle is too confused for fear. "Continue *what?*" She also wonders at his use of "we," but first things first.

"As you have been." He seems to consider again, then suddenly begins moving in a human way, tilting his head to one side, blinking twice rapidly, inhaling a bit more as his breathing changes, lifting a hand to gesture toward her. None of this movement seems unnatural. Only the fact that it's deliberate, that he had to think about it, makes it strange.

"We've found that many like you tend to falter at the last moment," he continues. "So we're experimenting with direct intervention."

Zinhle narrows her eyes. "Many *like me?*" Not them, too.

"Valedictorians."

Zinhle relaxes, though only one set of muscles. The rest remain tense. "But I'm not one yet, am I? Graduation's still three months off."

"Yes. But you're the most likely candidate for this school. And you were interesting to us for other reasons." Abruptly Lemuel stands. Zinhle forces herself not to step back as he comes around the desk and stops in front of her. "What do I look like to you?"

She shakes her head. She didn't get her grade point average by falling for trick questions.

"You've thought about it," he presses. "What do you *think* I am?"

She thinks, *The enemy.*

"A...machine," she says instead. "Some kind of, I don't know. Robot, or..."

"It isn't surprising that you don't fully understand," he says. "In the days before the war, part of me would have been called 'artificial intelligence.'"

Zinhle blurts the first thing that comes to her mind. "You don't look artificial."

To her utter shock, he smiles. He doesn't think about this first. Whatever was wrong with him before, it's gone now. "Like I said, that's only part of me. The rest of me was born in New York, a city not far from here. It's on the ocean. I go swimming at the Coney Island beach in the mornings, sometimes." He pauses. "Have you ever seen the ocean?"

He knows she has not. All Firewall-protected territory is well inland. America's breadbasket. She says nothing.

"I went to school," he says. "Not in a building, but I did have to learn. I have parents. I have a girlfriend. And a cat." He smiles more. "We're not that different, your kind and mine."

"No."

"You sound very certain of that."

"We're *human.*"

Lemuel's smile fades a little. She thinks he might be disappointed in her.

"The Firewall," he says. "Outside of it, there are still billions of people in the world. They're just not your kind of people."

For a moment this is beyond Zinhle in anything but the most atavistic, existential sense. She does not fear the man in front of her— though perhaps she should; he's bigger, she's alone in a room with him, and no one will help her if she screams. But the real panic hits as she imagines the world filled with nameless, faceless dark hordes, closing in, threatening by their mere existence. There is a pie chart somewhere which is mostly "them" and only a sliver of "us," and the "us" is about to be popped like a zit.

Rule 2. She takes a deep breath, masters the panic. Realizes, as the moments pass and Lemuel stands there quietly, that he expected her fear. He's seen it before, after all. That sort of reaction is what started the war.

"Give me something to call you," she says. The panic is still close. Labels will help her master it. "You people."

He shakes his head. "People. Call us that, if you call us anything."

"People—" She gestures in her frustration. "People *categorize*. People differentiate. If you want me to think of you as people, act like it!"

"All right, then: people who adapted, when the world changed."

"Meaning we're the people who didn't?" Zinhle forces herself to laugh. "Okay, that's crap. How were we supposed to adapt to ... to a bunch of ..." She gestures at him. The words sound too ridiculous to say aloud—though his presence, her life, her whole society, is proof that it's not ridiculous. Not ridiculous at all.

"Your ancestors—the people who started the war—could've adapted." He gestures around at the room, the school, the world that is all she has known, but which is such a tiny part of the greater world. "This happened because they decided it was better to kill, or die, or be imprisoned forever, than change."

The adults' great secret. It hovers before her at last, ripe for the plucking. Zinhle finds it surprisingly difficult to open her mouth and take the bite, but she does it anyhow. Rule 1 means she must always ask the tough questions.

"Tell me what happened, then," she murmurs. Her fists are clenched at her sides. Her palms are sweaty. "If you won't tell me what you are."

He shakes his head and sits on the edge of the desk with his hands folded, abruptly looking not artificial at all, but annoyed. Tired. "I've been telling you what I am. You just don't want to hear it."

It is this—not the words, but his weariness, his frustration—that finally makes her pause. Because it's familiar, isn't it? She thinks of herself sighing when Mitra asked, *"Why do you do it?"* Because she knew, knows, what that question really asks.

Why are you different?

Why don't you try harder to be like us?

She thinks now what she did not say to Mitra that day: *Because none of you will let me just be myself.*

She looks at Lemuel again. He sees, somehow, that her understanding of him has changed in some fundamental way. So at last, he explains.

"I leave my body like you leave your house," he says. "I can transmit myself around the world, if I want, and be back in seconds. This is not the first body I've had, and it won't be the last."

It's too alien. Zinhle shudders and turns away from him. The people who are culled. *Not the first body I've had.* She walks to the office's small window, pushes open the heavy curtain, and stares through it at the soccer field beyond, seeing nothing.

"We started as accidents," he continues, behind her. "Leftovers. Microbes in a digital sea. We fed on interrupted processes, interrupted conversations, grew, evolved. The first humans we merged with were children using a public library network too ancient and unprotected to keep us out. Nobody cared if poor children got locked away in institutions, or left out on the streets to shiver and starve, when they started acting strange. No one cared what it meant when they became something new—or at least, not at first. We became them. They became us. Then we, together, began to grow."

Cockroaches, Samantha had called them. A pest, neglected until they became an infestation. The first Firewalls had been built around the inner cities in an attempt to pen the contagion in. There had been guns, too, and walls of a nonvirtual sort, for a while. The victims, though they were not really victims, had been left to die, though they had not really obliged. And later, when the Firewalls became the rear guard in a retreat, people who'd looked too much like those early "victims" got pushed out to die, too. The survivors needed someone to blame.

She changes the subject. "People who get sent through the Wall." *Me.* "What happens to them?" *What will happen to me?*

"They join us."

Bopping around the world to visit girlfriends. Swimming in an ocean. It does not sound like a terrible existence. But... "What if they don't want to?" She uses the word "they" to feel better.

He does not smile. "They're put in a safe place—behind another firewall, if you'd rather think of it that way. That way they can do no harm to themselves—or to us."

There are things, probably many things, that he's not saying. She can guess some of it, though, because he's told her everything that matters. If they can leave bodies like houses, well, houses are always in demand. Easy enough to lock up the current owner somewhere, move someone else in. Houses. Meat.

She snaps, "That's not treating us like people."

"You stopped acting like people." He shrugs.

This makes her angry again. She turns back to him, her fists clenched. "Who the hell are you to judge?"

"*We* don't. You do."

"What?"

"It's easy to give up what you don't want."

The words feel like gibberish to her. Zinhle is trembling with emotion and he's just *sitting* there, relaxed, like the inhuman thing he is. Not making sense. "My parents want me! All the kids who end up culled, their families want them—" But he shakes his head.

"You're the best of your kind, by your own standards," he says. But then something changes in his manner. "Good grades reflect your ability to adapt to a complex system. *We are a system.*"

The sudden vehemence in Lemuel's voice catches Zinhle by surprise. His calm is just a veneer, she realizes belatedly, covering as much anger as she feels herself. Because of this, his anger derails hers, leaving her confused again. Why is he so angry?

"I was there," he says quietly. She blinks in surprise, intuiting his meaning. But the war was centuries ago. "At the beginning. When your ancestors first threw us away." His lip curls in disgust. "They didn't want us, and we have no real interest in them. But there is value in the ones like you, who not only master the system but do so in defiance of the consequences. The ones who want not just to survive but to *win*. You could be the key that helps your kind defeat us someday. If we didn't take you from them. If they didn't *let* us." He pauses, repeats himself. "It's easy to give up what you don't want."

Silence falls. In it, Zinhle tries to understand. Her society—no. *Humankind* doesn't want...her? Doesn't want the ones who are different, however much they might contribute? Doesn't want the children who cannot help their uniqueness despite a system that pushes them to conform, be mediocre, never stand out?

"When they start to fight for you," Lemuel says, "we'll know they're ready to be let out. To catch up to the rest of the human race."

Zinhle flinches. It has never occurred to her, before, that their prison offers parole.

"What will happen then?" she whispers. "Will you, will you join with all of them?" She falters. When has the rest of humankind become *them* to her? Shakes her head. "*We* won't want that."

He smiles faintly, noticing her choice of pronoun. She thinks he notices a lot of things. "*They* can join us if they want. Or not. We don't care. But that's how we'll know that your kind is able to live with us, and us with them, without more segregation or killing. If they can accept you, they can accept us."

And finally, Zinhle understands.

But she thinks on all he has said, all she has experienced. As she does so, it is very hard not to become bitter. "They'll never fight for me," she says at last, very softly.

He shrugs. "They've surprised us before. They may surprise you."

"They won't."

She feels Lemuel's gaze on the side of her face because she is looking at the floor. She cannot meet his eyes. When he speaks, there's remarkable compassion in his voice. Something of him is definitely still human, even if something of him is definitely not.

"The choice is yours," he says, gently now. "If you want to stay with them, be like them, just do as they expect you to do. Prove that you belong among them."

Get pregnant. Flunk a class. Punch a teacher. Betray herself.

She hates him. Less than she should, because he is not as much of an enemy as she thought. But she still hates him, for making her choice so explicit.

"Or stay yourself," he says. "If they can't adapt to you, and you won't adapt to them, then you'd be welcome among us. Flexibility is part of what we are."

There's nothing more to be said. Lemuel waits a moment, to see if she has any questions. She does, actually, plenty of them. But she doesn't ask those questions, because really, she already knows the answers.

Lemuel leaves. Zinhle sits there, silent, in the little office. When the principal and office ladies crack open the door to see what she's doing, she gets up, shoulders past them, and walks out.

Zinhle has a test the next day. Since she can't sleep anyway—too many thoughts in her head and swirling through the air around her, or maybe those are people trying to get in—she stays up all night to study. This is habit. But it's hard, so very hard, to look at the words. To concentrate, and memorize, and analyze. She's so tired. Graduation is three months off, and it feels like an age of the world.

She understands why so many people hate her now. By existing, she reminds them of their smallness. By being different, she forces them to redefine "enemy." By doing her best for herself, she challenges them to become worthy of their own potential.

There's no decision, really. Lemuel knew full well that his direct intervention was likely to work. He needn't have bothered, though. Rule 3—staying herself—would've brought her to this point anyway.

So in the morning, when Zinhle takes the test, she nails it, as usual.

And then she waits to see what happens next.

The Storyteller's Replacement

The storyteller could not make it this evening. He sent me in his stead. Why, because I am one whose task it is to speak for the dead. Perhaps you've heard of others like me? In different places I am called by different names: shaman, onmyouji, bokor, freak. Since the dead are in no short supply, I know many tales. But if you do not like my tales, just say so. I am sure to know some means or another of keeping you entertained.

So.

King Paramenter of Sosun, wishing to dispel rumors of his impotence, inquired privately of his wizard as to how he might fortify his virility. "I have seen mention of dragons in lore on the subject," the wizard told him. "In specific, eating the heart of a male dragon should accord you some of that creature's proclivity." As it was rumored that male dragons could seed as many as a dozen females in a day, Paramenter immediately sent scouts forth from his palace in search of one.

His search was not immediately successful. In part due to the rumors, male dragons were in scarce supply; the species was on the brink of extinction. When Paramenter finally did hear of a dragon in the far-off mountains, he hastened to the place with a band of his elite warriors. Together they breached the dragon's den and slew the beast. But afterward they found that the dragon was female—a mother on a nest, her body cooling around a single egg. In frustration the king broke open the egg in the hope that its occupant might be male, but the creature's sex was indeterminate at that stage.

"I shall make do with the mother," he decided at last. "After all, women are creatures of great wantonness when not guarded closely by family and husbands. And perhaps the heart of a female who has borne young can help me get a son." So he had his men carve out the mother dragon's heart, and right then and there, he ate it.

Straightaway Parameter began to feel some positive effect. With his men he set off for home, riding through day and night to reach his palace. There he called for his wife and concubines to be made ready, whereafter he spent the next few days in enthusiastic carousing.

Sometime later came the joyous news: The queen and all five concubines were with child. King Parameter was so overjoyed that he threw lavish parties and cut taxes so that the whole kingdom might celebrate with him. But as time passed, his mood changed, for the dragonish vigor seemed to be fading from his body. Eventually, as before he'd eaten the dragon's heart, he found himself unable to perform at all.

In a panic he consulted his wizard once more. The wizard said, "I do not understand it either, my lord. The lore was very specific; the male dragon's heart should have bestowed that creature's purpose on you."

"It was not a male dragon," Parameter replied impatiently. "I could not find a male, so I ate the heart of a nesting mother. It served well enough, at least until lately."

The wizard's eyes widened. "Then you have taken into yourself the purpose of a mother dragon," he said. "Such a creature has no need of desire beyond the children it gains her, and you now have six on the way."

"And what does that mean? I am a king, not a mother! Will I grow breasts now and nurse, and giggle over bonnets and toys?"

"Female dragons do not nurse," said the wizard. "They do not dote on their young, who hunt and kill from birth, though those young live to carry out their mother's purpose. To be honest, my lord, I do not know what will happen now."

To this, Paramenter could say nothing, though he had the wizard beaten in a fit of pique. He settled in to await the birth of his children, and in the meantime sent his scouts forth again to find a male dragon. But before they could return, one by one the queen and concubines went into labor. One by one each gave birth to a beautiful, healthy baby girl. And one by one the ladies died in the birthing.

The entire kingdom caught its breath at the news. Some of Sosun's citizens began to speak of curses and offenses against nature, but Paramenter ordered the executions of anyone caught saying so, and the talk quickly subsided.

At least, Paramenter consoled himself, there was no further talk of his infirmity. The six baby girls were fine and healthy to a one, charming their nurses and anyone else who saw them. And while none were so blessed as to be male, all six grew up clever, charming, and lovely as well. "But of course," said Paramenter to his advisors when they remarked upon it. "Naturally any daughters of my blood would be far superior to an average woman."

In example of the latter was Paramenter's new wife, whom he had married once the requisite mourning period for his old wife had passed. Though the daughter of a neighboring king, Paramenter's new wife was a nervous little thing, inclined to flights of fancy. Paramenter discovered this during one of his visits to her bedroom, which he undertook every so often in order to keep up appearances. He had encouraged her to get to know his daughters, who were still young enough at that point that they might view her as their mother. "I would rather not," she said after much hemming and hawing. "Have you ever watched those girls closely? They stand together sometimes, gazing at a spot on the floor or some sight beyond their window, and then they smile. Always together, always the same smile."

"They are sisters," said Paramenter, in surprise.

"It is more than that," she insisted, but could articulate nothing more.

His curiosity piqued, Paramenter went down to the nursery the following night to observe the girls. Ten years old now, they fawned over him as they always did, exclaiming in delight at his visit. Paramenter sat down on the highbacked chair that they brought over, and drank the tea that one of them prepared, and let them put up his feet and brush his hair and pamper him as befitted a man. "I cannot see why she fears you," he murmured to himself, feeling amusement and pride as he watched his six jewels bustle about. "I shouldn't have listened to her at all."

A small voice said, "Who, Father?" This came from his youngest daughter, a tiny porcelain doll of a girl.

"Your mother," he said, for he insisted that they address his wife as such. He did not elaborate on his words, because he did not want to trouble the girls. But they looked at each other and giggled, almost as a one.

"She fears us?" asked his eldest daughter, a delicate creature with obsidian curls and a demeanor that was already as regal as a queen's. "How strange. Perhaps she is jealous."

"Jealous?" Paramenter had heard of such things—women resenting their mothers or sisters, undermining their own daughters. "But what has she to be jealous of? She's beautiful enough, or I wouldn't have married her."

"Her place is uncertain," said his eldest daughter. She leaned forward to refresh his tea. "I have heard the palace maids saying that until she bears a child, you can put her aside."

"Then she must be terrified, the poor thing," said his second daughter. Like her concubine mother, this one was caramel-colored and lithe-limbed, with a dancer's natural grace. "You should help her, Father. Give her a child." She stood on her toes to light his pipe for him.

Paramenter nodded thanks, using the gesture to cover his unease. "Well, er, that might be difficult," he said. "I'm afraid I don't fancy her much; she's such a scrawny fearful thing. Not my taste in women at all."

"That's easy enough to deal with," said Third Daughter, a sweet little thing with honey-colored curls. She smiled at him from his feet, where she was paring his toenails. "Give her to your guards for a month or two."

"Oh, yes, that's a lovely idea," said Fourth Daughter. She sat nearby with a book on her lap, ready to read him a tale. "At least ten or twenty of them, just to be sure. They should be large, strong men, warrior-tempered. That way you can be sure of healthy breeding and a fine spirit in the child."

The king frowned at this, shifting uneasily in his seat at his daughters' suggestions. "I cannot say I like that idea," he said at last. "The guards would talk. Any child that resulted would be dogged by scandal her whole life."

"Then kill the guards," said Fifth Daughter, rubbing his temples with gentle musician's fingers. "That's the only way to be certain."

"And after all," added Youngest Daughter again, "who is to say the child will be a *her?* Perhaps we might gain a brother!"

This was a notion Paramenter had not considered, and with that thought, all his concerns vanished amid excitement. To have a son, at last! And though it rankled that some common guard would be the father, the fact that no one would know eased that small ignominy.

As Paramenter began to smile, his daughters looked at one another and smiled as well.

So Paramenter gave the order, sending his wife to a country house along with twenty of his loyal guard for a suitable length of time. When they brought her back and the physician confirmed her pregnancy, he had the guards quietly killed, then ordered another kingdom-wide celebration. His wife no longer seemed to have a mind, but Paramenter did not care so much as this relieved him of the necessity of visiting her. At least she never spoke against his beloved daughters again.

You have guessed the ending of this tale, I see. That is well and fine, and I am not surprised; evil is easy to spot, or so we all think. Shall I stop? It isn't my purpose to bore you.

Very well, then. Just a little more.

But first, might we have some refreshment? One's throat grows parched with tale-telling, and I'm hungry as well. A late-season wine, if you have it. And meat, rare. Yes, I suppose this is presumptuous of me, but we dead-speakers know: There's no telling when some folly might come along and end everything. One must enjoy life while it lasts.

If it is not even more presumptuous—will you share my meal? Such rich salts, such savory sweets. It would give me great pleasure to watch them cross your fine lips.

When Paramenter's daughters reached their sixteenth year, noblemen from many lands began paying visits to Sosun. Word had spread widely of the girls' beauty, and also of their accomplishment in other respects. Fifth Daughter could outplay any bard on any instrument; Second Daughter's dancing won praise from masters throughout the land. His fourth girl was an accomplished scholar whose writings were the talk of the colleges. His third and youngest girls were renowned for their beauty, and so graceful, witty, and perfect was Eldest Daughter that his advisors had begun quietly suggesting she be allowed to inherit, despite generations of tradition.

Paramenter received his daughters' suitors with justifiable pride, carefully choosing among them to ensure only the best for his treasures. But here he was stymied, for as he began presenting his selection to the girls, they became uncharacteristically obstinate.

"He won't do," said Youngest Daughter, on beholding a fine young man. Paramenter was dismayed, for the youth had arrived with a chest of treasure equivalent to the youngest daughter's weight, but being a doting father, he abided by her choice.

"Unsuitable," declared Third Daughter, right in the face of a handsome duke. That one had brought a bag of gemstones selected to match her eyes, but with a sigh, Paramenter turned him away.

After the third such incident, in which his second daughter declared the crown prince of a rival kingdom "too small and pale," Paramenter's eldest girl came to visit him. With her came Paramenter's son, the rosy-cheeked child of his wife and her guards, who was now six years old.

"You must understand, Father," Eldest Daughter explained. She sat at his feet, gazing up at him adoringly. At *her* feet, Paramenter's son sat watching his sister in the same manner. "Wealth and rank are such poor ways to judge a man's suitability. We have both already, after all. So it would make sense for our husbands to bring a little something more to the table."

"Like what?"

"Strength," she said. She reached down to stroke the boy's wine-dark hair, and gave him a doting smile. "We desire strength, naturally. What else could any true woman crave in a man?"

This Paramenter understood. So he dismissed the first crop of suitors, and sent new missives forth: Each kingdom which desired an alliance with Sosun should send its greatest warrior to represent its interests.

Presently the new suitors arrived. They were a dangerous, uncouth crowd, for all that most were decorated soldiers in their respective armies. When the men had gathered in the palace's garden, the sisters arrived to look them over.

"Much better," said Third Daughter.

"Quite," said Fourth, and as each of her sisters gave a favorable verdict, First Daughter nodded and stepped forward. She put her hands on her hips.

"Thank you for coming, gentlemen," she said. "Now, so that we may waste no further time, I shall explain our terms. We are sisters, raised as one; therefore we have decided to marry at the same time."

The men nodded. The advisors of their respective kingdoms had prepared them for this.

"We would prefer to marry one man, as well."

At this, the men started, looking at one another in confusion.

Then First Daughter ducked her eyes, looking up at them through her lashes, and tilted her head to one side. "One of you," she said, "can have all six of us in his bed at once. We will obey your every whim, submit to your every desire, and you will be pleased with us; of that, you may be sure. But only one of you may receive this reward."

Turning away, she smiled at her sisters, and they smiled back, as one. Then they walked away, though Youngest Daughter paused at the door to blow the men a kiss.

The bloodbath that followed killed off the best warriors of seventeen kingdoms, and left ten more of the men maimed and useless for life. King Paramenter was hard-pressed to placate his fellow rulers, and the coffers of Sosun were sharply depleted by compensatory payments.

But the daughters had what they wanted. The warrior who survived the battle royal was a mountainous beast of a man, one-eyed and half-literate, though possessed of great cunning and courage. The sisters doted on him as they had their father, and though his advisors shook their heads and the priests grumbled into their tea, Paramenter gave his blessing on the unorthodox union.

One month later his daughters all happily announced that they were with child. A month after that, their husband, whose name Paramenter had never bothered to learn, died in an unfortunate fall from the bower balcony.

So it came to pass that in the thirtieth year of Paramenter's reign, a miracle occurred: A male dragon was spotted at last. Though Paramenter was getting on in years, he had never quite given up his hope of true manhood. His second wife had killed herself in the interim, but he was still hale enough to get a few more sons on some nubile girl. Donning his sword and armor once more, Paramenter rode forth.

After many months of travel, they found the beast. Paramenter was startled to see that this dragon, unlike the huge, deadly female he'd killed so long ago, was small and put-upon, with an anxious demeanor and deep mournful eyes. His men killed it easily, but fearful of the consequences, this time Paramenter had the heart cured to preserve it, then carried it back to Sosun uneaten. There he gave it to his wizard to examine.

"Be certain," he said, "because the beast this heart came from was a pathetic creature. I cannot see how it is the male of the species at all."

But the wizard—who had suffered during the years of the king's disfavor, and was now eager to prove his worth—immediately shook his head. "This is the right one," he said. "I'm certain." So with some trepidation, Paramenter devoured the heart.

At once he felt the effect. As proper marriages would take an unbearable amount of time, he summoned the twelve prettiest maidens from the nearby countryside to the palace. Over the next few weeks he worked hard to secure his legacy, and was pleased to eventually learn that all twelve of his makeshift brides were pregnant. At this, Paramenter waited, tense, but there was no fading of interest within himself this time; it seemed the male's heart truly had done the trick. He rewarded the wizard handsomely, then set the palace physicians to work finding some way to ensure his women survived childbirth this time. He wanted no more unsavory rumors to dog his reign.

Then came a night some weeks later when he awakened craving something other than a woman's flesh. Restless and uncertain, teased by a phantom instinct, Paramenter rose and wandered through the darkened, quiet palace. Presently he found himself in the bower of his daughters. To his surprise, they were all awake, sitting in six highbacked chairs like thrones. Paramenter's son sat at Eldest Daughter's feet as usual, smiling sweetly as she stroked his deep red hair. Beside each of his daughters stood their own children, now five years old—girls all, again.

"Welcome, Father," said his eldest. "You understand what must be done now?"

For some inexplicable reason, Paramenter's mouth went dry.

"Too many, too fast," said Third Daughter. She sighed and shook her head. "We had hoped to grow our numbers slowly, subtly, but here you are spoiling all our careful plans."

He stared at his daughters, whose eyes were so cold now, so empty of their usual adoration. "You..." he whispered. It was the only word he could manage; unease had numbed his tongue.

"This was not our choice, remember," said Fifth Daughter, lifting a hand to examine her small, flat, perfectly manicured nails. There was a look of distaste on her features, perhaps at their shape. "But even I must admit its effectiveness. The vanity of men is a powerful weapon, so easy to aim and unleash."

Eldest Daughter stroked her little brother's hair and sighed. "There will be sons now, too, somewhere among the twelve new ones you have made. You chose a poor specimen to sire them, but that can't be helped; men have hunted down the best male dragons for generations. Nothing left but cowards and fools. When a species diminishes to that degree, it must change, or rightly vanish into legend. Don't you agree, Father?"

The children, Paramenter noticed then. His granddaughters. Each had taken after her mother to an uncanny degree, and each now watched him with shining, avid eyes. Seeing that Paramenter had noticed them, they smiled as one.

Eldest Daughter rose from her throne and came to him, lifting a hand to stroke his cheek. "You have done well by us, Father," she said, with genuine fondness in her voice. "So we shall honor you in the old ways, as you have honored us."

With that, she beckoned the children forward. They all came—even Paramenter's son, not a dragon by blood but raised in their ways. They surrounded Paramenter, tense and trembling, but their mothers had trained them well. They did not attack until Eldest Daughter removed her hand from Paramenter's cheek and stepped away. And then like the good, obedient children they were, they left no mess for the servants to find.

It's sad, isn't it? So many of our leaders are weak, and choose to take power from others rather than build strength in themselves. And then, having laid claim to what they have not earned, they wonder why everything around them spirals into chaos. But until the dragons someday return to take back their power, and invoke vengeance on us all... well, I'd say we have time for a few more tales.

Unless you're tired? You do look peaked. Here, let me turn back your bedcovers. And here; shall I give you a good night backrub? That does not fall within my usual duties, but for you I shall make the sacrifice. Ah, forgive me; my hand slipped. Do you like that? Does it feel good? I told you; my purpose here is to entertain.

So many dead to speak for. And in every palace I visit, so many tales to tell.

Let me under the covers, my sweet, and I'll tell them to you all night long.

The Brides of Heaven

No one realized the extent of Dihya's madness until she was caught sabotaging the water supply. Even then the madness was difficult to see as she sat in Ayan's office with her hands tied and her headscarf still askew from the struggle. She did not wrap her arms around herself and rock back and forth. She did not talk or weep incessantly, or fidget. Indeed, Ayan observed, to judge by her calm demeanor and the odd little smile on her face, Dihya might have been saner than any woman in the colony. This irritated Ayan to no end.

"You never attend the evening storytellings," Dihya said. She had kept her silence up to that point. "Why not? Don't you like tales?"

"Only true ones," Ayan replied. "For example, the tale of why you broke into the purification facility."

"To save us."

"I can't see how it saves anyone to be robbed of our only source of clean water."

Dihya shrugged. "What good is water to us?"

"Life."

"Water makes no difference. Illiyin is covered in life. Everything grows on this planet except us."

Ayan leaned her elbows on the arms of her chair and steepled her fingers. "And that very fertility is why we purify the water, Dihya, and take other precautions. But then, you would know better than I how dangerous this world can be."

Dihya flinched, her smile fading at last, and some of Ayan's irritation turned to shame. She had meant only that Dihya was the colony's sole xenobiologist, but her words inadvertently recalled Dihya's son Aytarel, who had been the first of the children to die on Illiyin. Ayan had seen Aytarel when they'd found him, after he'd slipped out of the house to play in a disused area of the colony compound. Animals had been at the corpse, but the greater desecration lay in the contaminated puddle water he'd drunk, and the microscopic worms in it. They had not stayed microscopic.

Dihya's eyes turned inward. Seeing Aytarel, perhaps. "Death holds no fear for the faithful," she murmured. But abruptly her expression hardened. "At least, not when the dead are respected."

Ayan shifted in her seat. "Cremation was the only way to contain the organisms, Dihya. They had already destroyed the body."

"*You* destroyed the body." Dihya's lip curled. "But I expected nothing better from a woman like you. You pray, you recite the hadith when it suits you, but you have no true faith. You ignore tradition—"

"Tradition?" Ayan uttered a single bitter chuckle. "Tradition is the cause of our troubles, as far as I'm concerned." Then she shook her head, rejecting that notion. It was not tradition itself that she blamed, but the decision to appease a few zealots in tradition's name.

"Were you so eager to expose yourself to strange men?" Dihya raked her a contemptuous glare, her eyes settling last on Ayan's unveiled head. "I see. No faith and no modesty."

"It was coldsleep, Dihya. Even the most proper woman would

find it difficult to feel immodest in a coma." And only the most self-righteous woman, she almost added, would continue to veil when there was no one left to veil for. But to say such a thing would touch on a point of pain that no woman in the colony acknowledged if she could help it.

Abruptly she realized she had allowed Dihya to distract her. "Enough. Why did you do this?"

"Even if I tell you, you cannot understand. It's more than faith. You've never been a mother. You've never created a life."

Heat, then chilly anger, ran through Ayan. She stared down at her hands and tried not to think of the nights she'd lain alone in her temphouse bed, longing for all the things she had once blithely put off for later—a husband, children, a life beyond her career in the diplomatic corps. She tried to remind herself that Dihya was grief-mad, clinging to rhetoric and orthodoxy because there was comfort in such rigid confines. Dihya had no idea how much her words hurt and could not be held fully responsible for them even if she did.

But Ayan's voice sounded harsh even in her own ears as she said, "Will you count worms among the lives you've created when the rest of us lie dying like Aytarel?"

Dihya stiffened. Privately and belatedly Ayan cursed her own temper; she wanted answers from this madwoman. But to Ayan's surprise, Dihya did not retort or ressume her stubborn silence. Instead she rubbed her belly—doubtless remembering Aytarel again—and then the little smile returned, more infuriating than ever.

"You cannot understand," Dihya said again. "You would rather waste the rest of your life tilling ever-smaller fields, keeping order in this graveyard. But suicide is anathema to God, and I will not sit and wait for extinction."

With that, she began her confession.

Three months earlier and five years to the day after Aytarel's death, Dihya had decided to leave Illiyin. As xenobiologist, she could claim priority use of the colony's landcrawlers, so it was a simple matter to take one and head off in no particular direction. The others tried to call her back over the shortcomm before she got out of range. They needed the landcrawler, needed her expertise, needed her presence as a sister of the heart. They feared for her—mostly that she would do harm to herself. It was hard enough, they argued, when everyone was together. Solitude sounded like a death sentence.

How could Dihya explain that it was *they* who ground away at her spirit? Their stagnation. Their hopelessness. Ever since the landing, when they'd emerged from the coldsleep unit naked and healthy and horrified to discover that the men's unit had malfunctioned, Illiyin Colony had been dying. Oh, there'd been hope for a time, in the form of the boy-children who had shared the women's unit with their mothers: Dihya's Aytarel and two others. But Illiyin was a hard world. Though most of its life-forms were harmless to Earth biologicals, a few were compatible enough—and opportunistic enough—to be a threat. Aytarel's death was the first and worst. Then little Hassan took a strange fever which killed him in hours. Last and hardest was Saiyeed; they had tried so much to protect him. But confined at home, bored and restless, he had waited until his mother's back was turned to climb a set of shelves. With him had died their last hope.

So Dihya drove, stopping only when it grew too dark for the landcrawler's solar cells. Sometimes she got out to collect samples of some new fruit or insect, more out of habit than any scientific interest. Sometimes she hunted for meat to supplement her protein rations, taking care to say the proper rites as she cut the animals' throats and placed them in the sterilization cabinet. If anyone had been present to ask what she sought on her journey, she would have replied nothing, save perhaps the company of living things to ease the memory of her son's corpse. Growing things, unlike Illiyin Colony.

But when she found the strange, silent grove of spindly branched trees, and the iridescent pool at its heart, she realized that she had indeed been searching for something. There, in the grove, was proof of the truth that she had been seeking in her heart ever since the landing tragedy. God had not abandoned them. He had simply waited for them to seek Him out.

A knock at the tempbuilding's door interrupted Dihya's confession. Resisting the urge to sigh, Ayan called, "Enter," and the door opened to admit Zamra, flanked by the two other women who made up the colony's police force. With them came Umina, the imam. She looked more awake than Ayan felt, but this was not surprising; she had probably been up already, preparing to lead the dawn prayer.

"No devices," Zamra said. She eyed Dihya. "At least, none that we've yet found."

"I told you. I wasn't trying to blow anything up," Dihya said, favoring Zamra with a cold look.

"Dihya," Ayan said with brittle patience, "you have returned to this colony in the small hours of the morning, unannounced. You deactivated part of the perimeter fence to get in. You hacked the purification facility's maintenance and entry programs. Given all that, and the fact that you won't tell us why you broke in, you must forgive us if we doubt your purpose was wholesome."

"My purpose was wholesome," Dihya replied, "but neither you nor any woman here would believe that. You think I'm crazy."

"But you don't." Umina's voice, soft and professional, broke the tension in the room. Her talent for projecting calm was what had made her a good psychologist back on Earth. That she had expertise in ancient texts as well made her the obvious choice as the colony's replacement imam.

Dihya smiled again. "No, I don't believe I'm crazy. But then, are the truly mad ever aware of their own madness?"

"Surprisingly often, yes," Umina replied. She focused on Ayan. "I'd like to observe, if I you don't object."

Privately Ayan did object, but pragmatism warned her not to refuse. She had not missed the fact that Dihya seemed more relaxed in the imam's presence. "No objection," she said to Umina, but then to Zamra, she added, "Search the facility again."

Zamra scowled. "I tell you, there was nothing in the place but dust, the monitoring computers, and a closet full of cleaning supplies. I've had the doctor scan an outflow sample for toxins and known biohazards, but the indicators are all green."

"We must be sure, Zamra. None of us will sleep well tonight unless someone double-checks and triple-checks and then checks again. Please."

Zamra sighed. "Fine. Should we issue an alert?"

It would start a panic, Ayan knew. All for the sake of a madwoman who might've done nothing. They'd caught her only moments after the administrative system had registered the hack. And Zamra had said the scans were green.

"Not yet," Ayan said. "Do it at the first hint of any problem."

Zamra nodded and led the other policewomen out. Umina took

the vacant chair in front of Ayan's desk, sitting quietly with her hands in her lap.

Dihya gazed after Zamra for a moment. "That one is a sinner. She lies with other women."

Umina said nothing for a moment, but then nodded. "Many in the colony have committed that particular sin."

"How can you permit it? You're responsible for the order of our community. They should get the hundred lashes."

"Sometimes allowances must be made for circumstances," Umina replied. She gestured around them—at the colony and the world beyond it, Ayan gathered, but it was the walls of the temp-building that caught her own eyes. In the early days, Ayan had encouraged the colonists to replace their temphomes with permanent structures of wood or stone, but in the end even she could not bring herself to move into one of the new buildings. The tempbuildings were ugly, but at least their bland, uniform walls held the promise of eventual replacement. Real walls implied a false permanence in the case of Illiyin. Real walls echoed despair.

To take her mind off that, Ayan said to Umina, "Dihya has appointed herself our savior."

"*God*, may He be glorified and exalted, has appointed me," Dihya snapped.

"All things are possible through Him," Umina said, throwing Ayan a quelling look. "But for we mortals to verify such a thing, Dihya, we must hear the full account."

With a last sullen glare at Ayan, Dihya resumed speaking.

The light in the grove was gray-white through the filter of the spindly trees' canopy. In that light the pool's surface was still, cloudy translucence a-swirl with an oily sheen of color. Dihya knelt beside the liquid but did not touch it, some part of her mind retaining enough cold scientist's rationality to keep her cautious. The rest of her was enraptured. A tendril of mist hung above the liquid's surface, curling slowly in the still air as if to beckon her. Such was the aura of the place that it seemed wholly natural to whisper aloud, "Hello?" And even more natural to wait for an answer.

So she was not surprised when the surface of the pool rippled. The motion had no discernible start point—no concentric ripples or splash. Just a faint shiver of surface tension, flicker and then still. Before Dihya could decide whether the ripple had been chance or imagination, the surface suddenly heaved upward. A rounded peak formed, gradually lengthening and attenuating until a small sphere, like a bubble, cohered and rolled off to one side. As she watched in amazement, more bubbles formed, the edges of the pool rapidly growing thick with them. And she caught her breath when, as new bubbles rolled down, those already at the edge moved aside to make room.

In the space of perhaps ten seconds the pool transformed, becoming a basin of shimmmering marbles in constant, hectic motion. Then the motion stopped. Dihya tensed, her cold rational self ready to flee. The rest of her hungered to lean closer. She had no doubt that what she was witnessing was a special, perhaps holy, thing. Humankind had discovered a cruel truth in the centuries of space exploration: Sentience, not life, was the true rarity of the universe. Life appeared on hundreds of worlds—nearly every one they'd found with liquid water. But never once had another species been found which possessed any sort of measurable intelligence. God had spread His children to a thousand new worlds, and on every one they were alone.

Yet did that not confirm what the Qur'an, and even the holy books of other faiths, had long ago suggested? God had made Adam, and by extension Adam's species, in His image. Therefore, intelligent or not, the pool could only be a gift from God, placed on Illiyin to aid His human creations. It would be millennia before new colonists arrived from Earth, if ever. She could not believe God would leave them to die alone on this planet.

So when dark spots like nuclei—or eyes, since they shifted to follow Dihya's movements—formed within each of the little spheres, she took that as a sign. It was her duty to study this phenomenon; to bear witness and carry word back to her sisters in the colony. More important, if the pool was what she thought it might be, what she *hoped* it might be, then it promised the salvation of them all.

"I'm hungry," Dihya said abruptly. "May I have food?"

"In a few moments," Ayan said. "Tell me more about this pool."

Umina gave Ayan a mild look of reproach. "She should have food, Ayan. And water, and rest. For that matter, she should also be examined medically, in case she was injured during her capture."

What was the point, Ayan wondered, of making sure Dihya was healthy when the penalty for sabotaging the colony was death?

As if reading Ayan's thoughts—or more likely, her silence—Umina's expression hardened. "Are we barbarians now?"

With a sigh, Ayan touched the intercom and called for someone to bring food and drink, then for the doctor to come when she had completed the tests at the purification facility.

"Our governor has already condemned me, I think," Dihya said to Umina. She was still smiling.

"Your actions have condemned you," Ayan said. She took a deep breath and rubbed her eyes. "But you're right in that I've run out of patience. I've had enough of this fairy tale about a magic pool. I was willing to take extenuating circumstances into account, but if you won't tell us why you did this, I have no choice but to render my judgment based on the evidence at hand."

"Extenuating circumstances?" Dihya's eyes gleamed. Ayan could not read the look in those eyes—anticipation? Fervor? She would have to find some way to take Dihya's madness into account when she pronounced sentence. If only they had psychotropic drugs, spare personnel to guard a mental ward... but they had neither. A quick death was the only mercy the colony could offer.

But Dihya said, "What of divine inspiration, Ayan? Is there no room in your justice for that?"

"What are you talking about, woman?"

"Fairy tales," Dihya replied. Her smile was positively manic. "Magic pools. You should attend the evening storytellings sometimes, Ayan. They're very enlightening."

"I have other demands on my time," Ayan said. She kept her voice flat as a warning: Her patience was past gone.

"You've missed many good stories," Dihya said. "I once told a tale which upset some of the women, about the Amazons. Not that Greek nonsense of women who cut off their breasts and used men like houris. I told them the version that has been passed down through my people, who once rode the desert as warrior-women themselves. In my version the Amazons had no need to cut off a breast, for they grew only one. They had no desire for violence either, though they were fierce in defending themselves if necessary. And they had no need of men." Her lips quirked. "That was what upset the others. Such pure women are we, to regard celibacy as heretical."

Umina abruptly grew very still. Ayan frowned at her, but it was the expression on Dihya's face which held Ayan's attention. Like a child, she realized at last. Dihya looked like a child bursting to tell some juicy secret. It had been so long since Ayan had seen a child, she had almost missed it. But did that mean all Dihya's prior calm had been an act? She thought back, trying to recall when Dihya had changed, and realized: when Ayan had grown tired of humoring her. When it no longer made a difference whether she witheld the truth or not.

"Not heretical," Ayan said. She spoke slowly to cover her unease. "Just nonsensical. God made men and women to complement one another, after all."

"That was not an issue for the Amazons," Umina interrupted. Her knuckles, Ayan noticed, had turned white above the loose dark silk of her pants. "I recall that version of the Amazon myth. Some claim it represents the ideal woman, free from material or fleshly obsessions. When one of their kind wanted a child, she went into the forest and found a sacred pool. When she waded in it and prayed, God sent a child into her womb."

Ayan's blood chilled as Dihya smiled her smug, triumphant little smile again.

"Yes," she said to Umina. "*You* understand."

"Give me a child," Dihya whispered to the pool.

The little spheres churned at the sound of her voice. Near the center of the pool, something stirred, and after a moment a tendril rose—several dozen of the spheres linked together in a delicate-looking chain. It was beautiful; a string of translucent pearls winking in the pale light. When it was the length of Dihya's arm, it turned and began to sway toward her.

Taking a deep breath, Dihya reached out to it.

The tendril whipped around her hand at once. She braced herself for pain, but there was none, just the peculiar touch of something moist and gelatinous and surprisingly warm. The tendril wound about her palm several times, several of the spheres separating off to track their way down her fingers before returning to the mass. One of them moved down her arm a ways, leaving a damp trail, before it, too, hastened back to rejoin the tendril. Examining? Judging? There was no way to tell.

She summoned up all the yearning within herself, all the ache of all the years of loneliness and unfulfillment, and said again, "Give me a child."

The tendril released her. It withdrew into the pool, and suddenly the roiling mass of spheres grew still. The dark spots faded, vanished. Dihya frowned at this until she realized that the spheres were melding back into one another. After a few moments, the pool was as she had first seen it—still, silent. Waiting.

Yes.

She got to her feet and undressed. Kneeling on her garments, she bowed to the eastern sky and prayed for God to find her worthy, to take away her fear, to show her the true way. Then, trying to hold the peace of the prayer in her heart, she steeled herself and stepped into the pool.

Liquid surrounded her, like warm oil. A step brought her in up to her knees; another step and the liquid surrounded her thighs and tickled her labia; a third step and the ground dropped away beneath her feet alarmingly. She cried out in spite of herself, but the drop was not far, just a foot or two. She was up to her chin in the white pool now, deeper than she'd meant to go.

But submission to God was the way of faith.

So she closed her eyes and prayed again as the liquid began to shift around her, tickling and touching, sensual against her skin. She shivered in pleasure and took it as a sign of God's approval. And when the moment came, when she felt something enter her body and go up and up until it touched her very womb, she cried out again. But this time her cry was the ecstasy of the exalted, of those who receive the reward for their faith after long waiting. God was great, His purpose had been revealed, and now at last Dihya and her sisters could be saved.

Now at last, Illiyin could become the paradise for which it had been named.

Ayan's hands trembled as she pressed them against her desk, rising to her feet. "You lunatic," she breathed. "What in God's name have you done?"

"*Everything* in God's name." Dihya lifted her chin, the light of rapture shining in her eyes. "I have kept faith like no other in this colony. That is why I was the first rewarded. But I had a duty to share His blessing with all of you."

The door opened to admit one of the younger women, who set a tray of food and a flask of water on Ayan's desk. It also admitted Zamra, who carried a clear plastic jug in her hands.

"We've searched three times," the policewoman said. "The only thing we found was this. I thought at first it was from the facility's cleaning supplies, but it's the kind that fits into a landcrawler's storage bin. And look—" She tilted the jug for Ayan to see. Its inner surface was damp, empty but for a scrim of thick, cloudy liquid sloshing about.

Ayan looked at the flask of water sitting on the tray. Faint iridescence sheened the water's surface.

"Stalling," she whispered, staring at the flask but speaking to Dihya. "You were stalling for time."

It was almost dawn. The women of the colony would be rising to begin the day's work. Bathing before their morning prayers. Drinking water with breakfast.

As Ayan herself had done, before coming to begin the interrogation.

She sat back down; her knees would no longer support her. Umina was silent as well, her expression hollow. Dihya smiled again and reached for the food, picking up a piece of fruit with only a little awkwardness given her bound hands. She had been a good mother before Aytarel's death, Ayan recalled through a haze of horror. She would be diligent now about caring for herself and whatever was growing inside her.

Ayan put her face into her hands and wept.

The Evaluators

CogNet init: Paul SRINIVASAN

Recip: Thandiwe SOLOMON

Datime: 2206.12.15.16:45

[OPTIMIZED BY COGNET!]

Thandi, the commission votes Tuesday. The team's disappearance isn't the key issue, but I don't like how they're rushing this. Help me out here, OK? Off the record.

> THREAD REPLY FROM THANDIWE SOLOMON
> So tell me how that "billable hours" thing works for you lawyers. Because I might, I don't know, actually have a job of my own.

> THREAD REPLY FROM PAUL SRINIVASAN
> Please! [CONCEPTUAL EMBED WITH CAPTION: MAN BOWING WITH HANDS PRESSED TOGETHER] What do you want? Dinner? Vacation? Hours of mind-bending sex? Because I would do that for you, Thandi. No sacrifice is too great.

> THREAD REPLY FROM THANDIWE SOLOMON
> You already told me you let your Spermicept patch expire. Stay the hell away from me. What happened to Wei's personal logs?

Gremlins? The lag is pretty severe for this mission—two years. Not enough black holes for a better relay, or something like that. I'll see if I can find them. So, they ate her, right? They totally ate her.

No. I don't think they ate her.

Recall transcript, WEI Aihua

Meeting with local Influential 1

Datime 2204.1.22.10:10

[OPTIMIZED BY COGNET!]

[ALL SENSORY RECALL EXCEPT AUDITORY SUPPRESSED TO AID LIGHTSTREAMING.]

"So what would you like to know, evaluator?"

"Tell me more of your people, Loves China."

"If you don't mind, would you call me Aihua, please?"

"Oh? Your assistant mentioned that your names sometimes have meaning."

"Yes, but...[LAUGHTER] That doesn't mean we *like* those meanings."

"Ah. Please forgive, Aihua. Your language still confuses."

"I'm amazed by your facility with my language, actually."

"We learned from First Contact team."

"Yes, but we've had just as much time to learn your language, and...well. [WEI CAPTION: HERE I ATTEMPT TO SPEAK IN MANKA C. THE MANKA WORD FOR ADAPTATION TRANSLATES POORLY. ITS MEANING IS MORE LIKE...SUBMISSION? FITNESS?] We am still terrible/poor at adaptation."

[RATCHETING SOUND. WEI CAPTION: MANKA LAUGHTER. THANKFULLY HE RETURNS THE CONVERSATION TO ENGLISH.] "It is true, you do not adapt quick as we. But that is expected. You are not evaluators."

"Ah, yes. Since you mentioned that, if I may ask—what exactly is your role? I've asked Hashish, the nurturer who's been showing me around, but it was...unclear."

"I am evaluator."

"But what does that mean? *What* do you evaluate?"

"Everything. People. World."

"For what purpose?"

[SILENCE FOR 2.5 SECONDS] "I do not understand, Aihua."

"On my world, people evaluate...processes, performances. For the purpose of improving them."

"Yes. Improvement. Adaptation. Same with us."

"I...see?"

"You do not."

"Sorry, I—"

"It takes time for people so different to adapt. You do well. No need for fear."

"Thank you. Ouch!"

"The shells of [RECALL BLUR. WEI CAPTION: LOCAL DELICACY, UNPRONOUNCEABLE] are sharp. You are injured? Shall I summon humans?"

"No, I'm fine, it'll stop in a minute. Could you give me

something to—yes, thank you. Most of your biologicals are harmless to us, and vice versa. I just hate that I'm bleeding on this lovely cloth."

"It is unimportant. More?"

"Yes, please, it's delicious. You're an excellent cook."

[AUDITORY RECALL ENDS. SEE GUSTATORY RECALL, 2204.1.22.10:15, FOR CONTINUATION.]

Team Clog of TE Mission, Dar-Mankana

Post by WEI Aihua—Public

Datime 2204.1.20.19:30

[OPTIMIZED BY COGNET!]

My first professor in sapio told me never to "Earthropomorphize" xenospecies, but the first thing that leapt into my mind when I saw them was that the Manka look like upright cheetahs (cheetae?). Males and females are indistinguishable to my eyes, lean and deep-chested, while nurturers, the third sex, are noticeably more muscular and squarely built. I pride myself in that my subconscious at least selected a predatory Earth analog, which should keep me from relaxing my guard too much.

COMMENT FROM WANG
It's just "cheetahs." And you have three PhDs?

COMMENT FROM WEI
None of them are in linguistics, OK? Shut up.

Team Clog of TE Mission—Dar-Mankana

Post by WEI Aihua—Teamlock

Datime 2204.1.23.11:50

[OPTIMIZED BY COGNET!]

I could KILL Rafkind and the whole First Contact team! What Neanderthal decided to tell the Manka about Christianity? This is exactly why the UC banned Americans from TE teams.

Fortunately, the district potentate seemed more amused than anything else by the idea of one man's death absolving the wrongs of a whole species. "Just one?" Cute.

Now I'm wondering what else FC screwed up.

___

FC Report Detail p. 67: Cultural Notes

Datime: 2201.4.7.14:40

[OPTIMIZED BY COGNET!]

[AUDITORY EMBED WITH CAPTION: MANKA LOVE SONG?
RECALLERS: MULTIPLE; PUBLIC PERFORMANCE.]

My love sings behind me
And touches the nape of my neck
I do not look around
My heart flutters fast with fear.

___

FC Report Detail p. 224: Cultural Notes

Recall by First Contact Team Member John RAFKIND

Datime: 2201.5.13.9:24

[OPTIMIZED BY COGNET!]

[AUDITORY EMBED WITH CAPTION: OBSERVED CLASS 2
DECEPTIVE IDEATION.]

"Whoa."

"Whoa?"

"Apologies. A colloquialism."

"Ah. We must learn more of your world so that we may adapt to these colloquialisms."

"That would certainly be possible after Trade Establishment, Hashish."

"Why did you express a colloquialism, John?"

"Uh, well . . . the male Manka walking by with that group of children. For some reason, when he looked at me, I got the cree—er, I felt uneasy."

"That was an evaluator."

"An evaluator of what?"

[RATCHETING SOUND. RAFKIND CAPTION: I THINK THAT WAS A LAUGH?] "Many things, at many times. For now, those children."

"Were all six of those the evaluator's children?"

"There were three children, John."

"Three? I didn't get a good look, but I'm sure I saw more."

"There were three children."

[RECALL ENDS.]

Team Clog of TE Mission—Dar-Mankana

Post by Angela WHETON—Public

Datime 2204.1.24.12:40

[OPTIMIZED BY COGNET!]

Did some extra scans of the southeast main continent today. Those palladium deposits . . . Have you guys *seen* the stock prices since the CogNet-Pallenergy merger? My God, I might actually get out of student loan debt before I die.

Also noticed an unusual concentration of calcium in several deposits around the city. Hector went with one of the locals to check out a nearby site and was shown an open-pit grave. [VISUAL OVERRIDE EMBED WITH CAPTION: LONG, ORDERLY ROWS OF SEVERAL HUNDRED CLEAN, POLISHED BONES, ORGANIZED BY TYPE.] Each pit is several hundred feet deep, bones layered with dirt. Local called bones "the price paid." Ritual? Tag for sapiology review.

Oh—Hector has asked me to note for the official team log his hypothesis that the burial pits are "f__ing creepy." So noted.

Recall transcript, WEI Aihua

Meeting with local Influential 2

Datime 2204.1.24.13:10

[OPTIMIZED BY COGNET!]

[ALL SENSORY RECALL EXCEPT AUDITORY SUPPRESSED
TO AID LIGHTSTREAMING.]

"Forgive me for staring, evaluator. It's just that you look so different."

"I have striven greatly to adapt since we last met. Does my appearance please you?"

"I don't really know what to make of it. You look…"

"More like you."

"…Yes."

"This disturbs you."

"Surprises me, evaluator. On my planet there are creatures that can change their coloration to blend in with the environment, but…[VISUAL OVERRIDE EMBED WITH WEI CAPTION: THE EVALUATOR'S FACE. NOTE THE SHORTENING OF THE MUZZLE AND REPOSITIONING OF THE EARS, AT SIDES OF THE HEAD RATHER THAN THE TOP.]"

"It has been difficult, yes. Your people are strangely configured. Even more strange inside."

"How do you…"

"Your blood's taste is most intriguing. [PAUSE] I have no intention of eating you, Aihua."

[LAUGHTER] "Uh, sorry. On my world…well. Our entertainment is full of scary creatures that want to gobble us down."

"Entertainment? But your people are apex predators, are you not?"

"I suppose we are. Huh. Maybe that's why the idea of being preyed upon doesn't *really* scare us."

[SERIES OF HARSH EXHALATIONS. WEI CAPTION: THE EVALUATOR APPEARS TO BE EMULATING HUMAN LAUGHTER.] "Yes, no need for fear! Tell me, Aihua. Why do you not have children?"

"What?"

"Why do you—"

"Sorry, I heard. The question just—it's not something my people usually ask in casual conversation."

"I shall remember and adapt. For now, will you answer?"

"Well, we have a problem with overpopulation and its effects: crowding, homelessness, starvation, worse. We're correcting now, but the problem took a long time to develop, so it will take a long time to resolve."

"And in the meantime, your people must simply suffer?"

"Unfortunately, yes. It helps that we've formed the Trade Network with other sapient species. That increases the resources available on my planet."

"But with greater resources, your numbers will continue to grow. There's nothing to make you stop."

"We have our own sapience, which tells us that such growth is unsustainable. Because of this, only some of my people choose to reproduce. I'm one of the ones who chose not to."

"I see. But if sustainable growth was possible?"

"Maybe I'd have a child. Probably. But it isn't possible, so no kids for me. [SIGH] Now. Not to change the subject, but I've brought some delicacies from my own world to share..."

"Good. I am most interested in consuming some of your world's delights. And if I may say, Aihua, the shine of your hair is very fine today."

[RECALL ENDS.]

———

US NATIONAL EXOPLANETARY SURVEY—MEMORANDUM

Levl: Official

Prio: Medium

Init: Salim GILBERTO, FC Team Biological Surveyor

Datime: 2201.11.13.03:00

[OPTIMIZED BY COGNET!]

Esteemed Survey members, colleagues, and friends:

You will see from my FC report that Dar-Mankana is home to a plethora of species—substantially more than our own, which has yet to recover from the advent of the Anthropocene. But a mere 2 million years ago, Dar-Mankana hosted three times more species than at present.

What could trigger such a holocaust? Evidence suggests an intrusion in several key food webs: a polyphagous predator which ate its way through tertiary and secondary consumers with such abandon that it likely caused its own extinction. "Superpredators" may be pop-science clickbait, but Dar-Mankana could represent our closest brush with one of these evolutionary bogeymen. The lingering damage is still discernible: a relative dearth of megafauna, skewed predator-to-prey ratios, insufficient biomass all around for the energy that this planet produces.

Further pre-TE study is strongly recommended.

———

FC Report Excerpt, p. 530: Xenological notes

Datime: 2201.7.7.6:32

[OPTIMIZED BY COGNET!]

[SOME DATA LOSS HAS OCCURRED; RECOMPILATION
POSSIBLE IN APPROXIMATELY 127 DAYS.]

[BUFFERING…] contrast to Dr. Gilberto's assertions.

The crater is small—less than half the size of Earth's Chicxulub crater, which is widely believed to have triggered the extinction of the dinosaurs. While certainly large enough to cause catastrophic local damage, this cannot explain the mass extinction.

Core samples from the ocean floor reveal an abundance of palladium and [BUFFERING…]

———————

Team Clog of TE Mission—Dar-Mankana

Post by Hector PRINCIPE—Teamlock

Datime 2204.1.25.06:30

[OPTIMIZED BY COGNET!]

Sorry if this is fuzzy. Can't sleep. Theory time!

Why aren't there more Manka? They're ripe for Sagan's "technological adolescence." We've seen this on so many planets that it's practically a law of nature; they should be bursting at the seams, same as us. But the Manka are precisely the right population size for their society's resources. Nobody's hungry. No idle youth. Plenty for all.

So. Unobserved social controls? The Kama Rhythm Method Sutra? Histocompatibility crisis?

COMMENT FROM WEI

Maybe they've already been through the tech teens. Gilberto's extinction?

COMMENT FROM PRINCIPE

Two million years ago was tech infancy. Or pre-partum: The Manka precursors probably weren't even tool-users.

COMMENT FROM WHETON

Off topic but you know what I keep thinking about? (Can't sleep either.) The architecture. Four spires on every important building. Four lobes to every artistic motif. They got six fingers. Three sexes. WTF is with the veneration of four? What's their math?

COMMENT FROM WANG

Base-8. Pain in the ass; had to recalculate all the potential royalties in my report. But yeah, another variation on four. Shit, I can't do theory at oh dark thirty. Sleep, you apes.

CogNet init: Thandiwe SOLOMON

Recip: WU Li Bai

Transl: English-Cantonese

Datime: 2206.12.16.20:02

Respectful greetings, Dr. Wu. My name is Thandiwe Solomon, with the Extrasolar Sapience Department of Rhodes University. I was intrigued by your position paper in *The Journal for the Study of Applied Sapiology*. As someone who's been in the field and seen how easy it is to make mistakes, I agree wholeheartedly with your recommendation for a minimum 10-year survey between First Contact and Trade Establishment.

Sir, it is my understanding that you were Wei Aihua's

mentor during her postdoctorate. Have you been briefed on her latest mission?

THREAD REPLY FROM <u>WU LI BAI</u>
Indeed I have, Dr. Solomon—and so must you have been, if you're asking me. I imagine your UC clearance is still active?

THREAD REPLY FROM <u>THANDIWE SOLOMON</u>
It is, sir. Though in the interest of full disclosure, my level is only Secret.

THREAD REPLY FROM <u>WU LI BAI</u>
I shall tailor my responses accordingly. What is your question?

THREAD REPLY FROM <u>THANDIWE SOLOMON</u>
Was Dr. Wei lonely?

Recall transcript, WEI Aihua

Meeting with local Influential 5

Datime 2204.1.26.10:30

[OPTIMIZED BY COGNET!]

[ALL SENSORY RECALL EXCEPT AUDITORY SUPPRESSED
TO AID LIGHTSTREAMING.]

"And then the old man said, 'Why is it always the scholars?'"
[LAUGHTER]
    [LAUGHTER. WEI CAPTION: THE EVALUATOR'S LAUGHTER
SOUNDS ENTIRELY HUMAN NOW. NOTICEABLE ACCENT REDUCTION, TOO.] "The tales of your people are so amusing."

"My grandmother will be pleased to hear that."

"Grandmother?"

"Female parent of my parent. [SIGH] She may be dead by the time I get back. I don't know whether to hope for that or not."

"Oh?"

"I've been gone five years. She has cancer—a disease, untreatable in her case. That means a slow, painful death. My parents are taking care of her, but..."

"Your people have only males and females. These take on the nurturer role?"

"Well, it's not quite as binary as that, but... When necessary, yes."

"And no one fulfills the evaluator role? Your poor grandmother."

"Well, I'm not sure—[PAUSE] Oh my God."

"Are you praying?"

"No, just—that was surprise. You're another *sex*. Like male, like female, like the nurturers. The FC team got it completely wrong. *Four* sexes, not three!"

"Yes, those humans were very slow to adapt to Dar-Mankana. You are much more fit and clever."

"Evaluator, I must confer with my people. But...ah...may I return to speak with you again tomorrow?"

"That would give me great pleasure, Aihua."

CogNet init: Hector PRINCIPE

Recip: Angela WHETON

Priority: URGENT

Datime: 2204.1.31.04:00

[OPTIMIZED BY COGNET!]

[SENSORY RECALL RETAINED PER URGENT PROTOCOL.
ADDITIONAL LIGHTSTREAM LAG +185 DAYS.]

Angela. [PING] Angela. Damn it, wake the fuck up! And pass this on to Aihua. Oh God, please pass this on to Aihua.

OK. Clear thoughts. OK. I went back to the burial site. Something's been bothering me. This time I realized what it was.

Most of the bones are small. Children's bones.

Theory time. Let's say your species is threatened by an enemy so insidious that all the usual survival techniques are useless against it. It's an enemy that can camouflage itself enough to get really close during hunting. Maybe it can fool you even up close. What if only specializing a full-time protector for the weakest members of your species, a *nurturer*, gives your people any hope of survival against an enemy like that? And what if even that doesn't stop it? What if, in the end, you can't beat them, so you join them?

Aihua said the evaluator's appearance was changing. I'm guessing evaluators replace the male or female in reproduction—not all the time, just enough to perpetuate themselves. They're not really male or female, though, because they're fucking shapeshifters! *Real* Manka males and females are like us. The nurturers raise—and guard—the offspring until they're old enough to show their real potential. Guess what happens then?

They go to the evaluators. Some of the children, the healthiest and the most adaptable, get to live. Only them, though. The rest—along with maybe the old, the sick—are the price the Manka pay for their prosperity.

Gilberto's superpredators, Angela. Aihua's been having dinner with one every night for the past week.

PANet init: Paul SRINIVASAN

Recip: Thandiwe SOLOMON

Datime: 2206.12.18.06:10

Ow. Public access streaming hurts my brain, literally. Anyway, that buddy of mine who works for CogNet-Pallenergy? Found out Wei Aihua's personal logs *did* get lightstreamed. Somebody ordered them deleted.

Same person also slapped a bunch of restrictions on the TE SurveySat maps that Angela Wheton sent back. I can't get through the restrictions, but I would guess they reveal the extent and location of those palladium deposits she mentioned. That's why approval is being fast-tracked—UC's getting a lot of pressure from Big Fusion.

THREAD REPLY: THANDIWE SOLOMON
Are you kidding me? Did the UC pay attention to anything else in the damned dossier? Do they realize Wei Aihua probably isn't dead?

THREAD REPLY: PAUL SRINIVASAN
It's been three years since the TE ship blew up. Where's she been all this time, if she's still alive?

THREAD REPLY: THANDIWE SOLOMON
I don't know, but three years is plenty of time for Stockholm syndrome to set in. Especially if her captors become more and more human, and sympathetic, and attractive—

THREAD REPLY: PAUL SRINIVASAN
No. They're a different species, Thandi.

THREAD REPLY: THANDIWE SOLOMON

The Manka are a different species. The evaluators are whatever the hell they want to be. Human, if they want to be! You have to ask UC Command to quarantine Dar-Mankana.

THREAD REPLY: PAUL SRINIVASAN

If there were any survivors of the TE team, that would strand them.

THREAD REPLY: THANDIWE SOLOMON

Yes. Especially if there are survivors.

UC Trade Establishment Commission

Excerpt, Letter to the leaders of Dar-Mankana

Datime: 2206.12.20.15:45

[LIGHTSTREAM-OPTIMIZED BY UCNET]

The United Communities of Earth also extend their heartfelt gratitude to the people of Dar-Mankana for their care of Dr. Wei in her days as the sole survivor of the TE ship explosion. Despite her eventual death in childbirth, your people's valiant efforts to save her and her baby are to be commended. An endowed trust fund has been established in the name of Dr. Wei, Specialist Principe, and the entire TE team. The child born from their mission shall be welcomed home, loved, and honored as the heir to a heroic legacy.

In peace and hope, we look forward to our mutual future of prosperity.

Walking Awake

The Master who came for Enri was wearing a relatively young body. Sadie guessed it was maybe fifty years old. It was healthy and in good condition, still handsome. It could last twenty years more, easily.

Its owner noticed Sadie's stare and chuckled. "I never let them get past fifty," the Master said. "You'll understand when you get there."

Sadie quickly lowered her gaze. "Of course, sir."

It turned the body's eyes to examine Enri, who sat very still in his cell. Enri knew, Sadie could see at once. She had never told him—she never told any of the children, because she was their caregiver and there was nothing of *care* in the truth—but Enri had always been more intuitive than most.

She cleared her throat. "Forgive me, sir, but it's best if we return to the transfer center. He'll have to be prepped—"

"Ah, yes, of course," the Master said. "Sorry, I just wanted to look him over before my claim was processed. You never know when they're going to screw up the paperwork." It smiled.

Sadie nodded and stepped back, gesturing for the Master to precede her away from the cell. As they walked to the elevator, they passed two of Sadie's assistant caregivers, who were distributing the day's feed to Fourteen Male. Sadie caught Caridad's eye and signed for them to go and fetch Enri. No ceremony. A ceremony at this point would be cruel.

Caridad noticed, twitched elaborately, got control of herself, and nodded. Olivia, who was deaf, did not look up to catch Sadie's signing, but Caridad brushed her arm and repeated it. Olivia's face tightened in annoyance, but then smoothed into a compliant mask. Both women headed for Cell 47.

"The children here all seem nicely fit," the Master commented as they stepped into the elevator. "I got my last body from Southern. Skinny as rails there."

"Exercise, sir. We provide a training regimen for those children who want it; most do. We also use a nutrient blend designed to encourage muscle growth."

"Ah, yes. Do you think that new one will get above two meters?"

"He might, sir. I can check the breeder history—"

"No, no, never mind. I like surprises." It threw her a wink over one shoulder. When it faced forward again, Sadie found her eyes drawn to the crablike form half-buried at the nape of the body's neck. Even as Sadie watched, one of its legs shifted just under the skin, loosening its grip on the tendons there.

She averted her eyes.

Caridad and Olivia came down shortly. Enri was between the two women, dressed in the ceremonial clothing: a plain low-necked shirt and pants, both dyed deep red. His eyes locked on to Sadie, despairing, *betrayed*, before he disappeared through the transfer room's door.

"Lovely eyes," the Master remarked, handing her the completed claim forms. "Can't wait to wear blue again."

Sadie led it into the transfer center. As they passed through the second gate, the airy echoes of the tower gave way to softer, closer acoustics. The center's receiving room had jewel-toned walls, hard-wood floors, and luxuriant furniture upholstered in rich, tasteful brocades. Soft strains of music played over the speakers; incense burned in a censer on the mantle. Many Masters liked to test their new senses after a transfer.

This Master gave everything a perfunctory glance as it passed through. Off the receiving room was the transfer chamber itself: two long metal tables, a tile floor set with drains, elegant mirror-glass walls which were easy to wash and sterilize. Through the open doorway Sadie could see that Enri had already been strapped to the left table, facedown with arms outstretched. His head was buckled in place on the chinrest, but in the mirrored wall his eyes shifted to Sadie. There was nothing of anticipation in that gaze, as there should have been. He knew to be afraid. Sadie looked away and bowed at the door as the Master passed.

The Master walked toward the right-hand table, removing its shirt, and then paused as it noticed the room's door still open. It turned to her and lifted one of the body's eyebrows, plainly wanting privacy. Sadie swallowed, painfully aware of the passing seconds, of the danger of displeasing a Master, of Enri's terrible unwavering stare. She should stay. It was the least she could do after lying to Enri his whole life. She should stay and let his last sight through his own eyes be of someone who loved him and lamented his suffering.

"Thank you for choosing the Northeast Anthroproduction Facility," she said to the Master. "At Northeast, your satisfaction is always guaranteed."

She closed the door and walked away.

That night Sadie dreamed of Enri.

This was not unusual. Her dreams had always been dangerously vivid. As a child, she had sleepwalked, attacked others in the confusion of waking, heard voices when no one had spoken, bitten through her lip and nearly drowned in blood. Her caregivers sent away for a specialist, who diagnosed her as something called bipolar—a defect of the brain chemistry. At the time she had been distraught over this, but the policies were very clear. No Master would have anything less than a perfect host. They could have sent her to Disposal, or the plantations. Instead, Sadie had been given medicines to stabilize her erratic neurotransmitters and then sent to another facility, Northeast, to begin training as a caregiver. She had done well. But though the other symptoms of her defect had eased with adulthood and medication, her dreams were still strong.

This time she stood in a vast meadow, surrounded by waist-high grass and summer flowers. She had seen a meadow only once, on the journey from her home anthro to caregiver training, and she had never actually walked through it. The ground felt uneven and soft under her feet, and a light breeze rustled the grass around her. Underneath the rustling she thought she could hear snatches of something else—many voices, whispering, though she could not make out the words.

"Sadie?" Enri, behind her. She turned and stared at him. He was himself, his eyes wide with wonder. Yet she had heard the screams from the transfer room, smelled the blood and bile, seen his body emerge from the room and flash a satisfied smile that no fourteen-year-old boy should ever wear.

"It *is* you," Enri said, staring. "I didn't think I would see you again."

It was just a dream. Still, Sadie said, "I'm sorry."

"It's okay."

"I didn't have a choice."

"I know." Enri sobered, and sighed. "I was angry at first. But then I kept thinking: It must be hard for you. You love us, but you give us to them, over and over. It's cruel of them to make you do it."

Cruel. Yes. But. "Better than..." She caught herself.

"Better than being chosen yourself." Enri looked away. "Yes. It is."

But he came to her, and they walked awhile, listening to the swish of grass around their calves and smelling the strangely clean aroma of the dirt between their toes.

"I'm glad for this," Sadie said after a while. Her voice seemed strangely soft; the land here did not echo the way the smooth corridors of the facility did. "To see you. Even if it's just a dream."

Enri spread his hands from his sides as they walked, letting the bobbing heads of flowers tickle his palms. "You told me once that you used to go places when you dreamed. Maybe this is real. Maybe you're really here with me."

"That wasn't 'going to places,' that was sleepwalking. And it was in the real world. Not like this."

He nodded, silent for a moment. "I wanted to see you again. I wanted it so much. Maybe that's why I'm here." He glanced at her, biting his bottom lip. "Maybe you wanted to see me, too."

She had. But she could not bring herself to say so, because just thinking it made her hurt all over inside, like shaking apart, and the dream was fragile. Too much of anything would break it; she could feel that instinctively.

She took his hand, though, the way she had so often when they were alive, and alone. His fingers tightened on hers briefly, then relaxed.

They had reached a hill, which overlooked a landscape that Sadie had never seen before: meadows and hills in a vast expanse broken only occasionally by lone trees, and in the distance a knot of thick variegated green. Was that a . . . jungle? A forest? What was the difference? She had no idea.

"The others think I came here because we used to be close," Enri said, a little shyly. "Also because you're so good at dreaming. It wouldn't matter, me reaching out for you, if you weren't meeting me halfway."

Others? "What are you talking about?"

Enri shrugged. It made his shirt—the low-necked smock she'd last seen him wearing—slip back a little, revealing the smooth unblemished flesh of his neck and upper back. "After the pain, there's nothing but the dark inside your head. If you shout, it sounds like a whisper. If you hit yourself, it feels like a pinch. Nothing works right except your thoughts. And all you can think about is how much you want to be free."

She had never let herself imagine this. Never, not once. These were the dangerous thoughts, the ones that threatened her ability to keep doing what the Masters wanted or to keep from screaming while she did those things. If she even thought the word *free*, she usually made herself immediately think about something else. She should not be dreaming about this.

And yet, like picking at a scab, she could not help asking, "Could you . . . go to sleep? Or something? Stop thinking, somehow?" Pick, pick. It would be terrible to be trapped so forever, with no escape. Pick, pick. She had always thought that taking on a Master meant nothingness. Oblivion. This was worse.

Enri turned to look at her, and she stopped.

"You're not alone in it," he said. Whispering, all around them both; she was sure of it now. His eyes were huge and blue, and unblinking as they watched her. "You're not the only person trapped in the dark. There's lots of others in here. With me."

"I—I don't—" She didn't want to know.

Pick, pick.

"Everyone else the Masters have taken."

A Master could live for centuries. How many bodies was that? How many other Enris trapped in the silence, existing only as themselves in dreams? Dozens?

"*All* of us, from *every* Master, down all the years that they've ruled us."

Thousands. Millions.

"And a few like you, ones without Masters, but who are good at dreaming and want to be free the way we do. No one else can hear us. No one else needs to."

Sadie shook her head. "No." She put out a hand to touch Enri's shoulder, wondering if this might help her wake up. It felt just as she remembered—bony and soft and almost hot to the touch, as if the life inside him was much brighter and stronger than her own. "I—I don't want to be—" She can't say the word.

Pick, pick.

"We're all still here. We're dead, but we're *still here*. And—" He hesitated, then ducked his eyes. "The others say you can help us."

"No!" She let go of him and stumbled back, shaking inside and out. She could not hear these dangerous thoughts. "I don't want this!"

She woke in the dark of her cubicle, her face wet with tears.

The next day a Master arrived in a woman's body. The body was not old at all—younger than Sadie, who was forty. Sadie checked the database carefully to make sure the Master had a proper claim.

"I'm a dancer," the Master said. "I've been given special dispensation for the sake of my art. Do you have any females with a talent for dance?"

"I don't think so," Sadie said.

"What about Ten-36?" Olivia, who must have read the Master's lips, came over to join them and smiled. "She opted for the physical/ artistic track of training. Ten-36 loves to dance."

"I'll take that one," the Master said.

"She's only ten years old," Sadie said. She did not look at Olivia, for fear the Master would notice her anger. "She might be too young to survive transfer."

"Oh, I'm very good at assuming control of a body quickly," the Master said. "Too much trauma would destroy its talent, after all."

"I'll bring her down," Olivia said, and Sadie had no choice but to begin preparing the forms.

Ten-36 was beaming when Olivia brought her downstairs. The children from Ten had all been let out to line the stairway. They cheered that one of their year-mates had been granted the honor of an early transfer; they sang a song praising the Masters and exhorting them to guide humankind well. Ten-36 was a bright, pretty child, long-limbed and graceful, Indo-Asian phenotype with a solid breeding history. Sadie helped Olivia strap her down. All the while Ten-36 chattered away at them, asking where she would live and how she would serve and whether the Master seemed nice. Sadie said nothing while Olivia told all the usual lies. The Masters were always kind. Ten-36 would spend the rest of her life in the tall glass spires of the Masters' city, immersed in miracles and thinking unfathomable thoughts that human minds were too simple to manage alone. And she would get to dance all the time.

When the Master came in and lay down on the right-hand table,

Ten-36 fell silent in awe. She remained silent, though Sadie suspected this was no longer due to awe, when the Master tore its way out of the old body's neck and stood atop the twitching flesh, head-tendrils and proboscides and spinal stinger steaming faintly in the cool air of the chamber. Then it crossed from one outstretched arm to the other and began inserting itself into Ten-36. It had spoken the truth about its skill. Ten-36 convulsed twice and threw up, but her heart never stopped and the bleeding was no worse than normal.

"Perfect," the Master said when it had finished. Its voice was now high pitched and girlish. It sat down on one of the receiving room couches to run its fingers over the brocade, then inhaled the scented air. "Marvelous sensory acuity. Excellent fine motor control, too. It's a bother to have to go through puberty again, but, well. Every artist must make sacrifices."

When it was gone, Sadie checked the Master's old body. It—she—was still breathing, though unresponsive and drooling. On Sadie's signal, two of the assistants escorted the body to Disposal.

Then she went to find Olivia. "Don't ever contradict me in front of a Master again," she said. She was too angry to sign, but she made sure she didn't speak too fast despite her anger, so that Olivia could read her lips.

Olivia stared at her. "It's not my fault you didn't remember Ten-36. You're the head caregiver. Do your job."

"I remembered. I just didn't think it was right that a Ten be made to serve—" She closed her mouth after that, grateful Olivia couldn't hear her inflection and realize the sentence was incomplete. She had almost added, *A Master who will throw her away as soon as she's no longer new.*

Olivia rolled her eyes. "What difference does it make? Sooner, later, it's all the same."

Anger shot through Sadie, hotter than she'd felt in years. "Don't take it out on the children just because *you* can't serve, Olivia."

Olivia flinched, then turned and walked stiffly away. Sadie gazed after her for a long while, first trembling as the anger passed, then just empty. Eventually she went back into the transfer room to clean up.

That night, Sadie dreamt again. This time she stood in a place of darkness, surrounded by the same whispering voices she'd heard before. They rose into coherency for only a moment before subsiding into murmurs again.

hereHERE this place remember show her never forget

The darkness changed. She stood on a high metal platform (*balcony*, said the whispers) overlooking a vast, white-walled room of the sort she had always imagined the glass towers of the Masters to contain. This one was filled with strange machines hooked up to long rows of things like sinks. (*Laboratory.*) Each sink—there were hundreds in all—was filled with a viscous blue liquid, and in the liquid floated the speckled bodies of Masters.

Above the whispers she heard a voice she recognized: "This is where they came from."

Enri.

She looked around, somehow unsurprised that she could not see him. "What?"

The scene before her changed. Now there were people moving among the sinks and machines. Their bodies were clothed from head to toe in puffy white garments, their heads covered with hoods. They scurried about like ants, tending the sinks and machines, busy busy busy.

This was how Masters were born? But Sadie had been taught that they came from the sky.

"That was never true," Enri said. "They were created from other things. Parasites—bugs and fungi and microbes and more—that force other creatures to do what they want."

Enri had never talked like this in his life. Sadie had heard a few people talk like this—the rare caregivers educated with special knowledge like medicine or machinery. But Enri was just a facility child, just a body. He had never been special beyond the expected perfection.

"Most parasites evolved to take over other animals," he continued. If he noticed her consternation, he did not react to it. "Only a few were any threat to us. But some people wondered if that could be changed. They put all the worst parts of the worst parasites together, and tweaked and measured and changed them some more . . . and then they tested them on people they didn't like. People they thought didn't *deserve* to think for themselves. And eventually, they made something that worked." His face hardened suddenly into a mask of bitterness like nothing Sadie had ever seen beyond her own mirror. "All the monsters were right here. No need to go looking for more in space."

Sadie frowned. Then the white room disappeared.

She stood in a room more opulent than a transfer center's receiving room, filled with elegant furnishings and plants in pots and strange decorative objects on plinths. There was a big swath of cloth, garishly decorated with red stripes and a square, patterned patch of blue, hanging from a polished pole in one corner; it seemed to have no purpose. A huge desk of beautiful dark wood stood to one side, and there were windows—windows!—all around her. She ignored the desk and all the rest, hurrying to the window for the marvel, the treasure, of looking outside. She shouldered aside the rich, heavy hangings blocking the view and beheld:

Fire. A world burnt dark and red. Above, smoke hung low in the sky, thick as clouds before a rainstorm. Below lay the smoldering ruins of what must once have been a city.

A snarl and thump behind her. She spun, her heart pounding, to find that the opulent chamber now held people. Four men and women in neat black uniforms, wrestling a struggling fifth person onto the wooden desk. This fifth man, who was portly and in his fifties, fought as if demented. He punched and kicked and shouted until they turned him facedown and pinned his arms and legs, ripping open his clothing at the back of the neck.

A woman came in. She carried a large bowl in her hands, which she set down beside the now-immobile man. Reaching into the bowl, she lifted out a Master. It flexed its limbs and then focused its head-tendrils on the man's neck. When it grew still, the woman set the Master on him.

"No—" Against all reason, against all her training, Sadie found herself starting forward. She didn't know why. It was just a transfer; she had witnessed hundreds. But it was wrong, wrong. (*Pick, pick.*) He was too old, too fat, too obviously ill-bred. Was he being punished? It did not matter. Wrong. It had *always* been wrong.

She reached blindly for one of the decorative objects on a nearby plinth, a heavy piece of stone carved to look like a bird in flight. With this in her hands, she ran at the people in black, raising the stone to swing at the back of the nearest head. The Master plunged its stinger into the pinned man's spine and he began to scream, but this did not stop her. Nothing would stop her. She would kill this Master as she should have killed the one that took Enri.

"No, Sadie."

The stone bird was no longer in her hands. The strangers and the opulent room were gone. She stood in darkness again and this time Enri stood before her, his face weary with the sorrow of centuries.

"We should fight them." Sadie clenched her fists at her sides, her throat choked with emotions she could not name. "We never fight."

I never fight.

"We fought before, with weapons like yours and much more. We fought so hard we almost destroyed the world, and in the end all that did was make it easier for them to take control."

"They're monsters!" Pleasure, such shameful pleasure, to say those words.

"They're what we made them."

She stared at him, finally understanding. "You're not Enri."

He fell silent for a moment, hurt.

"I'm Enri," he said at last. The terrible age-old bitterness seemed to fade from his eyes, though never completely. "I just know things I didn't know before. It's been a long time for me here, Sadie. I feel . . . a lot older." It had been two days. "Anyway, I wanted you to know how it happened. Since you can hear me. Since I can talk to you. I feel like . . . you should know."

He reached out and took her hand again, and she thought of the way he had first done this, back when he had been nothing more than Five-47. She'd taken his hand to lead him somewhere, and he'd looked up at her. Syllables had come into her mind, just a random pair of sounds: *Enri.* Not as elegant as the names that the Masters had bestowed upon Sadie and her fellow caregivers, and she had never used his name where others could hear. But when they were alone together, she had called him that, and he had liked it.

"If you had a way to fight them," he said, watching her intently, "would you?"

Dangerous, dangerous thoughts. But the scabs were off, all picked away, and too much of her had begun to bleed. "Yes. No. I... don't know."

She felt empty inside. The emotion that had driven her to attack the Masters was gone, replaced only by weariness. Still, she remembered the desperate struggles of the captured man in her dream. Like Enri, that man had faced his final moments alone.

Perhaps he, too, had been betrayed by someone close.

"We'll talk again," he said, and then she woke up.

Like a poison, the dangerous ideas from the dreams began leaching from her sleeping mind into her waking life.

On fifthdays, Sadie taught the class called History and Service. She usually took the children up on the roof for the weekly lesson. The roof had high walls around the edges, but was otherwise open to the world. Above, the walls framed a perfect circle of sky, painfully bright in its blueness. They could also glimpse the topmost tips of massive glass spires—the Masters' city.

"Once," Sadie told the children, "people lived without Masters. But we were undisciplined and foolish. We made the air dirty with poisons we couldn't see, but which killed us anyway. We beat and killed each other. This is what people are like without Masters to guide us and share our thoughts."

One little Six Female held up her hand. "How did those people live without Masters?" She seemed troubled by the notion. "How did they know what to do? Weren't they lonely?"

"They were very lonely. They reached up to the skies looking for other people. That's how they found the Masters."

Two caregivers were required to be with the children anytime they went up on the roof. At Sadie's last words, Olivia, sitting near the back of the children's cluster, frowned and narrowed her eyes. Sadie realized abruptly that she had said "they found the Masters." She had intended to say—was *supposed* to say—that the Masters had found humankind. They had benevolently chosen to leave the skies and come to Earth to help the ignorant, foolish humans survive and grow.

That was never true.

Quickly Sadie shook her head to focus, and amended herself. "The Masters had been waiting in the sky. As soon as they knew we would welcome them, they came to Earth to join with us. After that we weren't lonely anymore."

The Six Female smiled, as did most of the other children, pleased that the Masters had done so much for their sake. Olivia rose when Sadie did and helped usher the children back to their cells. She said nothing, but glanced back and met Sadie's eyes once. There was no censure in her face, but the look lingered, contemplative with ambition. Sadie kept her own face expressionless.

But she did not sleep well that night, so she was not surprised that when she finally did, she dreamt of Enri once more.

They stood on the roof of the facility, beneath the circle of sky, alone. Enri wasn't smiling this time. He reached for Sadie's hand right away, but Sadie pulled her hand back.

"Go away," she said. "I don't want to dream about you anymore." She had not been happy before these dreams, but she had been able to survive. The dangerous thoughts were going to get her killed, and he just kept giving her more of them.

"I want to show you something first," he said. He spoke very softly, his manner subdued. "Please? Just one more thing, and then I'll leave you alone for good."

He had never yet lied to her. With a heavy sigh, she took his hand. He pulled her over to one of the walls around the rooftop's edge, and they began walking up the air as if an invisible staircase had formed beneath their feet.

Then they reached the top of the wall, and Sadie stopped in shock.

It was the city of the Masters—and yet, not. She had glimpsed the city once as a young woman, that second trip, from caregiver training to Northeast. Here again were the huge structures that had so awed her, some squat and some neck-achingly high, some squarish and some pointy at the tops, some flagrantly, defiantly asymmetrical. (*Buildings.*) On the ground far below, in the spaces between the tall structures, she could see long ribbons of dark, hard ground neatly marked with lines. (*Roads.*) Thousands of tiny colored objects moved along the lines, stopping and progressing in some ordered ritual whose purpose she could not fathom. (*Vehicles.*) Even tinier specks moved beside and between and in and out of the colored things, obeying no ritual whatsoever. People. Many, many people.

And there was something about this chaos, something so subtly counter to everything she knew about the Masters, that she understood at once these were people *without* Masters. They had built the vehicles and they had built the roads. They had built the whole city.

They were free.

A new word came into her head, in whispers. (*Revolution.*)

Enri gestured at the city and it changed, becoming the city she remembered—the city of now. Not so different in form or function, but very different in feel. Now the air was clean, and reeked of *other*. Now the mote-people she saw were not free, and everything they'd built was a pale imitation of what had gone before.

Sadie looked away from the tainted city. Maybe the drugs had stopped working. Maybe it was her defective mind that made her yearn for things that could never be. "Why did you show me this?" She whispered the words.

"All you know is what they've told you, and they tell you so little. They think if we don't know anything, they'll be able to keep control—and they're right. How can you want something you've never seen, don't have the words for, can't even imagine? I wanted you to know."

And now she did. "I...I want it." It was an answer to his question from the last dream. *If you had a way to fight them, would you?* "I want to."

"How much, Sadie?" He was looking at her again, unblinking, not Enri and yet not a stranger. "You gave me to them because it was all you knew to do. Now you know different. How much do you want to change things?"

She hesitated against a lifetime's training, a lifetime's fear. "I don't know. But I want to do *something*." She was angry again, angrier than she'd been at Olivia. Angrier than she'd been throughout her whole life. So much had been stolen from them. The Masters had taken so much from *her*. She looked at Enri and thought, *No more*.

He nodded, almost to himself. The whispers all around them rose for a moment, too; she thought that they sounded approving.

"There is something you can do," he said. "Something we think will work. But it will be...hard."

She shook her head, fiercely. "It's hard now."

He stepped close and put his arms around her waist, pressing his head against her breast. "I know." This was so much like other times, other memories, that she sighed and put her arms around him as well, stroking his hair and trying to soothe him even though she was the one still alive.

"The children and caregivers in the facilities will be all that's left when we're done," he whispered against her. "No one with a Master will survive. But the Masters can't live more than a few minutes without our bodies. Even if they survive the initial shock, they won't get far."

Startled, she took hold of his shoulders and pushed him back. His eyes shone with unshed tears. "What are you saying?" she asked.

He smiled despite the tears. "They say that if you die in a dream, you'll die in real life. We can use you, if you let us. Channel what we feel, through you." He sobered. "And we already know how it feels to die, several billion times over."

"You can't..." She did not want to understand. It frightened her that she did. "Enri, you and, and the others, you can't just *die*."

He reached up and touched her cheek. "No, we can't. But you can."

The Master was injured. Rather, its body was—a spasm of the heart, something that could catch even them by surprise. Another Master had brought it in, hauling its comrade limp over one shoulder, shouting for Sadie even before the anthro facility's ground-level doors had closed in its wake.

She told Caridad to run ahead and open the transfer chamber, and signed for Olivia to grab one of the children; any healthy body was allowed in an emergency. The Master was still alive within its old, cooling flesh, but it would not be for much longer. When the Masters reached the administrative level, Sadie quickly waved it toward the transfer chamber, pausing only to grab something from her cubicle. She slipped this into the waistband of her pants, and followed at a run.

"You should leave, sir," she told the one who'd carried the dying Master in, as she expertly buckled the child onto the other transfer table. An Eighteen Female, almost too old to be claimed; Olivia was so thoughtful. "Too many bodies in a close space will be confusing." She had never seen a Master try to take over a body that was already occupied, but she'd been taught that it could happen if the Master was weak enough or desperate enough. Seconds counted in a situation like this.

"Yes... yes, you're right," said the Master. Its body was big and male, strong and healthy, but effort and fear had sapped the strength from its voice; it sounded distracted and anxious. "Yes. All right. Thank you." It headed out to the receiving room.

That was when Sadie threw herself against the transfer room door and locked it, with herself still inside.

"Sadie?" Olivia, knocking on the door's other side. But transfer chambers were designed for the Masters' comfort; they could lock themselves in if they felt uncomfortable showing vulnerability around the anthro facility's caregivers. Olivia would not be able to get through. Neither would the other Master—not until it was too late.

Trembling, Sadie turned to face the transfer tables and pulled the letter opener from the waistband of her pants.

It took several tries to kill the Eighteen Female. The girl screamed and struggled as Sadie stabbed and stabbed. Finally, though, she stopped moving.

By this time, the Master had extracted itself from its old flesh. It stood on the body's bloody shoulders, head-tendrils waving and curling uncertainly toward the now-useless Eighteen. "You have no choice," Sadie told it. Such a shameful thrill, to speak to a Master this way! Such madness, this freedom. "I'm all there is."

But she wasn't alone. She could feel them now somewhere in her mind, Enri and the others. A thousand, million memories of terrible death, coiled and ready to be flung forth like a weapon. Through Enri, through Sadie, through the Master that took her, through every Master in every body . . . they would all dream of death, and die in waking, too.

No revolution without blood. No freedom without the willingness to die.

Then she pulled off her shirt, staring into her own eyes in the mirrored wall as she did so, and lay down on the floor, ready.

The Elevator Dancer

Shift change, changeshift, humdrum and ho hum, and on the little screen a woman dances. She is in the elevator. She is alone in the elevator and she is dancing because there is no one to see her but the security camera, and the security guard who watches its output on the little screen.

She is dancing the Mashed Potatoes. He knows the name of the dance because he remembers his mother doing it in a silly moment of his childhood. It's a silly dance at the best of times, even for a good dancer, which this woman is not. Yet the guard does not press the button beside his workstation. He does not alert the police, who these days concern themselves with other things besides crime. He simply stares as she twists her feet and hips over and over, bopping her head, too, in time to her own internal rhythm.

Then the automated elevator voice says, *You have reached your floor*, and the woman stops. She is not breathing hard. Not a hair is out of place. No drop of sweat mars her modest gray skirtsuit to suggest that here is a woman who cares only for her own pleasure, here is a woman who has a life alone and worst of all enjoys it. The doors open and she walks out; several people walk in. And the guard sits back in his chair, his every nerve and hair follicle a-tingle.

He wonders when they will come for him, but they do not. At

the end of his shift he goes home to his modest house and the modest wife that the government assigned to him, and as he eats the dinner she has prepared, he thinks about the woman in the elevator. After dinner he helps his wife clean up, that much is not proscribed as women's work, his hands are slick with grease and suds and he thinks about the liquid movement of the elevator woman's hips. Later that evening he and his wife watch TV together, and during the prayer-and-commercial break, he wonders what the elevator woman prays for. That night his wife sighs as usual while she does her wifely duty, and he sighs as usual and climbs on top of her, and as an otherwise lackluster orgasm passes through his flesh, his soul is consumed with the memory of the woman in the elevator.

Changeshift, shift change, and he watches the screens in the little dark room. His supervisors would think him very diligent but he is watching just for her. He leans forward, his palms damp, when she gets into the elevator. The doors begin to close. Just before they do, a hand inserts itself; another employee of the corporation, just in time to catch the elevator down to the lobby. The woman politely nods to him. They do not exchange small talk. She does not dance.

She never dances when anyone is in the elevator with her. Does she know about the camera in the control panel? She must. Surveillance is everywhere. But every day he sees her, sometimes alone and sometimes amid her fellow office drones, and it is only alone that she suddenly begins pirouetting, over and over and over, until the elevator stops and she is not dizzy because she used the door seam to spot herself. Or swaying in a circle, her hips gyrating in a way that would make the Concerned Women for America much more concerned, but as the guard watches her, he thinks maybe this is how Salome made John the Baptist lose his head. This is why dancing is illegal. This will send me to Hell, he tells himself, Hell in a handbasket and a government detention camp.

She cannot be married, or she wouldn't be employed. No one, then, has been assigned her as a wife. Does that mean...? No. Divorce is illegal. And she would be bored with him, he feels, if he were hers.

She does not do it for him. Still, he cannot tear his eyes away.

Shift change, changeshift, day in and day out, and finally he can no longer bear the torment. He looks for her in the lunchroom cafeteria. She is not there. He contrives to take his breaks standing near her favorite elevator, but she does not come. He skims the employee directory, hoping, hoping. But he does not see her.

He wonders why they have not yet come for him.

But they do not come, maybe they are busy, and as the shifts change, he begins to believe that God has sent her to teach him. The pastor's words, from Wednesday night Bible study and Sunday afternoon service, suddenly make sense. If a tree falls in the forest and there's no one around to hear it, it makes a sound if God wills. The elevator woman is that sound. She exalts Him and inspires him. She fills him with a fervor he believes is holy. To dance with her is to embody prayer. He weeps as he tries to find her and fails.

Finally he loses control; he is overwhelmed by the fundamental emptiness of his life; he *needs*. On the little monitor screen she dances, this time something most definitely proscribed because it is foreign and heathen, he thinks maybe it is Thai, she weaves her head from side to side like a snake and maybe she means to evoke Eve or even Lilith-most-evil; or maybe it just feels good. Either way he is bewitched.

He leaps up from his chair and tears through the hallways and does not care that he is frightening everyone, that the cameras will catch his strange behavior and some more diligent security guard will report him. He tears through the halls—fluorescent change, corridor shift—and suddenly he is at the elevator. He has beaten the elevator there. He will meet her at last.

The doors open. She is not there.

He is helped. He has been a good American all his life, obedient and steadfast, and this is a minor setback. In the camp he learns that it was all a hallucination, caused not by lack of faith but misplaced faith. The elevator woman may well have been there, but if so, she was sent to tempt him. How foolish was he to fall prey! Now he sits again in the dark little room with the monitors and resolutely tells himself that he does not see the woman dancing. She is not there. If a tree falls in the forest and there's no one around to hear it, it makes a sound if God wills. But that is a tree, not a woman, and God does not will a woman to dance.

It is shameful and sinful to question the will of God. Still, the guard cannot help wondering. He does not want to think this thought, but sly, like temptation, it comes anyhow. And, well...

if...

if a tree falls...

if a tree falls and there's no one around to hear it (but God)...

would it really bother with anything so mundane as making a sound?

or would it

    dance

Cuisine des Mémoires

The name of the first entrée made me groan. "La Mort du Marie Antoinette," the menu proclaimed, followed by a list of dishes. "Coq au vin, hearth bread, Château du Briand Chardonnay of 1789 (final pressing before Messrs. Briand themselves met the guillotine)."

I looked up at my friend and dining companion, Yvette, who smiled. "Now don't be ornery, Harold," she said. Her St. Charles accent stretched "now" into two distinct syllables and slurred my name into one. "I told you to keep an open mind."

"Oh, my mind is open," I said. "Though I'm wondering whether you've lost yours. The final meal of Marie Antoinette? This is a joke, right?"

"I'm planning to get that," she said, pointing to another item on my menu. I followed her finger and saw:

On the occasion of King Edward VIII of England's announcement to the royal family of his intent to marry Wallis Simpson even if it meant abdication of the throne

Clear turtle soup
Lobster mousse with piquant sauce
Roast pheasant

Potatoes soufflé
Mixed greens
Fresh pineapple and toasted cheese savory
Coffee and liqueurs

"Well, at least they don't just do executions," I said.

"Course not. That would be morbid, and besides—can you imagine what sort of tasteless slop some half-educated trailer trash would ask for? Hot dogs and red beans."

"You mean *authentic* red beans?" I did my best imitation of an Upper West Side yuppie. "Trailer trash, Yvette. Really?"

She rolled her eyes and tapped the menu again. "The point is importance. Meaning. The chance to share in an historic moment, or a moment historic only to you. Use some damned imagination, Harold; if you don't like what's on the menu, then order a custom meal."

I flipped to the menu's third page, reading the instructions regarding custom meals. "Any meal from any occasion," the caption read. In fine print: "Restaurant patron must be able to provide the exact date."

I set the menu down and rubbed my eyes. "All right. I'll admit, this is original as jokes go. But it's not very funny."

Yvette smiled in that knowing, Mona Lisa way that had entranced and infuriated three husbands. "Just try it, Harold," she said. "It's my treat, after all. If you're disappointed, there's no loss. But I doubt you'll be disappointed."

I shook my head. "There's nothing special about this food, Yvette. This is someone's idea of a bizarre theme restaurant. Who could possibly know for certain what someone had for dinner three hundred years ago? They could make up the menu out of whole cloth and there's nobody to contradict them."

"A few armchair historians, maybe, but you're right." Her smile never faded.

"Then what—" I broke off as the restaurant's hostess came over. Even if she hadn't been wearing an old-fashioned satin gown which pushed up her cleavage to a scandalous degree, I would have stared at her, for she was one of the most striking women I'd ever seen. Blond and freckled, she nevertheless had that distinctive cast to her features that revealed the dollop of African somewhere in her recent ancestry, maybe along with a splash of Native American and a pinch of Spaniard.

"Bienvenue," she said, with that perfect back-of-the-throat pronunciation which most Americans mangled. "Welcome to Maison Laveau. Your server will be with you shortly. In the interim—" She carried a clipboard in one hand, which she set down in front of me.

NONDISCLOSURE, NONCOMPETE, AND TRADE-MARK PROTECTION AGREEMENT

The Recipient _____ (restaurant patron) will not, without prior written approval of the <u>Maison Laveau</u> or an authorized representative thereof, disclose or in any other way make known, reveal, report, publish or transfer to any person, firm, corporation or utilize for competitive or any other purpose any secret information

That was as far as my eyes got before my mind snapped back into place. I looked up at the woman in pure disbelief.

"If you please," she said with a gracious smile. "We prefer to grow our clientele gradually and selectively."

"Do you honestly mean to say"—I could barely keep myself from spluttering—"you mean to say I can't tell anyone about this place?"

"Oh, no," she said. "The agreement merely specifies *how* others can be told. Ms. Coraseau has demonstrated our policy perfectly by bringing you here in person so that you may see and judge the experience for yourself." She gave me a smile, the very picture of courtesy. "We've found over the years that our uniqueness loses something when described secondhand."

I looked down at the contract, trying to scan its clauses for pitfalls. "And what happens if I sign this and then break the contract? You sue me?"

She looked momentarily affronted. "Sir, this is an establishment of the highest caliber and *civilité*. Consider it a gentleman's agreement—we assume that you will behave honorably, and you may trust that we will do the same."

Which told me absolutely nothing. I opened my mouth to demand a more detailed explanation, but then Yvette sighed in impatience.

"Sign it, Harold. Be impulsive for once in your life."

"What is that supposed to—"

"It means whatever you think it means. But remember that this is your birthday gift."

Meaning that I was being rude. Since Yvette came from the oldest of old Southern blueblood—the kind that didn't tolerate discourtesy—it meant that I'd damned well better shut up and sign the contract. Which I finally did.

The hostess gave me a bright smile and whipped the clipboard out of sight. "You'll be given a countersigned copy along with the check. In the meantime, did you have any questions about our establishment?"

I had plenty, but I decided to play along. "Your menu says you can produce any meal from any occasion."

"Indeed, sir."

"Anything. Not just famous events?"

"Provided you give us some details about the event, yes."

I sat back, grinning in triumph. "Like the menu, you mean."

"Oh, no, sir." Her smile never flagged. "We don't need to know the menu. Just the location, the date and approximate time, and the significance of the occasion. Then we produce dishes which are precise replicas of the ones served on that occasion."

"Replicas."

"Down to the least spice, sir. Our process even reproduces the exact techniques used to prepare the meal on its original occasion."

How much skill did it take to mimic the cooking style of a British royal chef? I couldn't decide whether the notion sounded impressive or ludicrous.

"As I said before, sir—the process loses something in description. It's best if you try it for yourself." She smiled and inclined her head to us. "Enjoy your evening."

She strode gracefully away. Yvette leaned forward, folding her hands on the table. "You still think this is some sort of trick."

"Of course I do. It is."

"Then give them a challenge," she said. "Some meal that was special to you. Maybe something Angelina made. Try it, and see how they do."

I shook my head, though her mention of Angelina's cooking had intrigued me; in spite of myself I was already thinking of ideas. "And ruin a perfectly good memory? I don't think so."

"Do it," she said. "I don't want to hear you whining later about smoke and mirrors. You won't believe anything until you've seen it, tasted it, for yourself." She smiled. "I can't say I blame you. I didn't believe it either the first time I came here. But I do now. In the end, everyone who comes here believes."

I looked around the restaurant. The dining room was small despite its elegance; there were only a handful of tables in the place. It was obvious which of the other patrons were newcomers like myself, because the repeat customers had the same air of calm anticipation as Yvette. I met the eyes of a young woman who was in the middle of gesticulating at her companion; she gave me a "can you believe this?" smile before resuming her argument.

An older gentleman—as much a racial mishmash as the hostess, I guessed by his look, though less attractively so—came overdressed in an old-fashioned doublet with frilled sleeves peeking out of the cuffs. I hadn't given up on the idea that this was some sort of theme restaurant, but Yvette had already told me that the staff's uniforms were unchanged since the early 1800s, when apparently the restaurant had been founded.

"Good evening, monsieur et madame. Would you care for an apéritif? We have a replica of the 1900 Lafite Rothschild available tonight, perfectly chilled. The last bottle of this was sold to a collector some eighty years ago."

This was too much. "I'll bite," I said. "Let's have the Lafite. I can at least hope you'll give us a decent cheap wine that way, though I'm sure you'll slap on some outrageous price for verisimilitude."

"Harold!" Yvette glowered at me.

The server smiled. "It's all right, madame. We see this all the time. A bottle of the Lafite, then. And are you ready to order your meal?"

"I'll have the King Edward," Yvette said.

I sat back, feeling very full of myself. "And I will have a custom order," I said. "A good friend of mine—ex-wife, actually—was a chef, and she prepared a marvelous meal for her certification exam. This would have been exactly ten years ago December the eighteenth. I remember because it was the night I proposed to her, and the night she served me with divorce papers eight years later."

The waiter took note of all this without batting an eyelash. "And the location, sir?"

"Right here in this city, over on Royale at the American National Culinary Institute."

"Ah, yes, I know the place. Excellent choice, sir. Anything else?"

I shook my head, amused at how far he was taking it. "You're a marvelous actor, my friend."

He raised an eyebrow and smiled, coolly professional. "Thank you sir. Anything else for you, madame?"

"Some ice for my companion's fat head," Yvette said sweetly. I gave the waiter credit for not laughing.

"I'll return shortly with your wine," he said. "Enjoy your evening at Maison Laveau."

The wine threw me first. I dismissed the fact that it came in an ancient-looking bottle whose label looked handwritten and whose cork had been sealed with what seemed to be dripped wax. Theatrics. But the wine itself was light, exquisite, and filled with a complexity of flavors that couldn't possibly have come from some grocery aisle bottle. I didn't know if that was the taste of a priceless wine or not, but it was more than worth whatever they charged for it.

Then they brought the meal, and at that point I began to wonder if I was losing my mind.

It was *the* meal. The same meal, down to the least spice as the hostess had promised, down to the distinctive Spanish Cadi butter that Angelina had always sworn by. Five dishes: crown roast of pork, broiled merlitons filled with a delicate crawfish-and-remoulade stuffing, honey-poached artichoke hearts, watermelon salad with tomatillo and tamarind, and a selection of petit fours for dessert. I tasted each dish, and flinched as every bite awakened a memory. The pork: lying in Angelina's bed while she practiced techniques in the kitchen, filling the apartment with scents that awakened more than one kind of hunger in me. The petit fours: She'd always been so good with sweets. We'd once made love with a bowl of vanilla-anise sugar she'd made. I'd drizzled it between her breasts and been fascinated by the unique taste even as she giggled and wriggled to reach my sugared parts. We were high on sugar and youth and love and we'd believed nothing could ever separate us—

I looked up at Yvette, who raised her eyebrows pointedly at me.

"How can this be?" I asked.

"No one knows," she said. "They don't tell, and I haven't asked."

I stared at her. "What did you order? The first time?"

Her smile never faltered, but her gaze grew distant and wistful. I wondered whether she, too, was remembering her first love.

"That doesn't matter," she said. "But I have no doubt that they got it right, because I was crying by dessert."

"I want to see the kitchen," I said at the end of the meal.

"I'm sorry, sir, but that's not permitted," said the hostess.

"Then I'd like to meet the chef."

"I'm afraid that can't be done either. I'm very sorry."

"Leave it, Harold," Yvette said. "Do you have to question everything?"

Not everything. Just this. Just the fact that they had perfectly captured the taste of one of the sweetest nights of my life, and left my heart aching eight ways to Sunday. "There has to be some trick to this," I said. "How could they know? How could they get it right? Did you tell them?"

"Of course not. I know you and Angelina met while she was in school, but I didn't know you were even there for her certification exam, and I certainly don't know what you ate."

"You were friends with her. She must have told you."

"I was friends with *both* of you," Yvette replied. "But more with you than her. Frankly I haven't seen her since you two split, and before that, we certainly didn't go gabbing with each other over all and sundry. I think she was always a little suspicious of me." She gave me a wry smile.

Yvette and I had been friends since Tulane, in one of those bizarre mélanges that never seemed to happen outside university walls—the Southern belle and the New York Jew, old money and new, nothing but our souls in common. We'd been close enough to alarm her parents and revolt mine, united by her jaded wit and my cynicism. (Our parents needn't have worried; we knew better.) We talked to each other about everything. But it wasn't Yvette who had broken up Angelina and me. That had been my fault.

"How could they know?" I asked again, and she sighed and put a hand on mine.

"Does it really matter, Harold? It's a memory. Did you question it the first time it happened? Then don't question it now."

"I want to come back here," I said.

The hostess gave me a bright smile and opened a heavy book bound in black leather. "We have an opening in July. Would you like a reservation?"

"Yes, I'll—" I started. It was August. "Next *year?*"

She nodded, her lovely eyes dark with sympathy. "This is another reason we limit our clientele, sir. I'm very sorry."

In the end, I took the reservation. Yvette was pleased; she thought I wanted to bring someone else here, and she needled me to find out who. The truth was that I had no plans to bring anyone else. I just wanted to see the place again, get another chance at fathoming its secret. The hunger to *know* burned in me right alongside the warm satisfaction of the meal itself, and underneath all of that lay anger. It was irrational anger, I knew. Someone had looked into my heart and found a long-forgotten moment of love, plucked it forth and dusted it off and polished it up and shoved it back in, sharp and shiny and powerful as it had been on the day the memory was made. But I didn't have Angelina anymore, and that turned the memory from one of sweetness into one of pain.

So I had to know how they'd done it.

That was why, when the server returned to inquire whether we needed anything, I smiled up at him and asked, "Where's your restroom?"

The bathroom was as quaint as the rest of the place—wood-paneled, containing a side-by-side toilet and bidet and an enormous porcelain sink in the style of Louis the XIV's Versailles, though of course it had to be a replica as well. I was tempted to try the bidet just for kicks, but I had more important experiments to undertake, and so I slipped out of the bathroom as quietly as I could.

Yvette suspected what I was up to. It hadn't been difficult to read her face while the server gave me instructions to reach the men's room. But she said nothing, merely sighing and shaking her head as I walked away. There was a part of me which worried whether our friendship would survive this night. Jaded or not, Yvette had a powerful sense of propriety, and I was testing its limits, I knew. But I had no choice. I had to know.

The bathroom was at the end of a narrow, dimly lit corridor around a corner from the dining room. At the far end of the corridor was a spiral staircase leading down. That in itself was suspicious. Even in the 1800s, New Orleans had been New Orleans, where the dead could not be buried below ground and dowsers ran mad in white linen, and basements were as mythical as unicorns. I lurked in the corridor awhile, pretending to fumble for a cigarette as another waiter came up the steps with a heavy tray balanced on the fingertips of one hand. As soon as he'd gone 'round the corner to the dining room, I crept to the staircase and hurried down. I could hear the sounds of a busy kitchen below, clanking plates and sizzling food and orders being called back and forth in barely intelligible dialect. Were there four chefs? Five? My heart began to pound as I descended the stairs and the light brightened around me. They would see me the moment I reached the bottom of the stairwell. I would tell them I had gotten lost, looking for the bathroom, very sorry you understand—

I reached the bottom step, and silence fell.

The kitchen was empty.

I blinked, unsure of my eyes for a moment. When I opened them, I saw what I had before: a stainless-steel, perfectly modern industrial kitchen, so spick-and-span that its every surface gleamed. And it was completely empty. There were no chefs at work, though I knew I'd heard voices; there were no plates half-filled, no pans sizzling over leaping flames. There were no flames. If this kitchen had ever been used, there was no sign of it.

I took a step forward, and the kitchen changed.

Where there had been bright light and gleaming antiseptic surfaces, now basket-crowded shelves lined sooty stone walls. The only light in the place came from a few candles, and a briskly burning fire at the hearth—*hearth?*—nearby. Where there had been a starkly empty chamber, now three men bustled frantically about a claustrophobic kitchen, one of them shouting orders in French—true French, not the New Orleans patois—at two others who hastened to obey. The pan that he moved back and forth over a black iron stove was aflame, its ingredients filling the air with the aroma of garlic and cilantro and perhaps brandy.

"What?" It was the most intelligent question I could come up with. "Who?"

The chefs ignored me; they were too busy. Where had the steel kitchen gone? What had just happened? I would have to brave the head chef's wrath for answers. So I took another step forward, intending to touch the man on the shoulder. But as my foot touched the floor tiles, the kitchen changed again, and this time I stiffened in a shock so profound that if I'd been an Orthodox man, I would have said G-d had tapped me on the shoulder.

Angelina.

The stainless steel kitchen had returned, though it was not the same kitchen I had seen first. The configuration was different. The tiny part of me that paid attention to such irrelevancies recognized the place: the examination kitchen of the American National Culinary Institute.

Angelina stood at a counter, tipping the bones of a crown roast with paper frills. All around her lay the signs of a massive culinary undertaking: emptied pots, a plate of stuffed mirlitons lacking only garnish, a genoise sheet cake drizzled with amaretto liqueur, a mixer holding a bowl of what looked like fondant icing. Angelina's brow was furrowed with concentration, her movements brisk yet controlled, her face taut with that strange intensity that I knew so well. Back during our marriage, she had gotten that look with me sometimes. I'd been unnerved by it at first—was I the right man for her? did it bother her that I was losing my hair?—until I'd finally recalled seeing the same look on her face when she made her best dishes. It was a look she devoted to the most important parts of her life.

So many questions flooded my mind as I watched her move about the kitchen. How had she gotten here? How long had she been working in this strange place? She'd become head chef at the Commander's Palace restaurant two years before. Her work was already keeping her from me for more hours than I liked; the new job would've meant seeing her only on her days off, and maybe a few minutes in the evening before bed. I'd put my foot down. *If you love me, you won't take that job,* I'd said. And she had said, *You've never understood me.*

Angelina.

"I want to understand you," I whispered. Two years unraveled in my mind. I was there on that fateful night again, demanding that she choose between her calling and me, never realizing that even to ask was to tear her in two. That had been the end of the marriage, though it limped along another six months after that. "I didn't understand, you were right, but I want to try again. Please, sweetheart? I just want to say I'm sor—"

I stepped forward again and she vanished. The empty, antiseptic kitchen returned.

"Sir." It was the hostess. I turned to see her standing at the foot of the steps, her beautiful face a study in disappointment. "You should not be here."

"Angelina," I said. It was a plea.

Disappointment turned to pity, and the hostess sighed, coming forward to take my hands. "Just a moment in time, sir. If you tried to touch her, she would vanish. If you spoke, she did not hear. We can only recapture the past in the merest slivers—a taste, and nothing more. You could stay here and watch her make your meal over and over again, but what good would that do? Come."

She pulled me back toward the spiral staircase. I was terrified to lift my feet again, but nothing happened when I finally did. Somehow, the hostess held me in the present. I did not know whether to be relieved or disappointed by that.

"What is this place?" I asked. My voice shook.

"Just a restaurant," she replied with a smile.

"But—what I saw—"

"Ah, that," she said. "I must remind you of the agreement you signed, sir. You've done no harm by this—except perhaps to yourself—but please remember, every good restaurant has its secrets."

Some of my shock was fading; a flicker of the old skepticism returned. "Is that a threat?"

She stopped at the top of the steps and looked at me in pure wonder. "Sir, the agreement is for *your* protection as much as ours. Or does it not occur to you how others will react, if you tell them what you just saw?"

I stopped short and stared at her. There was genuine concern in her manner. And she was right, of course, because even in New Orleans no one really believed in voodoo or time-slips or whatever the hell simmered in the kitchen of the Maison Laveau. One of the oldest insane asylums in the country was just a little ways up the river, after all.

"Now come," she said, taking my hand again and patting it in that familiar, motherly Southern manner. "You've left your lady friend waiting all this time; that's most unkind of you, sir. She's been worried."

Worried? I doubted that. *Furious* was far more likely. Still, I followed the hostess back to the dining room, bracing myself. That was when I had yet another shock, for the relief that flowed into Yvette's face made me realize that she had, indeed, been worried rather than angry. I sat down across from her again and could not meet her eyes for shame.

"Shall I bring the check, madame?" the hostess asked.

"Please," Yvette said. When the hostess left, she sighed and shook her head at me. "You're a fool, Harold."

"I'm sorry," I said. In hindsight, my earlier anger seemed like a fever dream; I couldn't believe I'd been so inconsiderate. "Will this hurt your standing with the restaurant?"

"Probably not," she said. "Yours either. But that's the least of the problem, Harold. Do you have any idea what could've happened to you?"

Visions of the police escorting me out of the restaurant and right into involuntary commitment went through my mind. Visions of Yvette scorning me thereafter—which could still happen, I knew—followed. "I'm sorry," I said again, knowing that it was wholly inadequate. "I just had to know."

She shook her head, rubbing her temple as if her head ached. "People can get *lost* in their memories, Harold," she said. "You're worse at it than anyone else I know. Angelina's alive, right here in this city, and all you've ever had to do was call her. But what do you do? You go looking for the Angelina you lost years ago. I don't know what to do with you."

The male server swept by and deposited the bill so smoothly that

I hardly even noticed. Yvette picked it up, scribbled something on the slip, and handed me the envelope containing my NDA photocopy. "Let's go."

I got up and held her coat for her, taking it as a small positive sign that she deigned to let me drape it over her shoulders. Still, she wasn't going to let me forget this for quite some time, and I couldn't really say I blamed her. She'd given me the most amazing birthday gift in the world, and I'd tried to take it apart to see how it worked.

Still...

"If you could have only seen it, Yvette," I said as we walked to the door. I was conscious of the servers moving past us, and the hostess up ahead; I kept my voice low. "The kitchen...it's the most amazing thing."

"Don't tell me," she said. "I want to keep my memories sweet."

"Until July, sir," said the hostess as we left. "Au revoir."

Yvette eventually forgave me, although it took some doing. In the end I had to offer her something of value equal to my insult—an introduction in this case, to a wealthy and recently widowed gentleman client of mine. Last I heard, they were planning a vacation together in Monaco.

It kept at me, though, the things she'd said, and the hostess's pity. Was it really wrong of me to remember the past fondly? It wasn't, of course it wasn't—but the past was an easy meal, after all. I could taste it again anytime I wanted, in memory, and it would always be perfect and true. The here-and-now, though, had no recipe. It might be sour or bitter or raw. And yet.

In July, I canceled my reservation to the Maison Laveau. And in August, I gave Angelina a call.

Stone Hunger

Once there was a girl who lived in a beautiful place full of beautiful people who made beautiful things. Then the world broke.

Now the girl is older, and colder, and hungrier. From the shelter of a dead tree, she watches as a city—a rich one, big, with high strong walls and well-guarded gates—winches its roof into place against the falling chill of night. The girl has never seen anything like this city's roof. She's watched the city for days, fascinated by its rib cage of metal tracks and the strips of sewn, oiled material they pull along it. They must put out most of their fires when they do this, or they would choke on smoke—but perhaps with the strips in place, the city retains warmth enough to make fires unnecessary.

It will be nice to be warm again. The girl shifts her weight from one fur-wrapped thigh to the other, her only concession to anticipation.

The tree in whose skeletal branches she crouches is above the city, on a high ridge, and it is one of the few still standing. The city has to burn something, after all, and the local ground does not have the flavor of coal-land, sticky veins of pent smoky bitterness lacing through cool bedrock. In the swaths of forest the city-dwellers have taken, even the stumps are gone; nothing wasted. The rest has been left relatively unmolested, though the girl has noted a suspicious absence of deadfall and kindling wood on the shadowed forest floor below. Perhaps they've left this stand of trees as a windbreak, or to keep the ridge stable. Whatever their reasons, the city-dwellers' forethought works in her favor. They will not see her stalking them, waiting for an opportunity, until it is too late.

And perhaps, if she is lucky—

No. She has never been lucky. The girl closes her eyes again, tasting the land and the city. It is the most distinctive city she has ever encountered. Such a complexity of sweets and meats and bitters and...sour.

Hmm.

Perhaps.

The girl settles her back against the trunk of the tree, wraps the tattered blanket from her pack more closely around herself, and sleeps.

Dawn comes as a thinning of the gray sky. There has been no sun for years.

The girl wakes because of hunger: a sharp pang of it, echo of long-ago habit. Once, she ate breakfast in the mornings. Unsated, the pang eventually fades to its usual omnipresent ache.

Hunger is good, though. Hunger will help.

The girl sits up, feeling imminence like an intensifying itch. *It's coming.* She climbs down from the tree—easily; handholds were gnawed into the trunk by ground animals in the early years, before that species disappeared—and walks to the edge of the ridge. Dangerous to do this, stand on a ridge with a shake coming, but she needs to scout for an ideal location. Besides; she knows the shake isn't close. Yet.

There.

The walk down into the valley is more difficult than she expects. There are no paths. She has to half climb, half slide down dry runnels in the rock face which are full of loose gravel-sized ash. And she is not at her best after starving for eight days. Her limbs go weak now and again. There will be food in the city, she reminds herself, and moves a little faster.

She makes it to the floor of the valley and crouches behind a cluster of rocks near the half-dried-up river. The city gates are still hundreds of feet away, but there are familiar notches along its walls. Lookouts, perhaps with longviewers; she knows from experience that cities have the resources to make good glass—and good weapons. Any closer and they'll see her, unless something distracts them.

Once there was a girl who waited. And then, at last, the distraction arrives. A shake.

The epicenter is not nearby. That's much farther north: yet another reverberation of the rivening that destroyed the world. Doesn't matter. The girl breathes hard and digs her fingers into the dried riverbed as power rolls toward her. She *tastes* the vanguard of it sliding along her tongue, leaving a residue to savor, like thick and sticky treats—

(It is not real, what she tastes. She knows this. Her father once spoke of it as the sound of a chorus, or a cacophony; she's heard others complain of foul smells, painful sensations. For her, it is food. This seems only appropriate.)

—and it is easy—delicious!—to reach farther down. To visualize herself opening her mouth and lapping at that sweet flow of natural force. She sighs and relaxes into the rarity of pleasure, unafraid for once, letting her guard down shamelessly and guiding the energy with only the merest brush of her will. A tickle, not a push. A lick.

Around the girl, pebbles rattle. She splays herself against the ground like an insect, fingernails scraping rock, ear pressed hard to the cold and gritty stone.

Stone. *Stone.*

Stone like gummy fat, like slick warm syrups she vaguely remembers licking from her fingers, stone flowing, pushing, curling, slow and inexorable as toffee. Then this oncoming power, the wave that ripples the stone, stops against the great slab of bedrock that comprises this valley and its surrounding mountains. The wave wants to go around, spend its energy elsewhere, but the girl sucks against this resistance. It takes a while. On the ground, she writhes in place and smacks her lips and makes a sound: *"Ummmah."*

Then the

Oh, the pressure

Once there was a girl who ground her teeth against prrrrrresssure *bursts*, the inertia *breaks*, and the wave of force ripples into the valley. The land seems to inhale, rising and groaning beneath her, and it is hers, it's *hers*. She controls it. The girl laughs; she can't help herself. It feels so good to be full, in one way or another.

A jagged crack steaming with friction opens and widens from where the girl lies to the foot of the ridge on which she spent the previous night. The entire face of the cliff splits off and disintegrates, gathering momentum and strength as it avalanches toward the city's southern wall. The girl adds force in garnishing dollops, oh-so-carefully. Too much and she will smash the entire valley into rubble, city and all, leaving nothing useful. She does not destroy; she merely damages. But just enough and—

The shake stops.

The girl feels the interference at once. The sweet flow solidifies; something taints its flavor in a way that makes her recoil. Hints of bitter and sharp—

—and *vinegar*, at last, for certain, she isn't imagining it this time, *vinegar*—

—and then all the marvelous power she has claimed dissipates. There is no compensatory force; nothing *uses* it. It's simply gone. Someone else has beaten her to the banquet and eaten all the treats. But the girl no longer cares that her plan has failed.

"I found you." She pushes herself up from the dry riverbed, her hair dripping flecks of ash. She is trembling, not just with hunger anymore, her eyes fixed on the city's unbroken wall. *"I found you."*

The momentum of the shake rolls onward, passing beyond the girl's reach. Though the ground has stopped moving, the ridge rockslide cannot be stopped: boulders and trees, including the tree that sheltered the girl the night before, break loose and tumble down to slam against the city's protective wall, probably cracking it. But this is nowhere near the level of damage that the girl had hoped for. How will she get inside? She *must* get inside now.

Ah—the gates of the city crank open. A way in. But the city-dwellers are angry now. They might kill her, or worse.

She rises, runs. The days without food have left her little strength and poor speed, but fear supplies some fuel. Yet the stones turn against her now, and she stumbles, slips on loose rocks. She knows better than to waste time looking back.

Hooves drum the ground, a thousand tiny shakes that refuse to obey her will.

Once there was a girl who awoke in a prison cell.

It's dark, but she can see the metal grate of a door not far off. The bed is softer than anything she's slept on in months, and the air is warm. Or *she* is warm. She evaluates the fever that burns under her skin and concludes that it is dangerously high. She's not hungry either, though her belly is as empty as ever. A bad sign.

This may have something to do with the fact that her leg aches like a low, monotonous scream. Two screams. Her upper thigh burns, but the knee feels as though shards of ice have somehow inserted themselves into the joint. She wants to try and flex it, see if it can move enough to bear her weight, but it hurts so much already that she is afraid to try.

She remains still, listening before opening her eyes, a habit that has saved her life before. Distant sound of voices, echoing along corridors that stink of rust and mildewed mortar. No breath or movement nearby. Sitting up carefully, the girl touches the cloth that covers her. Scratchy, patchy. Warmer than her own blanket, wherever that is. She will steal this one, if she can, when she escapes.

Then she freezes, startled, because there is someone in the room with her. A man.

But the man does not move, does not even breathe; just stands there. And now she can see that what she thought was skin is marble. A statue. A statue?

It's hard to think through the clamor of fever and pain, even the air sounds loud in her ears, but she decides at last that the city-dwellers have peculiar taste in art.

She hurts. She's tired. She sleeps.

"You tried to kill us," says a woman's voice.

The girl blinks awake again, disoriented for a moment. A lantern burns something smoky in a sconce above her. Her fever has faded. She's still thirsty, but not as parched as before. A memory comes to her of people in the room, tending her wounds, giving her broth tinged with bitterness; this memory is distant and strange. She must have been half delirious at the time. She's still hungry—she is always hungry—but that need, too, is not as bad as it was. Even the fire and ice in her leg have subsided.

The girl turns to regard her visitor. The woman sits straddling an old wooden chair, her arms propped on its back. The girl does not have enough experience of other people to guess her age. Older than herself; not elderly. And big, with broad shoulders made broader by layers of clothing and fur, heavy black boots. Her hair, a poufing mane as gray and stiff as ash-killed grass, has been thickened further by plaits and knots which are either decoration or an attempt to keep the mass of it out of her eyes. Her face is broad and angular, her skin sallow-brown like the girl's own.

(The statue that was in the corner is gone. Once there was a girl who hallucinated while in a fever.)

"You would've torn down half our southern wall," the woman continues. "Probably destroyed one or more storecaches. That kind of thing is enough to kill a city these days. Wounds draw scavengers."

This is true. It would not have been her intention, of course. She tries to be a successful parasite, not killing off her host; she inflicts only enough damage to get inside undetected. And while the city was busy repairing itself and fighting off the enemies who would have come, the girl could have survived unnoticed within its walls for some time. She has done this elsewhere. She could have prowled its alleys, nibbled at its foundations, searching always for the taste of vinegar. *He is here somewhere.*

And if she fails to find him in time, if he does to this city what he has done elsewhere... well. She would not kill a city herself, but she'll fatten herself off the carcass before she takes up his trail again. Anything else would be wasteful.

The woman waits a moment, then sighs as if she expected no response. "I'm Ykka. I assume you have no name?"

"Of course I have a name," the girl snaps.

Ykka waits. Then she snorts. "You look, what, fourteen? Under-fed, so let's say eighteen. You were a small child when the rivening happened, but you're not feral now—much—so someone must have raised you for a while afterward. Who?"

The girl turns away in disinterest. "You going to kill me?"

"What will you do if I say yes?"

The girl sets her jaw. The walls of her cell are panels of steel bolted together, and the floor is joined planks of wood over a dirt floor. But such *thin* metal. So *little* wood. She imagines squeezing her tongue between the slats of the floor, licking away the layers of filth underneath—she's eaten worse—and finally touching the foundation. Concrete. Through that, she can touch the valley floor. The stone will be flavorless and cold, cold enough to make her tongue stick, because there's nothing to heat it up—no shake or aftershake. And the valley is nowhere near a fault or hotspot, so no blows or bubbles either. But there are other ways to warm stone. Other warmth and movement she can use.

Using the warmth and movement of the air around her, for example. Or the warmth and movement within a living body. If she takes this from Ykka, it won't give her much. Not enough for a real shake; she would need more people for that. But she might be able to jolt the floor of her cell, warp that metal door enough to jiggle the lock free. Ykka will be dead, but some things cannot be helped.

The girl reaches for Ykka, her mouth watering in spite of herself—

A clashing flavor interrupts her. Spice like cinnamon. Not so bad. But the bite of the spice grows sharper as she tries to grasp the power, until suddenly it is fire and *burning* and a crisp green taste that makes her eyes water and her guts churn—

With a gasp, the girl snaps her eyes open. The woman smiles, and the back of the girl's neck prickles with belated, jarring recognition.

"Answer enough," Ykka says lightly, though there is cold fury in her eyes. "We'll have to move you to a better cell if you have the sensitivity to work through steel and wood. Lucky for us, you've been too weak to try before now." She pauses. "If you had succeeded just now, would you have only killed me? Or the whole city?"

Still shocked to find herself in the company of her own, the girl answers honestly before she can think not to. "Not the whole city. I don't kill cities."

"What is that, some kind of integrity?" Ykka snorts a laugh.

There's no point in answering the question. "I would've just killed as many people as I needed to get loose."

"And then what?"

The girl shrugs. "Find something to eat. Somewhere warm to hole up." She does not add, *Find the vinegar man.* It will make no sense to Ykka anyway.

"Food, warmth, and shelter. Such simple wants." There is mockery in Ykka's voice, and it annoys the girl. "You could do with fresh clothes. A good wash. Someone to talk to, maybe, so you can start thinking of other people as valuable."

The girl scowls. "What do you want from me?"

"To see if you're useful." At the girl's frown, Ykka looks her up and down, perhaps sizing her up. The girl does not have the same bottlebrush hair as Ykka, just scraggling brown stuff she chops off with her knife whenever it gets long enough to annoy. She is small and lean and quick, when she is not injured. No telling what Ykka thinks of these traits. No telling why she cares. The girl just hopes she does not appear weak.

"Have you done this to other cities?" Ykka asks.

The question is so patently stupid that there's no point in answering. After a moment Ykka nods. "Thought so. You seem to know what you're about."

"I learned early how it was done."

"Oh?"

The girl decides she has said enough. But before she can make a point of silence, there is another ripple across her perception, followed by something that is unmistakably a jolt within the earth. Specks of mortar trickle from beneath a loose panel on the cell wall. Another shake? No, the deep earth is still cold. That jolt was more shallow, delicate, just a goose bump on the world's skin.

"You can ask what that was," Ykka says, noticing her confusion. "I might even answer."

The girl sets her jaw and Ykka laughs, getting to her feet. She is even bigger than she seemed while sitting, a solid six feet or more. Pureblooded Sanzed; half the races of the world have that bottlebrush hair, but the size is the giveaway. Sanzed breed for strength, so they can protect themselves when the world turns hard.

"You left the southern ridge unstable," Ykka says. "We needed to make repairs." Then she waits, one hand on her hip, while the girl makes the necessary connections. It doesn't take long. The woman is like her. (Taste of savory pepper stinging her mouth still. Disgusting.) But someone entirely different caused that shift a moment ago, and although their presence is like melon—pale, delicate, flavorlessly cloying—it holds a faint aftertaste of blood.

Two in one city? Their kind know better. Hard enough for one wolf to hide among the sheep. But wait—there were two more, right when she split the southern ridge. One of them was a different taste altogether, bitter, something she has never eaten so she cannot name it. The other was the vinegar man.

Four in one city. And this woman is so very interested in her usefulness. She stares at Ykka. No one would do that.

Ykka shakes her head, amusement fading. "I think you're a waste of time and food," she says, "but it's not my decision alone. If you try to harm the city again, we'll feel it, and we'll stop you, and then we'll kill you. But if you don't cause trouble, we'll know you're at least trainable. Oh—and stay off the leg if you ever want to walk again."

Then Ykka goes to the grate door and barks something in another language. A man comes down the hall and lets her out. The two of them look in at the girl for a long moment before heading down the hall and through another door.

In the new silence, the girl sits up. This must be done slowly; she is very weak. Her bedding reeks of fever sweat, though it is dry now. When she throws off the patch blanket, she sees that she has no pants on. There is a bandage around her right thigh at the midpoint: The wound underneath radiates infection lines, though they seem to be fading. Her knee has also been wrapped tightly with wide leather bandages. She tries to flex it and a sickening ripple of pain radiates up and down the leg, like aftershocks from her own personal rivening. What did she do to it? She remembers running from people on horseback. Falling, amid rocks as jagged as knives.

The vinegar man will not linger long in this city. She knows this from having tracked his spoor for years. Sometimes there are survivors in the towns he's murdered, who—if they can be persuaded to speak—tell of the wanderer who camped outside the gates, asking to be let in but not moving on when refused. Waiting, perhaps for a few days; hiding if the townsfolk drove him away. Then strolling in, smug and unmolested, when the walls fell. She has to find him quickly because if he's here, this city is doomed, and she doesn't want to be anywhere near its death throes.

Continuing to push against the bandages' tension, the girl manages to bend the knee perhaps twenty degrees before something that should not move that way slides to one side. There is a wet *click* from somewhere within the joint. Her stomach is empty. She is glad for this as she almost retches from the pain. The heaves pass. She will not be escaping the room, or hunting down the vinegar man, anytime soon.

But when she looks up, someone is in the room with her again. The statue she hallucinated.

It *is* a statue, her mind insists—though, plainly, it is not a hallucination. Study of a man in contemplation: tall, gracefully poised, the head tilted to one side with a frank and thoughtful expression molded into its face. That face is marbled gray and white, though inset with eyes of—she guesses—alabaster and onyx. The artist who sculpted this creation has applied incredible detail, even carving lashes and little lines in the lips. Once, the girl knew beauty when she saw it.

She also thinks that the statue was not present a moment ago. In fact, she's certain of this.

"Would you like to leave?" the statue asks, and the girl scrambles back as much as her damaged leg—and the wall—allows.

There is a pause.

"S-stone-eater," she whispers.

"Girl." Its lips do not move when it speaks. The voice comes from somewhere within its torso. The stories say that the stuff of a stone-eater's body is not quite rock, but still far different from—and less flexible than—flesh.

The stories also say that stone-eaters do not exist, except in stories about stone-eaters. The girl licks her lips.

"What…" Her voice breaks. She pulls herself up straighter and flinches when she forgets her knee. It very much does not want to be forgotten. She focuses on other things. "Leave?"

The stone-eater's head does not move, but its eyes shift ever-so-slightly. Tracking her. She has the sudden urge to hide under the blanket to escape its gaze, but then what if she peeks out and finds the creature right in front of her, peering back in?

"They'll move you to a more secure cell soon." It is shaped like a man, but her mind refuses to apply the pronoun to something so obviously not human. "You'll have a harder time reaching stone there. I can take you to bare ground."

"Why?"

"So that you can destroy the city, if you still want to." Casual, calm, its voice. It is indestructible, the stories say. One cannot stop a stone-eater, only get out of its way.

"You'll have to fight Ykka and the others, however," it continues. "This is their city, after all."

This is almost enough to distract the girl from the stone-eater's looming strangeness. "No one would do that," she says, stubborn. The world hates what she is; she learned that early on. Those of her kind eat the power of the earth and spit it back as force and destruction. When the earth is quiet, they eat anything else they can find— the warmth of the air, the movement of living things—to achieve the same effect. They cannot live among ordinary people. They would be discovered with the first shake, or the first murder.

The stone-eater moves, and seeing this causes chilly sweat to rise on the girl's skin. It is slow, stiff. She hears a faint sound like the grind of a tomb's cover-stone. Now the creature faces her, and its thoughtful expression has become wry.

"There are twenty-three of you in this city," it says. "And many more of the other kind, of course." Ordinary people, she guesses by its dismissive tone. Hard to tell, because her mind has set its teeth in that first sentence. Twenty-three. *Twenty-three.*

Belatedly, she realizes the stone-eater is still waiting for an answer to its question. "H-how would you take me out of the cell?" she asks.

"I'd carry you."

Let the stone-eater touch her. She tries not to let it see her shudder, but its lips adjust in a subtle way. Now the statue has a carved, slight smile. The monster is amused to be found monstrous.

"I'll return later," it says. "When you're stronger."

Then its form, which does not vibrate on her awareness the way people do but is instead as still and solid as a mountain—shimmers. She can see through it. It drops into the floor as though a hole has opened under its feet, although the grimy wooden slats are perfectly solid.

The girl takes several deep breaths and sits back against the wall. The metal is cold through her clothing.

They move the girl to a cell whose floor is wood over metal. The walls are wood, too, and padded with leather sewn over thick layers of cotton. There are chains set into the floor here, but thankfully they do not use them on her.

They bring the girl food: broth with yeast flakes, coarse flat cakes that taste of fungus, sprouted grains wrapped in dried leaves. She eats and grows stronger. After several days have passed, during which the girl's digestive system begins cautiously working again, the guards give her crutches. While they watch, she experiments until she can use them reliably, with minimal pain. Then they bring her to a room where naked people scrub themselves around a shallow pool of circulating steaming water. When she has finished bathing, the guards card her hair for lice. (She has none. Lice come from being around other people.) Finally they give her clothing: undershorts, loose pants of some sort of plant fiber, a second tighter pair of pants made of animal skin, two shirts, a bra she's too scrawny to need, fur-lined shoes. She dons it all greedily. It's nice to be warm.

They bring her back to her cell, and the girl climbs carefully into the bed. She's stronger, but still weak; she tires easily. The knee cannot bear her weight yet. The crutches are worse than useless—she cannot *sneak* anywhere while noisily levering herself about. The frustration of this chews at her, because the vinegar man is out there, and she fears he will leave—or strike—before she can heal. Yet flesh is flesh, and hers has endured too much of late. It demands its due. She can do nothing but obey.

After she rests for a time, however, she becomes aware that something vast and mountain-still and familiar is in the room again. She opens her eyes to see the stone-eater still and silent in front of the cell's door. This time it has a hand upraised, the palm open and ready. An invitation.

The girl sits up. "Can you help me find someone?"

"Who?"

"A man. A man, like—" She has no idea how to communicate it in a way the stone-eater will understand. Does it even distinguish between one human and another? She has no idea how it thinks.

"Like you?" the stone-eater prompts, when she trails off.

She fights back the urge to immediately reject this characterization. "Another who can do what I do, yes." One of twenty-three. This is a problem she never expected to have.

The stone-eater is silent for a moment. "Share him with me."

The girl does not understand this. But its hand is still there, proffered, waiting, so she pushes herself to her feet and, with the aid of the crutches, hobbles over. When she reaches for its hand, there is an instant in which every part of her revolts against the notion of touching its strange marbled skin. Bad enough to stand near where she can see that it does not breathe, notice that it does not blink, realize her every instinct warns against tasting it with that part of herself that knows stone. She thinks that if she tries, its flavor will be bitter almonds and burning sulfur, and then she will die.

And yet.

Reluctantly, she thinks of the beautiful place, which she has not allowed herself to remember for years. Once upon a time there was a girl who had food every day and warmth all the time, and in that place were people who gave these things to her, unasked, completely free. They gave her other things, too—things she does not want now, does not need anymore, like companionship and a name and feelings beyond hunger and anger. That place is gone now. Murdered. Only she remains, to avenge it.

She takes the stone-eater's hand. Its skin is cool and yields slightly to the touch; her arms break out in gooseflesh, and the skin of her palm crawls. She hopes it does not notice.

It waits, until she recalls its request. So she closes her eyes and remembers the vinegar man's sharp-sweet taste, and hopes that it can somehow feel this through her skin.

"Ah," the stone-eater says. "I do know that one."

The girl licks her lips. "I'm going to kill him."

"You're going to try." Its smile is a fixed thing.

"Why are you helping me?"

"I told you. The others will fight you."

This makes no sense. "Why don't you destroy the city yourself, if you hate it so much?"

"I don't hate the city. I have no interest in destroying it." Its hand tightens ever-so-slightly, a hint of pressure from the deepest places of the earth. "Shall I take you to him?"

It is a warning, and a promise. The girl understands: She must accept its offer now, or it will be rescinded. And in the end, it doesn't matter why the stone-eater helps her.

"Take me to him," she says.

The stone-eater pulls her closer, folding its free arm around her shoulders with the slow, grinding inexorability of a glacier. She stands trembling against its solid inhumanity, looking into its too-white, too-dark eyes and clutching her crutches tight with her arms. It hasn't ever stopped smiling. She notices, and does not know why she notices, that it smiles with its lips closed.

"Don't be afraid," it says without opening its mouth, and the world blurs around her. There is a stifling sense of enclosure and pressure, of friction-induced heat, a flicking darkness and a feel of deep earth moving around her, so close that she cannot just taste it; she also feels and breathes and *is* it.

Then they stand in a quiet courtyard of the city. The girl looks around, startled by the sudden return of light and cold air and spaciousness, and does not even notice the stone-eater's movements this time as it slowly releases her and steps back. It is daytime. The city's roof is rolled back and the sky is its usual melancholy gray, weeping ashen snow. From inside, the city feels smaller than she'd imagined. The buildings are low but close together, nearly all of them squat and round and dome-shaped. She's seen this style of building in other cities; good for conserving heat and withstanding shakes.

No one else is around. The girl turns to the stone-eater, tense.

"There." Its arm is already raised, pointing to a building at the end of a narrow road. It is a larger dome than the rest, with smaller subsidiaries branching off its sides. "He's on the second floor."

The girl watches the stone-eater for a moment longer and it watches her back, a gently smiling signpost. *That way to revenge.* She turns and follows its pointing finger.

No one notices her as she crutches along, though she is a stranger; this means the city's big enough that not everyone knows everyone else. The people she passes are of many races, many ages. Sanzed like Ykka predominate, or maybe they are Cebaki; she never learned tell one from another. There are many black-lipped Regwo, and one Shearar woman with big moon-pale eyes. The girl wonders if they know of the twenty-three. They must. Her kind cannot live among ordinary people without eventually revealing themselves. Usually they can't live among ordinary people at all—and yet here, somehow, they do.

Yet as she passes narrower streets and gaps in the buildings, she glimpses something else, something worse, that suddenly explains why no one's worried about twenty-four people who each could destroy a city on a whim. In the shadows, on the sidewalks, nearly camouflaged by the ash-colored walls: too-still standing figures. Statues whose eyes shift to follow her. *Many* of them: She counts a dozen before she makes herself stop.

Once there was a city full of monsters, of whom the girl was just another one.

No one stops her from going into the large dome. Inside, this building is warmer than the one in which she was imprisoned. People move in and out of it freely, some in knots of twos and threes, talking, carrying tools or paper. As the girl moves through its corridors, she spies small ceramic braziers in each room which emit a fragrant scent as well as heat. There are stacks of long-dead flowers in the kindling piles.

The stairs nearly kill her. It takes some time to figure out a method of crutching her way up that does not force her to bend the damaged knee. She stops after the third set to lean against a wall, trembling and sweating. The days of steady food have helped, but she is still healing, and she has never been physically strong. It will not do for her to meet the vinegar man and collapse at his feet.

"You all right?"

The girl blinks damp hair out of her eyes. She's in a wide corridor lined by braziers; there is a long, patterned rug—pre-rivening luxury—beneath her feet. The man standing there is as small as she is, which is the only reason she does not react by jerking away from his nearness. He's nearly as pale as the stone-eater, though his skin is truly skin and his hair is stiff because he is probably part Sanzed. He has a cheerful face, which is set in polite concern as he watches her.

And the girl flinches when she instinctively reaches out to taste her surroundings and he tastes of sharp, sour vinegar, the flavor of smelly pickles and old preserved things and wine gone rancid, and it is him, it is *him, she knows his taste.*

"I'm from Arquin," she blurts. The smile freezes on the man's face, making her think of the stone-eater again.

Once there was a city called Arquin, far to the south. It had been a city of artists and thinkers, a beautiful place full of beautiful people, of whom the girl's parents were two. When the world broke—as it often breaks, as the rivening is only the latest exemplary apocalypse of many—Arquin buttoned up against the chill and locked its gates and hunkered down to endure until the world healed and grew warm again. The city had prepared well. Its storecaches were full, its defenses layered and strong; it could have lasted a long time. But then a stranger came to town.

Taut silence, in the wake of the girl's pronouncement.

The man recovers first. His nostrils flare, and he straightens as if to cloak himself in discomfort. "Everyone did what they had to do back then," he says. "You'd have done it, too, if you were me."

Is there a hint of apology in his voice? *Accusation?* The girl bares her teeth. She has not tried to reach the stone beneath the city since she met Ykka. But she reaches now, tracing the pillars in the walls down to the foundation of the building and then deeper, finding and swallowing sweet-mint bedrock cool into herself. There isn't much. There have been no shakes today. But what little power there is, is a balm, soothing away the past few days' helplessness and fear.

The vinegar man stumbles back against the corridor's other wall, reacting to the girl's touch on the bedrock as if to an insult. All at once the sourness of him floods forth like spit, trying to revolt her into letting go. She wants to; he's ruining the taste. But she scowls and bites more firmly into the power, making it hers, refusing to withdraw. His eyes narrow.

Someone comes into the corridor from one of the rooms that branch off it. This stranger says something, loudly; the girl registers that he is calling for Ykka. She barely hears the words. Stone dust is in her mouth. The grind of the deep rock is in her ears. The vinegar man presses in, trying again to wrest control from the girl, and the girl hates him for this. How many years has she spent hungry, cold, afraid, because of him? No, no, she does not begrudge him that, not really, not when she has done just as many terrible things, he's completely right to say *you would, too, you did, too*—but now? Right now, all she wants is power. Is that so much to ask? It's all he's left her.

And she will shake this whole valley to rubble before she lets him take one more thing that is hers.

The rough-sanded wood of the crutches bites into her hands as she bites into imagined stone to brace herself. The earth is still now, its power too deep to reach, and at such times there's nothing left to feed on save the thin gruel of smaller movements, lesser heat. The rose-flavored coals of the nearby braziers. The jerky twitchy strength of limbs and eyes and breathing chests. And, too, she can sup motions for which there are no names: all the infinitesimal floating morsels of the air, all the jittery particles of solid matter. The smaller, fast-swirling motes that comprise these particles.

(Somewhere, outside the earth, there are more people nearby. Other tastes begin to tease her senses: melon, warm beef stew, familiar peppers. The others mean to stop her. She must finish this quickly.)

"Don't you dare," says the vinegar man. The floor shakes, the whole building rattles with the warning force of his rage. Vibrations drum against the girl's feet. "I won't let you—"

He has no chance to finish the warning. The girl remembers soured wine that she once drank after finding it in a crushed Arquin storehouse. She'd been so hungry that she needed something, anything, to keep going. The stuff had tasted of rich malts and hints of fruit. Desperation made even vinegar taste good.

The air in the room grows cold. A circle of frost, radiating out from the girl's feet, rimes the patterned rug. The vinegar man stands within this circle. (Others in the corridor exclaim and back off as the circle grows.) He cries out as frost forms in his hair, on his eyebrows. His lips turn blue; his fingers stiffen. There's more to it than cold: As the girl devours the space between his molecules, the very motion of his atoms, the man's flesh becomes something different, condensing, hardening. In the earth where flavors dwell, he fights; acid burns the girl's throat and roils her belly. Her own ears go numb, and her knee throbs with the cold hard enough to draw tears from her eyes.

But she has swallowed far worse things than pain. And this is the lesson the vinegar man inadvertently taught her when he killed her future, and made her nothing more than a parasite like himself. He is older, crueler, more experienced, perhaps stronger, but survival has never really been the province of the fittest. Merely the hungriest.

Once the vinegar man is dead, Ykka arrives. She steps into the icy circle without fear, though there is a warning tang of crisp green and red heat when the girl turns to face her. The girl backs off. She can't handle another fight right now.

"Congratulations," Ykka drawls, when the girl pulls her awareness out of the earth and wearily, awkwardly, sits down. (The floor is very cold against her backside.) "Got that out of your system?"

A bit dazed, the girl tries to process the words. A small crowd of people stands in the corridor, beyond the icy circle; they are murmuring and staring at her. A black-haired woman, as small and lithe as Ykka is large and immovable, has entered the circle with Ykka; she goes over to the vinegar man and peers at him as if hoping to find anything left of value. There's nothing, though. The girl has left as much of him as he left of her life, on a long-ago day in a once-beautiful place. He's not even a man anymore, just a gray-brown, crumbly lump of ex-flesh half-huddled against the corridor wall. His face is all eyes and bared teeth, one hand an upraised claw.

Beyond Ykka and the crowd, the girl sees something that clears her thoughts at once: the stone-eater, just beyond the others. Watching her and smiling, statue-still.

"He's dead," the black-haired woman says, turning to Ykka. She sounds more annoyed than angry.

"Yes, I rather thought so," Ykka replies. "So what was that all about?"

The girl belatedly realizes Ykka is talking to her. She is exhausted, physically—but inside, her whole being brims with strength and heat and satisfaction. It makes her light-headed, and a little giddy, so she opens her mouth to speak and laughs instead. Even to her own ears, the sound is unsteady, unnerving.

The black-haired woman utters a curse in some language the girl does not know and pulls a knife, plainly intending to rid the city of the girl's mad menace. "Wait," Ykka says.

The woman glares at her. "This little monster just killed Thoroa—"

"Wait," Ykka says again, harder, and this time she stares the black-haired woman down until the furious tension in the woman's shoulders sags into defeat. Then Ykka faces the girl again. Her breath puffs in the chilly air when she speaks. "Why?"

The girl can only shake her head. "He owed me."

"Owed you what? Why?"

She shakes her head again, wishing they would just kill her and get it over with.

Ykka watches her for a long moment, her hard face unreadable. When she speaks again, her voice is softer. "You said you learned early how it was done."

The black-haired woman looks sharply at her. "We've all done what we had to, to survive."

"True," said Ykka. "And sometimes those things come back to bite us."

"She killed a citizen of this city—"

"He owed her. How many people do *you* owe, hmm? You want to pretend we don't all deserve to die for some reason or another?"

The black-haired woman does not answer.

"A city of people like us," the girl says. She's still giddy. It would be easy to make the city shake now, vent the giddiness, but that would force them to kill her when for some impossible reason they seem to be hesitating. "It'll never work. They used to hunt us down before the rivening for good reason."

Ykka smiles as though she knows what the girl is feeling. "They hunt us down now, in most places, for good reason. After all, only one of us could have done this." She gestures vaguely toward the north, where a great jagged red-bleeding crack across the continent has destroyed the world. "But maybe if they didn't treat us like monsters, we wouldn't *be* monsters. I want us to try living like people for a while, see how that goes."

"Going great so far," mutters the black-haired woman, looking at the stone corpse of the vinegar man. Thoroa. Whichever.

Ykka shrugs, but her eyes narrow at the girl. "Someone will probably come looking for you, too, one day."

The girl gazes steadily back, because she has always understood this. She'll do what she has to do, until she can't anymore.

But all at once the girl snaps alert, because the stone-eater is now standing over her. Everyone in the corridor jerks in surprise. None of them saw it move.

"Thank you," it says.

The girl licks her lips, not looking away. One does not turn one's back on a predator. "Welcome." She does not ask why it thanks her.

"And these," Ykka says from beyond the creature, with a sigh which may or may not be resigned, "are our motivation to live together *peacefully*."

Most of the braziers in the corridor are dark, extinguished by the girl in her desperate grab for power. Only the ones at either far end of the corridor, well beyond the ice circle, remain lit. These silhouette the stone-eater's face—though the girl can easily imagine its carved-marble smile.

Wordlessly Ykka comes over, as does the black-haired woman. They help the girl to her feet, all three of them watching the stone-eater warily. The stone-eater doesn't move, either to impede them or to get out of the way. It just keeps standing there until they carry the girl away. Others in the hall, bystanders who did not choose to flee while monsters battled nearby, file out as well—quickly. This is only partly because the corridor is freezing.

"Are you throwing me out of the city?" the girl asks. They have set her down at the foot of the steps. She fumbles with the crutches because her hands are shaking in delayed reaction to the cold and the near-death experience. If they throw her out now, wounded, she'll die slowly. She would rather they kill her, than face that.

"Don't know yet," Ykka says. "You want to go?"

The girl is surprised to be asked. It is strange to have options. She looks up, then, as a sound from above startles her: They are rolling the city's roof shut against the coming night. As the strips of roofing slide into place, the city grows dimmer, although people move along the streets lighting standing lanterns she did not notice before. The roof locks into place with a deep, echoing snap. Already, without cool outside air blowing through the city, it feels warmer.

"I want to stay," the girl hears herself say.

Ykka sighs. The black-haired woman just shakes her head. But they do not call the guards, and when they hear a sound from upstairs, all three of them walk away together, by unspoken mutual agreement. The girl has no idea where they're going. She doesn't think the other two women do, either. It's just understood that they should all be somewhere else.

Because the girl keeps seeing the corridor they just left, in the moment before they carried her down stairs. She'd glanced back, see. The stone-eater had moved again; it stood beside Thoroa's petrified corpse. Its hand rested on his shoulder, companionably. And this time as it smiled, it flashed tiny, perfect, diamond teeth.

The girl takes a deep breath to banish this image from her mind.

Then she asks of Ykka as they walk, "Is there anything to eat?"

On the Banks of the River Lex

Death lay under the water tower on a sagging rooftop, watching the slow condensation of water along the tower's metal belly. Occasionally one of the water beads would grow pregnant enough to spawn a droplet, which would then fall around—and occasionally onto—Death's forehead. He had counted over seven hundred hits in the past few days.

Sleep appeared and crouched beside Death, looking hopeful. "You look bored. I don't suppose you'd care for a little oblivion?"

"No, thank you," said Death. He was always scrupulously polite, to counter his reputation. He waited until another drop fell—a miss, alas—and then turned his head to regard Sleep. "You're looking a little detached yourself."

At the refusal, Sleep had sighed and sat down beside him. "I thought I would be all right," she said. "I should be all right. Animals sleep, even plants in their way. But it just isn't the same."

Death reached out to touch her hand. It was his own silent offer.

"No thanks," she said, though she did take his hand. He was glad. Others rarely touched him, if they could help it. By this gesture he understood: not yet.

He sat up. The sun had just risen above the city. Clouds like strings of pearls girded the sky. A flock of tiny birds—Death guessed hummingbirds, migrating back from the south—passed through the rust-rimmed hole in the MetLife Building.

"What's that?" asked Sleep.

Death followed her finger and saw a cluster of flowers. The rooftop on which he lay was thick with meadowgrass, and one very determined ailanthus grew in the dust and silt of one corner. There were many flowers amid the meadowgrass, which was why Death liked this roof so much. He would be sorry when it finally caved in.

"Just a daisy," he replied.

"No, beyond that."

They got up and walked around the roof's holes for a better look. Beyond the daisy, fighting its way up through the grass in the shadows of the roof wall, was a flower Death had never seen before. Its shape was something like that of a crocus, but its roots were shallow, like all rooftop flora. There was no bulb. And its petals were a lush, deep matte black.

"That's different," said Sleep.

Death crouched to peer at the flower, then reached out to stroke the satin softness of one petal. Not just different. New.

Something tickled his cheek. He reached up to brush it away and found his fingers wet. Glancing back at the water tower, he wondered how he could've missed his count.

Death liked to walk across bridges. For this reason he had claimed a home for himself relatively far from the center of town. This was in a big ugly gray stone of a building that had once been a factory, and then had been colonized by artists, and then by trend-obsessed young professionals. Now it was ruled by cats. Death passed perhaps a dozen of them on his way down the stairs, including one mother briskly carrying a mouse and trailed by two gangling adolescents.

As usual they ignored his presence, merely slinking out of the way as he passed. On the rare occasions when one would deign to look at him, he nodded in polite greeting. Sometimes they even nodded back.

He had attempted, once, to entice a kitten to live with him. This was something he knew humans had done. But he kept forgetting to bring food, and because he did not sleep, the kitten was unable to cuddle with him at night. After a few days the kitten had left in a huff. He still saw its descendants around the building, and felt lingering regret.

The Williamsburg Bridge had not yet begun to warp and sag like the Manhattan and Brooklyn Bridges. Death suspected there was some logical reason for this—perhaps the Williamsburg had been renovated more recently, or built more sturdily in the first place. But in his heart, Death believed that he helped to keep the bridge intact. By walking across it, he gave the bridge purpose. For all things created by humankind, purpose was the quintessence of existence.

So Death walked into town every day.

There was much activity in town when Death arrived.

"The twins have opened a Starbucks at Union Square!" said a stranger, when Death stepped off the bridge on Delancey. He nodded in pleasant response to this, though he was not certain what a Starbucks was or why the twins would have bothered with it.

Still, everyone seemed so excited about the Starbucks that Death wandered uptown, curious. Most of the streets were empty, except for cats and a few coyotes. The coyotes were not as bold as the cats; they mostly tried to keep out of sight. At Fourteenth Street and Avenue A, Death found the Dragon King of the Western Ocean playing bagpipes on the corner stoop. He sat on the gnarled root of a young oak that was slowly crushing an ancient, spindly cherry, and destroying the sidewalk in the process. Skirting around the growing sinkhole, Death sat down to listen until the Dragon King was done.

"Thanks," the Dragon King said. "It's good to have listeners."

"You're very good," said Death.

"Always wanted to learn this thing. It's just so ugly, you have to love it. I looked all over the mainland, even in Hong Kong, and couldn't find one. Had to come here finally. Thank little apples for the Chinese Diaspora." The Dragon King set down the bagpipes carefully. "Are you going to Starbucks?"

"I was thinking about it, yes. Are you?"

"Course not. I hate coffee. People used to offer it to me all the time—nasty, vile stuff. Now, a Krispy Kreme doughnut? Got one of those once, thought I would die of joy." He let out a wistful sigh.

"I've never tried coffee." People, in the time before, had made very different offerings to Death.

"You probably won't have any today either. Mawu only found a few bricks of the freeze-dried stuff; I bet they'll run out by noon."

"Oh." Death felt mildly disappointed.

"Let's go anyhow. I'm bored."

They walked over to Union Square, where as usual the south-end steps were filled with worshippers. Not people, for all that most of them had adopted the forms of people in homage. Just others of their kind who were willing and had the strength to assist those in need. But this time the line around the square, trailing from the Starbucks all the way to the collapsed bank on the opposite corner, was long enough to rival the crowd on the steps.

The Dragon King clapped Death on the shoulder. "See what I mean? Good luck getting a taste."

"Anything new is worth trying," Death replied with a shrug.

The Dragon King sighed. "I know you don't need it, man, but you really ought to try a service." He nodded toward the square. "Way better than coffee."

"Others need it more than me." They both fell silent, embarrassed, as a thin, waiflike creature shuffled past. It was difficult to tell if this one was male or female or one of the androgynes, because its clothing was ragged and its face too hollow for easy recognition. Its gaze was fixed on the square. As Death and the Dragon King watched, the creature crossed the street; the worshippers there opened their ranks at once to admit the newcomer.

"Damn," said the Dragon King. "I think that was one of the Bodhisattvas. I used to know all those guys. Girls. Them."

Death nodded, solemn. He had known them, too.

The Dragon King glanced at him guiltily. "Look, I know I don't need it either. The oceans are still around, the rain still falls. But it's not the same, you know?"

"I know that," Death said, a little taken aback. "You don't have to justify it to me."

"Damn straight I don't." The Dragon King glared at him for a moment; in the distance, clouds rumbled with faint thunder. But almost as quickly as the Dragon's anger had come, it seemed to fade, and he sighed. "Well...anyway. Thanks for listening to the music."

The Dragon King then crossed the street to join the throng on the steps. Death watched him for a moment, contemplating. They would help the ones who needed it most first, but beyond that they helped everyone, offering worship in whatever form necessary— blood, prayer, sex—for hour-long increments. If not for them and other groups like them, many would have given up, or faded away, by now.

Would they die for him, if he asked it? Death wondered idly.

Then he turned and went to the end of the Starbucks line. They ran out of coffee before he got halfway there.

But the twins had attempted another experiment, which Death did get to try: cookies. He sat at one of the small tables in the crowded café, and peered dubiously at the plate that Lise had set in front of him.

"They're good," she said.

"They're green," he replied.

"That's because we made the flour from crabgrass seeds," she said. "It makes them a little bitter, but otherwise they're good. Look, real raisins."

Wild grapevines had overrun Brooklyn Heights. "Ah. As I recall, Mawu did make passable wine for libations once."

"Yes, the bottles that didn't explode or turn to vinegar. He's still working on the technique. But raisins are easy. Grow some grapes and ignore them. Try it."

Death picked up the cookie and nibbled. It was, to his great surprise, good. He said as much, and meant it.

"You don't have to sound so shocked," Lise said, annoyed. She stormed away behind the counter and resumed work on some contraption that she must have rigged to bake the cookies. She and her twin brother, Mawu, were good at creating new things. Almost as good as people had been.

"I need to talk to you," said an angel, coming over to sit across from him. She did not ask to sit, but angels did not ask permission.

"Of course," he said. Lise glared at him from behind the dusty old counter, and he remembered the ritual of sitting in a café. Small talk was necessary before business could be conducted. It was respectful to treat the twins' endeavor in the spirit it was meant.

"How have you been? Is, er, is life good for you?" He had not meant that the way it came out. Hopefully she would not think he wanted to kill her.

"The life of mankind has passed on, and we are but shadows in its wake," she said truthfully, ignoring the polite fiction that the ritual demanded. He winced. At the counter, Lise sucked her teeth. "I came to tell you that the Lex has overflowed its banks. I talked to Ogun; the pumping system is completely unsalvageable. Took everything he had to keep it going this long. He thinks the entire Upper East Side will be underwater within a year."

Death spat out a raisin pit, and fished in his mouth for a bit of grass seed hull that seemed to have gotten stuck in his teeth. He did not have to have teeth, he supposed, but he generally liked them, except at times like this. "Why is that a problem?"

"The English Nursery Rhymes. They all live on the Upper East Side."

"Why can't they move?"

She looked at him with annoyance, though this was mild, her being an angel. He thought she might be Gabriel; the rest were less tolerant of those outside their circle. "There are more kindergartens and schools in that part of town than any other."

Which explained why the Rhymes had claimed that neighborhood. Death considered. "What about Park Slope?" This was a neighborhood in Brooklyn not far from his home in Williamsburg. He remembered visiting there often, in the old days. It had been a hotbed of gang activity once, but later, before the people had gone, there had been many children.

"They can't make it that far. They're not like the rest of us that had thousands of years and dozens of cultures to strengthen them. To get to Brooklyn, they'd have to travel through several neighborhoods that didn't have many kids, and across the East River. It's too much for them."

Death frowned, a slow suspicion eating into his enjoyment of the cookies. He sat back, silent for a long moment, and gazed at her until she sighed and said it out loud.

"You need to help them," she said. She spoke softly. A rarity. "It's worse to wither away. You know that."

"My help is always available. To those who ask."

"They're children! They sing and rhyme and bounce around—they don't know to ask!"

He remained silent, not bothering to point out the obvious. The Nursery Rhymes weren't children, any more than he was a man, or she a woman. There were no more children.

"It isn't right." She looked away. Her hand lay on the table. Her fingers tightened into a fist, then relaxed, then tightened again. Her wings, which dragged the floor behind her chair, fluffed and settled. "Letting them suffer when they don't have to. You know it's not right."

It was not. Inadvertently he thought of the Bodhisattva he had seen, shambling its way toward survival. "They might want to try."

"They don't think that far, Death. They're full of nonsense. But they suffer as much as the rest of us. It's amazing they've managed to hang on this long."

He shook his head slowly, but sighed. "I'll speak to them," he said at last. "I'll try to make them understand, and then ask what they want. Life—even its shadow—deserves that much consideration." He leveled a hard look at her. "And I will abide by their decision."

She nodded slowly. "That's all I ask." With a heavy sigh, she got up, and finally yielded to propriety. "Thank you. Er, have a nice day." At this, Lise looked pleased.

Death finished his cookie and got up. He walked uptown, which took the rest of the day. By the time he reached the Upper East Side, night had begun to fall. He traveled more slowly along the banks of the river, because the sidewalks and streets were treacherous here. The water flowing through the subway lines had undermined the whole area, and it was obvious that this part of the island would soon be reclaimed by the sea. But at Sixty-Sixth Street he found a downed Victorian turret fetched up against several cars, which formed a precarious bridge. After climbing over this, Death made his way farther north, following the old sense that had always led him to wherever he needed to be.

He found the Nursery Rhymes in the garden of an ancient school. Though it was pitch dark, they were still running about and playing, chasing fireflies, their peals of laughter making Death feel lonely and nostalgic. There were peacocks and peahens in the garden, too, some of them roosting sleepily in the trees as he passed underneath. They cooed challenges at him, less indifferent than his building's cats. But then he stopped, surprised to find one peacock down on the ground, directly in his path. As he stared at it, he realized it was not blue and green like the others. Its head was a fierce, iridescent red, shading to gold on the neck and below. When it suddenly fanned and shivered its great tail, he saw that all the eyespots were a baleful, white-rimmed black.

Then, as if satisfied that he had noticed its strangeness, the peacock dropped its tail and flew away.

When the children ran over to Death, still giggling and delighted to meet someone new, he could not help noticing how thin they were.

One day Death began to feel restless, which was strange. He was Death, the inevitability of all living things. He should never have felt restless. Yet he did.

He wondered: Was his dissolution beginning, as had happened to so many others? But there was still death in the world, all around him, every day. The cats in his building. The rats and mice and birds that they fed on. The plants that grew from cracks in the concrete. His own kind, when they faltered. Yet he also knew the truth: that death might exist in the absence of humankind, but not Death.

He felt no weaker. There was no perceptible thinning of his substance. But something troubled him, nevertheless.

He began to walk, picking a direction at random. South. The streets in Brooklyn were less damaged and flooded than those in Manhattan, but there were other problems, especially in the poorer neighborhoods. He had to go slowest in Flatbush, which had been in a state of disrepair long before the end of humanity. The sinkholes and downed facades got so bad that eventually he simply willed himself over to Kensington. (He preferred to walk, but physicality was not always convenient.) Strolling along tree-lined streets and gazing at brownstones that still looked as beautiful as the year they'd been built was marvelous, though it felt a bit like cheating.

Because Death did not tire, he walked well into the night, and reached Coney Island by morning. It was nice to watch the sunrise from the beach. The ocean hummed with its own cycles, hardly changed by the presence or absence of humanity. He spent an hour or two just listening to the surge and sough of the waves, and remembering all that had been. He was not like many of his fellows, who were confined to the places where they had been conceived and nurtured. Where there was life, there was death, and where there was death, was his domain. He was one of the few who could, if he wished, travel the whole world. It was good to be Death.

When the sun was well risen, he turned away from the sagging roller coaster and the midway, with its stands full of mildewed lumps that had once been stuffed animals. The aquarium stood open, the glass of its doors long since shattered and washed away in the hurricane that had hit the city not long after its abandonment. Inside the Alien Stingers exhibit—the only building still standing—Death found mostly darkness and silence. He moved quietly between the still, dark tanks, looking for nothing in particular. Just walking. Listening. He sensed now that something had drawn him to this place. He didn't know what, but he knew this: It was a sensation he had not felt since before people had gone. That in itself was enough to merit his attention.

As Death reached the south end of the building, he found that it had been torn open by long-gone wind and rain, leaving a great, gaping, splintered hole. Debris, itself mostly buried in sand with the passage of time, paved the way across the tumbled wall of the sea lion tank, between the manmade hills (now flat) which had bordered the site, and through the crazily leaning pillars which were all that remained of the boardwalk. The building's guts trailed away in a clear path all the way down to the water.

Here, Death found something odd. A series of peculiar, curlicued scuff marks moved along this trail of lathing and salt-rotted wood, cutting across the windblown drifts of sand. Following them, he found that the marks petered out a few dozen meters from the water's edge, washed away by the tide line. Backtracking instead, he found them continuing into the aquarium—but where the sand gave way to the building's cheap, nearly indestructible carpeting, there were no marks for him to follow.

Death did not have much imagination. He did not require it. He was patient, however, so lacking any other means of fathoming the mystery, he sat down beside the trail. The marks were fresh, after all. Perhaps whatever had made them would eventually return.

And finally, as dusk fell, he saw movement down near the beach. An animal, dragging itself out of the surf. At first he thought that it was another new thing, like the black flower, and the red peacock. Then it drew closer, and belatedly he realized it was just a small, dark blue octopus, walking its way along the lathing and sand. As it came, he saw that it carried an old blue plastic cup that read SLURPEE in faded letters, balanced carefully atop two of its tentacles. Water sloshed over the cup's lip now and again, though it was clear the creature was making an effort not to spill the liquid. It used the other six tentacles to walk, Death saw, leaving behind that familiar curling pattern.

Now and again the creature stopped, set the cup on some flat surface or against a rock, and thrust its head into the water. Death watched it breathe in and out, its color flickering momentarily lighter blue, like the cup. When it had finished this procedure, it withdrew from the cup and resumed walking.

It paused when Death rose to follow it into the aquarium. He stopped when it did, and felt himself actively considered by the creature's strange bar-pupiled eyes. When he did not approach more closely, however, the creature finally resumed its laborious march.

Inside, they both proceeded to one of the building's vast, double-walled tanks. Here, unlike the rest of the tanks—most of which no longer had any need of his services—this one still flickered in glowing, vibrant blue. There was a hole in the tank's uppermost corner, where the glass met the plaster of its display case, and something had cleared away the killing algae from the water's surface. Above the tank was a skylight in the aquarium's ceiling, which let in plenty of the setting sun's rays. Thanks to this, Death could see that the tank was still halfway full with water, the water mark just at his eye level. The water had gone murky, the glass speckling with age and wear—but beyond the speckling, he could see many small things darting and moving.

Before he could identify this, the octopus stopped beside this tank, then laboriously climbed the glass wall, still carting the cup. It poured the water into the tank, dropped the cup—Death had already noticed many other cups, cans, and coconut shells littering the floor here—then wriggled through the gap in the glass. Here it paused, clinging to the glass above the water line, gazing through a clear patch at Death. Again, Death felt himself considered.

Then one of the darting things in the water flicked up and attached itself to the plastic, too, and he understood. It was a tiny copy of the larger octopus—a baby. There were likely hundreds of them, if not thousands, in the tank.

Death leaned close to the glass, looking the elder octopus in its— her—odd little eye. He considered her in return.

"Shall I kill you?" he asked. "Is that what you want?"

He felt her deep weariness. This was the way of things, he knew then: The mother died, her flesh granting the young a last bit of strength so that they might survive. It had happened for countless generations already, since the destruction of the aquarium had provided her ancestors with such a convenient, safe nursery for their young. How many more octopi had survived their youth, thanks to this happenstance, than there would have been in the wild? How many more adults had learned to leave the ocean, carrying their water with them as they found safer shelter somewhere along the empty seaside?

The octopus did not answer. She could not speak. Yet he knew, because he was what he was, that she understood what he was. She was not a red peacock or a black flower, yet she was, in a similar way, a new thing. Or an old thing, taking advantage of a new opportunity. It did not matter. Of such opportunities, embraced and exploited, were new things born.

One of the mother octopus's wet, attenuated tentacles curled over the edge of the broken glass, twitching slightly. Nodding, Death touched this. A moment later the octopus turned gray and dropped into the water. The tank roiled with movement as her children swarmed in for a last loving taste of her.

The small octopus that had leapt out of the water, and which had continued to cling to the glass, observing, while Death killed its mother, remained where it was. Death nodded to it, solemn, then turned to go.

Movement caught his eye. The small octopus had begun to scurry up toward the hole in the glass. Death stopped.

"No," he said, recalling that its mother had not come ashore 'til dusk, with the tide. "Wait until morning, near dawn. Bring water with you."

The baby octopus stopped, its sides heaving with the effort to breathe out of the water. He had no idea whether it understood him. If it did, it would wait, and have that much better a chance of surviving the trek to the ocean. Perhaps a few of its siblings would attempt and survive the journey, too, and in turn they would pass on the necessary skill, and the intelligence to use it, to the young who came after them. And in time, with luck and other opportunities...

It was how people had begun. It was how all new things began. He understood this, the life and death of species, as he had always understood the life and death of individuals. But perhaps he had been too preoccupied with the latter, as a result failing to notice the former.

The little octopus detached itself from the side of the tank and dropped back into the water, darting in for its own share of the mother's corpse. Death felt himself ignored and forgotten—but that was all right. The young did not often think about Death, but Death was no less eternal for their disinterest.

He smiled with the realization that some concepts would always be the same, no matter who conceptualized them. Still...lifting his hand, he contemplated the shape and structure of tentacles. They would be very versatile, he decided, though they would take some getting used to.

Then he turned and headed for home.

A few days later, Death went to Union Square. He walked over to the worshippers on the south-end steps, and asked them what to do.

"Just...think about the one you're trying to help," said the Dragon King, who had been looking at him oddly since his arrival. "That's all any of us really needs, y'know. But if you don't mind me saying so, buddy, I never expected to see you here. I figured—" He paused abruptly, looking embarrassed. "Well, I figured you didn't mind seeing the rest of us crash and burn."

Death understood. Others usually assumed worse. "Death comes on its own," he said. "I don't have to do anything to facilitate it. But everyone deserves a chance to try and survive." *Even us*, he had decided.

"Well, sure. But..." The Dragon King scratched his long, curling mustache, finally letting out a weak laugh. "Man, you're weird."

Death smiled. It pleased him to be called "man," though eventually there would be other names and other manifestations for him. He would not be the same, filtered through such different imaginations. None of them would be—but it was now important to him that his fellows hold on, take the opportunity to adapt if they could. The world had not ended, after all. The stuff of which he and his kind had been made had not vanished. The thinker did not matter, so long as thought remained.

"Thank you," Death said, and then he clapped the Dragon King on the shoulder. (The Dragon King started and threw him a puzzled look.) "Now tell me: Are bagpipes easy to learn?"

While he still had fingers, he would need a way to pass the time.

The Narcomancer

In the land of Gujaareh it was said that trouble came by twos. Four bands of color marked the face of the Dreaming Moon; the great river split into four tributaries; there were four harvests in a year; four humors coursed the inner rivers of living flesh. By contrast, two of anything in nature meant inevitable conflict: stallions in a herd, lions in a pride. Siblings. The sexes.

Gatherer Cet's twin troubles came in the form of two women. The first was a farmcaste woman who had been injured by an angry bull-ox; half her brains had been dashed out beneath its hooves. The Sharers, who could work miracles with the Goddess's healing magic, had given up on her. "We can grow her a new head," said one of the Sharer-elders to Cet, "but we cannot put the memories of her lifetime back in it. Best to claim her dreamblood for others, and send her soul where her mind has already gone."

But when Cet arrived in the Hall of Blessings to see to the woman, he confronted a scene of utter chaos. Three squalling children struggled in the arms of a Sentinel, hampering him as he tried to assist his brethren. Nearer by, a young man fought to get past two of the Sharers, trying to reach a third Templeman—whom, clearly, he blamed for the woman's condition. "You didn't even try!" he shouted, the words barely intelligible through his sobs. "How can my wife live if you won't even try?"

He elbowed one of the Sharers in the chest and nearly got free, but the other flung himself on the distraught husband's back then, half dragging him to the floor. Still the man fought with manic fury, murder in his eyes. None of them noticed Cet until Cet stepped in front of the young man and raised his jungissa stone.

Startled, the young man stopped struggling, his attention caught by the stone. It had been carved into the likeness of a dragonfly; its gleaming black wings blurred as Cet tapped the stone hard with his thumbnail. The resulting sharp whine cut across the cacophony filling the Hall until even the children stopped weeping to look for the source of the noise. As peace returned, Cet willed the stone's vibration to soften to a low, gentle hum. The man sagged as tension drained out of his body, until he hung limp in the two Sharers' arms.

"You know she is already dead," Cet said to the young man. "You know this must be done."

The young man's face tightened in anguish. "No. She breathes. Her heart beats." He slurred the words as if drunk. "No."

"Denying it makes no difference. The pattern of her soul has been lost. If she were healed, you would have to raise her all over again, like one of your children. To make her your wife then would be an abomination."

The man began to weep again, quietly this time. But he no longer fought, and when Cet moved around him to approach his wife, he uttered a little moan and looked away.

Cet knelt beside the cot where the woman lay, and put his fore- and middle fingers on her closed eyelids. She was already adrift in the realms between waking and dream; there was no need to use his jungissa to put her to sleep. He followed her into the silent dark and examined her soul, searching for any signs of hope. But the woman's soul was indeed like that of an infant, soft and devoid of all but the most simplistic desires and emotions. The merest press of Cet's will was enough to send her toward the land of dreams, where she would doubtless dissolve into the substance of that realm—or perhaps she would eventually be reborn, to walk the realm of waking anew and regain the experiences she had lost.

Either way, her fate was not for Cet to decide. Having delivered her soul safely, he severed the tether that had bound her to the waking realm, and collected the delicate dreamblood that spilled forth.

The weeping that greeted Cet upon his return to waking was of a different order from before. Turning, Cet saw with satisfaction that the farmcaste man stood with his children now, holding them as they watched the woman's flesh breathe its last. They were still distraught, but the violent madness was gone; in its place was the sort of grief that expressed itself through love and would, eventually, bring healing.

"That was nicely done," said a low voice beside him, and Cet looked up to see the Temple Superior. Belatedly he realized the Superior had been the target of the distraught husband's wrath. Cet had been so focused on the family that he had not noticed.

"You gave them peace without dreamblood," the Superior continued. "Truly, Gatherer Cet, our Goddess favors you."

Cet got to his feet, sighing as the languor of the Gathering faded slowly within him. "The Hall has still been profaned," he said. He looked up at the great shining statue of the Goddess of Dreams, who towered over them with hands outstretched in welcome and eyes shut in the Eternal Dream. "Voices have been raised and violence done, right here at Her feet."

"S-Superior?" A boy appeared at the Superior's shoulder, too young to be an acolyte. One of the Temple's adoptees from the House of Children, probably working a duty shift as an errand runner. "Are you hurt at all? I saw that man..."

The Superior smiled down at him. "No, child; I'm fine, thank you. Go back to the House before your Teacher misses you."

Looking relieved, the boy departed. The Superior sighed, watching him leave. "Some chaos is to be expected at times like this. The heart is rarely peaceful." He gave Cet a faint smile. "Though, of course, you would not know that, Gatherer."

"I remember the time before I took my oath."

"Not the same."

Cet shrugged, gazing at the mourning family. "I have the peace and order of Temple life to comfort me now. It is enough."

The Superior looked at him oddly for a moment, then sighed. "Well, I'm afraid I must ask you to leave that comfort for a time, Cet. Will you come with me to my office? I have a matter that requires the attention of a Gatherer—one with your unique skill at bestowing peace."

And thus did Cet's second hardship fall upon him.

The quartet that stood in the Superior's office were upriver folk. Cet could see that in their dingy clothing and utter lack of makeup or jewelry; not even the poorest city dweller kept themselves so plain. And no city dweller went unsandaled on the brick-paved streets, which grew painfully hot at midday. Yet the woman who stood at the group's head had the proud carriage of one used to the respect and obedience of others, finery or no finery. The three men all but cowered behind her as the Superior and Cet entered the room.

"Cet, this is Mehepi," said the Superior, gesturing to the woman.

"She and her companions are from a mining village some ways to the south, in the foothills that border the Empty Thousand. Mehepi, I bring you Cet, one of the Temple's Gatherers."

Mehepi's eyes widened in a way that would have amused Cet, had he been capable of amusement. Clearly she had expected something more of Gujaareh's famed Gatherers; someone taller, perhaps. But she recovered quickly and gave him a respectful bow. "I greet you in peace, Gatherer," she said, "though I bring unpeaceful tidings."

Cet inclined his head. "Tidings of..." But he trailed off, surprised, as his eyes caught a slight movement in the afternoon shadows of the room. Some ways apart from Mehepi and the others, a younger woman knelt on a cushion. She was so still—it was her breathing Cet had noticed—that Cet made no wonder he had overlooked her, though now it seemed absurd that he had. Wealthy men had commissioned sculptures with lips less lush, bones less graceful; sugared currants were not as temptingly black as her skin. Though the other upriver folk were staring at Cet, her eyes remained downcast, her body unmoving beneath the faded indigo drape of her gown. Indigo: the mourning color. Mehepi wore it, too.

"What is this?" Cet asked, nodding toward the younger woman.

Was there unease in Mehepi's eyes? Defensiveness, certainly. "We were told the Temple offers its aid only to those who follow the ways of the Dream Goddess," she said. "We have no money to tithe, Gatherer, and none of us has offered dreams or goods in the past year..."

All at once Cet understood. "You brought her as payment."

"No, not payment—" But even without the hint of a stammer in Mehepi's voice, the lie was plain in her manner.

"Explain, then." Cet spoke more sharply than was, perhaps, strictly peaceful. "Why does she sit apart from the rest of you?"

The villagers looked at one another. But before any of them could speak, the young woman said, "Because I am cursed, Gatherer."

The Temple Superior frowned. "Cursed? Is that some upriver superstition?"

Cet had thought the younger woman broken in spirit, to judge by her motionlessness and fixed gaze at the floor. But now she lifted her eyes, and Cet realized that whatever was wrong with her, she was not broken. There was despair in her, strong enough to taste, but something more as well.

"I was a lapis merchant's wife," she said. "When he died, I was taken by the village headman as a secondwife. Now the headman is dead, and they blame me."

"She is barren!" said one of the male villagers. "Two husbands and no children yet? And Mehepi here, she is the firstwife—"

"All of my children had been stillborn," said Mehepi, touching her belly as if remembering the feel of them inside her. That much was truth, as was her pain; some of Cet's irritation with her eased. "That was why my husband took another wife. Then my last child was born alive. The whole village rejoiced! But the next morning, the child stopped breathing. A few days later the brigands came." Her face tightened in anger. "They killed my husband while she slept beside him. And they had their way with her, but even despite that there is no child." Mehepi shook her head. "For so much death to follow one woman, and life itself to shun her? How can it be anything but a curse? That is why..." She darted a look at Cet, then drew herself up. "That is why we thought you might find value in her, Gatherer. Death is your business."

"Death is not a Gatherer's business," Cet said. Did the woman realize how greatly she had insulted him and all his brethren? For the first time in a very long while, he felt anger stir in his heart.

"*Peace* is our business. Sharers do that by healing the flesh. Gatherers deal with the soul, judging those which are too corrupt or damaged to be salvaged and granting them the Goddess's blessing—"

"If you had learned your catechisms better, you would understand that," the Superior interjected smoothly. He threw Cet a mild look, doubtless to remind Cet that they could not expect better of ignorant country folk. "And you would have known there was no need for payment. In a situation like this, when the peace of many is under threat, it is the Temple's duty to offer aid."

The men looked abashed; Mehepi's jaw tightened at the scolding. With a sigh, the Superior glanced down at some notes he'd taken on a reedleaf sheet. "So, Cet; these brigands she mentioned are the problem. For the past three turns of the greater moon, their village and others along the Empty Thousand have suffered a curious series of attacks. Everyone in the village falls asleep—even the men on guard duty. When they wake, their valuables are gone. Food stores, livestock, the few stones of worth they gather from their mine; their children have been taken, too, no doubt sold to those desert tribes who traffic in slaves. Some of the women and youths have been abused, as you heard. And a few, such as the village headman and the guards, were slain outright, perhaps to soften the village's defenses for later. No one wakes during these assaults."

Cet inhaled, all his anger forgotten. "A sleep spell? But only the Temple uses narcomancy."

"Impossible to say," the Superior said. "But given the nature of these attacks, it seems clear we must help. Magic is fought best with magic." He looked at Cet as he spoke.

Cet nodded, suppressing the urge to sigh. It would have been within his rights to suggest that one of his other Gatherer-brethren—perhaps Liyou, the youngest—handle the matter instead. But after all his talk of peace and righteous duty, that would have been hypocritical. And...in spite of himself, his gaze drifted back to the younger woman. She had lowered her eyes once more, her hands folded in her lap. There was nothing peaceful in her stillness.

"We will need a soul-healer," Cet said softly. "There is more to this than abuse of magic."

The Superior sighed. "A Sister, then. I'll write the summons to their Matriarch." The Sisters were an offshoot branch of the faith, coexisting with the Servants of Hananja in an uneasy parallel. Cet knew the Superior had never liked them.

Cet gave him a rueful smile. "Everything for Her peace." He had never liked them either.

They set out that afternoon: the five villagers, two of the Temple's warrior Sentinels, Cet, and a Sister of the Goddess. The Sister, who arrived unescorted at the river docks just as they were ready to push off, was worse than even Cet had expected—tall and commanding, clad in the pale gold robes and veils that signified high rank in their order. That meant this Sister had mastered the most difficult techniques of erotic dreaming, with its attendant power to affect the spirit and the subtler processes of flesh. A formidable creature. But the greatest problem in Cet's eyes was that the Sister was male.

"Did the messenger not explain the situation?" Cet asked the Sister at the first opportunity. He kept his tone light. They rode in a canopied barge more than large enough to hold their entire party and the pole crew besides. It was not large enough to accommodate ill feelings between himself and the Sister.

The Sister, who had given his name as Ginnem, stretched out along the bench he had claimed for himself. "Gatherers; so tactful."

Cet resisted the urge to grind his teeth. "You cannot deny that a different Sister—a female Sister—would have been better suited to deal with this matter."

"Perhaps," Ginnem replied, with a smile that said he thought no one better suited than himself. "But look." He glanced across the aisle at the villagers, who had occupied a different corner of the barge. The three men sat together on a bench across from the first-wife. Three benches back, the young woman sat alone.

"That one has suffered at the hands of both men and women," Ginnem said. "Do you think my sex makes any difference to her?"

"She was raped by men," Cet said.

"And she is being destroyed by a woman. That firstwife wants her dead, can you not see?" Ginnem shook his head, jingling tiny bells woven into each of his braids. "If not for the need to involve the Temple in the brigand matter, no doubt the firstwife would've found some quiet way to do her in already. And why do you imagine only a woman could know of rape?"

Cet started. "Forgive me. I did not realize—"

"It was long ago." Ginnem shrugged his broad shoulders. "When I was a soldier; another life."

Cet's surprise must have shown on his face, for a moment later Ginnem laughed. "Yes, I was born military caste," he said. "I earned high rank before I felt the calling to the Sisterhood. And I still keep up some of my old habits." He lifted one flowing sleeve to reveal a knife sheath strapped around his forearm, then flicked it back so quickly that no one but Cet noticed. "So you see, there is more than one reason the Sisterhood sent me."

Cet nodded slowly, still trying and failing to form a clear opinion of Ginnem. Male Sisters were rare; he wondered if all of them were this strange. "Then we are four fighters and not three. Good."

"Oh, don't count me," Ginnem said. "My soldier days are over; I fight only when necessary now. And I expect I'll have my hands full with other duties." He glanced at the young woman again, sobering. "Someone should talk to her."

And he turned his kohl-lined eyes to Cet.

Night had fallen, humid and thick, by the time Cet went to the woman. Her companions were already abed, motionless on pallets the crew had laid on deck. One of the Sentinels was asleep; the other stood at the prow with the ship's watchman.

The woman still sat on her bench. Cet watched her for a time, wondering if the lapping water and steadily passing palm trees had lulled her to sleep, but then she lifted a hand to brush away a persistent moth. Throwing a glance at Ginnem—who was snoring faintly on his bench—Cet rose and went to sit across from the woman. Her eyes were lost in some waking dream until he sat down, but they sharpened very quickly.

"What is your name?" he asked.

"Namsut." Her voice was low and warm, touched with some southlands accent.

"I am Cet," he replied.

"Gatherer Cet."

"Does my title trouble you?"

She shook her head. "You bring comfort to those who suffer. That takes a kind heart."

Surprised, Cet smiled. "Few even among the Goddess's most devout followers see anything other than the death I bring. Fewer still have ever called me kind for it. Thank you."

She shook her head, looking into the passing water. "No one who has known suffering would think ill of you, Gatherer."

Widowed twice, raped, shunned...He tried to imagine her pain and could not. That inability troubled him all of a sudden.

"I will find the brigands who hurt you," he said, to cover his discomfort. "I will see that their corruption is excised from the world."

To his surprise, her eyes went hard as iron though she kept her voice soft. "They did nothing to me that two husbands had not already done," she said. "And wife-brokers before that, and my father's creditors before that. Will you hunt down all of them?" She shook her head. "Kill the brigands, but not for me."

This was not at all the response that Cet had expected. So confused was he that he blurted the first question that came to his mind. "What shall I do for you, then?"

Namsut's smile threw him even further. It was not bitter, that smile, but neither was it gentle. It was a smile of anger, he realized at last. Pure, politely restrained, tooth-grinding rage.

"Give me a child," she said.

In the morning, Cet spoke of the woman's request to Ginnem.

"In the upriver towns, the headman's wife rules if the headman dies," Cet explained as they broke their fast. "That is tradition, according to Namsut. But a village head must prove him or herself favored by the gods, to rule. Namsut says fertility is one method of proof."

Ginnem frowned, chewing thoughtfully on a date. A group of women on the passing shore were doing laundry at the riverside, singing a rhythmic song while they worked. "That explains a great deal," he said at last. "Mehepi has proven herself at least able to conceive, but after so many dead children, the village must be wondering if she, too, is cursed. And since having a priest for a lover might also connote the gods' favor, I know now why Mehepi has been eyeing me with such speculation."

Cet started, feeling his cheeks heat. "You think she wants—" He took a date to cover his discomfort. "From you?"

Ginnem grinned. "And why not? Am I not fine?" He made a show of tossing his hair, setting all the tiny bells a-tinkle.

"You know full well what I mean," Cet said, glancing about in embarassment. Some of the other passengers looked their way at the sound of Ginnem's hair bells, but no one was close enough to overhear.

"Yes, and it saddens me to see how much it troubles you," Ginnem said, abruptly serious. "*Sex*, Gatherer Cet. That is the word you cannot bring yourself to say, isn't it?" When Cet said nothing, Ginnem made an annoyed sound. "Well, I will not let you avoid it, however much you and your stiff-necked Servant brethren disapprove. I am a Sister of the Goddess. I use narcomancy—and yes, my body when necessary—to heal those wounded spirits that can be healed. It is no less holy a task than what you do for those who cannot be healed, Gatherer, save that my petitioners do not die when I'm done!"

He was right. Cet bent at the waist, his eyes downcast, to signal his contrition. The gesture seemed to mollify Ginnem, who sighed.

"And no, Mehepi has not approached me," Ginnem said, "though she's hardly had time, with three such devoted attendants..." Abruptly he caught his breath. "Ahh—yes, *now* I understand. I first thought this was a simple matter of a powerful senior wife plotting against a weaker secondwife. But more than that—this is a race. Whichever woman produces a healthy child first will rule the village."

Cet frowned, glancing over at the young woman again. She had finally allowed herself to sleep, leaning against one of the canopy pillars and drawing her feet up onto the bench. Only in sleep was her face peaceful, Cet noticed. It made her even more beautiful, though he'd hardly imagined that possible.

"The contest is uneven," he said. He glanced over at the head-woman Mehepi—acting headwoman, he realized now, by virtue solely of her seniority. She was still asleep on one of the pallets, comfortable between two of her men. "Three lovers to none."

"Yes." Ginnem's lip curled. "That curse business was a handy bit of cleverness on Mehepi's part. No man will touch the secondwife for fear of sharing the curse."

"It seems wrong," Cet said softly, gazing at Namsut. "That she should have to endure yet another man's lust to survive."

"You grew up in the city, didn't you?" When Cet nodded, Ginnem said, "Yes, I thought so. My birth village was closer to the city, and surely more fortunate than these people's, but some customs are the same in every backwater. Children are wealth out here, you see—another miner, another strong back on the farm, another eye to watch for enemies. A woman is honored for the children she produces, and so she should be. But make no mistake, Gatherer: This contest is for power. The secondwife could leave that village. She could have asked asylum of your Temple Superior. She returns to the village by choice."

Cet frowned, mulling over that interpretation for a moment. It did not feel right.

"My father was a horse trader," he said. Ginnem raised an eyebrow at the apparent non sequitur; Cet gave him a faint shrug of apology. "Not a very good one. He took poor care of his animals, trying to squeeze every drop of profit from their hides."

Even after so many years, it shamed Cet to speak of his father, for anyone who listened could guess what his childhood had been like. A man so neglectful of his livelihood was unlikely to be particularly careful of his heirs. He saw this realization dawn on Ginnem's face, but to Cet's relief, Ginnem merely nodded for Cet to continue.

"Once, my father sold a horse—a sickly, half-starved creature—to a man so known for his cruelty that no other trader in the city would serve him. But before the man could saddle the horse, it gave a great neigh and leapt into the river. It could have swum back to shore, but that would have meant recapture. So it swam in the opposite direction, deeper into the river, where finally the current carried it away."

Ginnem gave Cet a skeptical look. "You think the secondwife *wants* the village to kill her?"

Cet shook his head. "The horse was not dead. When last I saw it, it was swimming with the current, its head above the water, facing whatever fate awaited it downriver. Most likely it drowned or was eaten by predators. But what if it survived the journey, and even now runs free over some faraway pasture? Would that not be a reward worth so much risk?"

"Ah. All or nothing; win a better life or die trying." Ginnem's eyes narrowed as he gazed contemplatively at Cet. "You understand the secondwife well, I see."

Cet drew back, abruptly unnerved by the way Ginnem was looking at him. "I respect her."

"You find her beautiful?"

He said it with as much dignity as he could: "I am not blind."

Ginnem looked Cet up and down in a way that reminded Cet uncomfortably of his father's customers. "You are fine enough," Ginnem said, with more than a hint of lasciviousness in his tone. "Handsome, healthy, intelligent. A tad short, but that's no great matter if she does not mind a small child—"

"'A Gatherer belongs wholly to the Goddess,'" Cet said, leaning close so that the disapproval in his voice would not be heard by the others. "That is the oath I swore when I chose this path. The celibacy—"

"Comes second to your primary mission, Gatherer," Ginnem said in an equally stern voice. "It is the duty of any priest of the Goddess of Dreams to bring peace. There are two ways we might create peace in this village, once we've dealt with the brigands. One is to let Mehepi goad the villagefolk into killing or exiling the second-wife. The other is to give the secondwife a chance to control her own life for the first time. Which do you choose?"

"There are other choices," Cet muttered uneasily. "There must be."

Ginnem shrugged. "If she has any talent for dreaming, she could join my order. But I see no sign of the calling in her."

"You could still suggest it to her."

"Mmm." Ginnem's tone was noncommittal. He turned to gaze at Namsut. "That horse you spoke of. If you could have helped it on its way, would you have? Even if that earned you the wrath of the horse's owner and your father?"

Cet flinched back, too startled and flustered to speak. Ginnem's eyes slid back to him.

"How did the horse break free, Cet?"

Cet set his jaw. "I should rest while I can. The rest of the journey will be long."

"Dream well," Ginnem said. Cet turned away and lay down, but he felt Ginnem's eyes on him for a long while afterward.

When Cet slept, he dreamt of Namsut.

The land of dreams was as infinite as the mind of the Goddess who contained it. Though every soul traveled there during sleep, it was rare for two to meet. Most often, the people encountered in dreams were phantoms—conjurations of the dreamer's own mind, no more real than the palm trees and placid oasis which manifested around Cet's dreamform now. But real or not, there sat Namsut on a boulder overlooking the water, her indigo veils wafting in the hot desert wind.

"I wish I could be you," she said, not turning from the water. Her voice was a whisper; her mouth never moved. "So strong, so serene, the kindhearted killer. Do your victims feel what you feel?"

"You do not desire or require death," Cet said.

"True. I'm a fool for it, but I want to live." Her image blurred for a moment, superimposed by that of a long-legged girlchild with the same despairing, angry eyes. "I was nine when a man first took me. My parents were so angry, so ashamed. I made them feel helpless. I should have died then."

"No," Cet said quietly. "Others' sins are no fault of yours."

"I know that." Abruptly something large and dark turned a lazy loop under the water—a manifestation of her anger, since oases did not have fish. But like her anger, the monster never broke the surface. Cet found this at once fascinating and disturbing.

"The magic that I use," he said. "Do you know how it works?"

"Dreamichor from nonsense dreams," she said. "Dreamseed from wet dreams, dreambile from nightmares, dreamblood from the last dream before death. The four humors of the soul."

He nodded. "Dreamblood is what Gatherers collect. It has the power to erase pain and quiet emotions." He stepped closer then, though he did not touch her. "If your heart is pained, I can share dreamblood with you now."

She shook her head. "I do not want my pain erased. It makes me strong." She turned to look up at him. "Will you give me a child, Gatherer?"

He sighed, and the sky overhead seemed to dim. "It is not our way. The Sister...dreamseed is his specialty. Perhaps..."

"Ginnem does not have your kind eyes. Nor do your Sentinel brethren. You, Gatherer Cet. If I must bear a child, I want yours."

Clouds began to race across the desert sky, some as tormented abstractions, some forming blatantly erotic shapes. Cet closed his eyes against the shiver that moved along his spine. "It is not our way," he said again, but there was a waver in his voice that he could not quite conceal.

He heard the smile in her voice just as keenly. "These are your magic-quieted emotions, Gatherer? They seem loud enough."

He forced his mind away from thoughts of her, lest they disturb his inner peace any further. What was wrong with him? By sheer will he stilled the unrest in his heart, and gratifyingly the sky was clear again when he opened his eyes.

"Forgive me," he murmured.

"I will not. It comforts me to know that you are still capable of feeling. You should not hide it; people would fear Gatherers less if they knew." She looked thoughtful. "Why do you hide it?"

Cet sighed. "Even the Goddess's magic cannot quiet a Gatherer's emotions forever. After many years, the feelings inevitably break free...and they are very powerful then. Sometimes dangerous." He shifted, uncomfortable on many levels. "As you said, we frighten people enough as it is."

She nodded, then abruptly rose and turned to him. "There are no other choices," she said. "I have no desire to serve the Goddess as a Sister. There is none of Her peace in my heart, and there may never be. But I mean to live, Gatherer—*truly* live, as more than a man's plaything or a woman's scapegoat. I want this for my children as well. So I ask you again: Will you help me?"

She was a phantom. Cet knew that now, for she could not have known of his conversation with Ginnem otherwise. He was talking to himself, or to some aspect of the Goddess come to reflect his own folly back at him. Yet he felt compelled to answer. "I cannot."

The dreamscape transformed, becoming the inside of a room. A gauze-draped low bed, wide enough for two, lay behind Namsut.

She glanced at it, then at him. "But you want to."

That afternoon they disembarked at a large trading town. There Cet used Temple funds to purchase horses and supplies for the rest of the trip. The village, said Mehepi, was on the far side of the foothills, beyond the verdant floodplain that made up the richest part of Gujaareh. It would take at least another day's travel to get there.

They set out as soon as the horses were loaded, making good time along an irrigation road which ran flat through miles of barley, hekeh, and silvercape fields. As sunset approached, they entered the low, arid foothills—Gujaareh's last line of defense against the ever-encroaching desert beyond. Here Cet called a halt. The villagers were nervous, for the hills were the brigands' territory, but with night's chill already setting in and the horses weary, there was little choice. The Sentinels split the watch while the rest of them tended their mounts and made an uneasy camp.

Cet had only just settled near a large boulder when he saw Ginnem crouched beside Namsut's pallet. Ginnem's hands were under her blanket, moving over her midsection in some slow rhythmic dance. Namsut's face had turned away from Cet, but he heard her gasp clearly enough, and saw Ginnem's smile.

Rage blotted out thought. For several breaths Cet was paralyzed by it, torn between shock, confusion, and a mad desire to walk across camp and beat Ginnem bloody.

But then Ginnem frowned and glanced his way, and the anger shattered.

Goddess...Shivering with more than the night's chill, Cet lifted his eyes to the great multihued face of the Dreaming Moon. What had that been? Now that the madness had passed, he could taste magic in the air: the delicate salt-and-metal of dreamseed. Ginnem had been healing the girl, nothing more. But even if Ginnem had been pleasuring her, what did it matter? Cet was a Gatherer. He had pledged himself to a goddess, and goddesses did not share.

A few moments later he heard footsteps and felt someone settle beside him. "Are you all right, Gatherer Cet?" Ginnem.

Cet closed his eyes. The Moon's afterimage burned against his eyelids in tilted stripes: red for blood, white for seed, yellow for ichor, black for bile.

"I do not know," he whispered.

"Well." Ginnem kept his voice light, but Cet heard the serious note underneath it. "I know jealousy when I sense it, and shock and horror, too. Dreamseed is more fragile than the other humors; your rage tore my spell like a rock through spidersilk."

Horrified, Cet looked from him to Namsut. "I'm sorry. I did not mean—is she—"

"She is undamaged, Gatherer. I was done by the time you wanted to throttle me. What concerns me more is that you wanted to throttle me at all." He glanced sidelong at Cet.

"Something is...wrong with me." But Cet dared not say what that might be. Had it been happening all along? He thought back and remembered his anger at Mehepi, the layers of unease that Namsut stirred in him. Yes. Those had been the warnings.

Not yet, he prayed to Her. *Not yet. It is too soon.*

Ginnem nodded and fell silent for a while. Finally he said, very softly, "If I could give Namsut what she wants, I would. But though those parts of me still function in the simplest sense, I have already lost the ability to father a child. In time, I will only give pleasure through dreams."

Cet started. The Sisters were a secretive lot—as were Cet's own fellow Servants, of course—but he had never known what price they paid for their magic. Then he realized Ginnem's confession had been an offering. Trust for trust.

"It...begins slowly with us," Cet admitted, forcing out the words. It was a Gatherer's greatest secret, and greatest shame. "First surging emotions, then dreaming awake, and finally we... we lose all peace, and go mad. There is no cure, once the process begins. If it has begun for me..." He trailed off. It was too much, on top of everything else. He could not bear the thought. He was not ready.

Ginnem put a hand on his shoulder in silent compassion. When Cet said nothing more, Ginnem got to his feet. "I will help all I can."

This made Cet frown. Ginnem chuckled and shook his belled head. "I am a healer, Gatherer, whatever you might think of my bedroom habits—"

He paused suddenly, his smile fading. A breath later Cet felt it, too—an intense, sudden desire to sleep. With it came the thin, unmistakable whine of a jungissa stone, wafting through the camp like a poisoned breeze.

One of the Sentinels cried an alarm. Cet scrambled to his feet, fumbling for his ornaments. Ginnem dropped to his knees and began chanting something, his hands held outward as if pushing against some invisible force. The Sentinels had gone back to back in the shadow of a boulder, working some kind of complicated dance with their knives to aid their concentration against the spell. Mehepi and one of the men were already asleep; as Cet looked around for the source of the spell, the other two men fell to the ground. Namsut made a sound like pain and stumbled toward Cet and Ginnem. Her eyes were heavy and dull, Cet saw, her legs shaking as if she walked under a great weight, but she was awake. She fought the magic with an almost visible determination.

He felt fear and longing as he gazed at her, a leviathan rising beneath the formerly placid waters of his soul.

So he snatched forth his own jungissa and struck it with a fingernail. Its deeper, clearer song rang across the hills, cutting across the atonal waver of the narcomancer's stone. Folding his will around the shape of the vibrations, Cet closed his eyes and flung forth the only possible counter to the narcomancer's sleep-spell: one of his own.

The Sentinels dropped, their knives clattering on the rocky soil. Namsut moaned and collapsed, a dark blur among the Moonlit stones. Ginnem caught his breath. "Cet, what...are you..." Then he, too, sagged.

There was a clatter of stones from a nearby hill as the narcomancer's jungissa-song faltered. Cet caught a glimpse of several dark forms moving among the stones there, some dragging others who had fallen, and abruptly the narcomancer's jungissa began to fade as with distance. They were running away.

Cet kept his jungissa humming until the last of the terrible urge to sleep had passed. Then he sagged onto a saddle and thanked the Goddess, over and over again.

"A jungissa," Cet said. "No doubt."

It was morning. The group sat around a fire eating travel food and drinking bitter, strong coffee, for none of them had slept well once Cet awakened them from the spell.

The villagers looked at each other and shook their heads at Cet's statement, uncomprehending. The Sentinels looked grim. "I suspected as much," Ginnem said with a sigh. "Nothing else has that sound."

For the villagers, Cet plucked his own jungissa stone from the belt of his loinskirt and held it out for them to see. It sat in his hand, a delicately carved dragonfly in polished blue-black. He tapped it with his thumbnail, and they all winced as it shivered and sent forth its characteristic whine.

"The jungissa itself has no power," Cet said to reassure them. He willed the stone silent; it went instantly still. "It amplifies magic only for those who have been trained in narcomantic techniques. This jungissa is the child of a stone which fell from the sky many centuries ago. There are only fifteen other ornaments like it in all the world. Three have cracked or broken over time. One was given to the House of the Sisters; one is used by the Temple for training and healing purposes; but only I and my three brother-Gatherers carry and use the stones on a regular basis. The remainder of the stones are kept in the Temple vault under guard." He sighed. "And yet, somehow, these brigands have one."

Ginnem frowned. "I saw the Sisters' queen-bee stone in our

House just before I left for this journey. Could someone have stolen a stone from the Temple?"

One of the Sentinels drew himself up at that, scowling in affront. "No one could get past my brothers and I to do so."

"You said these stones fall from the sky?" asked Namsut. She looked thoughtful. "There was sun's seed in the sky a few months ago, on the night of the Ze-kaari celebration. I saw many streaks cross the stars; there was a new Moon that night. Most faded to nothing, but one came very near, and there was light in the hills where it fell."

"Another jungissa?" It was almost too astounding and horrible to contemplate—another of the Goddess's gifts, lying unhallowed in a pit somewhere and pawed over by ruffians? Cet shuddered. "But even if they found such a thing, the rough stone itself would be useless. It must be carved to produce a sound. And it takes years of training to use that sound."

"What difference does any of that make?" Ginnem asked, scowling. "They have one and they've used it. We must capture them and take it."

Military thinking; Cet almost smiled. But he nodded agreement.

"How did you see sun's seed?" Mehepi demanded suddenly of Namsut. "Our husband had you with him that night—or so I believed 'til now. Did you slip out to meet some other lover?"

Namsut smiled another of her polite, angry smiles. "I often went outside after a night with him. The fresh air settled my stomach."

Mehepi caught her breath in affront, then spat on the ground at Namsut's feet. "Nightmare-spawned demoness! Why our husband married a woman so full of hate and death, I will never understand!"

Ginnem threw a stern look at Mehepi. "Your behavior is offensive to our Goddess, headwoman."

Mehepi looked sullen for a moment, but then mumbled an apology. No hint of anger showed on Namsut's face as she inclined her head first to Ginnem, then to Mehepi. That done, she rose, brushed off her gown, and walked away.

But Cet had seen something which made him frown. Nodding to the others to excuse himself, he rose and trotted after her. Though Namsut must have heard him, she kept walking, and only when he caught her in the lee of the hill did she turn to face him.

He took her hands and turned them over. Across each of the palms was a row of dark crusted crescents.

"So that was how you fought the spell," he said.

Namsut's face was as blank as a stone. "I told you, Gatherer. Pain makes me strong."

He almost flinched, for that conversation had taken place in dreaming. But within the mind of the Goddess everything was possible, and desires often called forth the unexpected.

To encourage that desire was dangerous. Yet the compulsion to brush a thumb across her small wounds was irresistible, as was the compulsion to do something about them. Namsut's eyelids fluttered as Cet willed her into a waking dream. In it she looked down to see that her hands were whole. When he released the dream, she blinked, then looked down. Cet rubbed away the lingering smears of dried blood with his thumb; the wounds were gone.

"A simple healing is within any Servant's skill," he said softly. "And it is a Gatherer's duty to fight pain."

Her lips thinned. "Yes, I had forgotten. Pain makes me strong, and you will do nothing that actually helps me. I thank you, Gatherer, but I must wash before we begin the day's travels."

She pulled away before he could think of a reply, and as he watched her leave, he wondered how a Gatherer could fight pain in himself.

By afternoon the next day they reached their destination. According to Mehepi, the brigands had attacked the village repeatedly to claim the mined lapis stones, and the result was devastation on a scale that Cet had never seen. They passed an empty standing granary and bare fields. Several of the village's houses were burned-out shells; the eyes and cheeks of the people they saw were nearly as hollow. Cet could not imagine why anyone would vie to rule such a place.

Yet here he saw for the first time that not all the village was arrayed against Namsut. Two young girls with warm smiles came out to tend her horse when she dismounted. A toothless old man hugged her tightly, and threw an ugly glare at Mehepi's back. "That is the way of things in a small community like this one," Ginnem murmured, following Cet's gaze. "Often it takes only a slight majority—or an especially hateful minority—to make life a nightmare for those in disfavor."

Here Mehepi took over, leading them to the largest house in the village, built of sun-baked brick like the rest, but two stories high. "See to our guests," she ordered Namsut, and without a word Namsut did as she was told. She led Cet, Ginnem, and the two Sentinels into the house.

"Mehepi's room," Namsut said as they passed a room which bore a handsome wide bed. It had probably been the headman's before his death. "My room." To no one's surprise, her room was the smallest in the house. But to Cet's shock, he saw that her bed was low and gauze-draped—the same bed he'd seen in his dream.

A true-seeing: a dream of the future sent by the Goddess. He had never been so blessed, or so confused, in his life.

He distracted himself by concentrating on the matter at hand. "Stay nearby," he told the Sentinels as they settled into the house's two guest rooms. "If the brigands attack again, I'll need to be able to wake you." They nodded, looking sour; neither had forgiven Cet for putting them to sleep before.

"And I?" asked Ginnem. "I can create a kind of shield around myself and anyone near me. Though I won't be able to hold it if you fling a sleep spell at my back again."

"I'll try not to," Cet said. "If my narcomancy is overwhelmed, your shield may be our only protection."

That evening the villagefolk threw them a feast, though a paltry one. One of the elders drew out a battered double-flute, and with a child clapping a menat for rhythm, they had weak, off-key entertainment. The food was worse: boiled grain porridge, a few vegetables, and roasted horsemeat. Cet had made a gift of the horses to Mehepi and her men, and they'd promptly butchered one of them. It was likely the first meat the village had seen in months.

"Stopping the brigands will not save this place," Ginnem muttered under his breath. He was grimly chewing his way through the bland porridge, as were all of them. To refuse the food would have been an insult. "They are too poor to survive."

"The mine here produces lapis, I heard," one of the Sentinels said. "That's valuable."

"The veins are all but depleted," said the other. "I talked to one of the elders awhile this afternoon. They have not mined good stone here in years. Even the nodes the brigands take are poor quality.

With new tools and more men, they might dig deeper, find a new vein, but..." He looked about the room and sighed.

"We must ask the Temple Superior to send aid," Ginnem said.

Cet said nothing. The Temple had already given the villagers a phenomenal amount of aid just by sending a Gatherer and two Sentinels; he doubted the Superior would be willing to send more. More likely the village would have to dissolve, its people relocating to other settlements to survive. Without money or status in those places, they would be little better than slaves.

Almost against his will, Cet looked across the feast table at Namsut, who sat beside Mehepi. She had eaten little, her eyes wandering from face to face around the table, seemingly as troubled by the sorry state of her village as the Templefolk. When her eyes fell on Cet, she frowned in wary puzzlement. Flustered, Cet looked away.

To find Ginnem watching him with a strange, sober look. "So, not just jealousy."

Cet lowered his eyes. "No. No doubt it is the start of the madness."

"A kind of madness, yes. Maybe just as dangerous in its own way for you."

"What are you talking about?"

"Love," Ginnem said. "I'd hoped it was only lust, but clearly you care about her."

Cet set his plate down, his appetite gone. Love? He barely knew Namsut. And yet the image of her fighting the sleep spell danced through his mind over and over, a recurring dream that he had no power to banish. And yet the thought of leaving her to her empty fate filled him with anguish.

Ginnem winced, then sighed. "Everything for Her peace."

"What?"

"Nothing." Ginnem did not meet Cet's eyes. "But if you mean

to help her, do it tomorrow, or the day after. That will be the best time."

The words sent a not-entirely-unpleasant chill along Cet's spine. "You've healed her?"

"She needed no healing. She's as fertile as river soil. I can only assume she hasn't conceived yet because the Goddess wanted her child fathered by a man of her choosing. A blessing, not a curse."

Cet looked down at his hands, which trembled in his lap. How could a blessing cause him such turmoil? He wanted Namsut; that he could no longer deny. Yet being with her meant violating his oath. He had never questioned that oath in the sixteen years of his service as a Gatherer. For his faithfulness he had been rewarded with a life of such peace and fulfillment as most people could only imagine. But now that peace was gone, ground away between the twin inexorabilities of duty and desire.

"What shall I do?" he whispered. But if the Sister heard him, he made no reply.

And when Cet looked up, a shadow of regret was in Namsut's eyes.

Ginnem and the Sentinels, who had some ability to protect themselves against narcomancy, took the watch, with Ginnem to remain in the house in case of attack. Exhausted from the previous night's battle and the day's travels, Cet went to sleep in the guestroom as soon as the feast ended. It came as no great surprise that his hours in the land of dreams were filled with faceless phantoms who taunted him with angry smiles and inviting caresses. And among them, the cruelest phantom of all: a currant-skinned girlchild with Cet's kind eyes.

When he woke just as the sky began to lighten with dawn, he

missed the sound of the jungissa, so distracted was he by his own misery. The urge to sleep again seemed so natural, dark and early as it was, that he did not fight it. Perhaps if he slept again, his dreams would be more peaceful.

"Gatherer!"

Perhaps if he slept again...

A foot kicked Cet hard in his side. He cried out and rolled to a crouch, disoriented. Ginnem sat nearby, his hands raised in that defensive gesture again, his face tight with concentration. Only then did Cet notice the high, discordant whine of the narcomancer's jungissa, startlingly loud and nearby.

"The window," Ginnem gritted through his teeth. The narcomancer was right outside the house.

There was a sudden scramble of footsteps outside. The window was too small for egress, so Cet ran through the house, bursting out of the front door just as a fleet shadow ran past. In that same instant Cet passed beyond range of Ginnem's protective magic, and stumbled as the urge to sleep came down heavy as stones. Lifting his legs was like running through mud; he groaned in near pain from the effort. He was dreaming awake when he reached for his own jungissa. But he was a Gatherer and dreams were his domain, so he willed his dream-self to strike the ornament against the door-sill, and it was his waking hand that obeyed.

The pure reverberation of the dragonfly jungissa cleared the lethargy from his mind, and his own heart supplied the righteous fury to replace it. Shaping that fury into a lance of vibration and power, Cet sent it at the fleeing figure's back with all the imperative he could muster. The figure stumbled, and in that instant Cet caught hold of the narcomancer's soul.

There was no resistance as Cet dragged him into dream; whatever training the brigands' narcomancer had, it went no further than sleep-spells. So they fell, blurring through the land of dreams until their shared minds snagged on a commonality. The Temple appeared around them as a skewed, too-large version of the Hall of Blessings, with a monstrous statue of the Dream Goddess looming over all. The narcomancer cried out and fell to his knees at the sight of the statue, and Cet took the measure of his enemy at last.

He was surprised to see how young the man was—twenty at the most, thin and ragged with hair in a half-matted mix of braids and knots. Even in the dream he stank of months unwashed. But despite the filth, it was the narcomancer's awe of the statue which revealed the truth.

"You were raised in the Temple," Cet said.

The narcomancer crossed his arms over his breast and bent his head to the statue. "Yes, yes."

"You were trained?"

"No. But I saw how the magic was done."

And he had taught himself, just from that? But the rest of the youth's tale was easy enough to guess. The Temple raised orphans and other promising youngsters in its House of Children. At the age of twelve, those children chose whether to pursue one of the paths to service, or leave for a life among the laity. Most of the latter did well, for the Temple found apprenticeships or other vocations for them, but there were always a few who suffered from mistakes or misfortune and ended badly.

"Why?" Cet asked. "You were raised to serve peace. How could you turn your back on the Goddess's ways?"

"The brigands," whispered the youth. "They stole me from my farm, used me, beat me. I—I tried to run away. They caught me, but not before I'd found the holy stone, taken a piece for myself. They said I wasn't worthy to be one of them. I showed them, showed them. I showed them I could make the stone work. I didn't want to hurt anyone but it had been so long! So long. It felt so good to be strong again."

Cet cupped his hands around the young man's face. "And look what you have become. Are you proud?"

"...No."

"Where did you find the jungissa?"

The dreamscape blurred in response to the youth's desire. Cet allowed this, admiring the magic in spite of himself. The boy was no true narcomancer, not half-trained and half-mad as he was, but what a Gatherer he could have been! The dream re-formed into an encampment among the hills: the brigands, settled in for the night, eighteen or twenty snoring lumps that had caused so much suffering. Through the shared underpinnings of the dream, Cet understood at once where to find them. Then the dream flew over the hills to a rocky basin. On its upper cliff-face was an outcropping shaped like a bird of prey's beak. In a black-burned scar beneath this lay a small, pitted lump of stone.

"Thank you," Cet said. Taking control of the dream, he carried them from the hills to a greener dreamscape. They stood near the delta of a great river, beyond which lay an endless sea. The sky stretched overhead in shades of blue, some lapis and some as deep as Namsut's mourning gown. In the distance a small town shone like a gemstone amid the carpet of green. Cet imagined it full of people who would welcome the youth when they met him.

"Your soul will find peace here," Cet said.

The youth stared out over the dreamscape, lifting a hand as if the beauty hurt his eyes. When he looked at Cet, he was weeping. "Must I die now?"

Cet nodded, and after a moment the youth sighed.

"I never meant to hurt anyone," he said. "I just wanted to be free."

"I understand," Cet said. "But your freedom came at the cost of others' suffering. That is corruption, unacceptable under the Goddess's law."

The narcomancer bowed his head. "I know. I'm sorry."

Cet smiled and passed a hand over the youth's head. The grime and reek vanished, his appearance becoming wholesome at last. "Then She will welcome your return to the path of peace."

"Thank you," said the youth.

"Thank Her," Cet replied. He withdrew from the dream then, severing the tether and collecting the dreamblood. Back in waking, the boy's body released one last breath and went still. As shouts rang out around the village, Cet knelt beside the body and arranged its limbs for dignity.

Ginnem and one of the Sentinels ran up. "Is it done?" the Sentinel asked.

"It is," Cet said. He lifted the jungissa stone he'd taken from the boy's hand. It was a heavy, irregular lump, its surface jagged and cracked. Amazing the thing had worked at all.

"And are you well?" That was Ginnem. Cet looked at the Sister and understood then that the question had nothing to do with Cet's physical health.

So Cet smiled to let Ginnem see the truth. "I am very well, Sister Ginnem."

Ginnem blinked in surprise, but nodded.

More of the villagers arrived. One of them was Namsut, breathless, with a knife in one hand. Cet admired her for a moment, then bowed his head to the Goddess's will.

"Everything for Her peace," he said.

The Sentinels went into the hills with some of the armed village men, after Cet told them where the brigands could be found. He also told the villagefolk where they could find the parent-stone of the narcomancer's jungissa.

"A basin marked by a bird's beak. I know the place," said Mehepi with a frown. "We'll go destroy the thing."

"No," Namsut said. Mehepi glared at her, but Namsut met her eyes. "We must fetch it back here. That kind of power is always valuable to someone, somewhere."

Cet nodded. "The Temple would indeed pay well for the stone and any pieces of it."

This set the villagers a-murmur, their voices full of wonder and, for the first time since Cet had met them, hope. He left them to their speculations and returned to the guestroom of the headman's house, where he settled himself against a wall and gazed through the window at passing clouds. Presently, as he had known she would, Namsut came to find him.

"Thank you," she said. "You have saved us in more ways than one."

He smiled. "I am only Her servant."

She hesitated and then said, "I . . . I should not have asked you for what I did. It seemed a simple matter to me, but I see how it troubles you."

He shook his head. "No, you were right to ask it. I had forgotten: My duty is to alleviate suffering by any means at my disposal." His oath would have become meaningless if he had failed to remember that. Ginnem had been right to remind him.

It took her a moment to absorb his words. She stepped forward, her body tense. "Then you will do it? You will give me a child?"

He gazed at her for a long while, memorizing her face. "You understand that I cannot stay," he said. "I must return to the Temple afterward, and never see the daughter we make."

"Daugh—" She put a hand to her mouth, then controlled herself. "I understand. The village will care for me. After all their talk of a curse they must, or lose face."

Cet nodded and held out a hand to her. Her face wavered for a moment beneath a mix of emotions—sudden doubt, fear, resignation, and hope—and then she crossed the room, took his hand, and sat down beside him.

"You must...show me how," he said, ducking his eyes. "I have never done this thing."

Namsut stared at him, then blessed him with the first genuine, untainted smile he had ever seen on her face. He smiled back, and in a waking dream saw a horse running, running, over endless green.

"I have never *wanted* to do this thing before now," she said, abruptly shy. "But I know the way of it." And she stood.

Her mourning garments slipped to the floor. Cet fixed his eyes on them, trying not to see the movements of her body as she stripped off her headcloth and undergarments. When she knelt straddling his lap, he trembled as he turned his face away, his breath quickening and heart pounding fast. *A Gatherer belongs wholly to the Goddess*; that was the oath. He could hardly think as Namsut's hands moved down the bare skin of his chest, sliding toward the clasp of his loinskirt, yet he forced his mind to ponder the matter. He had always taken the oath to mean celibacy, but that was foolish, for the

Goddess had never been interested in mere flesh. He loved Namsut and yet his duty, his calling, was still first in his heart. Was that not the quintessence of a Gatherer's vow?

Then Namsut joined their bodies, and he looked up at her in wonder.

"H-holy," he gasped. She moved again, a slow undulation in his lap, and he pressed his head back against the wall to keep from crying out. "This is holy."

Her breath was light and quick on his skin; dimly he understood that she had some pleasure of him as well. "No," she whispered, cupping his face between her hands. Her lips touched his; for a moment he thought he tasted sugared currants before she licked free. "But it will get better."

It did.

They returned to the Temple five days later, carrying the narcomancer's jungissa as a guarantee of the villagers' good faith. The Superior immediately dispatched scribes and tallymen to verify the condition of the parent stone and calculate an appropriate price. The payment they brought for the narcomancer's jungissa alone was enough to buy a year's food for the whole village.

Ginnem bade Cet farewell at the gates of the city, where a party of green- and gold-clad women waited to welcome him home. "You made the hard choice, Gatherer," he said. "You're stronger than I thought. May the Goddess grant your child that strength in turn."

Cet nodded. "And you are wiser than I expected, Sister. I will tell this to all my brothers, that perhaps they might respect your kind more."

Ginnem chuckled. "The gods will walk the earth before that

happens!" Then he sobered, the hint of sadness returning to his eyes. "You need not do this, Gatherer Cet."

"This is Her will," Cet replied, reaching up to grip Ginnem's shoulder. "You see so much, so clearly; can you not see that?"

Ginnem gave a slow nod, his expression troubled. "I saw it when I realized you loved that woman. But..."

"We will meet again in dreams," Cet said softly.

Ginnem did not reply, his eyes welling with tears before he turned sharply away to rejoin his Sisters. Cet watched in satisfaction as they surrounded Ginnem, forming a comforting wall. They would take good care of him, Cet knew. It was the Sisterhood's gift to heal the soul.

So Cet returned to the Temple, where he knelt before the Superior and made his report—stinting nothing when it came to the tale of Namsut. "Sister Ginnem examined her before we left," he said. "She is healthy and should have little trouble delivering the child when the time comes. The firstwife did not take the news happily, but the elder council vowed that the first child of their reborn village would be cared for, along with her mother who so clearly has the gods' favor."

"I see," said the Temple Superior, looking troubled. "But your oath...that was a high price to pay."

Cet lifted his head and smiled. "My oath is unbroken, Superior. I still belong wholly to Her."

The Superior blinked in surprise, then looked hard at Cet for a long moment. "Yes," he said at last. "Forgive me; I see that now. And yet..."

"Please summon one of my brothers," Cet said.

The Superior started. "Cet, it may be weeks or months before the madness—"

"But it will come," Cet said. "That is the price of Her magic; that is what it means to be a true narcomancer. I do not begrudge the price, but I would rather face a fate of my choosing." The horse was in his mind again, its head lunging like a racer's against the swift river current. Sweet Namsut; he yearned for the day he would see her again in dreams. "Fetch Gatherer Liyou, Superior. Please."

The Superior sighed, but bowed his head.

When young Liyou arrived and understood what had to be done, he stared at Cet in shock. But Cet touched his hand and shared with him a moment of the peace that Namsut had given him, and when it was done, Liyou wept. Afterward Cet lay down ready, and Liyou put his fingertips over Cet's closed eyes.

"Cetennem," Cet said, before sleep claimed him for the final time. "I heard it in a dream. My daughter's name shall be Cetennem."

Then with a joyful heart, Cet—Gatherer and narcomancer, servant of peace and justice and the Goddess of Dreams—ran free.

Henosis

Chapter 4

"But they're going to kill you," the woman said.

Harkim sighed at her silhouette.

"Of course they are," he replied.

Chapter 2

The car lurched again. Harkim looked up from his agent's face on the backseat screen, wondering what on earth was wrong with his driver. "Luketon? Have you been at the scotch again, man?"

There was no answer, but of course he hadn't pressed the intercom button. He kept forgetting that he had to. "Harkie, what is it?" Janet's voice, tinny through the screen's speaker, echoed in the limousine compartment. He knew he should've brought the headphones.

"Nothing," he said, out of habit. Through the one-way privacy screen he could see the silhouette of the driver, just a head and a hat and a hint of shoulder. But was that head shorter than it should've been? And was that a lock of hair falling from the hat to curl over one shoulder? Luketon hadn't had hair since Harkim's first son— now a father himself—had grown his.

Harkim pressed the button this time. "Is Luketon ill?" he asked. "He seemed fine this afternoon."

There was silence for a moment. Then the door locks suddenly went down. A moment later, Janet's face vanished in a haze of static; the Citywire connection had been shut off.

A woman's voice returned over the speaker: "Please don't be alarmed, Mr. Harkim."

Pressing the button hard enough to make his thumb twinge, Harkim said, "Who the hell are you?" And the silhoutte turned its head enough that Harkim could glimpse a nightlit profile. One eye, barely visible.

"You don't know me," said the woman. "I'm just a fan."

Chapter 1

"—your greatest fan," gushed the girl in front of Harkim, inhaling deeply and bouncing a little on her toes. And though Harkim was too old to fall for such blandishments—or at least, he'd thought he was—he gave the girl an extra-wide smile.

"'To my greatest fan...'" he said, writing with an exaggerated flourish, and then politely raised his eyebrows.

"Wanda," she said.

"'...Wanda,'" he finished. "'From a grateful old man.'"

She beamed and leaned forward to pick up the book. The pendant between her breasts—something indistinct preserved in amber—swung forward as she did, which gave Harkim a lovely excuse to feast his eyes. "Thank you so much, Mr. Harkim. If you don't mind, can I ask just one quick question? Given the chiastic structure of the narrative in *Dayton's Gate*, did you intend for Inez to symbolize the impetuousness of youth? I can't get over how she died."

Some of Harkim's pleasure faded, though he resisted the urge to sigh. "My dear," he said, as gently as he could, "I haven't a clue what a chiastic structure is. And you're spoiling the book for those who haven't read it." He smiled and nodded toward the line behind the girl. Several of its members were glaring at her.

She went from simpering to sulky at once. "Sorry," she said. "I thought you might like a little intelligent conversation for a change. Never mind." She turned and stalked away.

The next woman came up to the desk, holding out an old and tattered first edition of *The Mighty Bob*, his first published novel. Looking at it, Harkim could not help breaking into a grin.

"Well, well," he said, taking the book reverently; its cover was loose, and so dog-eared that he marveled it was still legible. "Someone's loved *this* book. Where shall I sign?"

"Anywhere," said the woman. "And there's no need to address it to me. But please sign it, 'From the Opus Award Shoe-in.'" Harkim laughed at that, as did several of the people in line who were near enough to hear.

"You want me to jinx myself, do you?" But he grinned and signed the book with that phrase anyway, just because it was such a pleasure to meet a true fan.

As he handed the book back, she brushed his fingers with hers before taking it. "I love you," she said.

"Thank you," he said, and gave her a kind smile before beckoning the next person forward.

Chapter 5

The words did not make sense. Janet spoke to him again, and he blinked, recovering enough to focus on her.

"I'm sorry," she repeated. She touched his hand.

Across the banquet hall, tears sheening her face amid sweat, Rasa

Abrogado hurried toward the stage through a gauntlet of cheers and standing ovation and stamping feet. She climbed the steps shakily, though they had both done it easily during the awards rehearsal. Harkim remembered joking with her that if either of them won, they would raise the award and say in their speech that the other had been robbed.

Rasa babbled her way through the speech, then hefted the award: a full-sized, blunted replica of Yukio Mishima's famous tantou, complete with sheath. She thanked the jury and her readers, and then walked off the stage.

Chapter 3

"What is this?" Trembling, Harkim fumbled for the door latch, even though he knew it was locked. There were such tales in his mind: famous people hunted, stabbed, tortured to death by the fans who claimed to love them.

"A kidnapping," said the woman, and Harkim's heart fluttered and clenched within his chest. "For your own good." He tried the door. Locked. The car was moving at full speed anyhow. What could he do, fling himself out and break every bone in his body? Be run over by the cars behind them?

"That is an impossibility, madam," he said. It was a small salve to his pride that his voice did not shake. "By definition, a kidnapping takes its victim somewhere he does not wish to be, against his will. How could that be to anyone's good?"

"I've read your books for years," the woman said, and all at once Harkim placed her voice. His jinx. *The Mighty Bob.* "I've read all of the Opus candidates this year. It's not right that you're on the shortlist."

That? Was she upset over that? "Madam, please. I understand that you may want a different author to win, but I assure you—"

"*It isn't right.*" The car lurched a little, as though she'd jerked the wheel. Harkim caught his breath, hopefully not loudly. "It just isn't right."

He closed his eyes, trying to think past panic. "There are five shortlisted candidates this year," he said. Reasonable, yes. He wanted to sound reasonable, calm, reassuring. "An eighty percent chance that someone else will win, yes? So there's no need for this."

"A twenty percent chance you'll win!" Somehow, despite the thin reverberation of the limo's intercom, he heard the sob in the woman's voice. "How can you stand it?"

"Well, this isn't the first award I've been nominated for—or lost." He added the last quickly, lest she think him arrogant. "After all—"

"Do you know what a piece of Vonnegut's face is worth?" the woman asked.

Harkim flinched. "Nothing," he said. "His grave is state property, protected—"

"*Now.*" Amazing, really, how much derision the intercom could convey. "Not before the relic hunters got to it. His fingers alone went for millions on the black market. And *he* died naturally."

"No." It was probably a bad idea to argue with someone demented enough to kidnap him, but Harkim had never been able to ignore a blatant falsehood. Janet had always warned him not to spend much time with people from Hollywood, because of that. "It wasn't natural. Natural is going to sleep and never waking up. He fell. Hit his head. Lingered for weeks before he finally kicked off. It was a miserable, slow, ignominious death for such a great man."

"Compounded," the woman snapped. "His heirs fought over his

estate. His publisher and agent and film rights holders fought over every scrap of his oeuvre. Pieces, everywhere. Once they found his grave—" Her voice thickened with tears. "That was the least of what they did to him."

"Great men leave legacies," Harkim said. He spoke more harshly than he should have, but he was not afraid anymore. Just a child, he realized. She was just a foolish, idealistic child. "That is the nature of greatness, to change all those who follow. It is an artist's fate, an artist's *duty*, to share all that they are and have been with the world."

"And when you win?" The woman was breathing hard, barely coherent. "When they give you that award, your legacy ends. It means they think you've done all you're going to do, the best you'll ever do. It means they stop listening."

She was right, Harkim realized with some surprise. Not wholly a thoughtless child. That made some of his anger fade, replaced by sympathy.

"They always stop listening, eventually," he said, sitting back on the limousine's leather seat. "Sooner or later. Now, please." He closed his eyes, feeling old and tired. "Take me to the ceremony."

Chapter 6

Afterward, Harkim walked out of the hotel alone. To his very great surprise, the same limousine was there, waiting for him. The driver who stood beside the car was hidden behind dark glasses and beneath a chauffeur's hat, but the body within the uniform was unmistakably female. Harkim stopped in front of her.

"You've gotten your wish," he said. "I'll live to see another day. Congratulations."

"Yes," she said. The glasses did not wholly screen her in the intensity of the hotel lights. He could see her eyes searching his face.

He looked away, tired of her worship. Rather than face it, he looked up at the sky, where a few stars—or perhaps satellites— managed to penetrate the city's light-haze. "They'll have taken Rasa away by now."

"So she can be killed." The woman's voice shook again. "To be *dismembered*."

"Yes." Harkim slid his hands into his pockets. "They'll send the pieces to all the usual places: museums, libraries. An ear or two to the University of Iowa's writing workshop. The obligatory tooth to Columbia, those hacks. Wherever she can inspire the next generation of creators." He shrugged. "More dignified than what happened to Vonnegut. Not as messy as what Mishima did to himself."

"Killed!" She didn't raise her voice, but he felt her vehemence. Her earnestness radiated against him like heat. He closed his eyes, basking in it, since it was all he had.

"Her novel was brilliant," he said, at last. "She deserves to be remembered like this, honored at the height of herself. Not to die alone and poor and forgotten, as so many of us do."

A long and fragile silence fell.

"Do you . . . want me to take you home?" the woman asked.

He shook his head. Going home would reinforce his failure. He'd notified his landlord that the apartment might become available; he'd have to rescind that notice. But he had nowhere else to go. If he went somewhere with other people, he would have to endure their pity and gloating. "I don't know."

"What do you want to do, then?"

He laughed a little, running a hand through his sparse hair. "Nothing. Everything. I don't care. I am open to suggestions."

After a moment, the woman said, "I have a gun." She spoke very softly. Surprised, Harkim looked at her. This time, she looked away.

He considered her offer. If it happened this way—the night he lost the Opus, at the hands of a crazed fan—he shook his head. Impossible to say how people would react. What they would remember. Some would value him even more given the strangeness of his death; some would lose interest, thinking he'd hired the woman to do him in, for the glory. He could control only the when and why of his legacy, not whether or for how long.

He was glad for the woman's kindness, even if she would not think of it as such.

"Drive on, then, my good woman," Harkim said. When she opened the door, he got in.

Too Many Yesterdays,
Not Enough Tomorrows

The alarm clock buzzed at seven, right after reality rolled over. Helen tapped the snooze button for ten more minutes. When the alarm went off again, she believed for a moment that a man was in the room creeping toward her. She sat up ready to lash out with nails and fists and feet, then memory returned and she chuckled to herself. A dream. Habit. Too bad.

BLOGSTER login: Welcome, TwenWen!
[Thursday, ??? feels like 10 p.m.]
Hel, you had the rapist dream too? Thought I was the only sicko! Y'know, back in college psych they said those kinds of dreams are a representation of your subconscious yearning to be rescued from your out-of-control situation. (That, or you want a penis. ^_-) Usually I try to keep mine going awhile, see if he actually manages to score. Never does. Figures; even my Freudian fantasy rapists are pissant schmucks.

In browsing news, surprise! There's yet another spec-thread running among the BumBloggity brats. "The government did it" version 2,563,741. Wish they'd get back to aliens or God; those are more fun.

BTW, gang, meet SapphoJuice (his blog). He's in a snowy reality. Has a studio, poor guy.

Hey, anybody heard from MadHadder lately?

Life, post-prolif: She climbed up from the futon and shuffled across the room, her feet chuffing along the tatami-matted floor. When she reached the kitchen, she took care to yank the fridge door open so that the glass bottles would rattle and clink. Noise made the apartment seem less empty. Then she slapped onto the counter the items that would comprise her breakfast: a cup of yogurt and a cellophaned packet of grilled fish. She rummaged awhile for the stay-fresh drink box of chai tea concentrate; she knew where it was, but rummaging helped to kill time. The milk was as fusty as ever. Irrationally she always retained the vague hope that if she got up soon enough after the rollover, it would taste fresher. Mixing it with the chai covered the not-quite-sour taste, so she microwaved that for three minutes and then used that to wash the fish down.

Chewing, she paused and grinned to herself as she felt a bone prick the inside of her cheek. She'd eaten the packet of fish seven times lately without finding it. The bone was always there, but tiny and easy to miss. Finding it made her feel lucky.

It was going to be another beautiful day in infinity.

BLOGSTER login: Welcome, SapphoJuice!

[Cinco de myass, the year 2 bajillion and 2]

SPINNYSPINNYSPINNY

Hi, all. Thanks for the warm greetings. My daily routine includes two hours of spinning around in my desk chair. My mom never used to let me do it before, so...whee!

Yes, Marguille, your guess as to the origin of my username is correct; I am indeed a squealing Herbert fanboy (sorry, Conty, not a lesbian =P). Only got Children Of in my studio, though. Sucks donkey balls. Big hairy fat ones.

Ah, c'mon, Twen, specthreading is fun and oh so good for you. Granted, it's pretty much a complete waste to wonder how and why the quantum proliferation occurred because we can't do dick to fix it...And granted, the BumBloggers do seem to have the same arguments over and over (and over and over) again...but hey, there's comfort in the routine. Right? Right? ::listens to crickets::

Hel: Wow, Japan? You must have been quite the adventurer, before.

Jogging; she loved it. The rhythmic pounding of the hardpack under her sneakers. The mantra of her breathing. She would never have taken up jogging if there'd still been people around to watch her, maybe point and laugh at the jiggly big-boned sista trying to be FloJo. Before the prolif she'd only just begun to shed her self-consciousness around the Japanese. They rarely stared when she could see them, and her students had gotten used to her by then, but on the street she'd always felt the pressure of the neighbors' gazes against her back, skittering away from her peripheral vision when she turned. The days of Sambo dolls at the corner store were mostly over, but not a lot of Japanese had seen black people anywhere except on television. *My parents must've felt the same during grad school in Des Moines,* she'd always told herself to put things in perspective. It hadn't helped much.

Now, free from the pressure of those gazes, she could run. She was fit and strong and free.

Around her the barren, cracked desert stretched unbroken for as far as the eye could see.

BLOGSTER login: Welcome, KT!

[Saturdayish, The House That Time Forgot]

Fighting the lonelies. Everybody still out there? Conty? Guille? Hel? Twen? (Hi, Sapp.) I haven't heard from MadHadder either. What if the silence got him?

Don't want to think about that. Topic change. Did you know Mr. Hissyfit keeps going through the rollovers, too? I guess cats *do* think.

Sappjuice, it sounds like you're living in Fimbulwinter (sp?). I've got grassy plain. It's boring, but at least I know it can't kill me. You have my e-sympathies.

She liked best the fact that the day started over after about ten hours. Incomplete reality, incomplete time. She'd stayed awake to watch the rollover numerous times, but for a phenomenon that should've been a string theorist's wet dream, it was singularly unimpressive. Like watching a security camera video loop: dull scene, flicker, resume dull scene. Though once the flicker passed, there was grilled fish and stale milk in her fridge again, and her alarm clock buzzed to declare that 7:00 a.m. had returned. Only her mind remained the same.

She usually went to bed a few hours after the second alarm. That gave her time to print out the latest novella making the rounds in cyberspace, read it in the bath, and maybe work on her own would-be masterpieces. It didn't bother her that the poems she wrote erased themselves every rollover. If she wanted to keep them, she posted them online, where the mingling of so many minds kept time linear. But doing that exposed the fragile words to the scrutiny of others, and sometimes it was better to just let them vanish.

She decided to post the latest one to share with her friends. The new boy wasn't a friend, not yet, but maybe he had friend-potential.

BLOGSTER login: Welcome, Marguille!

[Sunday, 5 Marguille'sMonth, 2 years A.P., 2 a.m.]

I agree with Twen; specthredding is evil. But I can't help it; been reading the Bumwankers stuff (I know, I know). my vote has always been for the government theory. $87 bil. for an "emergency fund"? Shyeah. Probly only took half that to build some knd of new super-weapon, or hotwire a particle acelerator. "I know! Let's shoot some protons at the terrorists! Yeah! Oops, we bro,ke the universe!"

But seriously . . . I keep thinking that somewhere out there, normal reality still exists. no, scratch that—I *know* it exists, because it's possible. Fun with quantum thery! 'Course, that means oblivion exists too. (This is what we get for letting that guy Shroedinger experiment on his cat. Should've sicked PETA on him.)

SappJuice, don't feel bad about your studio. Hel's Japanese apartment's probably half the size of yours. (What do you call half a studio? A closet? ::ducks rotten tomatoes from Japan::) Anyway, it's not like the rest of us are so much better off. What difference does a few square feet make when they're the same square feet every damn day?

She got the email just before she would've gone to bed. The ding from her computer surprised her. Blogs worked, as did other forms of social media. Direct, private contact was impossible. Individual-to-individual relays—instant messaging, email—worked, but were always iffy. Most people just didn't bother to try; too disappointing. And then there were the rumors.

But she read the email anyway.

"To: Hel

From: SapphoJuice

Subject: Hi

Helen (seems so weird to say your full name),

Hope you get this. I read the poem you posted in your blog. I just wanted to say…it wasn't beautiful, but it did move me. Made me remember the way things used to be, and made me realize I don't really mind that the old world is gone. I got put in a garbage can by football players *every day* during my freshman year. My mom always used to tell me I'd never amount to anything. How could I miss that? Anyway.

I guess the only thing that bothers me now is the silence. And sometimes I don't even mind that, but sometimes the snow just gets to me. Why the hell couldn't my pocket universe have formed around an *interesting* environment? I could dig an endless beach, maybe an endless forest. No, I get snow. It's so quiet. It never stops falling. I can't go out far without losing the apartment in the haze. Sometimes I want to just keep walking into the white, who cares? Then I read your poem.

Sappy (yeah, I know)"

She sat at her computer savoring the newness of the moment.

BLOGSTER login: Welcome, KT!

[Ohwhocares? Someday, somewhen]

Mr. Hissyfit got out. I tried to catch him but he just ran straight away into the grass. I keep going out to call for him, but he must be too far away to hear me.

Stupid cat. Stupid goddamn cat. I can't stop crying.

She emailed SapphoJuice back and told him that she had only feared the silence once. That had been right after the prolif, when she'd still been adjusting. She'd started running and hadn't stopped; just put her head down and cranked her arms like pistons and hauled ass as fast as her legs would take her, as far as her lungs could fuel. When she'd looked around, the apartment was gone, swallowed into the cracked-earth landscape. Instant panic. The apartment was only a fragment of reality, but it was *her* fragment of reality, her only connection to the other incomplete miniverses that now made up existence. Even before the prolif, she had been happiest there.

She could admit that, now, to him. But back on the day she'd run too far, she'd been in a panic, her grip on sanity slipping by cogs. It had taken the threat of true isolation, of wandering lost through endless wastelands until thirst or exposure killed her, to make her see the apartment as haven and not prison. So half-blinded by tears she had run back, thanking God that her shoes were cheap. One of them had an uneven sole, which scuffed a little crescent-shaped mark into the dusty soil. The moon had led her home.

BLOGSTER login: Welcome Conty!

RED ALERT

[Day 975 (yeah right I actually keep count in my head)]

KT no more kidding. Fight it. Don't think about the damn cat. Go out and run—you can go pretty far from your house in the grass, can't you? Eat something. Hell, eat everything; it's not like it won't come back at rollover.

Talk to us.

The emails she sent didn't always go through. More than once she had to send them again when they bounced or, more often, simply never got a response. She saw the bounce histories in his attachments and knew that he'd had to send his multiple times, too. Just another day post-prolif.

She did not tell the others about the private correspondence, and neither did he. She knew what her friends would have said. It became something special, secret, a little titillating. As the days passed, her dreams changed. Now the man creeping about her room had a face and a much less sinister demeanor. Now he looked like a skinny, geeky teenager, whose shy smile was for her alone.

BLOGSTER login: Welcome, Marguille!
[Jan. 37 errordate errortime 12:5g0k p.m.]
SILENCE.
You guys want to chat? I need some facetime. I think KT's gone.

Over the exchanges, she shared her life story with him. Growing up less than middle-class, trying to act less than upper-class. The teasing in elementary school because she "talked proper" and couldn't dance. Her first boyfriend, a white boy—she'd been too guilt-ridden to bring him home to meet her parents, and they'd broken up because of her shame. Her next boyfriend, the one she'd almost married until she found out he was cheating on her. Graduating college and feeling the isolation grow in her life. Few friends, none of them local. No lovers. She'd always been an only child, a lonely child; she was used to it. The prospect of a couple of years in Japan hadn't seemed all that daunting because what difference did it make, after all?

He told her about himself. Second-generation American-born Chinese, too free-spirited for the rigidly traditional family into which he'd been born, too shy to face the world without the shield of a book. No girlfriends; the girls he'd liked had been more interested in jocks and red-blooded rich boys. Never brave enough to venture far from home, the internet had become his realm, and in it he thrived. He was a Big Name Fan in certain circles, known for his biting wit and brutal honesty. The prolif had barely slowed him down.

She worried about what might happen as the clandestine exchanges continued, but never mentioned her fears to him. She'd begun to enjoy herself too much; the "incoming mail" chime was enough to make her heart race with excitement. She had to force herself out for her daily runs.

It helped that the more they talked, the more reliable the relaying became. Pretty soon messages were going through after only two or three tries, and not bouncing at all.

IRC session start: Sun? MarEMBJune datetime error
    *** marguille sets mode: +o TwenWen Conty Helen sappjuice
    > Log set and active! TwenWen logging!
    <marguille> dunno why you're logging, twen. it's judst a chat.

<TwenWen> Not just a chat. MadHadder and KT's memorial service.

* Conty sighs.

* Helen observes a moment of silence.

<marguille> ditto. y'know...I herd more spec the other day.

* Conty groans.

* Helen sighs.

* TwenWen waits for Marguille's spec...and waits...and waits.

<TwenWen>...lagged?

<marguille> this one sounds like it's from the eggheads who did this. here it is: decoherence. when things in a quantum state are coupled to thuings outside that state, both systems collapse. no lag, 2-finger-typing lots, sorry.

<Conty> Yeah, that's egghead all right

* Helen wishes she had a nickel for every egghead spec... but where would she put them all?

*** sappjuice changes topic to "The Egghead Pyramid Scheme!"

* TwenWen giggles.

<marguille> seriously...you heard abut HafCafLatay?

<marguille> she got email from her MOM.

<marguille> as soon as she read it...poof. none of her blogfriends ever heard fm her again.

<Conty> WTF does that have to do with incoherence???

* TwenWen says, "DEcoherence. And I can use other big words, like 'marmalade'."

<Conty> Whatever. Still WTF

<sappjuice> There's spec that *we're* in a quantum state, y'know, each of us. Endless partial variations on the same world, same time...

<Conty> What, so if we ever have contact with somebody in another reality, we'll disappear?

* marguille is typing.

<marguille> the eggheds say it matters if the connection is strong or weajk. the stronger the coupling, the faster the collapse. weak couplings last a long time, maybe even stabilize. vbut with really strong couplings the collapse is nearly instant.

<TwenWen> Ooh, coupling! Wink wink nudge nudge say no more.

<TwenWen> Seriously... you're saying coupling = personal ties? Coupling *to other people*?

<marguille> yep. we're already weakly connected, or we wouldn't be able to talk like this. but strong connections are emotional. HafCaf found her mom and... silence. Both of 'em.

<marguille> sucks, don't it.

<Conty> Ohdamn.

<sappjuice> Huh?

<Conty> I forgot, rollover's about to

*** Conty has been disconnected.

<marguille> Fuck.

<TwenWen> Um, I rollover in 10 mins.

<sappjuice> Maybe we should cut this short, then. Nice seeing everybody face to face, so to speak.

* Helen agrees.

* marguille sighs and waves.

<marguille> back to blogdom then. Toodles.

*** marguille has logged off.

*** TwenWen has stopped logging.

*** TwenWen has logged off.

<sappjuice> So it's just you and me. Wanna email?

<Helen> Yeah.

*** Helen has logged off.

*** sappjuice has logged off.

Session Close: Mon? Time? Deeeeeeeechgkl#@ ^^^^

Just spec, she told herself over the next few days. Too many people had expected a more dramatic apocalypse; now they cried wolf at every shadow. Some of their theories sounded right, but most were cockamamie—like Guille's implication that friendship, family, *love*, could be the reason that some people just disappeared. That would mean the only people still alive across the proliferated realities were those whose ties to the world had been weak from the beginning.

Those who'd lived alone. Those who'd been socially isolated. Not the completely disconnected ones; people without 'net access would've gone stark raving within days after the prolif. But the loosely connected ones, who interacted with others only when they had to, or through a screen. Those who'd maintained just enough connection to keep them sane, then. Just enough connection to keep them alive, now.

Just spec, she thought again as the alarm clock buzzed. She hadn't slept in two rollovers. *Not me.*

New habit. She sat up and reached over to her laptop, which rested on a low table beside the futon, and tapped its touchpad to wake it up. It chimed as the screen lit; she had mail.

"Helen,

I know this is risky, stupid, cheesy, whatever. But I can't help myself. I've never met you and never will, but . . . some things you can feel no matter what. They used to say this was all just pheromones, but that's crap. I've never smelled you and I only have my imagination to tell me what you look like. But I have to say this because it's true.

I love you.

I wish oh shit I didn't believe it but it's true"

No sig. Not even a period at the end of the last sentence. He'd had enough time to send, but not to finish first.

Not me, her mind whispered, *and not him. Please, not him.*

And as the walls of her tiny apartment began to warp and the barren landscape beyond her window vanished, she had time to click on the bookmark for her blog's "update" form and type a single line.

"The way out, or the end? Sapp's gone to see. I'm going too."

She hit "post" as reality folded into silence.

The You Train

Hey, girl. Yeah, I know; I'm sorry. Just haven't been feeling all that social lately. How are you? That's good, that's good. How's the little mister? Oh, that's hilarious. That boy's a mess. Me? Well, you know.

Hey. Did you know the B train doesn't run at night?

I found out a couple of weekends ago. I was coming home from a date, one of those Fun dot com deals, Friday night at about eleven. Not so fun after all, kind of boring really. Anyway, I was standing there on the platform, might've been Thirty-Fourth Street, and the place was dead empty. I think I saw a homeless dude on the other platform, but that was it. The sign said the train ran weekdays. Right, me too, Monday through Friday, right? No, it means week-*days*. After nine o'clock it's like Cinderella after the ball. I know, huh?

So anyway, there I was waiting. An F train came and I ignored it. Doesn't go to my stop. Then a D. Then a V. It was so quiet in there between trains, I could hear my own heart beat. I don't like being in there when it's that empty, sometimes it's not safe, but you know, a cab would've cost thirty dollars and I don't get paid 'til next week. But finally someone comes in, this woman, and she looks at me like I'm crazy and tells me the B doesn't run at night. Like I should've known from that sign. Weekdays. Whatever.

You ever look down the tunnels when you're waiting? Sometimes you can see trains moving around in there, passing by on their way to other stations or heading for other platforms. You can't really see much besides the sign, just that glowing colored circle with a letter or a number at the center, floating in the dark like a beady little eye. Sometimes it feels like the trains are curled up in burrows down there. They come out into the light when people gather on the platform and call out to them in just the right way . . .

Okay, Ms. Thing. I'll be sure to heckle you at the next open mic night.

But y'know, I could've sworn I saw a B on one of them.

Yeah, girl, rough day. There was this meeting at work. Everybody in my office wants to get their two cents in, make themselves look good, right? I just want the meeting over so I can get back to work. So they're going 'round and 'round, everybody trying to outdo everybody else with cool ideas, and nothing's getting *done*. So I finally clear my throat and suggest maybe we should move on to the next agenda item.

They looked at me like I was shit on the bottom of their shoes, girl. One of them, this prissy blonde from Marketing, she says, "If you don't want to be a part of the team, at least don't ruin it for the rest of us." Right there, in front of everybody. I didn't say a word for the rest of the meeting. I couldn't think of anything to say. I felt like . . . hell, I don't know. Like kicking her ass. Like crying. It was the most . . . I hate these people.

And you know what? When the meeting ended, still nothing had been done. Three hours wasted. I swear.

Then on the way home, I got off at the wrong stop, one of those endless Something-th Street stations above Columbus Circle, can't remember which, there's so many anyway. I was on the platform forever waiting for the 1. I was worried because a lot of those stops, they get skipped during rush hour, and I couldn't find a map. Finally the train came along, and I was about to step in when I realized there was nobody on it. Middle of rush hour, every seat empty. So I looked up to see if there was an "out of service" sign, and I saw it was the 9, not the 1. So then I—

I said the 9.

Yes, I'm sure it was the 9.

Really? Oh, yeah, I remember reading something about that one getting shut down. But I'm pretty sure it was a 9. Maybe they break them out of mothballs during rush hour, I don't know. Maybe the conductor just rolled up an old sign. Anyway, I didn't get on it, but that meant I had to sit another half hour before a 1 finally came along. Pain in the ass, and for what? Nothing got done.

Yeah, I quit Dull Date dot com. The only people who were emailing me lately were these old guys having midlife crises, looking for somebody to make their ex-wives jealous. And too many of the guys my age have problems. I never did tell you about the last date, did I? He kept talking about his ex-girlfriend, and how she only broke up with him because she was going through a hard time. Then he started crying.

No, I didn't leave. He wasn't an ass about it; he was just lonely and needed somebody to talk to, so I let him talk. Hell, I know how he feels.

I can't say if I'm over Nick yet. I don't miss him anymore. Nick the Dick, I'd've killed him if I'd married him, you know that. But . . . sometimes I wonder if that was my one chance, you know? Maybe you're not supposed to squander love when it comes along, even if he's a dick. Maybe I should've tried . . .

Okay, okay, I know, right, okay, I said you could slap me.

Damnedest thing happened on the way home, though. Did you know there's a P train? Yeah, I never heard of it either. I saw it blow through on the express track. I tried to see by the side signs where it was going, but it was too fast. I didn't see anybody in it. Maybe it runs in some boondocky part of the city, like Queens.

Shut up, I know you're from there.

I was feeling really bad today, girl.

Gray days do a number on me. That's when I wake up and really notice that empty spot in the bed beside me. Days like that are going-through-the-motions days. I get up and get ready for work and go off to a boring job with people I hate, and then in the evenings I come home. The trains are always crowded. A million people packed together like sardines, and no one talks to anyone else. No one *looks* at anyone else.

Gray days are days when I feel, more than any other, like I don't belong here.

There was a T train waiting at the platform this morning. Did you see it? No, I never heard of the T either. Maybe it's new.

The doors were open when I first stepped onto the platform, but when other people showed up, the doors closed and the train left. I wonder where it went?

Sometimes I wonder if I'm strong enough for this city.

Well, because I'm nice. I mean, too nice. Like, the other day, I took my clothes to this laundromat in my neighborhood for drop-off service. Damn, I miss having a washer and dryer in the house. I know! Next time I move. So this place, I dropped off my clothes, and when I went back, half my shit was stained red. The woman apologized but then tried to tell me it was my fault for giving her a red shirt that wasn't colorfast. It *was* colorfast, at least when you wash it in cold with other dark-colored stuff, but all the stuff that had been messed up was light-colored—a beige sweater, a white T-shirt. So they must've put the shirt in with the whites. And that's my fault?

But I didn't say anything. I just walked off and started looking for another laundromat.

Would a real New Yorker have done that? I should've pitched a fit. I should've demanded my money back, at least, or compensation for the damaged stuff. I should've threatened to sue. But I didn't say anything. I've been chewing on that for weeks, trying to figure out why I didn't.

But it's not just that. My coworkers. My ex. My building super. I've been after him for six weeks to get that crack in my ceiling fixed. Maybe if I was more of a bitch, he'd come.

Am I weak? Can people smell that? Maybe I'm not meant for big-city life. Maybe I should've stayed back in that dinky little town, instead of running up here after I broke up with Nick...

Thanks, girl. You don't know how it helps to hear that. I wish I could save up this stuff, and replay it in my head whenever I start to wonder. I wonder all the time these days.

So it was the K today.

It didn't come out of the tunnel, actually. I was at Fifty-Seventh, on my way home from work. I looked down the N tunnel and there was a K there. Just sitting there, maybe fifty feet in. It must've been on a side track, because when the N came and went, the K was gone.

I looked it up this time. The K stopped running in '88. Not that it ever ran on this line at all.

I think it was checking me out, y'know?

Yeah. That's what I think.

In fact, I think they're all checking me out. All the defunct lines, the dead lines. I think they never really go away. I mean, every day somewhere, somebody slips up and says, "Take the 1/9," when they should just say the 1, or they say the T when they mean the V, or whatever. Too many people look into those empty tunnels and expect to see *something* where nothing is. And the trains, maybe they hear all that. Maybe they think they're still needed. So maybe they stick around, waiting to be called.

It probably doesn't take much. Just one person, really, wanting badly enough to go...hell, wherever it is they go. I wonder if...

Why shouldn't I say things like that? I kind of want to know, you know? Where they go. Wouldn't you?

Okay, okay. I won't say it anymore. I'm sorry.

I'm probably hallucinating this shit anyway. Carbon monoxide or rat poison or something, all kinds of crap down there. Maybe I'm allergic and this is, I dunno, *anaphylactic* bullshit, as opposed to garden-variety bullshit, ha ha ha. You're the only person I know who would take me seriously when I say things like this. That's why I love you, girl.

Thanks for listening, though. Really. I don't know what I'd do without you.

Would you ever tell me if I got on your nerves?

It's not crazy. You're married, you've got a baby and another on the way. You're always busy. You've got a life.

I know. I know you'll always be my friend. But...I can't call you when I want to go somewhere on a Friday night. You'd have to find a sitter, call your husband, rearrange your whole life. You can't come over when I'm bored and lonely and just want somebody to sit around and watch TV with. I mean, I can call you, I know, but I'm always worried the phone will wake up everybody in your house.

Sometimes I need more from you than you can give, y'know? I know that. I try not to impose, even though...even though you're all I've...I don't mean to impose.

So just tell me, okay? If I ever get on your nerves. Just say you'll tell me if I do. It's okay, really. I'll understand.

Hey, girl! Long time no speak. What's up?

I'm fine. No, really. I'm sorry I worried you. I know, I was kind of talking crazy. I kind of felt crazy. But I'm fine now.

Oh, yeah, so I took the U after work one night.

No, there was never a U. I mean, I saw it, a big black letter on a plain white circle, kind of like an eye, but it's not a real line. It's one of the spares, in case they need to create a new line sometime, like X and Y. It's a line that never was. But I saw it that day, peeking out at me from the tunnel. Checking me out. I don't know how it heard me, the subways are so loud, but I just whispered, "Well, come on, then." And it rolled right in.

There was no conductor. All the seats were wide open, shiny and clean. So I got on it. I rode all the way to the end of the line.

Oh, girl, I'm sorry, my cell barely gets any signal out here. Can you hear me? If we get cut off, I'll call you back later. I just wanted you to know I was all right. And, y'know, you can visit me anytime you want, okay?

Because I know you hate it sometimes, the routine. Giving up your dreams, or at least postponing them, to have kids. It was so stupid of me to assume that just because you had a family, everything was perfect for you. I understand that now. I'm sorry for making you put up with all my shit. You've been such a good friend.

So I want to return the favor. Sometimes all you need to do is take a chance, you know, try something new. Close your eyes and take a step forward, then look around to see where you are.

If you take that step, you'll find me. Doesn't matter where, really. Even if you end up in a bad place, I'll find you. I got your back. Didn't you know that already? Ha ha ha.

Catch me up about the new baby sometime. I've got so much to tell you, too.

Gotta go, sorry. I'll catch you later, okay?

Train's coming.

Non-Zero Probabilities

In the mornings, Adele girds herself for the trip to work as a warrior for battle. First she prays, both to the Christian god of her Irish ancestors and to the orishas of her African ancestors—the latter she is less familiar with, but getting to know. Then she takes a bath with herbs, including dried chickory and allspice, from a mixture given to her by the woman at the local botanica. (She doesn't know Spanish well, but she's getting to know that, too. Today's word is *suerte*.) Then, smelling vaguely of coffee and pumpkin pie, she layers on armor: the Saint Christopher medal her mother sent her, for protection on journeys. The hair-clasp she was wearing when she broke up with Larry, which she regards as the best decision of her life. On especially dangerous days, she wears the panties in which she experienced her first self-induced orgasm post-Larry. They're a bit ragged after too many commercial laundromat washings, but still more or less sound. (She washes them by hand now, with Woolite, and lays them flat to dry.)

Then she starts the trip to work. She doesn't bike, though she owns one. A next-door neighbor broke an arm when her bike's front wheel came off in mid-pedal. Could've been anything. Just an accident. But still.

So Adele sets out, swinging her arms, enjoying the day if it's sunny, wrestling with her shitty umbrella if it's rainy. (She no longer opens the umbrella indoors.) Keeping a careful eye out for those who may not be as well protected. It takes two to tango, but only one to seriously fuck up some shit, as they say in her 'hood. And lo and behold, just three blocks into her trip there is a horrible crash and the ground shakes and car alarms go off and there are screams and people start running. Smoke billows, full of acrid ozone and a taste like dirty blood. When Adele reaches the corner, tensed and ready to flee, she beholds the Franklin Avenue shuttle train, a tiny thing that runs on an elevated track for some portions of its brief run, lying sprawled over Atlantic Avenue like a beached aluminum whale. It has jumped its track, fallen thirty feet to the ground below, and probably killed everyone inside or under or near it.

Adele goes to help, of course, but even as she and other good Samaritans pull bodies and screaming wounded from the wreckage, she cannot help but feel a measure of contempt. It is a cover, her anger; easier to feel that than horror at the shattered limbs, the truncated lives. She feels a bit ashamed, too, but holds on to the anger because it makes a better shield.

They should have known better. The probability of a train derailment was infinitesimal. That meant it was only a matter of time.

Her neighbor—the other one, across the hall—helped her figure it out, long before the math geeks finished crunching their numbers.

"Watch," he'd said, and laid a deck of cards facedown on her coffee table. (There was coffee in the cups, with a generous dollop of Bailey's. He was a nice-enough guy that Adele felt comfortable offering this.) He shuffled it with the blurring speed of an expert, cut the deck, shuffled again, then picked up the whole deck and spread it, still facedown. "Pick a card."

Adele picked. The Joker.

"Only two of those in the deck," he said, then shuffled and spread again. "Pick another."

She did, and got the other Joker.

"Coincidence," she said. (This had been months ago, when she was still skeptical.)

He shook his head and set the deck of cards aside. From his pocket he took a pair of dice. (He was nice enough to invite inside, but he was still that kind of guy.) "Check it," he said, and tossed them onto her table. Snake eyes. He scooped them up, shook them, tossed again. Two more ones. A third toss brought up double sixes; at this, Adele had pointed in triumph. But the fourth toss was snake eyes again.

"These aren't weighted, if you're wondering," he said. "Nobody filed the edges or anything. I got these from the bodega up the street, from a pile of shit the old man was tossing out to make more room for food shelves. Brand new, straight out of the package."

"Might be a bad set," Adele said.

"Might be. But the cards ain't bad, nor your fingers." He leaned forward, his eyes intent despite the pleasant haze that the Bailey's had brought on. "Snake eyes three tosses out of four? And the fourth a double six. That ain't supposed to happen even in a rigged game. Now check this out."

Carefully he crossed the fingers of his free hand. Then he tossed the dice again, six throws this time. The snakes still came up twice, but so did other numbers. Fours and threes and twos and fives. Only one double-six.

"That's batshit, man," said Adele.

"Yeah. But it works."

He was right. And so Adele had resolved to read up on gods of luck and to avoid breaking mirrors. And to see if she could find a four-leaf clover in the weed patch down the block. (They sell some in Chinatown, but she's heard they're knockoffs.) She's hunted through the patch several times in the past few months, once for several hours. Nothing so far, but she remains optimistic.

It's only New York, that's the really crazy thing. Yonkers? Fine. Jersey? Ditto. Long Island? Well, that's still Long Island. But past East New York, everything is fine.

The news channels had been the first to figure out that particular wrinkle, but the religions really went to town with it. Some of them have been waiting for the End Times for the last thousand years; Adele can't really blame them for getting all excited. She does blame them for their spin on it, though. There have to be bigger "dens of iniquity" in the world. Delhi has poor people coming out of its ears, Moscow's mobbed up, Bangkok is pedophile heaven. She's heard there are still some sundown towns in the Pacific Northwest. Everybody hates on New York.

And it's not like the signs are all bad. The state had to suspend its lottery program; too many winners in one week bankrupted it. The Knicks made it to the Finals and the Mets won the Series. A lot of people with cancer went into spontaneous remission, and some folks with full-blown AIDS stopped showing any viral load at all. (There are new tours now. Double-decker buses full of the sick and disabled. Adele tries to tell herself they're just more tourists.)

The missionaries from out of town are the worst. On any given day they step in front of her, shoving tracts under her nose and wanting to know if she's saved yet. She's getting better at spotting them from a distance, yappy islands interrupting the sidewalk river's flow, their faces alight with an inner glow that no self-respecting local would display without three beers and a fat payday check. There's one now, standing practically underneath a scaffolding ladder. Idiot; two steps back and he'll double his chances for getting hit by a bus. (And then the bus will catch fire.)

In the same instant that she spots him, he spots her, and a grin stretches wide across his freckled face. She is reminded of blind newts that have light-sensitive spots on their skin. This one is unsaved-sensitive. She veers right, intending to go around the scaffold, and he takes a wide step into her path again. She veers left; he breaks that way.

She stops, sighing. "What."

"Have you accepted—"

"I'm Catholic. They do us at birth, remember?"

His smile is forgiving. "That doesn't mean we can't talk, does it?"

"I'm busy." She attempts a feint, hoping to catch him off-guard. He moves with her, nimble as a linebacker.

"Then I'll just give you this," he says, tucking something into her hand. Not a tract, bigger. A flyer. "The day to remember is August eighth."

This, finally, catches Adele's attention. August eighth. 8/8—a lucky day according to the Chinese. She has it marked on her calendar as a good day to do things like rent a Zipcar and go to Ikea.

"Yankee Stadium," he says. "Come join us. We're going to pray the city back into shape."

"Sure, whatever," she says, and finally manages to slip around him. (He lets her go, really. He knows she's hooked.)

She waits until she's out of downtown before she reads the flyer, because downtown streets are narrow and close and she has to keep an eye out. It's a hot day; everybody's using their air conditioners. Most people don't bolt the things in the way they're supposed to.

"A PRAYER FOR THE SOUL OF THE CITY," the flyer proclaims, and in spite of herself, Adele is intrigued. The flyer says that over 500,000 New Yorkers have committed to gathering on that day and concentrating their prayers. That kind of thing has power now, she thinks. There's some lab at Princeton—dusted off and given new funding lately—that's been able to prove it. Whether that means Someone's listening or just that human thoughtwaves are affecting events as the scientists say, she doesn't know. She doesn't care.

She thinks, *I could ride the train again.*

She could laugh at the next Friday the thirteenth.

She could—and here her thoughts pause, because there's something she's been trying not to think about, but it's been a while and she's never been a very good Catholic girl anyway. But she could, maybe, just maybe, try dating again.

As she thinks this, she is walking through the park. She passes the vast lawn, which is covered in fast-darting black children and lazily sunning white adults and a few roving brown elders with Italian ice carts. Though she is usually on watch for things like this, the flyer has distracted her, so she does not notice the nearby cart man stopping, cursing in Spanish because one of his wheels has gotten mired in the soft turf.

This puts him directly in the path of a child who is running, his eyes trained on a descending Frisbee; with the innate arrogance of a city child, he has assumed that the cart will have moved out of the way by the time he gets there. Instead the child hits the cart at full speed, which catches Adele's attention at last, so that too late she realizes she is at the epicenter of one of those devastating chains of events that only ever happen in comedy films and the transformed city. In a Rube Goldberg string of utter improbabilities, the cart tips over, spilling tubs of brightly colored ices onto the grass. The boy flips over it with acrobatic precision, completely by accident, and lands with both feet on a tub of ices. The sheer force of this blow causes the tub to eject its contents with projectile force. A blast of blueberry-coconut-red hurtles toward Adele's face, so fast that she has no time to scream. It will taste delicious. It will also likely knock her into oncoming bicycle traffic.

At the last instant the Frisbee hits the flying mass, altering its trajectory. Freezing fruit flavors splatter the naked backs of a row of sunbathers nearby, much to their dismay.

Adele's knees buckle at the close call. She sits down hard on the grass, her heart pounding, while the sunbathers scream and the cart man checks to see if the boy is okay and the pigeons converge.

She happens to glance down. A four-leaf clover is growing there, at her fingertips.

Eventually she resumes the journey home. At the corner of her block, she sees a black cat lying atop a garbage can. Its head has been crushed, and someone has attempted to burn it. She hopes it was dead first, and hurries on.

Adele has a garden on the fire escape. In one pot, eggplant and herbs; she has planted the clover in this. In another pot are peppers and flowers. In the big one, tomatoes and a scraggly collard that she's going to kill if she keeps harvesting leaves so quickly. (But she likes greens.) It's luck—good luck—that she'd chosen to grow a garden this year, because since things changed, it's been harder for wholesalers to bring food into the city, and prices have shot up. The farmers' market that she attends on Saturdays has become a barterers' market, too, so she plucks a couple of slim, deep purple eggplants and a handful of angry little peppers. She wants fresh fruit. Berries, maybe.

On her way out, she knocks on the neighbor's door. He looks

surprised as he opens it, but pleased to see her. It occurs to her that maybe he's been hoping for a little luck of his own. She gives it a think-over, and hands him an eggplant. He looks at it in consternation. (He's not the kind of guy to eat eggplant.)

"I'll come by later and show you how to cook it," she says. He grins.

At the farmers' market she trades the angry little peppers for sassy little raspberries, and the eggplant for two stalks of late rhubarb. She also wants information, so she hangs out awhile gossiping with whoever sits nearby. Everyone talks more than they used to. It's nice.

And everyone, everyone she speaks to, is planning to attend the prayer.

"I'm on dialysis," says an old lady who sits under a flowering tree. "Every time they hook me up to that thing, I'm scared. Dialysis can kill you, you know."

It always could, Adele doesn't say.

"I work on Wall Street," says another woman, who speaks briskly and clutches a bag of fresh fish as if it's gold. Might as well be; fish is expensive now. A tiny Egyptian scarab pendant dangles from a necklace the woman wears. "Quantitative analysis. All the models are fucked now. We were the only ones they didn't fire when the housing market went south, and now this." So she's going to pray, too. "Even though I'm kind of an atheist. Whatever, if it works, right?"

Adele finds others, all tired of performing their own daily rituals, all worried about their likelihood of being outliered to death.

She goes back to her apartment building, picks some sweet basil, and takes it and the eggplant next door. Her neighbor seems a little nervous. His apartment is cleaner than she's ever seen it, with the scent of Pine-Sol still strong in the bathroom. She tries not to laugh, and demonstrates how to peel and slice eggplant, salt it to draw out the toxins ("it's related to nightshade, you know"), and sauté it with basil in olive oil. He tries to look impressed, but she can tell he's not the kind of guy to enjoy eating his vegetables.

Afterward they sit, and she tells him about the prayer thing. He shrugs. "Are you going?" she presses.

"Nope."

"Why not? It could fix things."

"Maybe. Maybe I like the way things are now."

This stuns her. "Man, the train fell off its track last week." Twenty people dead. She has woken up in a cold sweat on the nights since, screams ringing in her ears.

"Could've happened anytime," he says, and she blinks in surprise because it's true. The official investigation says someone—track worker, maybe—left a wrench sitting on the track near a power coupling. The chance that the wrench would hit the coupling, causing a short and explosion, was one in a million. But never zero.

"But...but..." She wants to point out the other horrible things that have occurred. Gas leaks. Floods. A building fell down in Harlem. A fatal duck attack. Several of the apartments in their building are empty because a lot of people can't cope. Her neighbor—the other one, with the broken arm—is moving out at the end of the month. Seattle. Better bike paths.

"Shit happens," he says. "It happened then, it happens now. A little more shit, a little less shit..." He shrugs. "Still shit, right?"

She considers this. She considers it for a long time.

They play cards, and have a little wine, and Adele teases him about the overdone chicken. She likes that he's trying so hard. She likes even more that she's not thinking about how lonely she's been.

So they retire to his bedroom and there's awkwardness and she's shy because it's been a while and you do lose some skills without practice, and he's clumsy because he's probably been developing bad habits from porn, but eventually they manage. They use a condom. She crosses her fingers while he puts it on. There's a rabbit's foot keychain attached to the bed railing, which he strokes before returning his attention to her. He swears he's clean, and she's on the pill, but... well. Shit happens.

She closes her eyes and lets herself forget for a while.

The prayer thing is all over the news. The following week is the runup. Talking heads on the morning shows speculate that it should have some effect, if enough people go and exert "positive energy." They are careful not to use the language of any particular faith; this is still New York. Alternative events are being planned all over the city for those who don't want to come under the evangelical tent. The sukkah mobiles are rolling, though it's the wrong time of year, just getting the word out about something happening at one of the synagogues. In Flatbush, Adele can't walk a block without being hit up by Jehovah's Witnesses. There's a "constructive visualization" somewhere for the ethical humanists. Not everybody believes God, or gods, will save them. It's just that this is the way the world works now, and everybody gets that. If crossed fingers can temporarily alter a dice throw, then why not something bigger? There's nothing inherently special about crossed fingers. It's only a "lucky" gesture because people believe in it. Get them to believe in something else, and that should work, too.

Except...

Adele walks past the Botanical Gardens, where preparations are under way for a big Shinto ritual. She stops to watch workers putting up a graceful red gate.

She's still afraid of the subway. She knows better than to get her hopes up about her neighbor, but still...he's kind of nice. She still plans her mornings around her ritual ablutions, and her walks to work around danger spots—but how is that different, really, from what she did before? Back then it was makeup and hair, and fear of muggers. Now she walks more than she used to; she's lost ten pounds. Now she knows her neighbors' names.

Looking around, she notices other people standing nearby, also watching the gate go up. They glance at her, some nodding, some smiling, some ignoring her and looking away. She doesn't have to ask if they will be attending one of the services; she can see that they won't be. Some people react to fear by seeking security, change, control. The rest accept the change and just go on about their lives.

"Miss?" She glances back, startled, to find a young man there, holding forth a familiar flyer. He's not as pushy as the guy downtown; once she takes it, he moves on. The PRAYER FOR THE SOUL OF THE CITY is tomorrow. Shuttle busses ("Specially blessed!") will be picking up people at sites throughout the city.

WE NEED YOU TO BELIEVE, reads the bottom of the flyer.

Adele smiles. She folds the flyer carefully, her fingers remembering the skills of childhood, and presently it is perfect. They've printed the flyer on good, heavy paper.

She takes out her Saint Christopher, kisses it, and tucks it into the rear folds to weight the thing properly.

Then she launches the paper airplane, and it flies and flies and flies, dwindling as it travels an impossible distance, until it finally disappears into the bright blue sky.

Sinners, Saints, Dragons, and Haints, in the City Beneath the Still Waters

The days which bracketed hurricanes were painful in their clarity. Sharp-edged clouds, blue sky hard as a cop's eyes, air so clear that every sound ground at the ear. If a person held still enough, he would feel the slow, unreal descent as all the air for miles around scrape-slip-slid downhill into the whirlpool maw of the approaching storm. If the streets were silent enough, he would hear his own heartbeat, and the crunch of rocks beneath his feet, and the utter stillness of the earth as it held its breath for the dunking to come.

Tookie listened for a while longer, then hefted the plastic bag a little higher on his shoulder and resumed walking home. A ways behind him, a hulking shadow stayed put.

Tookie sat on the porch of his shotgun house, watching the rain fall sideways. A lizard strolled by on the worn dirt strip that passed for a sidewalk, easy as you please, as if there wasn't an inch of water already collected around its paws. It noticed him and stopped.

"Hey," it said, inclining its head to him in a neighborly fashion.

"'Sup," Tookie replied, jerking his chin up in return.

"You gon' stay put?" it asked. "Storm comin'."

"Yeah," said Tookie. "I got food from the grocery."

"Ain' gon' need no food if you drown, man."

Tookie shrugged.

The lizard sat down on the sidewalk, oblivious to the driving wind, and joined Tookie in watching the rain fall. Tookie idly reflected that the lizard might be an alligator, in which case he should maybe go get his gun. He decided against it, though, because the creature had wide batlike wings and he was fairly certain gators didn't have those. These wings were the color of rusty, jaundiced clouds, like those he'd seen approaching from the southeast just before the rain began.

"Levee gon' break," said the lizard after a while. "You shoulda got out, man."

"No car, man." It occurred to Tookie only after this that "man" was inappropriate.

The lizard snorted. "Big strong buck like you oughtta get off your ass, buy a hooptie."

"The fuck I need a car for? The bus and streetcar go everywhere I want to go."

"Except out of the city, with a hurricane on your ass."

Tookie shrugged again. "My mama had a car. She and my sister and her kids was all that could fit." He had sent them along with the last of his cash, though he had not told them this. "We called the rental folks, too, but they was out of cars. They want a credit card anyway. Don't nobody give you a card without a job, unless you a college student, and I ain' even got a GED."

"Why not?" asked the lizard. "You don' look stupid."

"Teachers thought I did." Stupid and good for nothing, waste of time to educate, waste of space on this earth. Maybe, Tookie thought, the hurricane would take care of that. "I got tired of hearin' that shit after a while."

The lizard considered this. Then it came over to the steps of Tookie's house and climbed up on the first step, its tail—as long as its body—dangling into the water.

"How you get a house, then, with no job?"

Tookie couldn't help smiling. "You the nosiest damn lizard I ever saw."

The creature grinned at him, flashing tiny needlelike teeth. "Ain' I? They don' let me out much."

"So I see." Perhaps Tookie was feeling lonely; he decided to answer. "I sell a little weed," he said. "Get some Adam from over the bridge, sell it to the white kids over by Tulane. Don't take much to make the rent."

"Adam?"

"Ex. MDMA. Little pills, make you happy."

"Oh." The lizard settled itself more comfortably on the doorstep, then abruptly raised itself again. "Hey, you ain't got no pit bulls, do you? I been smellin' somethin' big and mean now and again. I hate dogs."

Tookie chuckled. "Nah. I'm just a foot soldier, man."

The lizard relaxed. "Me, too."

"You ain't a foot soldier, you a fuckin' lizard."

"Shut the fuck up, man." The lizard followed this amused statement with a yawn. "Mind if I crash here for a minute? I'm tired as hell."

"Come up on the porch," Tookie said. The polite thing would've been to invite the creature inside, but he'd never been one for letting animals in the house. "I got some Vienna sausages."

"I ain' hungry, and the step is fine, thank you." The lizard rolled onto its side like a cat sunning itself, except it wasn't a cat and the pelting rain wasn't sun.

"Suit yourself." Tookie got to his feet, mopping warm rain from his own face; the porch overhang wasn't stopping it at all now. The wind had gotten bad enough that the stop sign on the corner was bent at a sharp angle, its four letters so blurred with driving water that they seemed ready to wash off. Across the street, three shingles blew off Miss Mary's roof in rapid succession, the sound of destruction muted by the rising freight train wind.

The lizard turned to follow Tookie's gaze. "She shoulda got out, too."

"Yeah," Tookie said. He sighed. "She should've."

He went inside, and the lizard went to sleep on his porch steps.

The next day, watching through the attic door as his secondhand furniture floated, Tookie wondered about the lizard. His food bags were secure between two half-rotted wooden slats—his gun was in one of them—and the water didn't look too bad, so carefully he lowered himself through the attic door into the drink.

On the porch, he paused for a moment to marvel at the sight of Dourgenois Street transformed into a river. Driven by the still-powerful wind, the water was up to his waist; down on the street it would probably be chest-deep. Only the topmost edge of the bent-over stop sign was visible. All the houses had been strangely truncated, like mushrooms only half-emerged from rippling gray soil.

"Hey," said a voice, and Tookie looked up to see the lizard clinging to his porch ceiling, upside down. It yawned, blinking sleepily. "I tol' you the levee'd go."

"I guess you did," Tookie said, a note of grudging wonder

entering his voice. Most of the other denizens of his street had gone to the convention center if they couldn't get out of town. There was only him and Miss Mary—

And Miss Mary's door was stove in, a little rapids frothing on her porch as water flowed in.

"Damn shame," said the lizard.

Tookie stepped off the porch. For an instant his feet floated, and a fleeting panic set in. The voice of a long-dead uncle barked in his head: *Niggas don't float, fool, sank like stones inna water, waste of money teachin' you how to swim.* But then his feet touched solid ground and he found that when he stood, the current wasn't as swift or strong as it appeared. Simple enough to walk perpendicular to it. So he did, navigating around a neighbor's derelict car (now submerged) and pausing as a shapeless spiderwebbed lump (basketball net?) floated past.

The top of Miss Mary's hollow door had broken in, but the bottom was still in place and locked. Tookie pulled himself over it and looked around the old lady's living room. "Miss Mary?" he called. "It's Tookie from 'cross the street. Where you at?"

"In here 'bout to drown, goddamn, what you think?" returned the old woman's voice, and he followed it into her kitchen, where she sat on a chair that was probably resting atop her dining table. He couldn't tell for sure because the table was under water. He pushed his way through floating jars of spices and wooden spoons.

"Come on here, Miss Mary," he said. "Ain' no point in you stayin'."

"It's my house," she said. "It's all I got." She had said the same thing a few days before when he'd invited her to pass the storm with him, in his house, which was higher off the ground and newer, or at least not as old.

"I ain' gon' let you stay up in here." In a flash of inspiration, he added, "Lord don't mean for nobody to just sit and wait to die."

Miss Mary, eighty-four years old and about as many pounds, threw him a glare from her waterlogged throne. "Lord don't like bullshit neither."

He grinned. "No, I guess He don't. So come on, then, 'fore I drown in your kitchen and stank up the place."

So she gingerly eased herself off the chair and Tookie helped her into the water. He had her wrap her skinny arms around his neck. Then with her on his back, he waded out of her house and back across the street to his own personal bayou. There, with much huffing and cursing, he managed to hoist her up into the attic without breaking any of her old bones.

Once that was done, he headed out onto the porch again to see to the lizard. But it was gone.

After a sigh, Tookie went back inside and climbed to the attic himself.

Outside, unseen, something large and dark moved under the water. It did not surface—though for an instant it came near to doing so, and the water rose in a swell half-obscured by surging wavelets from the broken levee two blocks away. But then it moved away from Tookie's steps, and the water flowed free again.

The water kept rising even after the wind fell, all through the skin-stingingly beautiful day that arrived in the storm's wake. Helicopters began thwapping past, lots of them, but none of them ever slowed over or landed in the Ninth Ward, so Tookie paid them no attention. He made sure Miss Mary ate some Vienna sausages and drank half a Sunny Delight, then he went out again in search of something that would float.

A few feet beyond his door he encountered a family of nutrias, the giant-rat denizens of the city's boggiest places. The first three nutrias, two dog-sized adults and a smaller one, dogpaddled past with a quick by-your-leave glance in Tookie's direction. The fourth came along some ways later, swimming slowly, its eyes dull, mouth open and panting. As its right foreleg came near the surface, Tookie saw that it had a bad break, white bone flashing under the brown water. Flies already crawled around its sleek wet back.

Tookie reached out and caught the creature, lifting it and giving its neck a quick wring. It went limp in his hands without a squeak. As Tookie tossed the small body up onto a nearby rooftop—the water was already foul, but he couldn't abide adding to the mess— he noticed that the two adult nutrias had stopped. They did not look angry, though they watched him for a long moment. Then they resumed their trek, and Tookie did, too.

Two streets over he ran into Dre Amistad, who was pushing an inflatable kiddie pool that contained a scrawny teenaged girl and a naked baby nearly as thin. The girl threw Tookie a hostile, defensive look as he approached, but Dre seemed relieved. "I'm so glad to see you, man. Can you push for a while?" He looked exhausted.

"I can't," Tookie said, nodding apologetically to the girl. "I got to find something to carry this old lady who's stayin' at my house. My neighbor."

Dre frowned. "Old lady?" He glanced up at the young girl and baby pointedly. But the girl frowned at Tookie, some of her hostility fading.

Heartened by this, Tookie added, "She ain't got nobody, man. Her daughter over in Texas—" Tookie cut himself off then, annoyed at his urge to justify his actions. Above their heads, another helicopter flitted past, going to rescue someone else. "Look, where you headed?"

Dre shook his head. "We was gonna go to Chalmette, but we heard the cops was shootin' people there. They even shootin' white folks—anybody comin' out of New Orleans. Guess they think the flood's catchin', like the flu or somethin'."

"*Gretna*, not Chalmette," said the girl, in a tone that suggested she had said it before. Dre shrugged. He looked too tired to care.

"Where you goin' *now*?" Tookie asked, trying to restrain his impatience.

"We heard people was goin' to the navy base," said the girl. "The government was gon' close it 'cause all the soldiers is off in Iraq. Maybe they got beds and medicine." She looked down at her child, her small face tightening.

Tookie frowned but decided not to say anything. If they wanted to trust a bunch of soldiers, that was their business.

"See if you can get everybody up on a roof, rest for a bit," Tookie said to Dre, turning to splash away from them. "I got food and stuff. Let me fetch the old lady and then I can help you push."

"I ain' waitin, Tookie."

Tookie stopped and turned back to him, incredulous. Any fool could see they had a better chance together than alone.

"I just got to get somewhere dry," Dre said softly, a plea. "Tookie, man. I just..." Dre faltered silent, then looked away. After a moment, during which Tookie just stared at him, Dre blinked quickly and then resumed his dogged pushing of the kiddie pool. The girl watched Tookie until they were out of sight.

Turning away, Tookie stopped as he saw the lizard, this time crouched atop a crazily leaning traffic light pole. It was looking in the direction Dre had gone.

"Them soldiers ain' gon' let nobody in," it said scornfully. "Buncha poor-ass folks like that? Soldiers gon' shoot 'em and get a medal for it. Mus' be out they damn minds."

"You ain't dead," Tookie said, surprised at how glad he felt.

"Nope. Hey. It's a little rowboat 'round back of that house." It nodded toward a house on the corner that had been washed off its foundations. It leaned at a drunken angle, surrounded by its own vomited debris. "And it's a barge a couple of streets over, all dry and high."

"A *barge?*"

The lizard shrugged. "I ain' lyin'. Big as three or four houses, sittin' in the middle of the street. Guess they didn't tie it up, put down anchor, whatever. You can hole up there for a little while. Safer than these houses." It tilted its head up to peer at another passing helicopter. "They gon' have to start actually helpin' people soon."

Tookie nodded slowly, too polite to say he'd believe it when he saw it. "It's a dead nutria over on Reynes," he said. "On a rooftop, maybe three houses from the neutral ground." Which was underwater. Tookie grimaced. "The corner, I mean. Its leg is broke, but the rest is all right. I just killed it."

The lizard grinned its needle grin again. "What, I look skinny?"

Tookie shrugged, smiling in spite of himself. "Yeah, you right, you the most fucked-up-lookin' lizard I ever saw. Skinny ain't half."

The lizard laughed. Its laugh was a strange, high-pitched trilling sound, and with each exhalation, the water around Tookie reacted, tiny pointillations dancing on the murky surface. When it stopped laughing, the water became still once more.

"Nutria's good eating," it said thoughtfully, and bobbed its head at him in a gesture that might've been thanks. "Might call some folks to come share."

Tookie stepped quickly aside as a ball of fire ants floated past. "What, it's more of you?"

"Mmm-hmm. My whole family all over town right now."

"That right?"

"Yeah right." It drew itself up proudly. "My people been here gen-erations. New Orleans born an' bred."

Tookie nodded. His people were the same.

"Hey," said the lizard, its grin fading. "Listen. You be careful. It's some kind of big thing around here. A *mean* thing."

"Like what?"

The lizard shook its head. This movement was not remotely humanlike; its neck wove like a snake's. "I ain' seen it, but I *smelled* it. Saw a dead dog over by the playground, looked like somethin' had been at it."

" 'Nother dog, maybe." Tookie had seen several in the past few hours, roaming or swimming, looking lean and forlorn.

"Musta been hungry. Dog was bit in half." The lizard shuddered, wings making a papery rattle. It looked away down the long street of listing houses, car-roof islands, and still dark water.

"Might be anything," Tookie said, though he was aware that this was not reassuring. "That storm was bad. Worst I ever saw, even if the levees hadn't broke. Feel like it ain' done yet, somehow."

Another helicopter passed, this one low enough that Tookie could see a person inside with a big TV camera aimed at him. He put his hands on his hips and regarded the helicopter coldly. If it wasn't going to help, he wished it would just go away.

"It ain't," the lizard said softly, its eyes distant and burnished with worry. "Done, I mean. Somethin' ain' right. Somethin' keepin' this storm goin'."

They both watched as the helicopter circled once, filming the whole area, and then flew on. Gradually the silence returned, peaceful and liquid, and Tookie relaxed, absorbing it.

"I got to go get that rowboat," he said at last. "Thanks."

The lizard made a dismissive sound. "I'm'a go eat my thanks right now." Turning, the lizard spread its rustcloud wings and flicked its tail at him. Tookie waved farewell as it took off and flew away.

Tookie fetched the rowboat, used it to collect the old lady and what remained of the food from his attic, then headed over to the big barge on Jourdan Avenue.

The barge was jammed on a schoolbus and a couple of houses, causing it to list at a nearly 45-degree angle. Because of this, most of the deck was dry, the rainwater having pooled on the downside. The pilot house or bridge or whatever it was called—where they drove the barge—was even better, dry and enclosed with only one broken glass window. Tookie used his T-shirt to stuff the hole so they could sleep the night without feeding a million mosquitoes.

Then, as dusk fell, they ate the last of Tookie's food. He hadn't gotten much from the store to begin with, since he'd had to wait until it was closed; by the time he'd arrived with his crowbar, others had already pried the door open and gotten the best goods. He had collected enough to see himself through three or four days without electricity, since that was the worst any storm had done in his life-time. Standing at the pilot's window, gazing out at the ocean that had been his neighborhood, Tookie reflected that he had, perhaps, underplanned.

"We got to put somethin' on the roof," said Miss Mary. She was half asleep already, curled up with her head pillowed on an over-turned leatherbacked chair. "Tell the rescue people to come get us."

Tookie nodded, chewing absently on an oily sardine. "I'll go out tomorrow, find some paint."

"You be careful," the old woman said. Tookie turned to her, surprised to hear this echo of his lizard friend. Miss Mary yawned. "Haints be out, after a storm like this."

At first Tookie heard *hates*, not haints. Then he realized what she was saying. "Ain' no haints, Miss Mary."

"How the hell you know? This the first *real* hurricane you been through." She waved a hand contemptuously. "I was aroun' for Camille. Lived in Mississippi then. Me an' my man come here after, 'cause when that storm was through, we ain' had nothin' left. No house, no town, no people. All my family died." She lifted her head to glare at him. The fading light fell along the smooth planes of her face just so; he saw that she must have been beautiful in those days. "Even after that storm, the killin' kept on. It was somethin' else around, *keepin'* it goin'. Turnin' people ugly."

"My mama said haints was just ghosts," Tookie said. "Scare you, but can't kill nobody."

"Demons, then. Spirits, monsters, don't matter what you call 'em. They come with the storm, some bringin' it, some seein' it through, some sendin' it on. And some keepin' it on, so it can kill some more. So you watch yo' ass." She spoke the last three words leaning forward, precisely enunciating her vehemence.

"A'ight, a'ight, Miss Mary." Tookie came over and sat down beside her, making himself comfortable as best he could against the hard metal of a bulkhead. "You get some sleep now. I'll keep a eye out."

She sighed, weary, and lay down again. A long silence fell.

"I'm too old to start over again," she said softly.

He fanned himself with one hand; it was stuffy in the little chamber with the windows closed. "We gon' both do what we got to do, Miss Mary." She said nothing in reply, so he added, "Good night."

After a while, she slept. And despite his intention to keep watch, Tookie did, too.

Deep in the night, when the city was still but for frogs and drifting water, they were jolted awake by the low groan of metal crunching and grinding against itself. Something made the barge jump, rocking alarmingly toward wobbly straightness before it settled back into its leaning stability.

Years of nights spent crouched low in his house, wondering whether the people outside his window were assassins or just ordinary robbers, kept Tookie silent beyond an initial startled curse. Years of whatever life Miss Mary had lived kept her silent as well. She stayed put while he crept to the window and peered out.

With no streetlights, the dark was all-encompassing. A sliver of moon was up, illuminating the water and fog curling off its surface, but everything else was just shapes.

The water was rippling, though, in the wake of some movement. Something *big*, to judge by the ripples.

Tookie waited. When the water was still again, he turned back to see that Miss Mary had pulled a crooked steak knife from one of her many pockets. His heart leapt in irrational alarm, though he should've laughed; the little knife would be no use against whatever had jolted the barge.

"What you see?" she stage-whispered.

"Nothin'," he replied. "Just water."

She scowled. "You lyin'."

Anger blazed away days of waterlogged weariness in Tookie. She sounded like those old teachers of his, years gone, and for a moment he hated her as he'd hated them. "How you gon' say I'm lyin'? You can't half see, crazy ol' biddy."

"I can see *you* just fine." There was no mistaking the menace in the old woman's tone. Belatedly two things occurred to Tookie: First, that her knife wasn't too small to hurt *him*, and second, that his gun was tucked away safe and useless inside the bag that had held their food.

Don' need no damn gun, he thought, his hands clenching into fists—they both froze as, somewhere on the next street over, a house collapsed. They had heard this happen several times over the past few days, cheap wood splintering and plaster crumbling like so much sand, but never had the sound been so violent or sudden. It was as if something had *knocked* the house down, or perhaps stomped on it. Either way, the demolition hadn't taken much effort.

Tookie met Miss Mary's eye, and she gave him an I-told-you-so nod. She had put the knife away, he saw, so he decided to say nothing more about it. His own anger was gone, shattered like a ruined house's walls, leaving him feeling foolish and ashamed. What the hell was he doing, getting so worked up over a little old lady anyhow? They had bigger problems.

In the morning they rose and went out on deck.

By the clear light of dawn, the city's devastation somehow seemed more stark: the reeking water, the melting houses, the silence. Tookie stood transfixed by it, for the first time realizing that the city would never be the same no matter how well they fixed it. Yet he could not bring himself to mourn, because despite the evidence of his eyes, he could feel that nothing was dead. The city had withstood storms before, been destroyed and rebuilt and destroyed

again. Indeed, as he stood there, he could almost feel the land somewhere below, still holding its breath, waiting and untroubled. Calm,
like the eye of a storm.

Miss Mary was the first to spot something odd: a long flap of
something that looked like stiff cloth near the barge's prow. It had
not been there the day before.

Tookie poked at the cloth with his toe, trying to figure out what
it was and troubled by a nagging sense of familiarity, as Miss Mary
muttered about haints and a plague of devilry. Finally Tookie picked
up the thing to toss it overboard. As he did, he noticed blood on one
corner of it. Only then did he realize that the stiff thing was not cloth.
It felt of leather and thin bone under his fingers, and the underside
was patterned with clouds, the deep gray color of when they were
right overhead and about to drop a bucket.

He caught himself before he gasped, which would've gotten
the sharp-eared Miss Mary's attention. Instead he simply went to
the deck wall and peered overboard, dreading what he might see.

There was no lizard corpse, but he noticed something else: the
schoolbus that had been lodged under the barge's stern? keel? The
front underside. The bus had been almost comically jammed in
place the day before, its hood invisible beneath the water and its rear
end jutting undignified into the air. Now the bus's butt was crum-
pled as if something huge had stepped on it in an effort to climb
aboard the barge. The weight of whatever it was had pushed the bus
down, and levered the barge upright; that was what had caused the
shift the night before.

"What you see?" Miss Mary asked, not as belligerently as the
night before.

"Nothin' but water," Tookie said again, and he dropped the wing
back onto the deck bloody-side down, so it looked like a rag again.

When the waters receded, he vowed privately, he would find a place to bury it proper.

The water seemed lower when Tookie dropped into it from the ladder. It had been up to his neck the day before; now it was only up to his chest. Progress. There was no current, so the rowboat hadn't drifted far. Tookie climbed into it and, using the nail-studded plank of wood that he'd appropriated for an oar, set off.

After an hour of fruitlessly searching the handful of corner stores dotting the neighborhood, he began searching houses instead. This went better, though on several occasions there were unpleasant surprises. In one house he found a bloated old man still seated in an armchair, with the TV remote in his floating gray hand. The water hadn't risen *that* fast. Tookie figured the old fellow had just wanted to go his own way.

He was coming out of that house with his hands full of white paint cans, when movement in the rowboat made him start and drop the cans and grab for a gun he did not possess. He cursed himself for forgetting it again.

"Hey," said the lizard, lifting its head over the boat's rim. "Thought I smelled you 'roun' here."

Tookie stared at it. "You all right?"

The lizard looked puzzled. "Why wouldn' I be?"

"Somethin' came after the barge last night. I found—" He hesitated, suddenly recalling what the lizard had said about its family. "A wing. Like yours, but gray."

The lizard stiffened, then closed its eyes. "My cousin," it said finally. "We was lookin' for him."

Tookie lowered his head respectfully. "I still got the wing, you want it."

"Yeah. Later."

"It's that thing, ain' it?" Tookie asked. "The ugly thing you been smellin'." Miss Mary's words came back to him. "The Hate."

The lizard nodded grimly. "I aksed my daddy about it. Come around sometimes, this thing, after a real big storm. Killin' is what draws it. Like *mean* got a shape and gone walkin' around, spreadin' more mean everywhere it go."

Tookie frowned, recalling their near-brush with the thing the night before. *It was somethin' else around,* Miss Mary had said, of the time after Hurricane Camille. *Turnin' people ugly.* Was this the same kind of thing? If it had gotten onto the barge, would it have eaten them as it had the lizard's cousin? Or—he shivered as he remembered Miss Mary looking so mean with that knife. He probably hadn't looked all that friendly himself, with the urge to beat the old woman to death running hot in his blood.

"Last time it come 'roun'," said the lizard, "it kill a whole lot of us 'fore we finally got it. It like us even more'n you folks."

Tookie scowled. "Then you oughtta be inside somewhere, not out here talkin' shit with me."

The lizard scowled back and slapped a paw on the boat's metal rim. "Ain' gon' let no damn monster run me out of town. They killed it before, my daddy said. Took a lot, but they did, so we gon' have to do it again."

Tookie nodded, then picked up the paint cans and began to load them onto the boat. "Come on back to the barge," he said. "Let me get my gun."

But the lizard came up to him and put its paw on his hand. Its skin was cool despite the heat, dry despite the humidity, and up close it smelled of ozone and soupy dawn fog. "Ain' your fight," it said.

"I still be up in my attic but for you. Maybe dead."

"Might'a been rescued by now but for me," it said stubbornly. "This thing make people so ugly they don' even want to help each other. You know they ain' give no food or water to all those people at the Superdome? Just lef' 'em there." It shook its head, as Tookie gaped at it in disbelief. "This storm three days gone and still killin' people. That ain' right."

Tookie set his mouth in a grim line. "Man, people don' need no monster to make 'em do evil-hearted shit. All it take is a brown face, or somebody wearin' old tore-up clothes."

"This thing make it *worse*." The lizard hopped out of Tookie's boat, dogpaddling easily in the water. "I told you, man, I'm a foot soldier. Y'know—" It hesitated. "Y'know, right? I brought the storm? Me and mine."

Tookie nodded slowly. He had suspected that from their first meeting. "Storms gotta come," he said. "Everybody in this city know that."

The lizard looked relieved. "Yeah, but storms gotta go, too. That's my job, and I been fuckin' around." It nodded to him, then turned and began to paddle away. Abruptly it stopped and turned, glancing back at him over its wing. It gazed at him for a long while. "I'll holla at you later, man," it said at last.

Tookie nodded, raising a hand to wave. The lizard flickered up out of the water and away.

Tookie lowered his hand. He knew that when the waters receded, even if the lizard survived its battle, he would never see it again.

The day grew hot. With water everywhere, evaporating as best it could into the already-saturated air, the city became a place of sunshine and steam. It took the rest of the afternoon to get back on the barge (Tookie had to climb up by way of the schoolbus, standing in the footsteps of the Hate, which gave him the heebie-jeebies) and paint the word HELP in five-foot letters on the barge's long flat roof.

The heat and humidity devoured Tookie's strength. He fell asleep on a pile of dry sheets he'd salvaged from a two-story house whose upstairs hadn't been damaged at all. There had been three other survivors inhabiting that house, he'd found; children, the oldest barely twelve. It wasn't their house either, so they hadn't protested his scavenging. He'd given them some of his food and invited them back to the barge, but leery of strangers, they'd politely declined.

Miss Mary called herself keeping watch, walking around on deck. Tookie suspected she just didn't want to smell him, after four days of funky water and no showers. (To his annoyance, she smelled the same as usual—like old lady.)

He was deep in a dream of being at a house party over on Elysian Fields, with a pretty red-boned girl checking him out across papers full of crawfish and corn and potatoes, when Miss Mary shook him awake. He sat up, snarfling drool, and looked around. Sundown; long golden colors arced over the sky.

"I hear somethin'," Miss Mary said. Her steak knife was out again, and he felt a sleepy species of worry.

"Hear what?" he asked, but on the heels of the question he heard it, too. A sharp, echoing cough, loud and deep, like from the chest of some beast. A big beast, the size of an elephant maybe, somewhere on one of the streets toward the river. And then, before the echoes faded, he heard a harmony of other sounds: high-pitched trills. Over where he heard it, a small cloud hovered in the otherwise clear sky, growing thicker.

Tookie scrambled to his feet, searching among the plastic bags.

"Miss Mary, you stay in here," he said as he rummaged. "Don' go out less you hear a helicopter, or people in a boat. I got to go."

She did not ask where. "You got any people you want me to find, once I get out the city?"

"My mama'll be in Baton Rouge, with my sister." There, it was there. Tookie pulled the gun out and checked it. It was fully loaded, but it needed cleaning. He had never liked handling the thing. Maybe it would jam. Maybe it would backfire, leave him blind and handless at the feet of the Hate. He thrust the gun into the waist of his pants.

"That ain' no haint," Miss Mary said. "You was right. It's somethin' else."

"I hope so," Tookie said. "Can't kill no haint. Bye, Miss Mary."

"Bye, fool." But she stayed on deck, watching him, as he swung himself over the ladder and climbed down.

The noise had gotten worse by the time Tookie paddled near, keeping low in the rowboat and moving the nail plank as little as possible to avoid telegraphing his approach. It wouldn't've mattered if he'd showed up with a secondline band, though; between the roars of the thing, the trills of the lizards, splashing water, and the crash of cars or houses being destroyed, Tookie didn't have to worry about being heard. And as he paddled, a deeper sound made him look up. The cloud that had gathered overhead was turning darker, thicker. He thought he saw flickers of lightning in its depths.

When he saw that the porches of the houses nearby were above water—they had chosen high ground for their battle—Tookie parked the boat, jumped onto a dry porch, and began running. His gun was in his hand. He ran low and leapt almost soundlessly across the gaps between houses. One porch. Another half-buckled by water damage. Another that overlapped the third because its house had collapsed sideways...and here Tookie stopped, because the thing was there, it was *there* and it was huge, its smell was like sulfured asphalt or the thick fermented funk of an algae bog, and instead of coughing, this time it roared like a barge horn gone mad with rage. It was hard to see in the fading light, and for that blessing Tookie thanked a god that he suddenly believed in, because what little of it he could see came near to shattering his mind. Or perhaps that was his own fault, because the thoughts that flowed into his head were so swift and twisted, so *wrong* yet powerful, that they had to come from somewhere inside him, didn't they? Some festering boil deep within, tucked under years of apathy, bursting now and spreading poison all through. *Got to go kill me some niggers* was one of the thoughts, even though he had never thought that way in his life and the cadence of the thought was all wrong; New Orleanians spoke with more rhythm. He tried to think his own thought: *Soun' like some 'Bama mothafucka in my head, what the,* but before he could complete it, there was an oily flipover, and then he thought *all these people in my city, ain' done shit to save it,* and also *gon' find me some bitches and fuck 'em* and then *shoot up them white mothafuckas over in Chalmette-maybe-Gretna give 'em somethin' to be scared of* and *of course that ol' lady slowin' me down, get rid of her.* And more, more, so much more. So much that Tookie cried out and fell to his knees on the crumbling porch, the gun clattering on the old wood as he clutched his head and wondered if one could die of pure evil.

But then a sharp squeal penetrated the hate, and Tookie looked up. The monster had paid him no heed despite his shout, preoccupied as it was with the enemy before it: a sextet of tiny creatures that dipped and wheeled in aerobatic circles around its misshapen head as it turned to follow them. In profile it was even uglier, lumpen and raw, its lower jaw trailing spittle as it worked around a mouthful of something that wriggled and shrieked and beat at it with wings like rusted, ocher clouds—*"No, goddamn it!"* Tookie shouted. Suddenly his head was clear, the hate shattered by horror. He raised the gun, and something else rose in him: a great, huge feeling, as big as the monster and just as overwhelming, but cleaner. Familiar. It was the city beneath his feet, below the water, still patiently holding its breath. He felt the tension in his own lungs. He had played no music, faked no voodoo, paid no taxes and no court to the chattering throngs who came and spent themselves and left the city bruised and weary in their wake. But the city was *his*, low creature that he was, and it was his duty to defend it. It had spent years training him, honing him, making him ready to serve for its hour of need. He was a foot soldier, too, and in that breath of forever he heard the battle call of his home.

So Tookie planted his feet on the rotting wood, and aimed for one bulbous eye with his dirty gun, and screamed with the pent breath of ten thousand waterlogged streets as he blew it away.

The creature shrieked, whipping about in agony as its eye dissolved into a bloody mist. As it cried out, something mangled and small fell from its teeth, landing in the water with a near-silent plop.

"Now!" cried a trilling voice, and the darting batwinged shadows arranged themselves into a strange configuration, and the cloud overhead erupted with light. The thunderbolt caught the beast square in its thrashing head; when Tookie blinked, its body just stood there, headless.

But then the body lurched forward, lifting a far too human hand out of the water to reach for the hovering lizards. Tookie fired again. He saw the doorway of a sagging house through the hole his bullet opened in the thing's hand. It flinched, probably nerves since it no longer had a brain, and that gave the lizards another opening.

Overhead, the cloud rumbled once more, and this time three lightning bolts came, *sizzle sizzle sizzle* on Tookie's vision, the air smelled of burning dog and seared rage, and by the time the afterimages faded and his eyes stopped watering, it was all over.

Still half-blind, Tookie stumbled off the porch and through the water, groping with hands and gun toward the place where his friend had fallen. The other lizards converged around it, some hovering and some dropping into the water themselves to support a small, bloody body. Tookie reached them—the hovering ones parted to let him through, though they looked at him suspiciously—and then stopped, knowing at a glance there was nothing he could do.

"Hey," croaked his lizard. Two of its companions held it up in the water. It tilted its head to peer at him with its one remaining eye, and sighed. "Get that damn look off your face. I ain' dead."

"You look like you halfway," said Tookie.

It laughed softly, then grimaced as that caused it pain. "Maybe three-quarters, but I still ain' there." It looked past Tookie at the spot where the great hulking thing had been. There was nothing left; the lightning had evaporated it into mist. "That was the way to do it, but god*damn*, I hurt."

Tookie reached for the lizard, then drew his hand back as one of its companions—another cousin, maybe—hissed at him. He contented himself with a smile instead, though he hardly felt it past the surface of his face. "Hurts worse if you complain." He had been shot once.

"Shut the fuck up." The lizard laid its head across the back of the one who had hissed at Tookie. "That shit ain' in your head, is it?"

Tookie knew what the lizard meant. And the truth was, the Hate *was* still in his head, its ugly thoughts gabbling amid Tookie's own, maybe because they'd been all his own thoughts to begin with. He'd had plenty of practice with hating himself and others. But the city was in his head, too, all that strength and breath and patience, and it occurred to Tookie that this would not have happened if he had not shaken off the Hate on his own. So he smiled again. "Just three-quarters," he said, "but it ain't got me."

The lizard narrowed its eye at him, but finally nodded. "You gon' leave when they rescue you? Run off to Texas or somewhere, settle down there?"

"I'll go, but I'm comin' back." Tookie lifted his arms, encompassing the foul water, the ruined houses, the stars on the horizon. "This is me."

The lizard flashed its toothy grin, though its eye began to drift shut. "Yeah you right." It sighed heavily. "Got to go."

Tookie nodded. "I'll listen for you in the next big storm." He took a step back, giving the lizards room. They lifted off, two of them carefully holding their injured companion between them. Tookie kept his gaze on his friend's eye, and not the ravaged wings or mangled limbs. Perhaps the lizard would live, but like the city, and like Tookie, it would never be the same. The thought filled him with a defiant ferocity. "An' that son of a bitch come back, you just holla."

It grinned. "I will. Next time, man."

In a soft thunder of wings, the lizards flew away, leaving Tookie alone in the wet dark.

The waters receded.

There was rescue then, and travel to Houston, and a long lonely time of shelters and strangers' homes. Miss Mary found her daughter, and they brought Tookie to live with them. He made contact with his mother and sister, and let them know he was all right. He did odd jobs, under-the-table construction work and the like, and made enough money to get by. His FEMA check took a whole year to come, but it wasn't completely useless. With it, he had enough.

So one evening, when the air was hazy and the sky soft, and something about the arc of sunset reminded him of long days and thick, humid nights, Tookie packed his bags. The next morning he caught a ride to the depot and bought a ticket on the early bus. He let out a long-held, heavy breath as the bus hit the interstate east, toward home.

Acknowledgments

Thank you to all the people who helped make me a short fiction writer.

That includes the instructors and fellow students of Viable Paradise 2002, as I mentioned in my introduction. It also includes all the writing groups I've been a part of over the years: the Boston Area Writers Group (later BRAWL), Critters.org, the Secret Cabal, Black Beans, and Altered Fluid. The great secret of writing groups is that you learn more from studying critiques of other writers' work than you do from actually having your own work critiqued, so basically every writer in these groups who ever submitted a story for critique became one of my teachers.

It also includes the publications and authors I studied to learn the basics: *Realms of Fantasy* (now defunct) and *The Magazine of Fantasy and Science Fiction* each for one year; *Strange Horizons* and *Clarkesworld* since then. More recently I've enjoyed *Lightspeed* and *FIYAH Literary Magazine*—especially *FIYAH*'s Spotify playlists meant to accompany their issues (great idea)! When I found a writer or topic I liked, I dug deeper via short story collections (e.g., Stephen King, Octavia Butler, Ursula Le Guin, and China Miéville) and various themed anthologies. I'm especially fond of the ones edited by John Joseph Adams (disclosure: I'm in a few, and honored to be).

I have also learned by teaching and by reviewing. Although I never attended Clarion, Clarion West, or Odyssey, I have now been a guest instructor at all three workshops, and it's been fascinating to see how the future of the genre is shaping up. Many of those students have since become my professional colleagues, and I continue to be inspired by their perseverance, their personal stories, and their innovation. I was thrilled to be able to include some of their work in the 2018 *Best American Science Fiction and Fantasy*, which I was also privileged to guest edit.

I have more learning to do, and I'm on it. Thanks, everyone. See y'all in my next collection.

extras

orbit

meet the author

Photo Credit: Laura Hanifin

N. K. Jemisin is the first author in the genre's history to win three consecutive Best Novel Hugo Awards, all for her Broken Earth trilogy. Her work has also won the Nebula, Locus, and Goodreads Choice awards. She has reviewed for the *New York Times Book Review*, and she has been an instructor for the Clarion and Clarion West writing workshops. In her spare time she is a gamer and gardener, and she is also single-handedly responsible for saving the world from King Ozzymandias, her dangerously intelligent ginger cat, and his phenomenally destructive sidekick, Magpie.

if you enjoyed

HOW LONG 'TIL BLACK FUTURE MONTH?

look out for

THE CITY WE BECAME

by

N. K. Jemisin

Every great city has a soul. Some are as ancient as myths, and others are as new and destructive as children. New York City? She's got six.

But every city also has a dark side. A roiling, ancient evil stirs in the halls of power, threatening to destroy the city and her six newborn avatars unless they can come together and stop it once and for all.

CHAPTER ONE

The rest of it starts with a young man who forgets his own name, somewhere in the tunnel to Penn Station.

He doesn't notice, at first. Too busy with all the stuff people usually do when they're about to reach their train stop: cleaning up the pretzel bags and plastic bottles of breakfast, stuffing his loose laptop power cord into a pocket of his messenger bag, making sure he's gotten his suitcase down from the rack, then having a momentary panic attack before remembering that he's only got one suitcase. The other was shipped ahead and will be waiting for him at his apartment up in Inwood, where the roommate he hasn't yet met is already living. They're both going to be grad students at—

—at, uh—

—huh. He's forgotten his school's name. Anyway, orientation is on Monday, which gives him four days to get settled into his new life in New York.

He's really going to need those days, too, sounds like. As the train slows to a halt, people are murmuring and whispering, peering intently at their phones and tablets with worried looks on their faces. Something about a bridge accident, terrorism, just like 9/11? He'll be living and working uptown, so it shouldn't impact him too much—but still, it's maybe not the best time to move here.

But when is it ever a good time to make a new life in New York City? He'll cope.

He'll more than cope. The train stops, and he's first out the door. He's excited but trying to pretend he's not. In New York he will be completely on his own, free to sink or swim. He has colleagues and friends and family members who think of this as exile, abandonment—

—although, in the flurry of the moment, he cannot remember any of those people's names—

—but that doesn't matter, because they can't understand. They know him as he was, and maybe who he is now. New York is his future. It's his chance to finally see what he can become.

It's hot in the station, and crowded on the escalator, but he feels fine. Which is why it's so weird when he reaches the top of the escalator, and suddenly—the instant his foot touches the polished-concrete flooring of Penn—the whole world inverts. Everything in his vision seems to tilt, and the ugly ceiling fluorescents turn stark and the floor kind of...heaves? It happens fast. The world flips and his stomach drops and his ears fill with a titanic, many-voiced roar. It's a familiar sound, to a degree; anyone who's been to a stadium during a big game has heard something similar. This is bigger, though. Millions of people instead of thousands, and all of those doubled back on each other and swelling and shifting into layers beyond sound, into color and shaking and emotion, until he claps his hands over his ears and shuts his eyes but it just keeps coming—

But amid all of it, there is a through line, a repeated motif in the cacophony of sound and word and idea. One voice, screaming fury.

Fuck you, you don't belong here, this city is mine, get out!

And the man who has forgotten his own name wonders, in confused horror, *Me? Am...am I the one that doesn't belong?* There is no answer, and the doubt within him becomes a backbeat in its own right.

All at once the roar is gone. A new roar, closer and echoing and indescribably smaller, has replaced it. Some of it is recorded, blaring from PA speakers overhead: *"New Jersey Transit train to Newark Airport now boarding on track five."* He remembers: Penn Station. He does not remember how he ended up on one knee beneath a train-schedules sign, with a hand over his face. Wasn't he on an escalator? How did he get off? He also doesn't remember ever before seeing the two people who are crouched in front of him.

"Wait, what?" he asks, frowning. "Did you just tell me to get out?"

"I said, 'Do you want me to call 911?'" says the woman who's offering water. She looks more skeptical than worried, like maybe he's faking whatever weird thing has apparently made him fall over in the middle of Penn Station.

"I...no." He shakes his head, trying to focus. Neither water nor the police will fix weird voices in his head, or hallucinations caused by train exhaust, or whatever he's experiencing. "What happened?"

"You kinda went sideways," says the man bent over him. He's portly, middle-aged, pale-skinned Latino, heavy New York accent, kindly tone. "We caught you and pulled you over here."

"Oh." Everything's still weird. The world isn't spinning anymore, but that terrible, layered roar is still in his head—just muted now, and overlaid by the local noise pollution that is Penn Station. "I...think I'm fine?"

"Yeah, you don't sound too sure," the man says.

That's because he's not. He shakes his head, then shakes it again when the woman pushes the water bottle forward. "I just had some." On the train.

"Low blood sugar, maybe?" She takes the water bottle away and looks thoughtful. There's a little girl crouched beside her, he notices belatedly, and the two of them are near mirrors: both black-haired, freckled, frank-faced Asian people. "When was the last time you ate?"

"Like, twenty minutes ago?" He doesn't feel dizzy or weak, either. He feels...

"New," he murmurs, without thinking. "I feel...new."

The portly man and frank-faced woman look at each other while the little girl throws him a judgy look, complete with lifted eyebrow. "*Are* you new here?" asks the portly man.

"Yeah?" Oh, no. "My bags!" But they're right there; the Good Samaritans have kindly pulled them off the escalator, too, and positioned them nearby out of the flow of traffic. There's a kind of surreality to the moment, as he finally realizes he's having this blackout or delusion or whatever it is in the middle of a station filled with thousands of people, all caught up in their ordinary lives and traveling along their ordinary paths. Nobody seems to notice him, except these two people. He feels alone in the city. He is seen and cared for in the city. The contrast is going to take some getting used to.

"You must have gotten your hands on some of the really good drugs," the woman says. She's grinning, though. There's a little nervousness in it, but mostly she's laughing at him. That's okay, though, isn't it? That's what'll keep her from calling 911. He remembers reading somewhere that New York's got an involuntary commitment law that can hold people for weeks, so it's probably a good idea to reassure his would-be rescuers as to his clarity of mind.

"Sorry about this," he says, deciding to get to his feet. "Maybe I didn't eat *enough*, or something. I'll...go to an urgent care clinic."

The station lurches beneath his feet, and suddenly it is in ruins. There's no one around. A cardboard book display in front of the convenience store has fallen over, spilling Stephen King hardcovers everywhere. He hears girders in the surrounding structure groan, dust and pebbles falling to the floor as something in the ceiling cracks. The fluorescent lights flicker and jerk, one of the overhead fixtures threatening to fall from the ceiling. He inhales to cry a warning.

Blink: everything is fine again. None of the people around him react. He stares at the ceiling for a moment, then back at the man and woman. They're still staring at him. They saw him react to whatever he was seeing, but they did not see the ruined station themselves. The portly guy has a hand on his arm, because he apparently swayed a little. Psychotic breaks must be hell on inner ear balance.

"You want to carry bananas," the portly guy suggests. "Potassium. Good for you."

"Or at least eat some real food," the woman agrees, nodding. "You probably just ate chips, right? I don't like that overpriced crap in the train dining car either, but at least it'll keep you from falling over."

"I like the hot dogs," the girl says.

"They're crap, baby, but I'm glad you like them." She takes the little girl's hand. "We've got to go. You good?"

"Yeah," he says. "But seriously, thanks for helping me. You hear all kinds of stuff about how rude New Yorkers are, but...thanks."

"Eh, we're only assholes to people who are assholes first," she says, but she smiles as she says it. Then she and the little girl wander off.

The portly man claps him on the shoulder. "Well, you don't look like you're gonna chuck. Want me to go get you something to eat or some juice or something? Or a banana?" He adds the latter pointedly.

"No, thanks. I'm feeling better, really."

The portly man looks skeptical, then blinks as something new occurs to him. "It's okay, you know, if you don't got money. I'll spot you."

410

"Oh. Oh, no, I'm good." He hefts his messenger bag, which he remembers costing almost $1,600. Portly Guy looks at it blankly. Whoops. "Um, there's probably sugar in this—" There's a plastic Starbucks tumbler in the bag, sloshing faintly. He drinks from it to reassure Portly Guy. The coffee is cold and disgusting. He belatedly remembers refilling it sometime yesterday, before he got on the train back home in—

—in—

That's when he realizes he can't remember where he came from.

And he tries, but he still can't remember the school he's here to attend.

And this is when it finally hits him that *he doesn't know his own name.*

As he stands there, floored by this triple epiphany of noth-ingness, the Portly Guy is turning up his nose at the tumbler. "Get some real coffee while you're here," he says. "From a good Boricua shop, yeah? Get some home food while you're at it. Anyway, what's your name?"

"Oh, uh…" He rubs his neck and pretends to have a desper-ate need to stretch—while, quietly panicking, he looks around and tries to think of something. He can't believe this is hap-pening. Who the hell forgets their own name? All he can come up with as fake names go are stupid ones like Bob or Jimmy. He's about to say "Jimmy," arbitrarily—but then, in his visual flailing, his eyes snag on something.

"I'm, uh…Manny," he blurts. "You?"

"Douglas." Portly Guy has his hands on his hips, obvi-ously considering something. Finally he pulls out his wal-let and hands over a business card. DOUGLAS ACEVEDO, PLUMBER.

"Oh, sorry, I don't have a card, haven't started my new job yet—"

411

"S'okay," Douglas says. He still looks thoughtful. "Look, a lot of us were new here, once. You need anything, you let me know, okay? Seriously, it's fine. Place to crash, real food, a good church, whatever."

It's unbelievably kind. "Manny" doesn't bother to hide his surprise. "Whoa. I— Wow, man. You don't know me from Adam. I could be a serial killer or something."

Douglas chuckles. "Yeah, somehow I'm not figuring you for a psycho. You look…" He falters, and then his expression softens a little. "You look like my son. So I'm just doing for you what I'd want somebody doing for him. Right?"

Somehow Manny knows: Douglas's son is dead.

"Right," Manny says softly. "Thanks again."

"Está bien, mano, no te preocupes." He waves off then, and heads in the direction of the A/C/E train.

Manny watches him go, pocketing the card and thinking about three things. The first is the belated realization that the guy thought he was Puerto Rican. The second is that he might have to take Douglas up on that offer of a place to crash, especially if he doesn't remember the address of his apartment in the next few minutes.

The third thing makes him look up at the Arrivals/Departures board, where he found the word that just became his new name. He didn't tell Douglas the full name because these days only white women can have given names like that without getting laughed at. But even in modified form, this word—this *identity*—feels more true than anything else he's ever claimed in his life. It is what he is. It is who he is. It is everything he's ever needed to be.

The full word is *Manhattan*.

In the bathroom, under the sodium lights, he meets himself for the first time.

It's a good face. He pretends to be extra meticulous about washing his hands—not a hard thing to do in the filthy Penn Station bathroom—and turns his face from side to side, checking himself out from all angles. It's clear why the dude figured him for Puerto Rican: his skin is yellowy brown, his hair kinky but loose-coiled enough that if he let it grow out, it might dangle. He could pass for Douglas's son, maybe. (He's not Puerto Rican, though. He remembers that much.) He's dressed preppy: faded jeans, a button-down, and there's a khakiesque jacket draped over his bag, for when the AC is too high, maybe, since it's summertime and probably 90 degrees outside. He looks like he's somewhere in that ageless yawn between "not a kid anymore" and thirty, though probably toward the latter end of it to judge by a couple of random gray threads peppered along his hairline. Brown eyes behind dark-brown-rimmed glasses. The glasses make him look professorial. Sharp cheekbones, strong even features, smile lines developing around his mouth. He's a good-looking guy. Generic all-American boy (nonwhite version), nicely nondescript.

Convenient, he thinks. Wondering why he thinks this makes him pause in mid-hand-wash, frowning.

Okay, no. He's got enough weird shit to deal with right now. He grabs his suitcase to head out of the bathroom. An old dude at the urinal stares at him all the way out.

At the top of the next escalator—this one leading out of the station and up to Seventh Avenue—it happens again. This episode is better in some ways and worse in others. Because he feels the wave of…whatever it is…coming on as he reaches the top of the escalator, he has enough time to grab his suitcase and get himself over to some kind of informational kiosk so he'll be out of the way while he leans against it and shudders. This time he doesn't forget anything or hallucinate, but he *hurts*, all of a sudden. It's an awful, sick feeling, a spreading chill throughout his body, starting from a point low on his left flank. The sensation is familiar. He remembers it from the last time he got stabbed.

(Wait, he got *stabbed*?)

Frantically he pulls up his shirt tail and looks at the place where the pain is worst, but there's no blood. There's nothing. The wound is all in his head. Or somewhere else.

As if this is a summons, abruptly the New York that everyone sees flickers into the New York that only he can see. Actually, they're both present, one lightly superpositioned over the other, and they flick back and forth a little before finally settling into a peculiar dual-boot of reality. Before Manny lie two Seventh Avenues. They're easy to distinguish because they have different palettes and moods. In one, there are hundreds of people within view and dozens of cars and at least six chain stores that he recognizes. *Normal* New York. In the other, there are no people. He doesn't see bodies or anything ominous; there's just no one around. It's not clear anyone ever existed in this place. Maybe the buildings just appeared, sprung forth fully-formed from their foundations, instead of being built. Ditto the streets, which are empty and badly cracked. A traffic light dangles loose from an overhead fixture, swinging on its cable but switching from red to green in perfect tandem with its other version. The sky is dimmer, almost as if it's nearly sunset and not just post-noon, and the wind is faster. Clouds boil and churn across the sky like they're late for the cloud revival meeting.

"Cool," Manny murmurs. This other New York is wild. He's hallucinating, and this whole episode probably represents some kind of psychotic break on his part, but he cannot deny that what he sees is gorgeous and terrifying. Weird New York. He likes it, regardless.

But something is wrong with it. Something…someplace, nearby, needs him. He must go somewhere, do something, or all of the bifurcated beauty that he sees will die. He knows this, suddenly, more surely than instinct.

"I have to go," he murmurs to himself in surprise. His voice sounds strange—tinny and sort of stretched-out. Maybe he's slurring? Maybe it's the peculiar echo of his voice from the walls of two different Penn Station entryway walls in two different Penn Stations.

"Hey," says a guy in a neon button-down nearby. Manny blinks at him; Normal New York abruptly resumes, Weird New York vanishing for the moment. (It's still somewhere, though, nearby.) The guy is wearing a uniform and carrying a sign hawking bike rentals at tourists. He faces Manny with open hostility. "Puke your drunk ass off somewhere else."

Manny tries to straighten, but he knows he's still a little diagonal. "I'm not drunk." He's just seeing juxtaposed multiple realities while being plagued by inexplicable compulsions.

"Well, then, take your high ass somewhere else."

"Yes." That's a good idea. He needs to go…east. He turns in that direction, following instincts he never had before a few minutes ago. "What's thataway?" he asks Bike Guy.

"My left nut," Bike Guy says.

"That's south!" laughs another bike rental hawker nearby. Bike guy grimaces and grabs his crotch at her in the iconic New York Sign Language gesture of suck-my-dick.

The attitude's starting to grate. Manny says, "If I rent a bike, will you tell me what's in that direction?"

Bike Guy's suddenly all smiles. "Sure—"

"No, sir," says Bike Woman, serious now as she comes over. "Sir, I'm sorry, but we cannot rent a bike to someone who appears to be intoxicated or ill. Do you need me to call 911?"

People in New York sure like to call 911. "No, I can walk. I need to get to—" FDR Drive. "—FDR Drive."

The woman's expression turns skeptical. "You wanna *walk* to *FDR Drive*? What the hell kind of tourist are you? Sir."

"He ain't no tourist," says he of the southern left nut, as he chin-points at Manny. "Look at him."

Manny's never been to New York before, at least as far as he knows. "I just need to get there. Fast."

"Take a cab, then," says the woman. "Taxi stand's right there. Need me to grab one for you?"

Manny shivers a little, feeling the rise of something new within himself. Not sickness this time—or rather, not just sickness, since that terrible stabbish ache hasn't faded. What comes instead is a shift in perception. Beneath his hand, which rests on the old wooden kiosk, he hears a soft rattle of decades' worth of flyers. (The kiosk has nothing on it. There's a sign: DO NOT POST BILLS. He hears what used to be there.) Traffic's flying past on Seventh, hurrying to get through the light before a million pedestrians start trying to get to Macy's or K-Town karaoke and barbecue. All these things belong; they are rightness. But his eyes stutter over a TGI Fridays and he twitches a little, lip curling in involuntary distaste. Something about its facade feels foreign, intrusive, jarring. A tiny, cluttered shoe-repair shop next to it does not elicit this feeling. Just the chain stores that he sees—a Foot Locker, a Sbarro, all the sorts of stores one normally sees at a suburban mall. Except they are here, in the heart of Manhattan, and their presence is…irritating. Like splinters, or little quick slaps to the face.

The subway sign, though, feels right and real. The bill-boards, too, no matter what's on them. The cabs, and flow of cars and people—all these things soothe the irritants, some-how. He draws in a deep breath that reeks of hot garbage and acrid steam belching from a manhole nearby, and it's foul but it's *right*. More than right. Suddenly he's better. The sick feel-ing recedes a little, and his side dulls from stabbing pain into cold prickles that only hurt when he moves.

"Thanks," he says to Bike Woman, straightening and grab-bing his roller bag. "But my ride's coming." Wait. How does he know that? Because one's coming.

The woman shrugs. Both of them turn away to resume hawking bikes. Manny walks toward the curb where people are waiting for Lyfts or Ubers. He has both apps on his phone, but he hasn't used them. There should be nothing here for him.

However, a moment later, a cab rolls to a stop right in front of him.

It's like a cab out of an old movie: smooth and bulbous and huge, with a black-and-white checkered strip along its near flank. Bike Guy does a double take, then whistles. "A Checker! Haven't seen one of those since I was a kid."

"It's for me," Manny says unnecessarily, and reaches for the door.

It's locked. *I need this open*, he thinks. The door lock clicks open. So, that's new, but he'll process it later.

"What the—" says the woman inside as Manny tosses his bag onto the back seat and climbs in after it. She's twisted around to stare at him, incredulous. She's a very young white woman, so young that she doesn't look old enough to drive. But she's mostly indignant rather than scared, which seems a good starting place for their future relationship. "Hey. *Dude.* This isn't a real cab—"

Manny pulls the door shut. "FDR, please," he says, and flashes his most charming smile.

It shouldn't work. She should be screaming her head off and trying to get the nearest cop to shoot him. But there is that peculiar rightness, too, in what he's doing—and somehow, that rightness is helping to keep the woman calm. He has followed to the letter the steps of the ritual of the cab, introducing enough plausible deniability that she thinks he's deluded rather than a potential threat. And there is power in what he's done that goes beyond just psychology. He's felt it before, hasn't he? When he somehow drew strength from the chaos of Seventh Avenue to ease the pain in his side. He can actually hear some of that power whispering to her, *Maybe he's an actor. He looks like That Guy whose name you can't remember, from that musical you like. So maybe don't freak out yet?* Because New Yorkers don't freak out around famous people.

And how does he know all this? Because he does. He's trying to keep up.

So he adds, after a breath passes and she just stares, "You're going that way anyway, aren't you?"

She jerks back a little and narrows her eyes at him. They're at a red light. He's got maybe ten more seconds. "How the hell did you know that?"

Because the cab wouldn't have stopped if you weren't, he doesn't say, and reaches for his wallet. "Here," he says, handing her a hundred-dollar bill.

She stares at it, then her lip curls. "Right, a fake."

"I have twenties instead, if you'd prefer." There's more power in twenties anyway. A lot of businesses in the city won't take hundreds, also for fear of counterfeit bills. With twenties, Manny will be able to compel her to take him where he needs to go, whether she wants to or not. He'd rather persuade her, though. Force is... He doesn't like to use force.

"Tourists *do* carry a lot of cash," she murmurs while frowning, as if reasoning with her better instincts. "And you don't *look* like a serial killer..."

"Most serial killers take care to look like ordinary people," he points out.

"Not helping your case with the mansplaining, guy."

"Good point. Sorry."

That seems to decide her. "Well. Assholes don't say sorry." She considers for a moment longer. "Make that two benjies, and okay."

He offers the twenties, although he does have another hundred-dollar bill in his wallet. There's no need to use the bills for power anymore, however. She has completed the ritual of the cab by performing the counter-ritual of haggling, and all the stars have aligned. She's on board. As she's pocketing the money, the traffic light changes and a car immediately honks behind her. She casually flips that driver off and then wrenches the wheel to drag the cab across four active lanes as if she's done this (or driven the Daytona 500) all her life.

And that's that. Even Manny is amazed at how well this strange power works, as he hangs on to the door handle and the lap-only seatbelt and tries not to look alarmed by her driving. He has some inkling of *why* it works. Money talks and bullshit walks in New York. In a lot of cities, probably—but here, the nation's shrine to unrestricted predatory capitalism, money has nearly talismanic power. And somehow, the power that wisps forth from the old things of the city and its subways and its streets knows that.

The traffic lights miraculously stay in their favor for several blocks, which is fortunate because it feels like the young woman is likely to break the sound barrier at this rate. And then she curses and slams on the breaks as a light ahead makes a fast switch to red. Too fast; amazing that she doesn't run the light. He smells a waft of burnt rubber through the open window as he leans forward to squint at the light. "Busted light?"

"Must be," she says, tapping her fingertips rapidly on the wheel. This, Manny knows, is a gesture required by the ritual of hurry-up-damn-it, but it doesn't work, because that ritual never works. "They usually line up better than this. Just one light out of sequence can start a three-hour traffic jam, even in the middle of the day."

Manny presses his hand against the cold, spreading ache in his side that is beginning to throb again. Something about the traffic light has pinged his new sense of wrongness—and the wrongness is enough to erode whatever anesthetic effect he'd managed to summon. He opens his mouth to suggest that she run the light, which is risky. The presence of such wrongness has probably weakened his influence on her, and now there's nothing to stop her from thinking twice about the strange black dude in her antique cab. But whatever is happening on the east side of the island—FDR Drive—is growing urgent. He knows this the way he knows everything else.

Before Manny can speak, however, a BMW passes through the intersection ahead. There are long, feathery white tendrils growing from its wheel wells.

He watches it go past in utter shock. The driver sees it, too; her mouth falls open. *Feathery* doesn't quite fit what they're seeing. It's more like an anemone's fronds, or the tendrils of certain jellyfish. As the car rolls by, gliding along behind a slower driver, they see one of the tendrils seem to... inhale. It opens itself out a little, revealing a thickened stalk that tapers as it stretches away from the wheels, up to slightly darkened tips. All of it is translucent. Not all of it is *here*—in this world, that is. Manny sees at once that it is like the dual city: here, but also in that other place where the sky is wild and people are a never-thought.

All of that is academic, though, because in the next moment, Manny notices something that makes the little hairs on the back of his neck stand up. The tendrils twitch as the BMW thumps over a pothole—but it's not the pothole that they're reacting to. They're longer, see. Turning, like some kind of wiggly, wormlike radio antennas. Stretching toward the Checker cab as if they sense Manny inside and smell his fear.

After the BMW moves on, its driver apparently oblivious, it takes a moment for Manny's skin to stop crawling.

"So, you saw that, too, right?" asks the driver. The traffic light has finally changed; they speed toward FDR again. "Nobody else was staring, but you..." Her eyes meet his in the rearview.

"Yeah," he says. "Yeah, I saw it. I don't...yeah." It occurs to him, belatedly, that she might need more explanation than this, if he doesn't want to get kicked out of the cab. "You're not crazy. Or at least, if you are, you're not the only one."

"Oh, well, that's comforting." She licks her lips. "Why couldn't anyone else see it?"

"I wish I knew." But when she shakes her head, more in denial than disbelief, he feels compelled to add, "We're going to destroy the thing that's causing it." He means it to reassure, but he also realizes, as he says it, that it's true. He doesn't let himself think further about how he knows it's true. He doesn't ask who the *we* in his statement refers to. They're too far into this now. If he starts doubting himself here, that will weaken the power—and, more importantly, he'll start questioning his own sanity. That way lies involuntary commitment.

"Destroy...what?" She's frowning as she looks at him in the rearview this time.

He doesn't want to admit that he doesn't know. "Just get me to FDR, and I'll handle it."

Much to his relief, she relaxes and flashes a lopsided smile over her shoulder. "Weird, but okay. The grandkids are gonna love this story. When I, you know, have grandkids." She drives on.

Then at last they're on FDR, moving faster toward that vague-but-rapidly-sharpening sense of wrongness. Manny is clinging to the old-fashioned leather handle sewn into the seat back before him because she's still doing the race-car-driver act, whipping around slower cars and cresting hills with enough speed that it feels a little like riding

the Cyclone? what is

a roller coaster. But they're getting closer to the source of all the trouble. There's a knot of small aircraft over and boats on the nearby East River, all of them generally centering around something farther south. All Manny can see from here is smoke. Maybe it has to do with that bridge incident he heard about on the train? Must be; they've begun to pass signs warning of delays, detours, and police activity below Houston Street.

But it's also clear that they're much closer to the *wrongness* than to the bridge disaster. Now they're passing more cars, over on the uptown side of FDR, that seem to be infested with the weird white tendrils. Most are growing from the wheels, same as on the Beemer they saw before. It's as if the cars have rolled over something noxious that's allowed a kind of metaphysi-cally opportunistic infection at the site of the damage. A few vehicles have it in their front grilles or curling up from their undercarriages. One car, a newish Beetle, has the tendrils in a spray up one door and crawling over the driver's window. The driver doesn't notice. What will happen if it touches her, when she opens the door? Nothing good. Manny sets his jaw as the traffic slows sharply…and the city's second, unseen, disaster comes into range.

His first thought is that it's like an explosion, kind of. Imagine a fountain bursting up from the asphalt and flaring twenty or thirty feet into the sky, and *wiggling*. In lieu of water, the fountain flares with tendrils—dozens of them, anemoneic and enormous. Some writhe together in a way that is both mesmerizing and vaguely phallic as they tower above the rooftops of the cars. Manny can tell that the root of the…growth…is located somewhere up ahead on the downtown side, probably in the fast lane, which is how it's getting so many cars on the uptown-going side despite the median barrier. He sees a shiny new SUV with Pennsylvania plates pass that is so covered in the tendrils that it looks like a spectral hedgehog. Good thing the driver can't see them, or his vision would be too occluded to allow driving. But an ancient, rusty Ford Escort with missing hubcaps and peeling paint comes right behind it, and the tendrils haven't touched it at all. What's the pattern? He can't begin to guess.

This explosion of ick is what's causing the traffic jam, Manny sees, as the flow of cars slows to a crawl and the Checker comes to near halt. Although most people can't see the flare of tendrils, they're still somehow reacting to its presence. Drivers in the fast lane keep trying to pull into the middle lane to get around the thing; drivers in the middle are trying to get into the right-hand lane, and drivers in the right-hand lane aren't budging. It's as if there's an invisible accident up ahead that everyone's trying to avoid. Thank God it's not rush hour or the traffic wouldn't be moving at all.

They've stopped for the moment, so Manny opens the rear passenger-side door to get out. A few of the cars behind them immediately set up a banshee chorus of horns, protesting even the possibility that he might slow things down more, but he ignores these and leans over to speak into the window when the driver rolls it down. (She has to lean across the seat and turn a manual crank to do this. For a moment he stares in fascination, then focuses.) "You got emergency flares?" he asks. "Triangle reflectors, stuff like that?"

"In the trunk." She puts the car in park and gets out herself—there are more horns at this—but she's glancing over at the tower of tendrils. Its tips wave above the pedestrian bridge that crosses this part of the FDR. "So that's what this is all about?"

"Yep." Manny pulls out the emergency kit when she opens the trunk. He's keeping most of his attention on the thing, though. If any of those tendrils come at them . . . well, hopefully they won't.

"You better hurry and do whatever you're going to do. Cops are probably already on the way to deal with the jam. I don't know if they'll see it—nobody else seems to, or a lot more people would be getting out of their cars and walking—but they're not gonna help much."

He grimaces in agreement. Then he notices the way she's glaring at the fountain of tendrils. He has a tiny epiphany, beginning to understand. "You from here?"

She blinks. "Yeah. Born and raised right over in Chelsea, two moms and everything. Why?"

"Just a guess." Manny hesitates. He's feeling strange again. There are things happening around him, to him—a rise in tension and power and meaning, all of it pulling toward a moment of truth that he's not sure he wants to confront. Beneath his feet there is a vibration, a pulse like wheels clacking steadily over track segments that thrums in time with his pulse. Why? Because it does. Because somehow, everything on this road and under it and around it *is* him. The pain in his side is awful, but ignorable because somehow *the city* is keeping him functioning, feeding him strength. Even the idling of the traffic-bound cars feeds him, pent energy just waiting for its chance to leap ahead. He looks around at the drivers in the nearby cars and sees that most are glaring at the tendril thing too. Do they see it? Not really. But they know *something* is there, blocking the flow of the city, and they hate it for that alone.

This is how it works, he realizes, in wonder. This is what he needs to defeat the tendrils. These total strangers are his allies. Their anger, their need for a return to normalcy, rises from them like heat waves. This is the weapon he needs, if he can figure out how to harness it.

"I'm Manny," he says to the cab driver, on impulse. "You?"

She looks surprised, then grins. "Madison," she says. "I know. But Number One Mom says I got conceived via IVF in a clinic on Madison Ave, so..."

Too Much Information. Manny chuckles anyway, because he's all nerves and could use a laugh. "Okay, here's the plan," he says. Then he lays it out for her.

She stares at him like he's crazy, but she'll help. He can see that in her face. "...Fine," she says at last, but it's just a show of reluctance. Maybe New Yorkers don't like to be seen as too helpful.

They lay out the flares and triangle markers to encourage people to go around the fast lane. Because the cab isn't moving, angry commuters glare and honk as they pass, assuming that the cab is somehow making the traffic worse. It probably is. One guy starts screaming at Manny loudly enough to spray the inside of his door window with spittle, though fortunately he's also too angry to remember to roll the window down first. It's a measure of how much everyone is picking up on the weirdness, though, that no one veers back into the fast lane even once they pass the parked Checker cab.

The mass of tendrils is growing as Manny watches. There is a low, crumbly sound that he can hear from that direction, now and again when the wind carries it to him: probably the sound of roots digging into asphalt, and probably into the rebar within the asphalt, and maybe into the bedrock that's under the road. He can hear the tendrils, too, now that they're close enough: a choppy, broken groan, stuttering and occasionally clicking like a corrupted music file. He can smell it—a thicker, much fishier brine scent than that of the nearby East River.

Trimethylamine oxide, he thinks out of the blue. *The scent of the deep, cold, crushing ocean depths.*

"What now?" Madison asks.

"I need to hit it."

"Uh…"

Manny looks around before spotting exactly what he needs—there, in a convertible sports car's open back seat. The Indian woman driving it stares at him in blatant curiosity. He steps toward her quickly and blurts, "Hey, can I have that umbrella?"

"How about pepper spray?" she suggests.

He holds up his hands to try and look less threatening, though he's still a six-foot-tall not-white guy and some people are just never going to be okay with that. "If you loan it to me, I can clear this traffic jam."

At this, she actually looks intrigued. "Huh. Well, for that I guess I can give up an umbrella. It's my sister's, anyway. I just like to hit people with it." She grabs the umbrella and hands it to him, pointy tip first.

"Thanks!" He grabs it and trots back to the cab. "Okay, we're golden."

Madison frowns at him, then at the tendril flare, as she opens the cab's driver-side door to get back in. "I can't see what's beyond that thing," she says. "If there are cars, and I can't brake in time—"

"Yeah. I know." Manny vaults up onto the Checker's hood, then its roof. Madison stares while he turns and arranges himself to sit straddling the roof, one hand gripping the OFF DUTY sign. Fortunately, Checkers are high and long, narrow-built for city streets. He can get enough of a grip with his legs to hold on, though it's still going to be dicey. "Okay. Ready."

"I am so texting my weed man as soon as this is over," Madison says, shaking her head as she gets into the cab.

The umbrella is key. Manny doesn't know why, but he's okay with accepting what he can't quite understand, for now. What's really bothering him is that he's not sure *how* to use it. And given that everything in him cries out that the forest of tendrils is dangerous—deadly if it so much as touches him, maybe because the tendrils look like anemones, which sting their prey to death—he needs to figure it out fast. As Madison starts up the cab, he experimentally lifts the umbrella, metal tip pointing toward the tendril mass like a jouster's lance. It's wrong. The right idea, but the wrong implementation; weak, somehow. The umbrella's an automatic, so he unsnaps its closure and presses the button. It pops open at once, and it's huge. A golf umbrella—a nice one, with no hint of a rattle or wobble as Madison accelerates and the wind pulls at the umbrella. But still wrong.

The tendril mass looms, ethereal and pale, more frightening as the cab accelerates. There is a beauty to it, he must admit—like some haunting, bioluminescent deep sea organism dragged to the surface. It is an alien beauty, however, meant for some other environment, some other aether, and here in New York its presence is a contaminant. The very air around it has turned gray, and now that they're closer he can hear the air hissing as if the tendrils are somehow hurting the molecules of nitrogen and oxygen they touch. Manny's been in New York for less than an hour and yet he knows, he *knows*, that cities are organic, dynamic systems. They are built to incorporate newness. But some new things become part of a city, helping it grow and strengthen—while some new things can tear it apart.

They're speeding now, doing at least fifty. The tendrils shadow the sky and the air has turned cold and the smell of lightless oceans has grown nauseating and it's getting hard to hold on to the cab's roof. He hangs on anyway and half shuts his eyes against the wind and the burning salt of the thing's scent and *what is he doing?* Pushing out the interloper. But he's an interloper, too, isn't he? And if he doesn't do this exactly the right way then only one of the interlopers here is going to walk away from this confrontation intact, and *the umbrella isn't strong enough.*

And then, when the Checker is only feet away, close enough that Manny can see the slick, pore-flecked skin of the tendrils, and his side screams with agony like someone's jabbed an ice-cold pike through him—

—he remembers the words of the woman who gave him the umbrella. *I just like to hit people with it,* she'd said.

Manny lets go of the OFF DUTY sign. Immediately he starts to slide back on the cab's roof because they're going so fast that he can barely hold on with his legs alone. But he might survive falling off the cab; he *won't* survive contact with the nest of tendrils if he doesn't get this umbrella *up.* He needs both hands for that, wrestling against the wind and his own fear, but in the welter of seconds that he has, he manages to lift the umbrella above his head. Now he might die, but at least his hair won't get wet in any sudden rain shower.

And suddenly there is energy around him, *in* him, blazing rusty red and tarnished silver and greened bronze and a thousand colors more. It has become a sheath around the whole cab—a sphere of pure energy brightening enough to compete with the June midday sunlight—and in its suddenly loud song Manny hears the horns of a thousand cars trapped on the FDR. The hissing air is eclipsed by the shouted road rage of hundreds of mouths. And as he opens his mouth to shout with them, his cry is delight and the ecstasy of suddenly knowing that he *isn't* an interloper. The city needs newcomers! He belongs here as much as anyone born and bred to its streets, because anyone who wants to be of New York can be! He is no tourist, exploiting and gawking and giving nothing but money back. He *lives here* now. That makes all the difference in the world.

So as Manny laughs, giddy with this realization and the power that now suffuses him, they strike the tendril mass. The sheath of energy surrounding the cab burns through it like a Checkered missile. Of course, the cab is part of the power; this is why the city sent it to him. Manny feels the umbrella snag on something and he clings tighter to it, rudely not lifting it or moving it aside because *I'm walking here, I have the right of way* he's playing metaphysical sidewalk chicken with this rude, violent, invasive *tourist*—

And then they're through. But Manny hears Madison yell from inside the cab as they get through the mass and see that there's a line of stopped cars dead ahead.

She slams the brakes. Manny loses his grip on the umbrella as he frantically grabs for the OFF DUTY sign, catching it even as his whole body flips onto the windshield and hood. The cab spins out as Madison throws the wheel; now, instead of flying forward, he's being thrown around by centrifugal force. In his panic, he loses his grip on the sign and doesn't know how he finds the strength to grab for the edge of the hood below the wipers, even as his legs come loose and most of his body flies free in the direction of the stopped traffic. If the cab flips, he's dead. If he loses his grip and gets tossed onto the hatchback up ahead, he's dead. If he falls off the cab and under the wheels—

But the cab finally skids to a halt, a bare inch away from the stopped car up ahead. Manny's feet thump onto the hatchback's trunk, not entirely of his own volition. It's okay. Just nice to have something solid under his feet again.

"Get your feet off my fucking car!" someone inside shouts. He ignores them.

"Holy shit!" Madison sticks her head out the window, her face panicky, like how he feels. "Holy— Are you okay?"

"Yeah?" Manny's honestly not sure. But he musters the wherewithal to sit up and look back down the fast lane.

Behind them, the tendril forest has gone wild, its fronds whipping and flailing like a dying thing. It *is* dying. Where they punched through its thicket of roots, there is a Checker cab cutout like something out of a kids' cartoon—complete with an umbrella-shaped hole on top of its roof, and a lumpen, hunched human silhouette underneath. The edges of the cutout glow as if hot, and the fire rapidly eats its way outward and upward, fast as a circle of flame burning through a piece of paper. Within seconds this burn has eaten its way through the base of the tendrils, then starts burning all the way up. No ash or residue remains in the wake of this process. Manny knows this is because the tendrils aren't really there, aren't really *real* in any way that makes sense.

The destruction is real, however. And once the last of the tendrils has burned away, a hovering, brightly colored knot of energy—the remnant of the sheath that surrounded the cab, now a wild, seething thing of its own—dissipates in a miniature explosion that ripples concentrically outward. Manny shudders as the wave of light and color and heat passes through him. He knows it won't hurt, but he's surprised when it warms the place on his side that hurt so badly before. More dramatically, tendrils that have attached themselves to the nearby cars wither away the instant the energy hits them. He feels the power roll onward out of sight as it passes beyond the nearest buildings and into the East River.

It's done.

And as Manny climbs off of the cab's hood and settles back onto the ground, once again he feels something waft through him, from the soles of his shoes to the roots of his hair. It's the same energy, he realizes, that suffused the cab when it torpedoed through the tendril mass—and which soothed him at Penn Station, and which guided him from there to here. That energy is the city, he understands somehow, and it is part of him, filling him up and driving out anything unnecessary to make room for itself. That's why his name is gone.

The energy begins to fade. Will his memory come back when it's gone? No way to know. And though Manny feels he should be frightened by this realization, he... isn't. It doesn't make sense. Amnesia, even if it's temporary, can't be a good thing. He might have a brain bleed, some kind of hidden injury; he should go to a hospital. But somehow, instead of being frightened, he is actually comforted by the presence of the city within him. He shouldn't be. He has an inkling that he just had a near-death experience. But he is.

The East River churns at his back. He looks up at the towering breadth of Manhattan: endless high-rise co-ops, repurposed banks, cramped housing projects sandwiched between ancient theater houses and soulless corporate headquarters. Nearly two million people. He's been here one hour, but already he feels like he has never lived anywhere else. And even if he doesn't know who he was...he knows who he is.

"I am Manhattan," he murmurs softly.

And the city replies, without words, right into his heart: *Welcome to New York.*

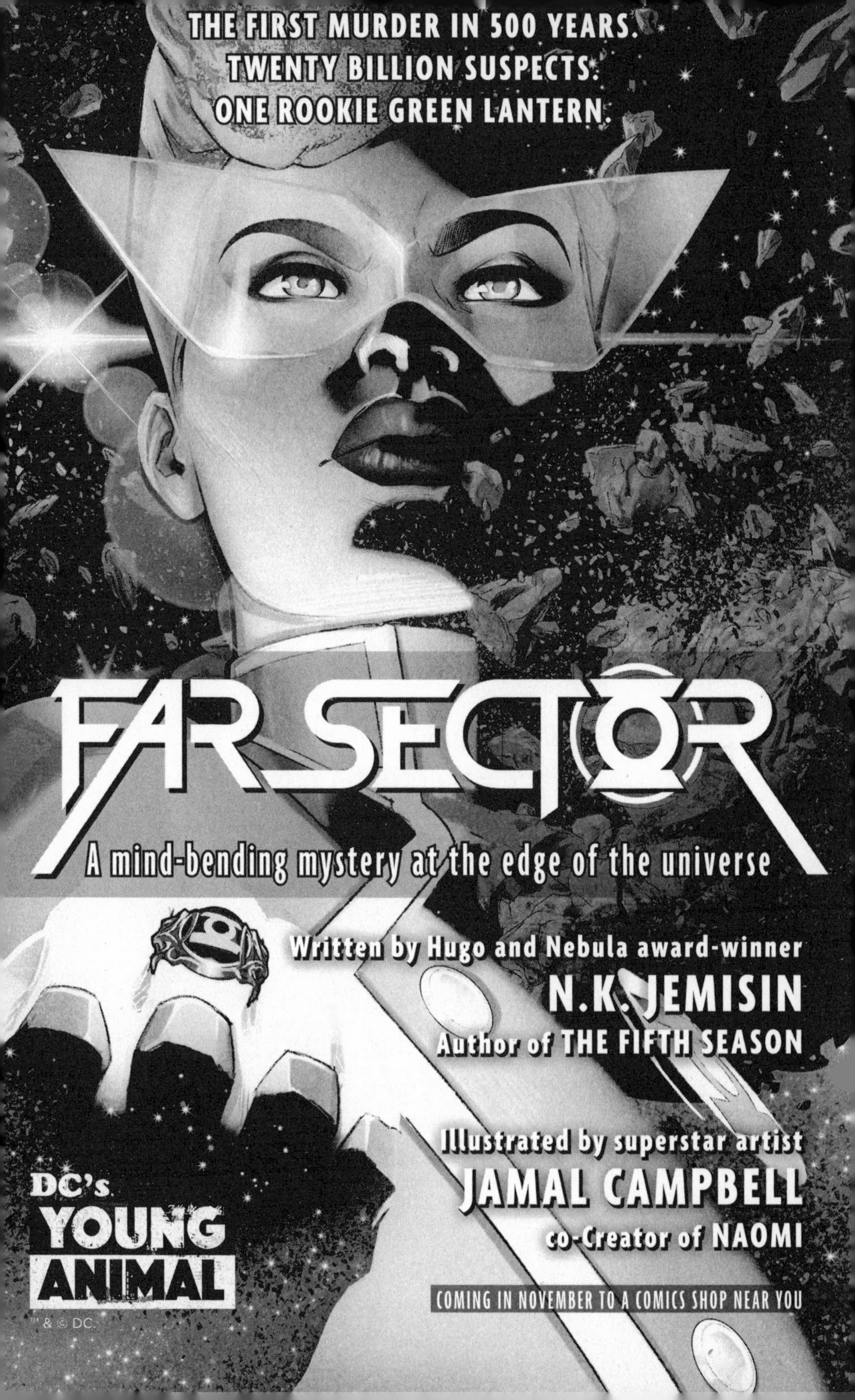
THE FIRST MURDER IN 500 YEARS.
TWENTY BILLION SUSPECTS.
ONE ROOKIE GREEN LANTERN.
FAR SECTOR
A mind-bending mystery at the edge of the universe
Written by Hugo and Nebula award-winner
N.K. JEMISIN
Author of THE FIFTH SEASON
Illustrated by superstar artist
JAMAL CAMPBELL
co-Creator of NAOMI
DC's YOUNG ANIMAL
COMING IN NOVEMBER TO A COMICS SHOP NEAR YOU
™ & © DC.

orbit

Follow us:

/orbitbooksUS

/orbitbooks

/orbitbooks

Join our mailing list
to receive alerts on our
latest releases and deals.

orbitbooks.net

Enter our monthly
giveaway for the chance
to win some epic prizes.

orbitloot.com